I0628728

Heir of Ether

HER DIVINE CHILDREN

ELENA HUEBERT

For the misfits that need a little extra sign to keep on going. Your passions are weird and that's a good thing. Your people will find you. The world needs you. I love you.

Copyright © 2025 by Elena Huebert All rights reserved.

No part of this publication may be reproduced, distributed, or transmitted in any form or by any means, including photocopying, recording or other electronic or mechanical methods, without the prior written permission of the publisher, except as permitted by Australian copyright law.

For permission requests, contact Elena Huebert at elenahuebertauthor@gmail.com

The story, all names, characters and incidents portrayed in this production are fictitious. No identification with actual persons (living or deceased), places, buildings, and products is intended or should be inferred.

No AI Training: Without in any way limiting the author's exclusive rights under copyright, any use of this publication to "train" generative artificial intelligence (AI) technologies to generate text is expressly prohibited. The author reserves all rights to license uses of this work for generative AI training and development of machine learning language models.

Book Cover by Etheric Designs

1st edition 2025

No AI was used in the creation of this story.

Prologue

Inanna felt a surge pulse through her that could only mean one thing; the baby was coming, and too soon.

She pushed on, through the thickening mist on her strong, white mare. She knew The Gate was soon within reach. The forest was dense and winding, but Inanna trusted that her mare could find the way. Few knew of this portal to the mortal lands. She prayed to The Divine Mother that her source did not deceive her, for there was no time for uncertainty now.

Another intense wave coursed through her, and it took all of her concentration not to scream out. There was no doubt that this baby was coming today. She breathed through the pain, and clutched onto Durga's mane for support until it began to ease. Inanna feared that being on horseback would not be an option for much longer but she could see no alternative. *He* was coming for them, they had to escape.

"This is happening too fast, Durga!" Inanna gasped. This was the only cue her horse needed to quicken into a gallop. The crunch of hooves and the heaving breaths of Durga rang through the forest like a beacon. They both knew that they must try to keep as quiet as they could and hope their stealth would save them, but going quickly was just as important now, so they pushed on.

Just as they came to the crest of a hill, finally breaking through the Tanglewood Forest's gnarled embrace, a piercing howl sounded behind them that sent dread shooting up Inanna's spine.

He had found her; and would rather rip her to shreds than let her leave.

A warm wetness burst onto her legs, soaking her skirts. Her waters had broken. She had to push through the fear, push through the pain to focus on saving her child.

"Make haste Durga! Take me to The Gate, to safety!" Inanna pleaded. With increased urgency, Durga continued at a full gallop through the dense mist with her ears flattened and sweat already glistening on her coat; the sound of growling was closing in on them.

The Mist felt tangibly thick here in the valley and she prayed to The Mother that it would hide them from the fast approaching creature, even if its power was something she had been told to fear as a child.

The density of the Mist pulled at them, forcing its way down their throats and into their noses. This was the last distracting defense before The Gate to keep the fae out... and the humans in. Inanna could feel the laboured wheezing of

Durga under her thighs and a wave of guilt passed through her with the knowledge that Durga could not return once she passed through.

I can continue on foot. You've done enough, Inanna said into the mind's eye of her steed.

I will serve you until my dying breath my Lady, Inanna heard Durga's deep, steady voice down the line of their mental bond; an overwhelming dizziness suddenly cut their communication off as the Mist clouded her mind. She could feel its smoky tendrils pulling at her thoughts and memories, worming its way to her core. Scenes flashed through her mind like lightning.

A high domed ballroom — women in glimmering dresses that twirled in unison to the melody of the eight piece band — the green eyed stare of a devastatingly handsome man from across the room — a kiss on the hand and a wink as he led her onto the dance floor.

Inanna fought the urge to pound the images out of her head. She did not wish to relive the heartbreak, but the Mist was relentless.

Skin on skin in a heated embrace that consummated their love — skin turned to fur and a courtesan's sweet smile morphed into sharp teeth and fangs — her father slashed down, blood staining the stone floor.

The visions wrenched open a still fresh wound within her heart. The Mist continued to push.

A cold, dark cell and a red-haired boy with fire in his eyes who smiled apologetically through the bars of her jail — the boy holding a loaf of bread, urging her to eat and pointing to her enormous pregnant belly — a key, baked into the bread — a fearful glance down the dark stone tunnel as she finally broke free from her prison.

The Mist tried to grasp her light, her essence and fed off her memories – it was wildly searching for her powers. It would feast upon her magic if she lingered too long within its grasp. She tried to distract the engulfing vapours with as many painful memories as she could.

Just as darkness began to creep into the sides of her vision and her hold on the reins slackened; they burst through the opening of a small cave at the base of a big mossy hill. Inanna's whimper of relief cut through the stillness of their drastically changed surroundings. Safety, at last.

They found themselves transported into a crisp, clear meadow full of wildflowers that bobbed and danced in the breeze. Here, the warm sun was shining through the rustling leaves of the aspen trees that encircled the space like sentries on guard, everything was calm and still. No Mists, no need for escape. Inanna and her mare both knew the creature would not follow them into the mortal realm for fear that he could never return. For the fae – both Elemental and Metamorph – were cursed to stay within their realm; while the creatures-of-fae and humans could roam freely between the two.

It was an ancient curse that the Earth, Herself, had placed upon those with a thirst for power; a curse of balance. A curse to protect the land in a time when the humans and creatures-of-fae cared for Her more than the fae did.

The humans could pass through The Gates, and were free to live and move between both realms. The ferocity and tricks of the fae realm was often what kept them out. If the fae passed through to the human realm they were stuck to live out a mortal life and unable to use their powers. Over the generations The Gates were widely forgotten, as was magic in the human realm.

Durga felt Inanna start to sag in the saddle so she slowed her pace, searching for a spot to let her down. Just through the other side of a copse of birch she could see the glistening flow of a little creek; with many moss covered boulders and stones lining the edges and soft, whispering grasses blowing in the light breeze. She kept searching until she found a patch of grass that looked quite soft, then knelt down to let Inanna slide off her back. Here, she could rest for a moment before the next contraction took hold of her.

Inanna took a steadying breath and let herself collapse against a big boulder, leaning her cheek on the downy, tickling moss. She had never seen anyone give birth before but she trusted that her body knew what to do. She knew fear would not help in this moment yet couldn't help but despair at what was to come.

Now that they were safe from the creature she tuned into her next contraction. She dove into the inner workings of her body; visualising the wave pushing down with the movements of her daughter, allowing a guttural moan to escape her lips as the baby dropped low in her pelvis.

"My daughter," she said out loud, realizing this was the first time she knew.

A dizzy spell started to blacken her vision and she felt as if the world was tilting and rumbling beneath her. *I must be about to faint*, she thought to herself but noticed Durga quickly stood up and whinnied as she nervously padded at the ground, throwing her nose up as if trying to point behind her. Inanna felt two cold, hard hands grasp her shoulders.

"Do not fear poppet, Granny Mog is here!" a gravelly voice grumbled behind her. She turned to see a hunched gnome with a big nose, tiny spectacles and fluffy moss for hair smiling at her. Many of the surrounding boulders and stones started to tremble, uncurling from their resting places by the creek and shaking the leaves and dust from their limbs.

"Gnomes! Durga, where are we?" Inanna exclaimed before another contraction took hold, forcing her to lurch forward and up onto her knees. This one didn't feel right. It felt as if a thousand knives were cleaving at her from the inside. Her scream broke free from her lips as she looked down to see a red patch blooming on her dress.

"Sisters, grab some leaves and water. The baby is coming!" Granny Mog commanded. The male gnomes began to curl into themselves to roll away, knowing it was not their place to be of witness. Granny Mog moved in front of Inanna, lifting Innana's nearly limp arms up onto her sturdy shoulders.

"I am made of stone my dear, push onto me as much as you need, you're almost there. The babe is coming!" the ancient gnome instructed as another contraction came tearing through. Inanna could not fight the urge to bear down. She sank her weight into the sturdy boulder gnome, crying out and seeing stars as the baby made its way through her.

A vision of a grown woman with Inanna's own features flashed in her mind. A man with fiery red hair leaned in to kiss her, the woman wore her necklace, the family heirloom her father gifted to her. The gem within it started to glow. Inanna let out a sob which the gnomes assumed was in the throes of pain but only Inanna felt the joy at seeing her yet unborn daughter in love; she also knew that her gift allowed her to see this vision because she must, at all costs, prevent it.

Inanna screamed as she felt herself being ripped in two. One more wave and the babe slid out, all red and glistening, wriggling on a bed of leaves the sister gnomes had placed on the forest floor.

She was born with her eyes wide open, already a piercing green.

The sound of the baby's sweet, little cry filled the glen and the gnomes cheered and rolled around in the grass and splashed in the creek in their excitement. It had been a very long time since they had seen a baby born. Durga kicked and whinnied in her elation, joining in the revelry of the frolicking boulders.

Inanna sat back with relief and reached out for her daughter but before their skin could touch an all-encompassing wave of dizziness took hold of her and everything went black.

Granny Mog quickly realized that there was too much

blood; the wound was too big for even a fae to self-heal. All merriment ceased as she huddled close trying to shake Inanna awake but life was slowly draining from her. With a sob of defeat Granny knew that Inanna was beyond repair.

Durga came to kneel next to her Lady, and gave her a gentle nudge of concern, which provoked some movement beneath Inanna's eyelids and caused her to briefly regain consciousness.

She leaned closer to Durga and spoke in a barely audible whisper. "My sweet Durga, I release you from your bond to me but ask humbly that you watch out for my daughter. Do not let her enter the fae realm. She has been born into the mortal realm so can choose to go back, but only danger and heartbreak awaits her. My gift of Sight foretold she will try. You must stop her..."

She winced slightly at the effort then muttered even more quietly, " her name is Nuria," before she slumped down, her skin turning a snowy white.

She looked as though she was made of the purest marble and had just lain down peacefully to sleep in the grass. Her long ebony curls created a stark contrast against her pale skin, which seemed as if it were glowing. If it weren't for the pool of startling red around her that had begun soaking into the earth, one would mistake her for sleeping peacefully. The gnomes could do nothing but stand silently, heads bowed in despair at the sudden passing of such a beautiful visitor.

Granny Mog sniffled then cleared her throat. "Let us clean her in the creek and move her to the resting stone sisters." She motioned for them to carry Inanna and place her onto a flat rock covered in the plushest moss. They would perform their burial ritual when the moon rose but for now, they attended to Nuria; *poor little Nuria who had entered into the wrong world, without her mother's warm embrace and only gnomes to care for her*, Granny thought to herself, worry creased her stoney brow.

"We may be made of stone but our hearts are as warm and beating as any other creature! Do not lose heart Granny, we can raise her!" Sister Marg, the gnome with pale blue lichen for hair, proclaimed as she looked down at the sweet, pink, wriggling child.

"We haven't seen a human child in a very long time but she can play and learn with our children just the same," Sister Iris agreed.

"I'm not sure she is human, sisters. I think they came from the fae realm, just look at her tiny little claws, and the colour of her eyes..." Granny said, lifting a pudgy little hand that was tipped in pointy nails wondering if they were the cause of irreparable damage to her mother.

"We must find a doe that is newly with child and willing to share her milk, for I do not believe human or fae babies eat as we do," she grumbled, realizing this may be more difficult than they had initially thought. Her sisters were just excited for a little play thing but Granny had been around long enough to know that when humans grow up they can become destructive and too inquisitive for their own good. It had been many years since man last travelled this far into the woods of the east, for superstition of the land being haunted and tales of unexplained disappearances kept them

9

at bay, yet there were still signs of their pillaging present. Ancient trees had been felled, leaving stumps that would take a dozen boulder gnomes to wrap their arms around. Animals of the human realm were content to make their homes within these stumps, but Creature-of-fae could feel the devastation of the trees and stayed away.

May be best to leave the babe to its fate, Granny contemplated as she turned to look towards the direction Inanna and Durga had come from.

"She is looking around Granny! And listen to her sweet sounds," Sister Iris exclaimed. At this reaction Granny turned to look into Nuria's cherubic face and knew she was doomed to love this child.

With a grunt, Granny Mog squared her shoulders and turned to the mare. "Durga, I task you with finding us a milk nurse. Be it doe, mare or vixen - I do not care but make haste." Durga dutifully nodded and galloped off into the woods.

The uncles, brothers, fathers and sons came rolling back in to see the fate of the mysterious woman and came upon Nuria, cooing and grasping out her little hands. She managed to grab ahold of Grandpa Jorg's nose and he yelped at the scratch of tiny claws. The gnomes burst out in laughter and all agreed they were going to enjoy having a little human... or *fae* baby around.

As night fell, Nuria was safely tucked away nursing in a nearby cave with a fiery red vixen whom Durga had found mourning the loss of her pups. Granny Mog and her sisters made their way back to the mossy rock where Inanna was laid to prepare her for their ritual of guidance back to The Mother.

They arrived to a startling sight, Inanna was no longer lying there upon the stone in human form but had transformed into a mound of cascading, white flowers; the scent of cinnamon and jasmine thick in the air.

"Granny, are those ghost orchids?" Sister Marg squeaked as she abruptly stopped in her tracks.

"Yes my sister, I believe they are. Quickly, go and check the spot where her blood has fallen. Are they sprouting there as well?" Granny asked; worry creasing her brow as Sister Marg rushed off.

"Yes Granny, they are here as well!" Marg called through the trees. Granny's sense of foreboding was strong as she knew all too well that this rare flower only bloomed upon the spilt blood of royalty...

THE YEARS FOLLOWING PASSED PEACEFULLY for the inhabitants of Granny Mog's glen. Other than the addition of a white horse and a squealing little childling, much stayed the same. The gnomes were the guardians of the gardens, the cutters of small creeks and hollowers of big logs. Some may even say they kept things balanced and right in their own ways. Many resembled big rocks but some also melded into trees or dissolved into puddles. They kept out of sight of the humans and fae but often delighted in aiding those who were more green-thumbed and kind. Nuria did not necessarily fit in but she grew up loving and cherishing the forest as much as her guardians did.

The life of a gnome was fairly simple. New creeks were dug throughout the forest to supply the ever growing trees with water, fallen logs were hollowed out for new homes for the many creatures of the glen, and little gardens of wild berries, mushrooms and herbs were tended to. Mother gnomes would harvest acorns to turn into flour for acorn and berry pies and teach the children the correct gnome ways; while father gnomes would design and build new additions to the forest floors. They would all come together to dance and sing to the plants, bugs and mushrooms; encouraging them to grow and co-exist in a most peaceful way.

The gnomes shared good relations with the sprites of the water, wind and fire and would help them create ecosystems that would benefit all. The water sprites, in one such instance, were awfully bored with a creek that was too calm. They desired some little waterfalls and whirlpools, which the gnomes would carefully craft by shifting boulders, digging up sand and toppling logs.

The sprites of the wind required enough foliage to rustle and holes in trees to whistle through; so, of course, the gnomes obliged by directing more water to the trees and encouraging the mycelium to help bring nutrients to the roots, so the leaves could be more abundant.

The fire sprites were a bit more mischievous, trying to burn deadfall when they pleased to satiate their need for ignition. To placate them, once a month on the new moon, the boulder gnomes would create a big bonfire in honor of the sprites; who would dance and crackle and spin around gleefully within the flames. This was Nuria's favourite night of the month for there was something about the flame that would draw her in, completely enchanted and unafraid.

At one such fete, Nuria seemed to be calling the fire sprites to her, letting the flames leap and swirl a little too close. The young gnomes were gathered listening to Granny Mog, who was busy telling stories of The Divine Mother; how She had created the gnomes to be Her stewards of the forest. When Granny briefly looked up she could have sworn she saw the face of a young red haired boy in the flames, speaking to Nuria.

"Nuria! Step away from there," Granny called, which seemed to have snapped Nuria out of a dream. She stumbled back and blinked around as if she knew not where she was, falling into Uncle Bog, who had been having a particularly good night enjoying the berry wine, causing his usually sturdy stance to falter. This in turn created a cascade of tumbling gnomes, the hilarity of it all bringing Nuria out of her stupor and distracting Granny from what she thought she may have seen. The night carried on in gnomely merriment however, Granny thought to keep an eye on Nuria, and maybe to get some new spectacles.

Nuria loved joining the other little gnomes in games: capturing frogs, skipping stones upon the nearby lake, and using the juice of berries to write secret notes on peeling birch bark. Sometimes Nuria would even get her stained little fingers onto Durga's shining white coat when the mare was napping. She would then wake to funny drawings all over her pristine coat and couldn't help but laugh before trotting off to the closest creek. The gnome children would not dare get so close to such a big creature though; they weren't a mischievous, thrill-seeking bunch. The biggest creature they'd encountered was the rare male buck, with antlers spanning wide as he strutted through the forest in springtime (though he was miniature compared to Durga).

The older Nuria grew the more curious and roguish she became. A few moons after her fourth birthday she managed to hop onto Durga's back while the mare was napping and even greater, managed to hold on. Durga sprang up from her slumber and bucked and kicked, thinking something sinister had landed upon her.

In that moment of excitement Nuria could only shriek and giggle but she thought to herself, *calm down Durga it's me, let's run through the forest!* Durga immediately calmed down but did not dare respond as she once could with her Lady. The shock of what this meant for Nuria worried the mare greatly.

Reflecting on what the knowledge of Nuria's inherited power could bring forth, Durga did not obey and gently lowered back down so the child could hop off instead; hoping Nuria didn't catch on that she had understood her. As she watched Nuria skip away memories of her vow to Inanna flashed into her mind.

Do not let her enter the fae realm. The Seers foretold she will try but you must stop her...

How could she have let Nuria stay so close to the portal

these past few years? The sense of safety the gnome community provided felt stripped away. Her duty to protect felt heavy upon her shoulders; fear of a sweet child stumbling upon the Mists through to a world in which she could not follow to protect her terrified Durga. The low growl of the creature awaiting on the other side filled her with even more terror. With a heavy heart, she knew what needed to be done.

A few months later, Durga waited for a particularly busy day for the gnome community to execute her plan. It was the first clear day after a week of heavy rains and the gnomes were hard at work creating a new tributary off the lake to help manage the overflow. A little forest of ferns had been eagerly awaiting this development, so excitement was in the air. This was hard, muddy work though and Nuria preferred to stay out of it on such a beautiful day. There were better adventures to be had.

When Durga knelt down beside Nuria, she knew the childling would not be able to resist hopping on. Nuria's exclamations of joy and wonder at all the surrounding beauty almost made up for the hurt in Durga's heart for what had to come next. They rode past the weeping willows that shaded the creek, that still had the haunting patches of ghost orchids, the grand oaks that housed the local chipmunks and burst through to a whispering meadow that was dotted with red poppies and pink corn flowers.

Nuria held on tightly and giggled as they flew through the trees. "I have never been out this way. Granny said not to wander too far, but it's so much fun! Let's see more!" Nuria gave Durga excited little kicks, urging her to speed up as they cantered past a thicket of blackberries. Durga knew this to be the border of how far the peaceful, non-thrill seeking boulder gnomes would go. All feelings of guilt at what she had planned were trumped by the promise she had made to Inanna years ago. They took a turn to the west, riding downhill for what felt like an eternity to Nuria. Her stomach was starting to grumble and it was getting chilly out.

"I'm ready to go home now, Durga. Let's go back," Nuria said.

Instead, Durga picked up the pace, forcing Nuria to hold tight as she quickened into a gallop. Just a little further and Durga could execute her plan. She had ventured out this way in the past few days, looking for signs of what she knew was the only answer to fulfilling her promise to Inanna.

Nuria screamed into Durga's ear , "put me down, put me down! Stop!" But all she could do was hold on tight in her growing terror. She was quite resolved that she had to get off and quickly. They were so far from home and Nuria had a sinking feeling that she had not experienced before. The safety of home was far away and Durga seemed completely alien to her. She longed for the warmth of the gnome caves and a slice of berry pie. She had to get back!

Nuria decided she would jump off just as soon as Durga slowed. All she needed to do was walk back uphill and surely the gnomes would be there waiting for her.

The aspens were soon traded for tall spruce trees and the air began to grow crisp and chilly. Even though they were headed downhill it was as if they were leaving summer behind and heading straight into autumn on a mountainside. They leapt over big mossy logs, swerved between trees and dodged low hanging branches as Durga surged on, frost crunching underfoot as she went.

As they crashed through a dense border of spikey gorse they suddenly came splashing into a wide river. The water was only up to Durga's knees but the current was quick enough to force her to slow down and focus as she began to wade in.

Nuria took the sudden slowed pace as her chance. She didn't think twice before she leapt off, splashing into the swift moving river and immediately losing her footing. The current had her racing downstream and out of Durga's sight before she could even react to Nuria's dismount.

Durga reared and spun back to shore. She tried her best to work her way down the rocky bank in the direction Nuria was being swept away but the brush was getting too thick and the current slowed her down too much, so she had to cut back inland.

The ice cold waters nearly shocked the breath out of Nuria as she gasped and sputtered, kicking her little legs and waving her little arms frantically, trying to keep her head above the water. None of the gnomes had taught her to swim in deep water (boulders do sink after all). She was going under too quickly. Her screams gurgled as water splashed over her head.

As a shallower part of the river approached, Nuria kicked down her feet to keep her head above water and looked around in the brief moments of respite, hoping to find something, anything to grab ahold of.

Just as she rounded a bend she could see a big tree up ahead that had toppled over on the far side of the river bank and was leaning just above the water. Relief washed over Nuria. It was fast approaching so she kicked and splashed as hard as she could, trying to direct herself to the opposite side when she noticed two large figures dressed in a shock of bright orange and yellow sitting by a campfire just beyond the toppled tree.

Nuria yelled out and waved, desperately hoping to catch their attention, not caring who or what they were. The larger of the two immediately jumped up from his seat and raced into the river, using the tree as an anchor as he leaned out and plucked Nuria out of the current, sweeping her into his arms. She grasped onto his neck and stared with wide eyes for a moment, realizing he looked like a big version of herself, before she gave into her exhaustion and collapsed, leaning her head on his big chest as she was carried back to shore.

"Paul, is she ok? Where did she come from? Why is she naked?" the other human shouted, increasing her pitch with each question.

"I don't know Jenny, I just grabbed her!" Paul shouted back. The peaceful morning they were having had been completely flipped on its head.

Paul and Jenny had made something of a monthly ritual during the warmer months, before winter set in, finding new backcountry spots to explore to escape the madness of the city. Each outing was as revitalizing and serene as the next and often involved spotting elusive wildlife that would never dare get so close to town, but a human child was the last thing to be expected.

"Take off your jacket and lay it down by the fire, we need to warm her up, she's hypothermic," Paul instructed, trying to remember the first-aid training he did years ago as he lay the now unconscious Nuria down by the fire. Jenny and Paul shared worried glances and huddled close to her, trying to shield her from the wind.

On the other side of the river Durga had heard shouting as she crashed her way around a bend, scratching her coat up on the thick bracken and getting twigs tangled in her mane as she went. When she poked her head through the brush she could see a tall man in a neon yellow jacket carrying Nuria out of the water towards a woman by a fire. She made sure to stay hidden as she watched on. She hadn't expected humans to be so far up but this could make her plan much easier than expected. She knew the humans were Nuria's only chance at a safe life. Her plan had been to get her as close to the nearest town as possible, which was another few hours' ride down the mountain. She prayed these two would do the trick.

Sure enough, after a few minutes of what looked to be a heated discussion, the humans grabbed their packs and the man scooped up the now limp Nuria, wrapped in a bright orange puffy coat, and they all headed west towards the town. Durga could only hope Nuria would end up well looked after and that Inanna would have approved.

Chapter One

16 YEARS LATER

"Nuria! We're going to be late! Where are you?" I can faintly hear the call of my mother through the forest that is our extended backyard. We live on a cul-de-sac that backs onto the state forest, the last whisper of civilization before the deep Wildwood Forest and the Easthelm Mountains beyond. She wants me to join her and my sister, Marissa, for this ridiculous luncheon with the other wives and daughters of the town council. It's all frills and puff. The hot topic being the new landscaper in town who has come equipped with all the latest technology in lawn maintenance, and the innovative genius of the council's decision to dig into the water basin to fortify our water supply in the ever growing drought. After all, Easthelm is best known for its glistening green lawns and cookie-cutter homes, we need water to maintain those lawns, right? Even though we have the wildest backcountry just at our back door the town seems to ignore this and focuses on the "beautification" of our spaces. I see it more as conformity but, regrettably, I am mostly alone in this perception.

I have conveniently forgotten about the luncheon and am definitely too covered in mud for such "high society". Earlier in the week I had stumbled upon the beginnings of the most perfect fairy circle of *Morchella esculenta* I have ever seen and had to document it for my nearly finished guide to mushroom foraging before they withered. University is starting back up in a few weeks and I promised Mr. Bugg, my botany professor, I'd have this done for him to edit at the start of term. He was equally excited about the discovery of the fairy circle and was eagerly awaiting my paintings and observations. My adoptive family thinks I'm strange for making such a dear friend in a seventy year old plant enthusiast. I'd rather talk to him about the changing ecosystems than to my peers, who care more about finding the best paying jobs so they can get their own cookie-cutter homes.

"Nuriaaaaaa!" I cringe at the tone of shriek and I know this will hurt me more later on if I don't haul ass back home now. I quickly pack up my paints and sketch pad and take one more appreciative look at the morels when, a sudden flash of a hand that is not my own reaching down to pick a mushroom sparks in my mind. I stagger back and try to blink away the image but instead, I am momentarily transported to a forest, much like this one, except the greens are much more vibrant and a faint humming sound fills the air.

I look down to see the mushroom in my hand has some mud on it, and turn around to wash it off in the pond behind me.

Wait, there has never been a pond back here, I think to myself, looking down.

My reflection takes me by surprise. Upon closer inspection, I see a man, not much older than me, with a shock of red hair looking back. He blinks once, pupils dilating, then I am abruptly snapped back into my own body.

"What in the actual..."

"Nuriaaaaaa!" I'm interrupted by my mother's shriek. I shake my head, staring at my now empty hand, before quickly hurrying back towards the house.

The scent of Mom's scones tempts me from even this far away. As I walk through the back gate I can already see perfect little Marissa with her soft blonde curls and flowing lilac dress leaning against the back door, smirking in anticipation of the impending entertainment from the deep shit I am in for being so late. I shove past her and walk through the kitchen, swiping a scone as I pass through, towards the stairs, where my mother is standing, arms crossed, with an impatient high heeled foot tapping on the hardwood floor. Her white blonde hair is swept back in a painfully tight looking bun and her crisp, cream coloured power suit seems to recoil from my grubby appearance.

"I'm here, Mom. Sorry, I lost track of time," I try to placate whilst shoveling the scone in my mouth. I had forgotten to eat breakfast in my excitement about the morels this morning.

My mother clicks her tongue at me. "We're going to be

late, and look at the state you are in! This is an important event darling and you're an embarrassment." I cringe at the use of the word *darling*, knowing she is trying her best to not go ballistic on me. After all, she must stay demure and respectable. Delia, my adoptive mother, would never 'lose her shit'.

"Maybe I should just stay behind. I don't fit in there and you all know it," I try to reason.

"Marissa, go help her fix all...this." Delia gestures from my feet to my head in a little waving motion, ignoring my last statement.

"You just gestured to all of me," I try to keep the dryness out of my tone.

"Precisely." Marissa chimes in with a little giggle, "come on I've got something that might fit you," she says with a devious look in her eye as she grabs onto my hand and drags me upstairs and into her room.

It always shocks me how different our rooms are. There are several posters of boy bands and her four poster bed looks as if it came straight out of a fairy tale, complete with draping white lace and twinkling lights. The light purple paint on the walls nearly matches the dress she is wearing and I can see more shades of purples and pinks scattered on her dressing table in the form of lipsticks, eye shadows and nail polishes. The mirror on the bureau is covered in polaroids of her and her many friends all smiling and hugging. The only things we both have in common in our rooms are our fencing epees and uniform.

As she is rummaging through her closet I take a quick

look at myself in the mirror and grimace at the state my hair is in. At one point I was lying on the forest floor to better see the underside of the morels and must have picked up a few leaves and twigs in the process.

"Here it is!" She whips around holding an outfit that scares the shit out of me.

A few minutes later I emerge from her room in an impractically tight, high-waisted, minty green silk skirt with a matching off the shoulder cropped blouse with long sleeves that cinch at the wrists before flaring out again in a frill. I'm sure the skirt fits her much more loosely but my curves are making it hug me in an uncomfortably revealing way. I stomp down the stairs as Marissa trails behind me, still pinning my dark hair up with a big clip that matches the green of the clothes.

"Ah, lovely work Marissa. The green really brings out her eyes. Quickly now ladies, get in the car," Mother says as she snaps her fingers at us.

"I can barely move in this. What if I need to run... or sit down?" I complain, already knowing it will get me nowhere.

"Ladies don't run, my dear," my mother responds while giving my back a little push out the door, towards the car.

"Shot gun!" Marissa quickly runs to the front seat and hops in before I can get there. I resist rolling my eyes. Already an instance where running was necessary...

As we drive towards the country club Marissa peers at me, over her shoulder. "Were you drawing those silly mushrooms again?"

"They aren't silly and it's for a university project that

could be *published* Mar. The findings could be used in an affront to our local politicians, proving the rapid decline of the mycorrhizal populous of the forests! You're too young to understand. You don't even care about your high school studies." I huff out a breath as I look out the tinted window at the suburban streets. In just a few minutes I've already counted five people spraying their lawns with a herbicide that has been the new popular way to keep weeds at bay and I can't help but worry, thinking of what other creatures it might be poisoning.

"We can't all be nerds like you, Nuria. I became captain of the fencing team a year before you did and at least I have friends my own age unlike someone..." Marissa quips back. In truth the only thing we have in common was our skill and passion for fencing.

Our father was a state champion back in his day and firmly believed fencing to be one of the oldest art forms of high society. He nurtured our passions at a young age by play fighting with us. Marissa would always be the princess and I her knight, fighting off our father, the evil king. She would often quickly forget the princess trope and join in the fight which would always end up with both of us piled on top of him in a tickle fight. This was back when he had time for such things. Now he rarely even makes it to our matches.

"Marissa, be nice. And Nuria, darling, please remember to not do that strange thing you do sometimes. It disturbs people," Delia says casually, trying not to make a big thing out of the fact that I can occasionally guess what others are thinking and can't help but say it out loud; especially when it's something judgmental. It's not as if I can actually hear their voices but rather, I get a feeling for what they are saying. It is almost like reading a book that flashes in my mind for a moment before disappearing again. Maybe I've just become good at reading people from spending my entire life as a wallflower. Some have said that they could have sworn they heard my voice in their heads though, which is a little harder to explain.

As we pull up and wait in the queue of cars for the valet I notice that Benji, my ex, is the one greeting cars. I let out a groan and sink low in the seat hoping he won't see me.

"Oh look there's your *lover*," Marissa snickers from the front seat. I can feel the heat rise up my cheeks.

"That is not what he is! Besides whatever that was, I ended it a couple of weeks ago..." I quickly reply, catching my mother's glance at me through the rear view mirror. She doesn't need to know I lost my virginity to one of the Jones boys or that he was a pretty good lover, not that I have much to compare him to.

Benji is the second oldest of six boys that poor Mrs. Jones was left with after their father split a few years back. They are a good bunch for the most part, as good as six mischievous boys who are always together could be, with Benji being the better of them, but his idea of a good life is staying put and never changing. Our relationship seemed to be just about sex near the end. Benji would travel all the way to my dorms, a few hours away, in his rusty old car just to scratch the itch. I could feel greater things pulling me away from settling for that. I could feel someone...*else*, pulling me away. Or perhaps it was the wilder parts of this world, calling my name.

"Go on then, leave before he gets to the car. We will meet you inside." Delia winks in the rear view before rolling down the window as Benji approaches. She has her nice moments and in this one I could kiss her. I quietly open the door and slide out as silently as I can.

"Hello Mrs. Piedmont, hello Marissa, lovely to see you. May I park your car?" Benji says as he tries to peer into the back seat. I hunch down on the other side of the car then run, or waddle, as quickly as I can to the front door while he is distracted holding the car door open for my mother. *Sometimes ladies do need to run after all!* I scoff to myself knowing I look like a ridiculous, elegantly dressed duck trying to run in this skirt.

Once inside, I am hit by a wall of floral perfume and a chorus of giggling women clinking their glasses. The front foyer opens up to a grand room that is set up with dozens of round, white-clothed tables leading up to a low stage with a podium set up on top. No doubt for the announcements and bragging of the ladies. I wait off to the side of the front door hoping to not be approached before Delia and Marissa arrive. Crowds are hard for me. I can never tell if all the voices are in my head or being spoken out loud and I often feel like I'm in a hazy cloud of sound.

"Ah, Delia, we've been waiting for you and the girls to begin," the leader of the council wives committee chimes in, her pink, floral chiffon skirt swishing as she saunters to the door with a flute of champagne held out for my mother.

"We are precisely on time darling Margo. We may begin now," Mother says with an air of superiority, grasping the champagne and not pausing in her step as she continues walking to our table. Margo may be the committee head but my mom is clearly the more revered. She has always had an aloofness to her that draws people in and makes them want to impress her or be her confidant.

The room seems to settle down upon our arrival and the women rush to their seats. The gathered women sit down simultaneously, keeping an eye on my mother as she sits. I must have missed the memo and am the awkward one left standing before quickly plopping down in my seat, feeling the heat rise to my cheeks.

The first course, which is a crisp, green salad with a lemon dressing, is brought out and the hum of conversation, thankfully, starts back up around the room. Seated at our table are a few of the ancient ladies of Easthelm, who are well respected but don't offer much in the way of conversational company, and Mrs. LaRue with her twin daughters June and Samantha. June and Sam were in my grade at high school and made sure to ignore me every chance they could. I don't see why now would be any different. They are both studying ballet at a fancy school somewhere out of state and were probably back visiting for the summer like me. I avoid eye contact and start to poke around at my boring salad.

"So, Delia, do tell us what your Hunt has been up to with the water management board? I hear we are moving forward with the drilling? How exciting!" Mrs. LaRue says as she claps her petite hands together in excited little taps. *Such a suck up.* I roll my eyes at my salad.

"Pfft if by exciting you mean disastrous," I let slip, immediately regretting it as everyone at the table turns to stare at me.

"And whatever could you mean by *that,* Nuria?" Mrs. LaRue questions me whilst scowling like she smelled something awful wafting by. I look to Delia for either guidance or disapproval but she has an unreadable mask on.

Right, I'm on my own here. I think to myself as I stare into her cool blue eyes. A glimmer of shock passes across her face before her mask of indifference snaps back into place. *Did she hear that?* My eyes widen for a moment before I address Mrs. LaRue.

"Only that draining the basin would steal the water out from under us. That water is what protects us from fire. We have already been facing unprecedented droughts and the dying of our flora and fauna at alarming rates because of the lack of water. The better use of our money would have been to create *more* water catchments... maybe even supplying each household with a water tank." I can't help my voice growing quieter and quieter as I explain the point I have been saying to my dad for the past year. He was never really present enough to hear me, always on a call or rushing off somewhere.

"Hmm what funny little ideas they seem to put into the heads of our youth at university these days," one of the ancient crones croaks in response as she reaches over to pat my hand, as if I am a child who had an embarrassing outburst.

I wonder if Delia regrets adopting this one. She is so odd, I can hear her voice in my mind, not trusting whether it is my own frustration fueling my inner dialogue or the actual thoughts of the old bag beside me. I bite my tongue regardless.

Marissa places her cutlery daintily down on her plate. "Please excuse me ladies, Nuria, would you join me?" she says as she pushes up from her chair and heads towards the washrooms. Thankful for the out, I give the ladies my best decorous smile and a little nod before darting after her. Once I enter the washroom Marissa's plastered on sweet smile has been wiped off for a frown.

"Come on Nuria, you've got to try harder out there. Reign in the savior of the planet crap. You know Mom is pushing for committee head in the fall and having a weirdo daughter won't help matters. Besides, Dad is the one spear-heading the basin drill. How does it look if his oldest daughter is rallying against him?" Marissa pleads, looking genuinely upset. I didn't realize she cared so much about keeping up the pretense that we were a perfect little family. She'd always seemed pretty content pretending to not know me when we were at the same school and now that she has had the place to herself for the past four years her social life seems to be soaring.

"What do you care what I say and do? It's not like anyone takes me seriously. I swear everyone in there sees me as a charity case that Mom took on sixteen years ago. You're the golden child, so they will barely look in my direction. Mom will get committee head whether I'm around or not to support her! I just can't get behind this backwards town. There are signs all over the forest that we are destroying things and this drill is going to make it so much worse!" I start to raise my voice as the all too familiar feeling of being misunderstood washes over me.

"I do not see you as a charity case, darling," Mom says from the now open door of the washroom. There is a look of hurt in her eyes. I didn't hear her come in and I immediately regret what I said. "You are my child and quite frankly, after all we have been through, I would have hoped you'd believe that by now." I do know she loves me in her own way but there will always be differences between me and Marissa.

I pinch the bridge of my nose and take a breath, trying to dispel my frustration. "Sorry Mom, I do... I just got caught up in the moment. These events are really insufferable for me. There is so much noise in my head. I need to step out. I'll wait for you in the gardens," I say, while heading for the door. I catch a knowing glance shared between Marissa and Delia; the glance that makes me feel like a nutter every time. I sigh and steel myself for the dining hall, hoping to make my escape without drawing too much attention.

I keep my gaze straight ahead to the exit door and my head held high as I walk slowly enough to not alert anyone to my rising panic but I get about half way when I can't help but look at all the staring faces. It all starts pouring in.

What was she saying about her own dad's project?
She thinks she is better than us.

Hunt is such a hottie. He probably has a mistress.

What an ungrateful brat.

Poor Marissa, how does she stand living with such a freak?

Delia should have sent her to a boarding school.

Is that a leaf in her hair? She's so feral.

I heard she was slumming it with that Jones boy.

Her only friend is an old man.

Such a weirdo. She used to believe in gnomes.

Freak.

Nerd.

All I can do is clasp my hands over my head and run. *I'm a freak...*

I slam into the door, pushing my way through, hoping on the other side I find peace and quiet, but instead, I find myself in a completely different building.

There are rough hewn, white stone bricks on the walls and floors and flickering flames propped up in old iron sconces lining the walls. I'm in a long corridor with a high, domed ceiling. There are multiple rounded wooden doors on either side of the hall and a grand double door that is taller than all the others at the very end.

Where am I? I shake my head and look around. There is light shining under the double door so I slowly make my way towards it. There are some strange, small statues sitting in little alcoves carved out of the rock, lining the hall. One appears to have the torso and head of a man and the lower body of a goat. Another is a bust of a regal looking man with pointed ears and canines that appear slightly too long to be normal. *Such strange art...*

As I inch my way down the corridor I notice my movement comes much easier than it should in that ridiculous skirt so I look down and see that I am in some sort of button down vest and trousers tucked into tall boots.

This is not my body, this is not me. Where am I? My stomach sinks, the few bites of salad I had are fighting each other back up my throat.

"You may enter Embrys!" I hear a deep growling voice call from beyond the doors. I do not want to go but I feel a pull to open the doors that I cannot resist. I grasp the curling iron handles and fling them open, more easily than I should've been able to judging by their size. Seated at the other end of a massive, high ceilinged hall is a man with the head of a wolf grinning back at me. His fanged mouth is all I can focus on. The look on his face makes me instantly nauseated. He looks as if I am the juiciest prey and he is ready to pounce. The moment our eyes meet there is a strange flicker of recognition but at that precise moment I am jolted back into my body like a snapping rubber band before I can step fully into the hall and face the wolfish nightmare.

Chapter Two

I can feel a throbbing in my head and the brightness of the neon lights overhead make my eyes sting as I crack them open. I am met with Benji and Marissa hovering over me and I swear it looks like they are holding hands.

"She's back! Make room!" Marissa nudges Benji out of the way as she kneels down, grasping her dress so as to not wrinkle it as she lets her bare knees hit the hardwood floor beside me.

"Nuria! Nuria are you ok? You bolted out of there like a jack rabbit!" Marissa clearly exaggerates whilst shaking my shoulders. I brush her off, coming up onto my elbows.

"I didn't bolt. I walked like a normal human. I'm fine, I think I just haven't eaten enough today," I lie as I push myself up onto my feet and dust off my clothes. My vision swims for a second, Benji leans in to grasp my arm but I pull it away before he can.

"Get back in there Mar, really I'm fine. I'll wait in the

car," I say with a little feigned smile and start walking towards the front door so she won't see my hands shaking.

I hesitate pushing the door open for fear that I will be transported back to wherever that place was.

"Here, let me get that for you," Benji offers, swinging the door open and letting the hot midday air wash over me. I give him a little nod then hurry towards the car.

"I've got the keys, remember... I'm the Valet," Benji chuckles whilst following me and swinging the keys around his finger. I grasp out for them but he pulls his hand away. Concern wrinkles his brow.

"What happened in there, Nuri?" he asks. I just shrug in response and try to grab the keys again but he pulls them away. "I think that happened once when we were together but you didn't collapse that time. You just kind of looked straight ahead and couldn't hear me. Also this time you said a name. You said Embrys. Is that your new boyfriend?" he questions me but I'm too shaken to deal with this right now.

Embrys... his name is Embrys. I feel my cheeks flush and my body warm despite the chilling scene I have just witnessed.

"Leave me alone Benji," I say through clenched teeth. He sighs and turns on his heel to walk back towards his Valet's podium. Annoyingly, he also took the keys with him. I decide I just need to get out of here, so begrudgingly I start my walk back home.

The entire walk is a blur as I go over every detail of what I saw when I was passed out. *Am I losing my mind?* These flashes used to happen for the briefest of moments when I was younger when I would enter a room or spin around suddenly but they would never last for more than a few moments. I remember enjoying the scenes I would see. Sometimes I was in a vibrant forest, others were on horseback. I know it sounds strange but I felt like a friend was taking me away from my reality, just for a moment, to show me another life. They all felt joyful and exciting as a kid but it happened less and less as I became a teen, to the point that I stopped believing they were anything other than childish dreams.

This one was different. This one felt sinister.

The visions seem to be getting stronger since my return from university, it feels so real. The hard stone beneath my feet and the cool iron door handles in my hands. It all felt so real! And that voice... Why do I know that voice? Fear sours my stomach.

When I finally get home I'm a bit of a sweaty mess and just want to dissolve into nature for a while. I peel off the skin tight skirt and frilly blouse right there in the foyer before running up to my room to put on my swimmers. I also grab my towel and sketch pad before I bolt out the back door, letting it slam behind me.

The midday heat is softened by the dense canopy of the forest just beyond our backyard, the call of the birds a familiar comfort. I find my well-hidden deer track that leads to my favourite swimming spot and pad my way down to the creek in my bare feet; the crackle of leaves and soft sponge of the mosses underfoot giving me a sensory delight; the tickling brush of the ferns on my shins are friends welcoming me home.

I've been coming here ever since I first arrived at the Piedmont's house. Delia and Hunt had to constantly keep an eye on me, otherwise I would race off into the forest. They would find me by the creek turning over boulders as if I was desperately looking for something and babbling away about gnomes. Just the grand imagination of a five year old they would joke.

The creek is just as I left it in its sweet bubbling glory; I drop my towel and sketch pad on the bank and wade in; the first touch of the cool water eliciting an audible sigh from my lips. There hasn't been any rain in weeks though so my swimming hole is more or less a spot to sit in with the water going just above my belly button when I am seated but it does the trick to cool me down both physically and mentally.

I lie down in the creek, using a big rock as a pillow and let the soft current flow over my shoulders. The waving, whispering leaves of the willows overhead lull me into deep relaxation, my eyes flutter closed by their own accord. I bask in the quiescence of the moment, audibly sighing.

The squirrels chitter at each other from different trees, proclaiming their territory and the sweet, yellow warblers call, searching for their mates. In the distance, there is the tap tap tap of the woodpecker and the lilting song of the robin. The songs of the forest all meld together in a symphony of balance that puts me into an easeful trance. The weirdness of the morning washes away in the serenity.

My consciousness is fading between dream and wakefulness as I soak in the cool tendrils of the creek when, out of nowhere, I hear a crash coming from deeper within the forest.

My eyes snap open, I notice that the sun has lowered significantly in the sky and there are some big clouds rolling in. *How long have I been here?* I wonder, looking down at my wrinkly hands. In that moment, a chill creeps down my spine as I take in the eerie silence of the forest. The birds have fallen silent and the squirrels seem to all be hiding or staying completely still. All I can hear is the soft bubbling of the creek as it tumbles around the rocks.

There must be something big nearby, I observe with a twinge of panic, scrambling out of the creek and grabbing my towel. I pause, listening closely and looking in the direction I heard the crash but everything is utterly still. *Surely a bear wouldn't come this far down the mountain,* I try to reassure myself, I grab my sketchbook and quickly tiptoe back up the deer track, not wanting to find out.

Once I begin to see the houses through the trees the birds start picking up where they left off, giving the illusion of safety again. Whatever that thing was, it must have headed back into the direction of the mountain. I sigh and slow my pace. I still need a bit of time before I step into what I know will be uncomfortable scrutiny from my family.

When I get back to the house it feels quiet. I realize with relief that it is only Delia who is home – interrogation avoided.

"Where is everyone?" I ask, putting my sketch pad and

towel down on the kitchen counter as I grab one of her famous chocolate chip cookies.

She startles at the sound of my voice. "Oh... Marissa is at her friend's place and your father will be home late... again. Just you and me, dear." She sounds far away and it feels like a punch to the heart. Ever since Dad was promoted within the council he is barely home and it's awful to see the effect it has on her. I often wonder who and what she was before she had me and Marissa in her life. She is an absolute badass when she is in front of people from town, but at home she just feels like an empty shell sometimes.

"That's ok. Let me help you cook dinner, it will be fun." I get a little nod and a meek smile in response, a small victory. We end up baking more cookies after dinner as well, cookies always fix things.

THE NEXT MORNING I leave the house early to document the morels but the heat is extraordinarily oppressive today so, before I know it, I find myself daydreaming by the creek instead. Thankfully there are no strange silences or feelings of being watched today. Just the sweet symphony of croaking frogs, chirping grasshoppers, and twittering birds – the soundtrack to my admiration of a spider performing her dance of geometrical magic.

When I return home the air-con is pumping and, while I usually despise the dry, recycled air, today I have to admit it is welcome. *Perhaps I will just catch up on my paintings.*

The day has well and truly turned into a rot day though, all productivity is fried away by the hot air outside and I find I am just mindlessly flipping through magazines, trying to avoid looking at my phone.

I look up from the new monthly Eco-Quirk magazine to find Marissa's head peering into my room; I sigh and wave her in.

"Hey Nuri, I brought some nail polish. I thought maybe we could hang." She plops down on the bed beside me. This feels strange, she never wants to just *hang*, or at least she hasn't for many years. We were inseparable when we were little. Puberty ruined everything.

"Okay... why?" I don't hide my confusion.

"I just... feel like we need some sisterly bonding time, or whatever." She rolls her eyes and starts flicking through the magazine I had been reading, landing on an article about medicinal weeds for a moment before quickly setting it back down. She probably thought it was an article about marijuana – to her disappointment, it was a spotlight on the resourcefulness and necessity of dandelions in urban gardens.

"Right, well the Marissa *I know* would rather be out with her friends than in here with me, so tell me what's up? Did something happen with Lucie or Taylor?" I may not spend much time with her these days but I do know when she wants something from me.

"No no nothing like that. It's just..." She blows a big sigh out through her lips, "it's just been kind of shitty this past year, okay? I feel like when you were around more we had each other's backs, you know? And this year, since you didn't come back for *any* of the other school holidays, Dad has been extra hard on me." Marissa gets up and starts pacing the room. I've never seen her like this. She usually has this *I don't give a damn* mask on and nothing fazes her. The assumption I made of her wanting something feels rotten in my stomach. *Am I a bad sister?*

"I'm sorry Mar... what has he been doing?" I know all too well that Hunt can be a bit of a pompous ass, but it is usually directed at me or his colleagues, never to Mom or Marissa. She comes and sits back down, staring at her hands.

"Nothing I do is good enough for him. Every report card, every fencing match, even every friend I make is not good enough, not that he ever actually attends my matches or takes time to interact with any of my friends." She aggressively unscrews the lid to the nail polish, which is a startling shade of purple I might add, and grabs my hand. I want to say, *at least he pays you any attention as he pretty much just ignores me*, but I'm trying a new thing, I'm going to be a *supportive*, older sister, maybe. I'll try...

"That does sound shitty. Well I'm here now Mar. I will try to be as annoying and disappointing as possible so he backs off. How does that sound?" This manages to elicit a snort out of her.

I relent to the supposed pampering Marissa is now supplying to my poor nails because the soft smile that has spread on her face reminds me that, despite having different parents, we are family and she is important to me. I want her to be happy.

We sit quietly while she glosses up my short and dirty nails, the pause in her usual chatty self has me feeling a bit awkward so I try to fill the silence.

"So... you seeing anyone?" *Is that a normal question to ask a sixteen, almost seventeen, year old?*

Judging by her facial expression, *it is not.* This is the first I think I have ever seen Marissa Piedmont blush. She does one more stroke on my pinky then quickly screws the cap back on the polish.

"There you go, much better. Those scraggly nails were an eye sore." She hops off the bed then promptly leaves the room, slamming the door as she goes. *Back to her normal self.*

"So is that a yes?" I call out after her but receive radio silence. *Great, I messed that one up.*

I look down and grimace at the purple monstrosity that is my finger nails and decide I will have to remove it once they dry. *Pfft, sisterly bonding my ass...*

I look longingly out the window and decide that the afternoon sun is low enough, I decide to brave the scorching day once again. I know that the fairy circle will disappear soon so I push myself to get out there.

Somehow, in this heat, fungi still seem to be thriving, so I go around to each mushroom and give its cap a little tap in hopes that the spores will spread and more will pop up after the next rains – *if* the rain ever comes again. It baffles me how it seems barely anyone in this town gives a damn about how bloody hot it has been. The protest I have planned in two weeks about the water basin drill has only managed to conjure up three other people that seem even remotely interested. Mr. Bugg was going to come all the way out to Easthelm for it but it just feels like an embarrassment now. If only I could bring the entire town out here to experience the precious serenity of the forest, maybe then they would understand. I also may be using the lack of protestors as an excuse to get out of public speaking. My fear of addressing a crowd unfortunately trumps my activism.

I slowly start rambling back home, dreaming about Easthelm's lawns turning into dynamic food and flower gardens, when I hear it – a low rumbling growl sounds behind me.

Shit... I don't dare to turn around and look, I just start running.

Come on legs move faster! I don't slow my pace until the back fence is in view, when I stop I listen out but nothing is following me. *I may need to start bringing bear mace out here...*

I'm lost in thought about what on earth that creature could be when I hear voices arguing in the backyard just beyond the back gate. It sounds like Marissa and a man.

"You can't just touch me like that in front of her! What if she saw?" Marissa sounds peeved.

"What are you afraid of? Come on, I want to be with you. You understand me more anyway," the male voice responds gently and I don't want to believe who it sounds like but when I peek through a crack in the fence I can see Benji there, holding my little sister's *waist*.

I see red. Rage and betrayal wash over me. In my fury, I

swing open the back gate and let it smash against the fence, a bit more dramatic of an entrance than I intended.

"What on earth is going on here?" I seethe, looking between Benji and Marissa as they quickly step away from each other. "She's only sixteen Benji! And we literally broke up only a few weeks ago!" I yell, as images of us in bed together flash through my mind. His mouth on mine and his wandering hands sliding between my legs. Then I picture my little sister and him together in that way and shake my head to quickly shut that thought down, suppressing my shudder.

"I'm turning seventeen in a few months! Don't be such a prude, Nuria," Marissa says, while pursing her lips and crossing her arms.

"I'll just go. Always a pleasure, Nuria." Benji winces before giving Marissa's hand a squeeze and heading around the side of the house, probably trying to avoid our parents. *Coward.*

"Seriously Marissa, you're too young for him and I would have assumed there would be some sort of sister code preventing us from dating the same guy..." I start saying but am soon cut off by Delia sticking her head out the back door.

"Ah, there you are, Nuria, dinner is ready girls, come inside," she calls before disappearing back inside. Marissa gives me a glare that I know means, *don't you dare tell Mom,* before running up the back steps and through the door. I stare after her knowing there is no way I am letting this drop but at least *I* am honourable to the sister code and won't tell our parents. Besides, this is between me and her. She always wants what I have, but this is taking it too far.

I realize in my shock that I dropped my towel and sketch pad outside the gate and walk back to pick them up when I notice the birds have gone silent again and my skin prickles. I feel like I'm being watched. I can hear the distant rumble of a storm as I quickly grab my stuff and run back towards the house. I don't dare to look back, having that feeling of terror I used to get as a little girl when I would have to go down into the cellar of the house to grab a bottle of wine for Mom. The kind of terror that if you don't move quick enough something is going to grab you from behind and drag you into the darkness. *I'm getting out of here!*

Once I'm inside I can already hear the deep rumbling laugh of my dad coming from the dining room, so I race upstairs to change out of my swimmers and start mentally preparing my rebuttal to the inevitable heated debate that's about to ensue.

I always looked up to him when I was younger. He seemed larger than life to me with his tall, strong body, a face that was all hard angles, and a deep authoritative voice. He would tell me of his travels, visiting many of the universities across the Continent and even getting out to a few of the large island chains in the south. He spoke of his interest in how cities were planned and of man's ingenuity across the world. I never thought a day would come where I would doubt him but the work he has been doing lately just isn't something I can get behind. Perhaps he was always this way and the whimsy of childhood just sheltered me from reality.

I change into a comfortable romper and hurry downstairs, knowing Delia takes personal offence when we let the food she cooks go cold, and slide into my seat at the big oak dining table.

"My dear Marissa, I hear congratulations are in order for a win at your match," my father announces while passing the potatoes, as if this wasn't last weekend's old news. Marissa looks elated at the mention.

"Thank you Father. I used the manoeuvers you showed me and schooled Gemma Hawkesbury. She thought she was going to take my spot as captain this year but I showed her," Marissa says, puffing herself up while flipping a curl over her shoulder. We share a knowing glance.

"Good good," he responds, giving her hand a little pat, already dismissing the conversation and turning his sharp eyes on me. "Nuria..." My eyes open wide in anticipation of his next words and I try to hide my gulp.

"Father..." I say back warily.

"Delia and I will be joining the Turnbulls this Saturday at their lake house. I want to get William on board with the new environmental proposal for the drill. It's the only thing holding us back from breaking ground at the moment. So I will need you here to watch out for Marissa. I know you had plans this weekend, some sort of hike I believe but you will need to cancel as this is of the utmost importance. Perhaps you two can practice your fencing," he says, using his stern voice. He is probably expecting a fight from me but I sigh in relief at avoiding yet another fruitless debate about what I think of the council's work. After what happened at the luncheon, my brain feels too scrambled anyway. So I give him a curt nod and we all slip back into our normal dinner time silence but as I glance at my sister I can see a cheeky little smirk on her lips and wonder what mischief she is planning.

LATER THAT NIGHT, I knock on Marissa's open door, leaning on the frame and peering into her bright room. She's sprawled on her massive bed, staring at her phone with that same cheeky smile from dinner.

"Whatever you're plotting, stop it."

"Whatever could you mean?" she says, rolling onto her stomach and batting her long, blonde eyelashes at me. I roll my eyes and sigh, knowing she'll do what she wants regardless of my protestations.

"Can we please talk about Benji? It kind of feels like you're just going after him because I dated him," I say, the hurt from before is bubbling up.

"That's not true Nuri. I actually really like him." She sits up, tossing her phone on the bed. "Look, I have had a crush on him since the seventh grade and then you started dating him out of the blue and it sucked. You don't even care about him, you said so yourself. Just let me live my life. There are probably loads of cute guys at your university anyway. Probably nerds just like you that you'd have more in common with," she says, wincing at the harshness of her last comment. I let it slide.

"It's just really strange for me, ok? Can you at least wait until I head off for university in the fall before pursuing anything?" I say, hoping she will get bored of him and move on to the guys at her school instead.

"Ok, ya, maybe." She shrugs and goes back to looking at her phone. I open my mouth to push on when instead I decide to cut my losses on this conversation. Not worth the headache, and I will be out of here soon enough.

"Good night girls! We are heading out early tomorrow so we most likely won't see you. Marissa, listen to your sister!" we hear our mother call from downstairs.

"Good night!" we call back in unison. I push off her door and head down the hall to my room.

I swing open the door to the pitch black of my room, flipping the light switch, but nothing happens. The light bulb must have burnt out so I feel my way over to my desk by the window that faces the backyard. As I lean down to flick on the lamp a sudden flash of lightning lights up the sky and illuminates the backyard, I see a hairy creature standing on two legs with freakishly long fingernails staring up at the window. Its knees are pointing backwards and its arms are too long to look natural. I scream and quickly feel for my lamp but when I turn it on and look back out the window, the creature that looked like death incarnate is gone.

"What? What is it!?" Marissa screeches as she comes tumbling in and sees me staring out the window.

"Uh...um, I don't know! Some sort of creature is out there!" I answer and can't keep the shake out of my voice.

"Like a fox or something?" she asks, scrunching her face up and looking at me like I'm ridiculous.

"No, not like a *fox or something*. You think I would scream at a bloody *fox*? It was standing on two legs and it was huge!" I yell back.

"Ya right. I think your brain has had a weird couple of days, Nuri. Get some rest," Marissa chuckles, leaving me alone in my terror.

Maybe I am seeing things. I feel like I'm unraveling at the seams but as I look back out the window, another lightning strike flashes and I can clearly see the back gate is wide open. *Didn't I close that behind me?* I shudder and yank my curtains closed, as if some flimsy fabric could keep out whatever the heck that thing was or maybe at least keep my sanity intact.

Chapter Three

True to their word, my parents are gone when I get up in the morning. It's already eleven and I'm annoyed at myself for the sleep-in, but after what I thought I saw last night, sleep didn't find me until well into the wee hours of the morning. I had wanted to get out early to document what the miniscule downpour we had last night might have sprouted and hoped the scorching heat hadn't dried everything up already. Surely some new mycelial specimens would have popped their little heads up overnight. When I stumble down the stairs, Marissa is giggling on the couch with three of her cronies, Lucie, Taylor and Annie. They all look up at me simultaneously and stop talking.

"Not suspicious at all..." I say as I swing myself around on the stair's banister and make my way to the kitchen.

"You know if you still wanted to go camping tonight I

would be totally fine by myself. Lou, Tay and Annie can keep me company, super low-key girl's night." Marissa bounces into the kitchen after me.

"Ya right. The four of you can never be classified as *low-key*," I respond as I rummage through the dishwasher looking for my favourite mug to brew my tea in.

"Well all right if you must know, we are planning a little get together. Just a few friends and some pizza I swear," she says, as quickly as she can, no doubt thinking that I would somehow miss what she just said.

"Absolutely not! Mom and Dad put me in charge specifically because they knew you'd pull something like this," I say crossing my arms.

"Come on, you can join us! I'll even order the smelly mushroom one from Zazzella's that you love so much. Mom left me one of her credit cards and said to order out anyway. Might as well be the good stuff and with some friends. I swear it will be chill," she pleads her case as her cronies come through the doorway to back her up. I sigh and contemplate her offer. I do really love Zazzella's pizza. The stuff we have on the university campus tastes like cardboard in comparison. I just can't imagine anything worse than hanging out with a bunch of teenagers at the moment. Maybe I can just pop in and out to make sure they aren't breaking into the liquor cabinet and catch up on my paintings in my room. Besides, after what I thought I saw last night, going solo camping is the last thing I want to do. Benji and I had planned to go together before the semester was over but for obvious reasons I will not be doing that anymore.

All four of the girls start pouting and batting their eyelashes at me. "Fine, only a few people though. Like ten, max. And I'm hiding Mom's liquor," I concede. They are satisfied enough with my reluctant response and run back into the living room squealing. I give up looking for my mug and settle for a travel thermos to take out to the woods on my quest for new fruiting mushrooms.

When my tea is brewed I grab my pack and a banana and head out through the back door to go see what I can find when I notice the back gate is closed again.

Maybe I did imagine the creature, relief washes over me, but there is also a chance that Mom or Dad closed it before they left this morning. Still, I decide to brave the woods hoping that daylight will keep anything malicious far away. At least my mind can't play tricks on me when there aren't as many shadows.

I stop just in front of the back gate, holding onto the handle, deciding that surprise is my best defense if there is something lurking back there as I whip the door open. I'm met with nothing but forest and let out a big sigh, realizing I had been holding my breath. *There is no such thing as monsters...*

I head in the opposite direction to the swimming hole and stay close to the fence line as I look for fallen logs and pine trees, hoping to find some new blooms. I keep my eyes peeled to the forest floor when I see something zoom by, out of the corner of my eye. I stop dead in my tracks, looking around the forest as my breath quickens and I start to hear my own heart pounding. A little further up there is another flash of something and I stifle a scream as I spin around to see a fawn jump out from a bush and stare at me before she bounds past to run deeper into the forest. I can see she has a limp and a smear of blood on her back leg and before I think twice about it I run in after her.

She looked to be only a few days old and if her mother isn't around then perhaps I can call wildlife services to come by; that is, if I can catch her. I use my minimal tracking skills that Benji's older brother Johno taught us when I'd go camping with their whole family. We would break off from the younger boys to try and hunt and once Johno even let me fire the rifle at a deer, which I was nowhere near hitting. I told him I'd stick to wielding my fencing swords if I ever needed to defend myself.

As I search, I occasionally pick up a hoof imprint in the mud and a little drop of blood here and there. I can tell she is slowing and when I finally catch up to her I step into a clearing and can see her sitting down in the high grass with her little ears poking up. A pretty good camouflage, but any predator would smell the blood immediately. I slowly tiptoe up to her, knowing any sudden movement will have her bolting again, even though she is clearly injured and her movement is limited. I lower myself down to her level.

"Hey sweet thing, it's okay I won't harm you. I'm just going to keep you company until someone can come help you. I wonder where your mom is," I say in my gentlest voice as I pull out my phone to get ahold of wildlife services. They pick up on the first ring.

"Hello you've reached Easthelm Wildlife Services, this is Andy speaking," a familiar voice eagerly replies.

"Yeesh, slow day there Andy? Hey, it's Nuria. I'm out the back of the Burgess' house, about half a kilometre in, north east, with an injured fawn. No sign of the mother and a visible wound on her back leg. Can you get someone out here?" I reply, knowing what to say from the summer I volunteered with them a few years back.

"Hey Nuri! Yes, can do, just waiting on the van. Steve's out chasing down a rabid raccoon at the Lawson's place so it shouldn't be too long, sit tight. Oh and Nuri?"

"Yes Andy?" I respond with a premonition of what is about to come next.

"I heard you and the Jones guy broke up so I was uh... wondering uh..."

"I've got to go Andy, the fawn is trying to get up..." I lie then quickly hang up, narrowly avoiding the request for a date. He's a good guy but I'll be gone in less than a month and just can't get caught up in anything right now. I know Andy has had a crush on me for years though, so I feel a twinge of guilt for not giving him a chance.

I sit quietly with the fawn as we wait and she even lets me give her a little pat on the head. When I look over her shoulders I can see she has sat down right next to an exquisite *Amanita muscaria* in full bloom.

"Oh wow!" I exclaim, causing the fawn to flinch away from me, and making me wince at my own outburst.

"Sorry, it's ok. I get excited about mushrooms some-times," I whisper and she seems to settle down at my soft tones. I guess that we will be waiting a while so I pull out my sketchpad and pencils from my pack and crouch down low to get a good look at the beautiful red mushroom with white polka dots. These always make me feel a wave of nostalgia that I can't quite place the origin of.

I'm about halfway done with my sketch of the underside of the mushroom, the fourth drawing I've done so far, when I hear a rustling coming from the east side of the clearing. The fawn's ears are on full alert, both facing towards the sounds and she starts squirming and trying to stand but falling back down as her back leg fails her.

"Stay down little one. Stay still. Everything is ok. It's probably just a rabbit, or better yet your mother coming to find you," I whisper to her, knowing she doesn't understand but in a way comforting myself and keeping from admitting it was stupid to come out here alone after last night.

All illusion of comfort is gone when it sounds as though the rustling is coming closer and is now accompanied by a low, barely audible growl that makes the hairs on my arms stand up. The kind of growl you can feel inching up your spine rather than hear.

"Ok that doesn't sound like a rabbit..." I squeak, quickly gathering up my supplies and shoving them in my pack. The growling grows to a very audible snarl and I can see the branches just behind the bushes that are lining the clearing being pushed out of the way, as if something large is clearing its way through. The pounding of my heart becomes audible when I see long claws poke out from the bush as they clasp onto the branches, slowly parting them.

"Yup, we are getting out of here now!" I screech as I bend down to scoop the fawn into my arms and turn around to dash out of here when I nearly run into Steve. I let out a scream and nearly drop the fawn as he takes a step back with his hands up.

"Woah there, just me young buck," Steve chuckles, "sorry it took me so long to get here. One rabid raccoon turned into a gang of them and I had to get Andy out there to help me. Here, let me take her off your hands," he says as he reaches out to take her into his arms. I hand her over and just stand there fear stricken and shaking.

"Come on, let's get to the van. She's not looking too good... and neither are you for that matter," he says, raising an eyebrow and giving me a once over. I give myself a little shake and take a deep breath.

"I just thought I heard something back there," I say as I look over my shoulder to a perfectly quiet and still scene. I shrug and keep close behind Steve as we walk back towards the fence line, still feeling skittish and like something is watching me.

I follow him through the Burgess' back yard and onto the street to where the van is waiting, with a stupidly grinning Andy. I sigh and ready myself for that date proposal.

"Hey Nuria!" Andy calls, waving at me from the front seat of the van. He is handsome in a quirky way I will admit. His black curls and dimples give him this utterly harmless aura and his new glasses suit his face better than the round ones he once had that made his face look moonshaped.

"Wowie, look at that back leg. Guess we're headed to the

vet eh?" Andy says as he gets out of the car. He's nearly half a foot taller than me and reaches out to give me a bear hug. I give him a little pat back, trying to hurry it up, but secretly I enjoy the all-encompassing Andy hug.

"Yup, let's load her up and head on over. Thanks for the call, Nuria. This little one would have been someone else's lunch in no time. Keep an eye out for the doe if you can," Steve instructs as he and Andy swaddle the fawn and put her in a big cage in the back of the van. As Steve moves over to the driver's door Andy comes to stand beside me with one hand rubbing the back of his neck and the other hand playing with a button on his shirt.

"Nuri... look I know you're headed back out to university soon, but I was wondering if maybe you'd like to hang out before then. Just hang out. Nothing implied. Maybe go for a hike or something?" Andy says, taking a step closer to me while dropping his hand and looking me straight in the eyes. The awkward Andy from a few summers ago seems to be traded in for someone more sure of himself. The dimpled smile is what gets me to consider the offer.

"Um... sure a hike would be nice. Send me a text or something," I say as I pat his arm and head back towards my house. I turn around to give them a little wave and can see the cheesiest grin on his face as he hops in the van, his voice chimes in my mind saying *Yes, finally!*

I let out a little groan and head back home. *Ah jeez, what did I just agree to?*

As I walk back I pull out my phone and notice my hands are shaking. It's already five. All I've eaten today is a banana and some tea, no wonder my nerves are a wreck. I pick up my speed as I also realize I have left my sister and her friends alone for five hours and genuinely fear that the house has been burned down. When I round the corner of the cul-de-sac everything looks normal, except for the half dozen cars parked outside our house.

As I step through the front door I am met with a literal hoard of teenagers scattered around. Five are crammed on the couch, playing video games, another four are lying on the rug in front of the T.V. playing cards and I can hear giggling coming from the kitchen. I drop my pack at the stairs and head into the kitchen and see Marissa, Lucie, Taylor and Annie pouring over some teen magazines and flicking through social media on their phones. Marissa is wearing my strappy, off-white linen dress and my annoyance bubbles below the surface of my tongue at how much better she looks in it than I do.

"Who starts a party at five?" I question as I quickly open the liquor cabinet to find everything still in its place. I start taking the bottles out and piling them in a laundry basket.

"Pfft, this isn't the party; these are just a few friends who are helping set up," Annie Lee responds with an unwarranted amount of sass.

I remember sweet little Annie with the pigtails and blouses buttoned all the way up to the neck coming to join the lapidary club when I was still in school. She was so enthusiastic about rocks and I immediately liked her for her passion, but I guess the pressure of this town got to her.

Now I have another blank-eyed, crop-topped teen, staring at me.

"Ok...well I'm going up to my room but that doesn't mean I am not here and I can't hear what's going on. I'll be in and out all night. You won't know when I'll just pop down here so keep it low-key and bring me my pizza when it's here," I say, as I quickly make myself a salad with some leftover roast chicken from the night before, realizing I'm verging on the level of hangry.

"Yes ma'am," they all say simultaneously then giggle and go back to their phones and magazines. The way they keep doing that freaks me out. Or maybe I've just never had close friends long enough to reach that level of synchronicity. I just roll my eyes and head back upstairs with the laundry basket full of liquor and my salad, grabbing my pack on the way. None of the other teens pay me any attention.

I devour the salad in my room and pop my headphones on to drown out the raucous voices as I settle into painting those beautiful Amanitas from earlier today. I can hear my phone pinging, guessing it's probably Andy already messaging me but decide to just let that sit for a while. I mix my paints and turn my music up.

It's easy for me to get lost in creation. Time warps and my senses hone into what I am working on; the smell of the paints, the feel of the wooden brush in my hand, smoothed from so much use, and the pictures in my mind coming to life on the paper is mesmerizing. Occasionally my botanical drawings take on animated forms and I find myself giving this particular mushroom a face and arms as well as animating the flowers and boulders around her. One stone character pops up quite often in my illustrations. She has a kind face with little spectacles and fluffy green moss for hair. I feel as though I can hear her gravelly laugh ringing through the air whenever I draw her.

As I pull back from the paper to take a better look at the woodland scene that has just poured out of me my gaze goes a bit hazy and I feel a bit dizzy, a purple haze spots my vision. When my eyes clear I am in a forest with gnarled, dark trees and high grasses that dance wildly with the wind. There is a thick mist swirling around, making it hard to see farther than a few meters. I look down and see the boulder creature I was just drawing looking up at me. *I must be dreaming!*

The creature reaches out to grasp my hand and I can feel the cool roughness of her stone fingers. *Nope, that's real...*

"What have you done boy! I will not let her pass through. You must call the varg back!" the creature begs as she tugs on my hand.

"It is too late, Mog. The varg is beyond my command now. You must trust me, this is for her own good. I would do nothing to harm her, she must be kept safe," I can hear a deep voice originating from my own lips.

What is going on here, who am I? I think I see shock in the creature named Mog's eyes, or is it recognition? She grabs onto my hands even harder and pulls me down to her level.

ELENA HUEBERT

"Don't let it take you, my child! You must fight back; it has orders not to harm you!" Mog quickly says and I feel she is talking directly to me before the body I am in pulls back and stumbles away, running into the dark, tangled forest. The next moment I am snapped back into my room.

I look down to see I am still holding my paint brush and have dripped bright red paint all over the hardwood floor and let out a groan. *What was that?* I think, shaking my head as I clean up the paint. I always felt removed from these episodes in the past, as if I am witnessing someone else's life in a dream, but that thing spoke directly to *me* this time. At least it sure felt as if she did. She told me to fight back. *What am I meant to fight?* I slide my headphones off and am accosted with a loud booming baseline and shouting, coming from downstairs. I look out the window to see it's already dark out and wonder at how long I must have just been standing there holding my paint brush, looking like an idiot. *Good thing no one walked in.*

I rip open my door and nearly run into Benji, who is standing there with one hand up, as if he was about to knock on the door and the other hand holding a pizza box.

"What are you doing here?" I bite out, a bit more harshly than I intended.

"Mar invited me to the party and told me to bring up your pizza. She also said to thank you for being so cool and not coming downstairs like you said you would," he laughs, pushing his way into my room and setting the pizza box down on my table. *Did she send him up purely to annoy me?*

"Woah cool, new piece?" he asks, leaning in to closely

look at my recent painting. The smell of the pizza has my stomach grumbling, so I grab a piece and shove it into my mouth.

"Um... yes it is. Thanks for the food, now would you kindly leave. Thank you," I say tersely through a full mouth as I shoo him out the door.

"Nuri, there is no need for the hostility, honestly. I'm not mad at you for breaking up with me," he says, clearly wanting to talk about it. *No thanks!* I just roll my eyes at him as I grab my phone to check the time.

"It's already eleven?!" I say, completely shocked, and I follow him out of my room, grabbing another slice of pizza on my way out. Downstairs, the vision I'm met with is pandemonium. The furniture has all been moved around to make room for a dance floor and I can see through the dining room door that a raucous game of beer pong is well under way. There are definitely more than ten people here and judging by the fact that Benji has come with his friends I'd guess that it's not just juice in all the red cups floating around.

Delia and Hunt are going to kill me if they find out. I worry as I try and navigate my way through all the flailing teens, looking for Marissa. First I push my way over to the fire place where I can see one of the guys has dismantled my dad's antique sword and is waving it around like some drunken pirate.

"Give me that you moron! Dad keeps it sharpened! You could kill someone!" I yell over the music as I rip the sword out of his hand and shove it behind the T.V. so no one else gets any crazy ideas of trying to sword fight in a mosh pit. I point my pointer finger and middle finger at my eyes then back at him, *I'm watching you*; what I hoped would be a menacing gesture just ends with the guy and his friends laughing as I storm off in search of my sister.

I find her in the middle of a beer pong game, with a big Sasquatch of a man that I have never seen before as her partner. I grab her arm, pulling her into the kitchen, she squawks out in protest.

"Who are all of these people Mar? And I said no drinking! You've got to shut this down now or the police will surely come shut it down for you and then we will both be in a heap of shit!" I yell at a clearly inebriated Marissa.

"All right, all right, fair enough, it is getting a bit crazy out there. But you've got to admit it's a pretty cool party, there are even university guys here!" she says, swaying a little bit, grabbing onto the kitchen counter to steady herself.

"Ok, you've had your fun. You'll be a legend for the whole first semester," I compliment her, hoping my request will take. "Now can you *please* help me shut it down and clean it up before Mom and Dad get back?"

"I'll help!" Benji pipes up as he saunters into the kitchen, "I'll go get Jimmy, he'll get them all out," he says as he heads toward the dining room. I catch Marissa's longing stare as he walks away and I do nothing to stifle my gag reflex.

A few moments later I can hear, who I assume to be Jimmy, yell, "Everyone out! Party's over!" The thumping music is immediately turned off and is replaced by a chorus of groans at the sudden stop. The Sasquatch man walks into the kitchen with a big smile on his face.

"I've always wanted to do that," he laughs.

"Ah, Jimmy I presume. Thanks," I reply, truly grateful at how easy that was.

"My pleasure. You must be Nuria? I'm Benji's cousin, in town for the weekend," he takes my hand in his massive grip and gives it a brisk shake. "Great party Mar, I'll see ya around," he says, shooting finger guns at Marissa before heading back out into the living room, herding a dozen teens out the door with his large arms as he goes.

Lucie, Taylor and Annie come stumbling in from the dining room with big pouts on their faces.

"Ugh, party poopers. It was just getting good!" Taylor complains.

"You four are menaces," I say in my driest tone, "I expect you to clean this all up before Mom and Dad get back tomorrow morning. I'm going to bed," I say, giving them all my best, *I mean it,* glare before heading back towards the stairs. I take one quick glance at the mess of the living room and I regret coming downstairs in the first place. Benji is at the front door ushering out the last of the stragglers and shuts the door with himself still inside the house.

"You can go too," I say, stopping at the base of the stairs

"Nuri, I'm going to stay back to help clean up. It's the least I can do," Benji shrugs.

"You're right, *it is* the least you can do," I snap.

"What do you mean by that? Why would it be *so bad* if

Mar and I started dating? I'm not that bad," he says as he leans against the door, propping one foot up behind him.

"You're not *bad* Benji, but Marissa has a bright future ahead of her and I'm not sorry for protecting her from getting stuck in this town," I explain, "and judging from past experiences, you're pretty complicit in the view of settling down and never changing."

"That isn't true!" He kicks off the door and steps up to me, getting in my personal space. "I believe in change and growth but I also believe that committing to making a home somewhere is just as good as gallivanting around the Continent. You're the one always preaching about caring for the land better. Well this is my version of that. My family has lived here for three generations. I want to *build* something in a place I *love* and I care for it. And yes, Marissa is still young, but have you ever stopped to ask her if maybe she wants to build something here as well? Now get off my back!" he fumes, only inches from my face before shoving past me towards where the others are starting to clean in the kitchen.

I let out a huff at his retreating back and storm upstairs. He never shared those thoughts with me when we were together. I kind of wish he had. I get it, that need to build something and protect it. I guess our only difference is that I don't consider Easthelm to be that place, and despite what he thinks, I do know what is best for Marissa. She is too wild for this place. Surely she needs more...

When I get to my room I shove one more slice of pizza in my mouth, put on my headphones and flop onto my bed. *Everything will be better in the morning.*

After what feels like only a few minutes I hear Marissa's friends call out from downstairs saying they are leaving and sarcastically thanking me for not being a bore.

"Always a pleasure!" I call back, knowing that the house is probably still a train wreck and I will have to get up to do some damage control. First, I lick the greasy goodness from the pizza off my fingers and reach for my phone and notice a bunch of missed texts and calls from Andy. He isn't usually this persistent and I have a sinking feeling that something is wrong. I click open my messages.

<u>Andy:</u>

6:12 p.m.

Hey Nuri, just reaching out to make sure you still have my number. This is Andy by the way.

6:54 p.m.

Hey we got a few more calls in today about some sort of animal out in the woods stealing pets. Have you noticed anything out there? Maybe that's what hurt the fawn.

7:15 p.m.

Let me know if you see anything and I can come out there.

8:15 p.m.

There is something or a pack of somethings out there that is seriously hungry. I just got another call from the Martins saying their Doberman got into a fight with something big. The other guys have gone home for the night though so there isn't anything I can do until morning.

10: 22 p.m.

Hey so we got another call in, not that long ago from the Burgess', saying they saw something big like a bear headed your way. Maybe stay out of the back yard and keep the gate closed.

I snap the phone shut, my eyes go wide and my heart quickens. *I knew I saw something yesterday, but that was no bear!* I think in a panic. I haven't heard Marissa come upstairs yet and notice through my bedroom window that the back light is still on. I rush over to my window to see if anyone is back there. Half the backyard is illuminated, leaving the back half in shadows. I can't tell whether the gate is closed or open.

Shit, did I leave that closed or open? Closed or open!?

I can see Benji walking out, headed to the side of the house holding a full garbage bag when Marissa comes prancing out behind him. She grabs his hand and whispers something in his ear that makes him laugh. He drops the garbage bag and they stumble towards the direction of the back gate and stop just outside of where the light reaches and turn to face each other. All I can see is their feet and judging by their closeness, they are kissing.

My panicked gaze darts to the left side of the yard as the creature emerges, out from under the oak tree, stepping into the full light. Its back is to me but I can see it is easily over six feet tall and has freakishly long arms and dripping nails. *No doubt the blood from all those missing pets Andy warned me about.* It seems to be sniffing the air, trying to scent Marissa and Benji. I can see its plan is to block their way back into the house so I bolt out of my room and down the stairs to try and intercept it, not thinking twice about how on earth I am going to face something so large. *Not my baby sister!* Is all

I can think as I jump the last four steps feeling a sharp pain shoot up my shins.

I hear a scream and as I run past the living room, I grab my dad's antique sword that I'd stashed away earlier. Now it's violence is exactly what I need to face this nightmare. *Better to be armed*, I rush on to save my sister.

Tentatively, I scan the courtyard – Benji is down, his runners are poking out of the shadows. I'm praying to whatever gods might be out there that he isn't dead. Gripping the sword harder in my sweat slicked hands, I slowly make my way to where he is lying down, swinging my gaze side to side, looking for Marissa and the beast.

"Benji?" I whisper as I crouch down beside him, "Benji!" I say a bit louder, shaking him with my non-sword wielding hand. I feel something warm and sticky and pull my hand away to see bright red. For a moment, in my confusion, I'm wondering why my paint from earlier is on him before, to my horror, I realize it's blood.

"Nuri! It took her... into the woods," he sputters. I wipe my shaking, blood covered hand on the grass.

"Thank fuck you're alive! Benji, stay still. I'm calling you an ambulance. Where is your phone?" I command, already rummaging in his pockets.

"Back pocket," he replies as he tries to sit up, groaning at the effort.

"Stay down, It's ringing!" I say, panic rising in my voice as my eyes adjust to the darkness and I start to see just how torn up his torso is. *No, no, no, no!* I'm trying to keep those slices of pizza down and have to look away.

"Here, give me the phone," he says, reaching out with one hand while the other puts pressure on the slash across his front. "You have to go after her, there's no time to wait for the bloody police Nuri! Bring her back, please..." he says, making a good point that I wish I wasn't about to listen to. His trust in my skills with a sword should reassure me but still, I falter.

Shit, what am I waiting for? She's my sister!

"Marissaaaa!"

Chapter Four

I stumble out from the back gate, sword in hand and take a moment to let my eyes adjust to the darkness.

Marissa's screams ring through the forest. "No, no no! Put me down! Benji help!" I don't waste a second, starting out at a full speed run, plunging into the dark forest.

"Marissa! Keep making noise, I'm coming!" I yell out, realizing afterwards that that *thing* could always double back and slice me open like it did to Benji.

"Nuria!" I hear her call, sounding farther away than before. I stop to see if I can hear more but everything has gone quiet. It's as if the crickets are holding their breath and the leaves of the trees are keeping themselves still so I can hear.

There. Straight ahead.

I hear a crash through the brush. It's going up the mountain. This won't be an easy task in the dark but I push on, stopping every now and again to listen out.

Her shrill screams stop after a while and I am now relying solely on the faint light of the moon to reveal where the creature is going. It seems to be running in a panic and not caring about making tracks, but I know I'm falling farther and farther behind every time I stop and examine broken branches and footprints in the mud. My night vision has always been exceptional but having to decipher tracks in the dense forest is proving difficult even for me. Hours pass this way, but time and the distance from home means nothing to me right now. *Hang in there Mar!*

I run on, my lungs heavily protesting. When I stop for a breath I realize I haven't heard anything or seen any tracks in a long time. The darkest part of the night looms over me like an oppressive dome and even the moon seems to have given up on aiding me in the search. If I keep blindly running on, I might lose the trail for good. I decide to hunker down under an overhanging rock to wait out the few remaining hours of the night and see if I can find a trail in the morning. There is no use stumbling around when I might end up going in the wrong direction. My body vehemently thanks me for stopping.

As I lay on the hard lumpy ground, thoughts of what my parents will come home to in the morning keep playing through my mind. I can't help but feel that for some reason this is all my fault. All I can do is pray that Marissa is still alive.

Out of nowhere the vision from earlier passes through my mind –

"The talking boulder said that the creature had orders not to harm me!"

Ok, I'm sounding crazier and crazier; a bloody talking boulder? Come on Nuria... but I hold onto the thought that maybe it was real and maybe that *thing* thinks Marissa is me and won't hurt her. I curl up, nestled far against the back of the rock wall and welcome sleep.

I wake with a start. The sun is already peeking through the trees, my only clue to the time. I quickly get up and stumble over to a nearby creek that I hear babbling nearby. I splash icy water on my face and take a long drink from my cupped hands. *I should've brought my hiking pack with me.* I realise I might not always be near a creek, and having at least a water bottle would have been a smart move. *How many things could I have done differently to keep Marissa safe?*

I start my hike uphill, to the protest of my legs from the night before, when I notice the leaves of the birch and aspen are already starting to turn into their startling yellow and oranges up here. I pause a moment to appreciate the golden sight, wishing that the circumstances of this discovery were in a less dire situation. I wish I could be allowed a moment to sit and paint what I saw, but I shake my head and carry on, all too aware of the importance of my mission. I scan the bush nearby and can't see anything immediately so keep making my way north-east, in the direction I last heard them crashing through the forest.

After a few minutes of fruitless searching I start to lose hope. I begin to wonder whether not waiting for the police was a stupid idea, when I see something shimmering out of the corner of my eye. I rush up to it and bend down to find one of Marissa's stick on nails, light purple with glittery tips, lying on the ground. *Mar, you genius!* I look up to find some very distinct tracks leading straight up a steep incline. The added weight of carrying Marissa is making the creature's feet sink into the ground more than it normally would, making the tracks much easier to see. I strengthen my grasp on the sword and start my climb.

I'm coming for you Marissa, I think to myself over and over, letting the mantra keep me steady.

The trees slowly change as the sun passes into the west and I gain altitude, with pines and spruces becoming more and more abundant. The air grows colder as well, the pine scented, cool mountain breeze is a welcome sensation as I am sweating and huffing my way up this particularly steep and rocky section. I am not graced with any more footprints amongst the rocks but every now and again there is a snapped branch on the low lying juniper bushes, showing signs of something big trying to pull itself up. The stick on nails stopped littering the forest floor a few kilometres back when, I'm guessing, she ran out. But I can feel that I am still on track.

I hope I'm still on track... Marissa I'm coming for you!

Holding onto a sword whilst scrambling up rocks is proving harder and harder but any thought of leaving it behind is met with the memory of the deep gash in Benji's chest, and I think better of it. When there is a brief respite from the steep incline I take a moment to search for some sort of water to quench my extremely parched mouth when

I come across the most beautiful patch of wild blueberries I've ever seen. A late season bush that must have been missed by the resident bears and squirrels. At the sight of their juicy ripeness I hear my stomach grumble and let myself pause long enough to gorge on handfuls of them. There is no water in sight but the juice from the berries should keep me from dehydration if I slow my speed and try not to sweat so much.

Up this high I have a better view of where the sun is in the sky as the canopy is starting to thin out. I pause, realizing it is much farther into the afternoon than I thought.

I should probably find shelter soon. I feel guilty for not trying to search through the night again but my body is aching and my feet are bleeding through my canvas shoes. I know I'll lose the ability to track soon anyway.

Better to let my body rest so I have my strength tomorrow, I reassure myself. It doesn't look like there will be any rain so I flop down beside a big rock that shields the cool wind, for the most part, but knowing with some dread, that I will be cold tonight. So many things I should have thought about before blindly running off, I know that this was the right choice though. *The useless Easthelm police would never have found the tracks... I had to go.*

I carefully peel off my shoes, hoping that airing them out overnight will help them heal. The cool air on my open blisters feels amazing, but the sight of them makes my stomach churn. I lean back against the cold, hard stone and close my eyes. Despite the discomfort, I am already starting to drift from sheer exhaustion.

I have the feeling of falling, my eyes flick open but all I see is darkness. Someone else is there though, they are familiar somehow... almost comforting.

Do not fear. You will be safe soon; the male voice from my visions speaks to me. I try to respond but I am suddenly jerked awake by the sound of a snapping twig. It is dark outside, with the faintest hint of light cresting the eastern horizon.

Is it almost morning already? I'm shocked at how deeply I must have been asleep and I wipe at my mouth feeling a good amount of crusted drool in the corner and wish I had a creek nearby to rinse it off. I quickly pull on my shoes and wince at the sting as they slide over my now scabbed over blisters when I hear another twig snap, even closer. I am now on full alert.

The snapping twig sounded way too close for comfort. I grab onto my sword and stay as still as I can, listening out for more movement. Something clicking on the stones approaches from behind the rock I am leaning on. The element of surprise is on my side; that is, if whatever is stalking me doesn't know I am hiding here. The steady rhythm of clicking on stone gets closer and closer until it sounds as if it is right behind the rock. I have to take my chance–

I jump up and spin around, "you will not take me!" I yell whilst brandishing my sword. I am shocked to see a massive white horse staring at me. The yelp I let out startles us both and I stumble back, tripping over a boulder and landing flat on my back. The horse shakes its head and whinnies, looking as if it is laughing at me as it steps around the boulder. It looks happy to see me and seems docile enough that I wonder if its rider is near-by, but notice it has no saddle or reins.

"What on earth are you doing all the way up here?" I ask, shaking my head and laughing out loud as I realize I am talking to a horse. She saunters right over to me and lowers her head, giving my shoulder a nudge with her nose. I tentatively reach out to give her a little scratch but as she huffs a big breath on my hand, I pull away. I have had an irrational fear of horses for as long as I can remember. I used to have nightmares about falling off the back of one when I was first staying with Delia and Hunt but they didn't know anything of my past, other than that I had been found in the woods by some hikers with no other people in sight. I was nearly hypothermic and couldn't remember much myself. The search for my parents went on for a few years but nothing ever came of it.

"You're the biggest horse I've seen. It makes no sense for you to be up here." I feel silly talking to a horse, and push back up onto my feet, taking a big step away. The bruise already forming on my tailbone smarts a bit as I stand hesitatingly. I can now fully see how truly massive the horse is, at least seven feet to my five seven. She is stunning, with her pristine white, shining coat, long wavy mane and fluffy fur around her ankles. It wouldn't shock me if she'd have had a horn in the centre of her head because she looks as though she came straight out of a fairytale.

The majestic mare takes a few steps towards me and

lowers herself down onto her knees. I believe I understand what she wants when she starts flipping her nose towards her back.

"No way, I am *not* getting on your back! Look, you're very beautiful and I am sure someone is missing you but I am not that person and I am on a mission so... shoo..." I wave my hands at her, she looks up to me with bashful eyes. I just shake my head and step around her to begin my search for some signs of my trail. I can hear her get up behind me and a moment later she is stamping her feet in my path.

"Hey! I'm trying to locate some tracks so I can find my sister and your bloody stomping around is not going to help. Shoo!" I'm trying to push past her, giving her a little shove on her side, but as my hands meet her coat a vision strikes me. A vision of a big, white horse and a little girl with green eyes, like mine, playing in a stream. The girl is giggling and the horse is splashing her with its hooves. The vision blurs then I am suddenly on the back of the horse and she is in full gallop, crashing through the forest, a wave of gut wrenching terror washes over me. Next, I am lying on the bank of a big river, shivering in front of a fire. The white horse is peering out from behind a bush on the far side of the river bank before the vision clears and I am snapped back into the present moment.

I know you, I stand in awe as I look into her big black eyes.

My name is Durga. I am here to protect you. You must return to the humans. I hear a deep, yet feminine voice reply in my mind. I take a step back, washing my hands over my eyes.

I truly am going crazy now. I turn away and start running uphill, I hope, in the right direction.

She keeps up to me easily but doesn't try and get in my way again. My body is starting to tire from the long stretch of uphill climbing and the lack of food and water when finally, mercifully, the hill starts to level out. As I reach its crest I am met with the gurgling sound of a big river. I can just make out the bank at the bottom of the hill and begin my search around the forest floor again to see if I can see any tracks.

I pick up a trail a bit more north to where I had been walking and I follow it down to the river's edge. When I look up, the scene from my vision flashes into my mind and I know I have been here before. The horse stops beside me and gives me a look as if to say, *I told you so,* and as our eyes meet I can hear her saying, *Nuria, you must return to the humans. It is not safe for you to venture any further.*

You know my name? I question, realizing that she can actually hear me and I can hear her.

All those times I thought I could hear other people's thoughts... *They were real.* I feel as though a veil has been lifted but I am met with confusion and fear rather than clarity. *All those hateful comments from the council luncheon, all the judgement... it was all real...*

Durga blinks her long dark lashes at me, *yes my childling, I have known you since birth. I made a promise to your mother to keep you safe.*

You knew my mother? The shock of this does not stop me from the next question that tumbles out of me – *Why did she leave me?* A deep pain that I thought I had mastered long ago, bubbles up.

She did not mean to, dear one. She died trying to save you. Now please, I implore you to turn around and return to safety! Durga says as she nudges me with her nose, urging me to take a step back.

Why is it not safe? I must go on; I have to save Marissa, I push back.

It's a long tale my dear. Please put your trust in me. Your sister is lost to you, return from whence you came. Durga pleads.

"No! I don't have time for this! My mother abandoned me and I *will not* do the same to my sister!" I side step Durga and search the bank for an easy crossing, wiping at the tears that escaped with my trembling hand. I shove down the good old abandonment wound; there is no time for this right now, and I am well versed in ignoring it.

The current looks pretty strong but there hasn't been any substantial rain in weeks, so the water level should be quite low. *Should be...* I find a spot with some big rocks poking out of the middle of the river and hope that means it's shallow at this spot and start wading in, if only to get away from this bloody horse.

The shockingly cold water makes me suck in a breath as it quickly rises up my legs. I'm not yet half way across when the water starts to reach my waist, I can feel the current yank at my balance every time I lift my foot to take a step. The rocks are slippery and uneven so I have to feel around with my toes before placing any weight on my newly placed foot with each step. My pace slows exponentially when I reach the first big rock jutting out, I grab on, taking a moment to centre myself. The water is just above my belly button and I fear there may be another drop in depth up ahead, but the shore seems so close so I push on.

When I leave the safety of the last rock I step out and feel my foot slip out from under me and I flail out both arms, still wielding my dad's sword in one hand, as I feel the other foot slip away too. *No, no, no!* A memory of gasping for air and a chill that permeated my bones flashes before my eyes.

I have *been here before... Durga, help!*

I get dunked under the water for a moment before something bites down hard on my arm and yanks me up. I scream at the agony of my skin tearing. Durga is the one pulling me up onto my feet. She drags me back to the rocks in the middle of the river and lets me scramble on top of one as she loosens her bite.

"Aah my arm!" I moan. I can barely stand looking down at the torn flesh. I don't see my bone, thankfully, but she may have bitten through the muscle because it is hard to move my fingers.

At least you didn't bite my sword arm; I give her now red stained mouth a wary glance.

Climb on my back and I'll get you back on the shore. Durga turns to line her back up with the rock facing in the direction I had already come from.

"No way, I am going that way with or without you," I say, pointing my sword to the opposite bank and making moves to hop off the rock. Durga huffs a big sigh and turns around so she is now facing the way I want to go, still within reach for me to get onto her back. I know this is my best chance at survival so I shove down my fear of being on a horse and I awkwardly fling myself sideways across her back with my head and legs dangling off her sides. With my now useless left arm and my right arm holding the sword I can't really get myself properly seated.

"Just go!" I yell so she doesn't wait for me to try to sit up. She lurches forward, pushing her big body against the current. I notice I'm staining her immaculate coat red where my arm dangles and worry about how much blood I'm losing. *I'll have to find something to bandage this,* I think as we are nearing the opposite bank. My vision starts to go blurry as Durga steps up onto the rocky shore.

"Durga, I'm losing too much blood. I think you hit a vein or something," I groan, not really knowing my anatomy very well but knowing enough to judge that the rapidly growing red stain now trickling down Durga's leg is a bad sign. She doesn't stop to let me down and picks up the pace instead, racing through the undulating hills at a gentle trot so she doesn't accidentally fling me off her back.

"Where are you taking me?" I try to protest but the throbbing pain in my arm (and my darned logic) is keeping me from trying to jump off a rapidly moving, seven foot tall horse.

"Wait, stop for a second! I'm slipping off!" I call out and

she slows to a walk, but doesn't fully stop. I place the blade of the sword in between my teeth and reach my right arm around to yank on her mane as I swing my right leg up and over, hauling myself into a seat. I take the blade from my teeth and let myself slump forward onto her neck, a wave of dizziness really grabbing hold of me now. I don't know if I trust this horse but I don't think I would make it very far on my own at this point so I let her guide the way. Although, what could possibly be up here to save me – I do not know. *Shit, this is bad...*

We ride on like this for what feels like a long time, weaving through a forest of massive trees that I notice have started to change again. *I swear I just saw a copse of birch and aspen, and the big jagged trunk of a douglas fir. These trees shouldn't be growing at this altitude,* I ponder, making a mental note; my botanist's intrigue is piqued even though I feel like I may pass out. Not the most useful information when you're bleeding profusely.

The wind rushing against my wet clothes makes my teeth chatter and the throb in my arm turns into a steady ache as I feel my whole body going cold. I get a shock of deja vu about this very same ride through this very same forest and a wave of nausea hits – I lean over to throw up the bile of my empty stomach, barely missing Durga's now blood spattered shoulder. *Horseback riding, plus searing pain, plus no breakfast equals a very upset stomach,* my head is spinning.

"Durga, I need water, please we have to stop," I say weakly, leaning forward to speak in her big ears. She slows her speed as we pass a big blackberry bush with a few big juicy berries still holding on, untouched by the birds. My stomach gurgles so audibly that I'm sure Durga can hear it as she abruptly stops on the other side of the bush and kneels down so I can slide off. I look into her big black eyes, with their long soft eyelashes, and can hear her say, *stay here and eat something, I will be back shortly,* before getting up and trotting away, leaving me alone.

The realization that she hasn't been able to communicate with me this whole time because I have not been looking into her eyes dawns on me. I wonder to myself if that is how the channel of communication is opened but before I can ponder on that further I find myself distracted by the very real hunger that is flipping my stomach over and the awful taste in my mouth so I grab a few blackberries to eat.

The sweet, juicy blackberries are a momentary reprieve from the throb of my arm; the sugars from the fruit seem to revive me enough for me to become even more aware of the dire situation I have gotten myself into. My arm is ripped open, but thankfully has stopped gushing, my feet are wrecked, my clothes are all wet, I've lost the trail of my sister and I have no idea where I am. A deep panic starts to build in my chest. My heart quickens and my breath comes in shallow bursts.

Is this what a panic attack feels like? I recall seeing Mom coach Marissa through these when she was younger. When she first entered middle school she was having them every week and sometimes they really scared me. I thought she was going to suffocate as she would stare blankly ahead and just gasp for air. Mom would tell her to say one thing she could see, one thing she could hear, one thing she could touch and one thing she could smell and it would almost always work to settle her heart down. So, in this moment, I try to do the same.

"Ok, ok, ok, I can feel the sword in my hand," I say out loud, the sound of my own voice a comfort as I try to take in a normal breath, clenching the sword, the firm, cool metal grounding me.

"I can hear a creek nearby... I can smell cedar trees... I can see... I see... boulders rolling towards me?!" I drop my sword to rub my hand over my eyes, not believing what I'm seeing but there are, in fact, boulders rolling straight at me!

The next moment, Durga bursts out of the bush on the far side of the meadow that lies in front of me and I see even more boulders rolling in after her. I jump up onto my feet wondering if I should run, when a big moss covered boulder uncurls and springs up onto two feet, right in front of me.

"Hello poppet! Don't fear, Granny Mog is here!" the big moss haired, bespectacled rock exclaims. I scream and my head spins and my vision goes dark. It feels like my feet are swept out from under me and I hit the ground.

Chapter Five

"Oh dear, oh dear, I seem to have frightened the poor thing," I can hear a gravelly voice say as I come back into consciousness. I keep my eyes closed, not wanting to acknowledge that there are actual talking boulders, like the ones from my vision a few days ago, standing in front of me.

Was that only two days ago? It feels as though time has warped on this journey as I think back to the painting I made with the very same creature in it that is standing before me now.

"Quick, Sister Buttercup, go and fetch us some yarrow and plantain. She has sustained a deep wound that we must attend to!" The one called Granny Mog instructs as I crack open an eye to see who she is addressing. A taller, thinner rock creature with light green, curling old man's beard lichen for hair nods and scurries off into the meadow.

"Ah, she's awake. Welcome back, Nuria!" A boulder even bigger than Granny Mog reaches out a stone hand to help me up.

"Who... what are you?" I stammer as I tentatively reach out to feel its scratchy, cold, hard hand grasp onto mine and pull me upright.

"It is I, Brother Willow, do you not recall? We were gnome childlings together. I guess I am a tad larger now eh?" Willow chuckles back. The name rings a bell but with no clear memories. Despite the thought that he could crush me with one squeeze if he wanted to, I feel at ease hearing his deep voice.

"I'm sorry I don't remember... gnomes?!" I question, shaking my head.

"Oh dear, she has forgotten all about us," a plump, rosy cheeked gnome squeaks.

"Dear child, you were born here, right in this glen," another gnome with a scraggly moss beard and an Amanita mushroom as a hat butts in.

"We raised you as one of our own but one day you wandered off and we could not find you anywhere. Brother Spruce ventured far, much farther than us boulder gnomes would ever dare to go and he found signs of *humans*," a tall, thin gnome that looks much like Sister Buttercup adds next, and I feel my head is swimming as it snaps from gnome to gnome.

"We thought perhaps they had taken you and there was nothing we could do," Granny Mog laments as she takes hold of my hand and gives it a tender pat. I sit with this information for a moment while Sister Juniper returns with the plants Granny Mog had asked for. Granny pops them into her mouth, chews them up, spits them back into her hands, creating a paste, then she reaches out to put it on my arm. I flinch away but she gives me a glare that makes me feel like a child being scolded and some subconscious part of my brain tells me to submit.

Yarrow and plantain she said... I've read about these somewhere. I recall that yarrow was used on battlefields to staunch bleeding. The kind of information you tuck away, never expecting to have to use it. My curiosity trumps my squeamishness, so I watch her apply the paste to my ripped up arm.

"If I was born here... then where is my mother buried?" I question cautiously, wincing as she smooths the paste over my ripped up arm. I realize maybe I do not want to know, *maybe they are the ones who killed her.*

"We did nothing of the sort! boulder gnomes do not harm. We create and maintain!" Granny snaps at me as she grasps my hand tighter and starts to pull me along with her. The ease at which I transferred that thought to her surprises me. *There must be some way to moderate this, or am I just doomed with having my inner dialogue on display?*

"Come child, I will show you," she says as I try to keep up with her startling speed, considering she has very small, stubby legs. The other gnomes roll into tight balls and start rolling along after us and Durga keeps up pace easily with her long, elegant, now blood stained, legs.

We pass through a copse of rustling birch trees, hop over a babbling creek and walk past a glistening lake that has swans lazily floating on top of it. I realize how much warmer it is up here. *What a strange microclimate,* I marvel at my surroundings as we follow a larger creek that branches off the lake.

A small patch of beautiful white flowers catches my notice. An intoxicating jasmine scent is coming off of them. I wish we could stop and examine them for just a brief moment but before I can make the request I am pulled along. Up ahead, in a small meadow with poppies and cornflowers dancing in the breeze, there is a mound of white flowers all clustered together just like the ones by the creek, except here there are hundreds of them. The scent of jasmine and cinnamon fill the meadow and the sun is illuminating the spot with a bright column of glittering, gold light. We all stop at the foot of the mound and the boulders uncurl from their balls and stand with heads bowed. Durga looks at me then bows her head as well.

"What is this?" I ask, confused as to why we have stopped when I thought they were bringing me to my mother.

"This is your mother's resting place. We had planned to give her a proper ceremony sending her back to The Divine Mother but she transformed into this before we could," Granny Mog says, with a sympathetic look mixed with something else, a secret perhaps that she is not sharing. She refuses to meet my eyes, so the answer to that is lost from me.

"She *transformed?* Into flowers? How does someone just

transform?!" I ask with disbelief in my voice. "People don't just transform into flowers. They decompose, they rot and are eaten by bugs and animals and mycelium," I say, my confusion clearly written on my face as I turn to Durga for confirmation.

She was of the fae. As are you and I, Nuria. We do not return to The Mother in the same way that humans do. I can hear Durga say in my mind, but her words don't register as anything remotely logical.

Is this some strange joke? Am I dreaming? Did I bleed out and am actually lying by that blackberry bush – dead?

"Fae... as in faeries? I'm a fairy? Ya right!" I laugh out loud in disbelief, but the fact that I have been told this piece of information by reading the mind of a horse and speaking with gnomes makes my disbelief suddenly turn into shock. *This cannot be true!*

"If you need more reassurance young one then take that paste off your arm. I'm sure you will find it is already perfectly healed. fae heal very quickly," Sister Buttercup chimes in and sure enough as I scrape away the green goop I can see my wounds have closed, leaving only a slight pink scar. I can freely wiggle my fingers without pain.

"But you put that on me. It must be some sort of magic. You are a gnome after all... you're a magical creature," I say, trying to deny what they have said I am capable of.

"We are no more magic than the humans. We have our duties to The Earth Mother and execute them well, yes, but we have no special healing magic like the fae. Those were healing herbs poppet; gifted to us by The Mother herself, a gift that all may use. It only aided in your innate ability," Granny Mog replies.

"Wait a moment, Durga, you are fae as well? But you're a horse! Why do *I* look like a human? And don't fairies have pointy ears and wings?" The questions tumble out of me as all the fairytale stories I once read as a child pop into my head.

"There are many types of fae, dear. Durga is a Meta-morph who, unfortunately, cannot turn into her humanoid form since she passed into the human realm. You, my dear, are what they call an Etherealist, which has come to be a very rare gift amongst the Elemental fae. They have an affinity over the ruling element of the mind... the Ether," Granny Mog replies, talking in calming tones as if I am a skittish baby deer that is about to bolt.

"An Etherealist?" I say, testing the word out on my tongue. *Is that why I can sometimes read minds and communicate through thoughts?* I chew on my nails as I ponder what this means. My whole strange childhood is making more and more sense but at the same time, completely overwhelming me.

Fairies... I laugh out loud, earning a few curious looks.

Endless questions are racing through my mind and my voice fails me as I stare wide eyed at Granny Mog's warm features. *What else can an Etherealist do? Was my mother an Etherealist? Is my father fae as well? Why was I brought to the human realm? Why can't Durga change back? Does any of this have to do with my sister being taken? My sister... I've been here too long! I need to find Marissa!*

Granny Mog squeezes my hand, drawing me back into focus. "Slow down Nuria, I cannot answer all you have asked dear child as I do not have the answers. What I can tell you is that we saw a varg come through here carrying an unconscious girl." The surrounding gnomes shudder at the name of the creature. "We feared it had gotten *you* but I could tell it had made a mistake and taken another poor soul. I am truly sorry that the varg has taken your sister but my dear you must not follow them! Your mother warned us you would try to return but the fae realm is cruel and tricky. No place for someone raised by humans," Granny Mog pleads.

"You... you tried to warn me about the varg in my vision. Why is it after me?" I question, looking around as if I may see a sign of where the creature has taken Marissa.

"It is a minion of The Wolf King. One of his young lackeys sent it through. I do not know why it was sent for you though; I only know that your mother was running from something when she came through The Gate. My child you must stay here," Granny Mog warns.

"Don't go, Nuria, stay with us!" Brother Willow exclaims and several other gnomes call out in agreement.

"I must go! I will not abandon Marissa. She puts up a tough front but she is probably terrified and you said that thing had orders not to harm *me*, but what happens when it figures out *she* is not *me*? No, I have to go, please help me!" I beg, gripping onto my sword for strength. I look several of the gnomes in the eye before landing on Durga.

"You! You can take me! You came from there and you

said so yourself that you were tasked to protect me!" I try to reason with her, remembering her vow to my dead mother.

I cannot return. Durga huffs and bows her head low. I step up to her and grasp her head, lifting her chin to make our eyes meet.

"Can you take me to The Gate?" I ask, looking straight into her big eyes and I can see a flash of what I can only assume is my mother in her memories, impossibly beautiful with her golden eyes and cascading ebony curls, asking her the same question years ago. Her face is blurred, as if the memory is too distant to recall. Durga nods her head gently and kneels in front of me, bowing down low.

"The sun will soon be setting my dear, at least stay the night with us to get your strength back," Granny Mog reasons with me and I feel that a solid rest may be what I need before venturing into the unknown. So I nod and let them lead me to their caves.

There is already something delicious smelling, bubbling over the fire pit just outside the cozy entrance and my stomach does a little jump for joy, gurgling loud enough for everyone to hear. Little boulder gnome children come rolling out to greet me, giggling as one grabs my newly healed arm and another takes my sword and waves it around in awe.

"Hey, I'm going to need that back you little rascal," I tease, all tension already easing away as I am welcomed into the wholesome boulder gnome family. *Maybe I should just stay here,* the thought comes up but I quickly shove it aside, knowing I have a greater duty towards my own family.

~

I SLEEP DEEPLY through the night with the deep rumbling of the snoring gnomes lulling me into a dreamless slumber. The next morning I wake up to find a water vessel and a sheath for my sword crafted out of bark lying beside my pillow, a gift from one of the gnomes, too modest to take credit for the kind gesture. I get up to see everyone else is already gone from the cave and gather up my gifts and stumble out into the bright sun.

"Ah, you're awake. I did not want to disturb you, my dear," I hear Granny Mog say, my eyes are still adjusting to the blaring light and all I see are blurry figures. It must be well into the morning which gives me a wave of panic.

"I have to get going. Thank you for your hospitality," I say looking around for Durga and seeing her sitting in the middle of a group of gnome childlings that are playing with her hair.

"Before you go dear, I have something we found in the flowers years ago. I am sure she would have wanted you to have it." Granny holds out a beautiful necklace with a pendant of a little golden eye with delicate feathers encircling it. On closer inspection I notice it has a small, purple crystal gleaming in the iris.

"She left this for me? Thank you, truly," I say, pushing back the tears that are threatening to overflow as she puts it around my neck, a piece of my mother that I could have never wished for. The cool metal soon turns warm and I swear I hear it hum for a split second. I look around but no one else seems to be reacting to the sound, *must be hearing things*. Durga walks up to my side and kneels down for me to hop on.

Granny grabs my hand before I hop on. "Look for the boulder gnomes in the fae realm, my dear; they tend to the hills on the other side of the Tanglewoods. Tell them I sent you and they will give you guidance," Granny instructs, and I can see tears threatening to spill down her stone cheeks. I realize with a pang of guilt that she has probably had to mourn me once before. I give her a tight hug and look into her kind eyes.

"Thank you for your help Granny, I am sorry I could not stay." I give a nod to the gathered crowd before I hop on the back of Durga, taking a deep breath, having to steel my nerves as she fully stands up and starts trotting, taking us out of sight of the gnomes and onward to The Gate.

We ride on in silence for a while before questions start to plague my mind again.

"Let me down Durga, I want to walk," I say, giving her mane a gentle stroke as she stops and kneels down so I can slide off her large back. As she stands I look her in the eye.

"Why can you not return to the fae realm? Will I be able to return to the human realm?" I ask, my unanswered question weighing heavy on my mind. We keep our eyes locked as we keep walking through the forest.

It is a very old curse that we no longer know the details of.

We, the fae, are taught as children that if we cross over we will be stuck forever. We were told The Divine Mother Earth herself placed the curse upon us as punishment for our greed. I had always believed it to be a tale told to keep children close but I have tried to return many times without success. Durga explains, her voice sounding heavy and resigned in my head. *You were born in the human realm so can return to the fae realm but I am unsure whether you can cross back. I have never known a fae to be born on this side.* Durga admits.

Dread washes over me. I know I must search for Marissa but accepting that I may never return shatters a little piece of me. Is my home a place I am willing to leave forever? Why would Durga leave her home so willingly?

"Who were you to my mother Durga? Why did you sacrifice yourself for her?" I ask, trying to keep the pity off of my face.

I was her lady-in-waiting. She rescued me from a violent master that I had been traded to when I was a young foal. He had a charm that kept me trapped in my morphed form and would use me as a workhorse on his lands. I thought that was to be my horrible lot in life, until she freed me. She took me to her home to live freely. I owed her my life. When she first fell pregnant, her husband—your father, would not let her leave the house and I was cast out by the servants. I was never even permitted to meet her husband. He kept her locked in there and would not allow any visitors. There was unrest amongst the court, fae were going missing and there was word of a rebellion against The King. Perhaps he was shielding her from whatever danger there may have been but why he would not permit me to be with her, I do not know. The next time I saw her, she was large with you in her belly and running from that same house, in fear. Durga says, her strong voice cracking slightly at the memories.

I have so many questions but as I am about to ask more, we step into a sweeping meadow with wildflowers dancing in the breeze and tall green grasses that sing with the passing wind. At the far side of the clearing there is a big hill that has a small cave at the base. The mouth of the cave is so dark it seems to swallow all the light. A twinge of fear skitters up my spine.

"Is that The Gate?" I ask, swallowing down the lump that has formed in my throat. Durga nods her head, snorting a huff of air through her nostrils. We walk on through the meadow but when we are halfway across, Durga stops suddenly. I look into her eyes and can hear her say, *this is as far as I can go.* I nod and look forward, clasping onto my sword, feigning bravery. *Am I ready for this?*

I take a deep breath, "thank you for all you have done Durga, I hope to see you again. I have so much I want to ask you but I fear I've already spent too much time here. I have to find her..." I say, turning back to face her and giving her soft cheek a stroke.

Wait, one last piece of advice; beware of the Mists when you first enter into the realm. They will worm into your thoughts and memories. Just keep walking, whatever you do, do not stop.

I nod, taking on her advice but not entirely understanding what to expect.

I'm ready. I'm coming for you Marissa!

I take a deep breath to centre myself, then walk on. I start to run, hoping that the speed will help keep my nerves steady, but as I near the mouth of the cave I can feel my sword hand start to shake. I close my eyes and shield my face with my arms as I blindly sprint into the darkness.

Chapter Six

Rather than the rocky ground that I would expect to be inside a cave, I am met with the soft sponge of moss and open my eyes to see I am facing another meadow, except this one is dark and full of a thick, tangible mist. I look behind me to see a cave at my back and realize I am on the other side, *the fae realm*.

Something ancient that was slumbering deep in my bones cracks open and my mother's necklace hums faintly. I feel all my senses perk up at the crackle of energy that runs through the air, I inhale deeply. Immediately the Mist shoves its way up my nose, making my eyes tear.

I remember Durga's warning so I start sprinting forward. The ground starts to incline as I run up a hill much like the one the cave was hidden in and then tumble back down the other side into a valley. I feel as though I am wading through water, but I keep running. If I stop, something terrible is bound to happen. My head starts to throb as the Mist tangles into my memories and pieces of my past start to flash before my eyes.

Marissa whispers to her friends at my old high school, pretending to not know me as we pass in the halls – judgemental giggles pierce my ears as if they are right behind me.

A young boy is clasping his ears, yelling at me to get out of his head in the middle of a birthday party – Delia is crouching down and telling me to stop – horror is on all the surrounding faces.

The Mist is working its way to my earliest memories. I swipe away the tears that are pooling on my eyelids and keep running.

Delia and Hunt are having a heated argument over whether or not to adopt me . Both of their heads snap to where I am eavesdropping at the top of the staircase – my finger nails leave indents in the wood of the railing from my white knuckled grasp – Delia fervently advocates for me to stay while she rocks baby Marissa in her arms – Hunt crosses his arms, looking sceptical.

The pain of rejection stings freshly. *Did he ever want me?* The Mist seems to relish my despair and pushes even further into my past.

I am on the back of a big, white horse and my tiny hands clasp the horse's mane as we tumble through the forest. My own shrill scream rings in my ears.

A cold, dark feeling as my mother slips away from me...

I crest the top of a hill and stumble into a deep, dark forest. The Mist immediately clears, shying away from the oppressive presence that lurks here. I lean over with my hands on my knees to take a few deep breaths, shaking off the memories that usually only resurface during fitful nights. The faces of all those that have judged or feared me continue to flash behind my eyes, although less vividly as the seconds tick by. The dark void in my chest that felt as if it was healing over when I put on my mother's necklace has been ripped open anew. *Come on Nuria, get it together...*

I take a moment, letting the ache in my chest ease before I scan my surroundings. I'm not sure which is a more fearful sight, the Mist behind me or the clearly haunted forest that lies ahead.

The trees look as though they are caught in battle with each other; striving for the blocked out sun above the canopy. The white moss hanging from the branches gives off the illusion of a forest full of ghosts. *This must be the Tanglewood Forest.* I take a breath and shake off all that has just flashed before my eyes.

"Nasty stuff, that mist," I say to myself as I sheathe my sword at my hip and set off through the forest.

"Look for the gnomes on the other side of the Tanglewoods she said... pfft, but what about navigating this bloody forest of death?" I mutter as I dodge the wispy moss and duck under branches – that I swear are moving to try and hit me in the head purposely.

There is absolutely no wind in this forest and the moist air feels suffocating. There isn't any bird song either which naturally leaves my nerves on high alert, thinking there may be something sinister lurking around each corner.

Perhaps I am the thing they are shying away from, I hope

as I sly foot my way forward. I have no way to navigate in here so I try my best to keep a straight path. However, some of the trees are three times my arm span in width and I am constantly met with impassable thickets of spiky brush that force me to veer off course.

It feels like a few hours have now passed in this eerie place and I fear I am utterly lost. I have no scope for the size of these woods and worry they may stretch on forever.

"I should have asked for better directions. This place is a maze." I am mumbling to myself when I hear a sharp laugh behind me. I whirl around and I unsheathe my sword to find a funny looking little creature standing before me. It is only waist high and it looks as if its skin is made of bark. It has long spindly arms, twigs for fingers and small beady, black eyes.

"Who are you?!" I yelp, as I point the sword towards the creature.

"I am Barnaby Sprout of the Tanglewoods! Who are you?" it demands back, placing its twig hands on its hips.

"I'm Nuria Piedmont... of Easthelm," I cautiously say back, trying to mimic its form of introduction. "What exactly *are* you?"

"Well that is a very rude question. But if you must know, I am a wood sprite," it huffs, crossing its arms and tapping its little tree-stump foot, clearly annoyed at me.

"So sorry for the question Mr. Sprout, I am new here and very lost. Could you, perhaps, guide me out of the Tanglewoods?" I ask, cringing, I am not sure what the proper etiquette is in these lands.

"Hmmmm, I suppose... for a price," he replies, giving me a cheeky grin. Not sure what else to do, I nod to his request.

"What is the price?" I cautiously question.

"Hmmm either a nibble on your pinky toe or five hairs and one eyelash from your pretty head," he sneers, wiggling his twiggy fingers, looking as if he is up to no good.

"Um, I think I will go with the eyelash and hairs..." I respond, thinking that his first request must mean the wood sprites snack on humans. I try to suppress a shudder.

"Deal!" he shouts out before I can think twice about what I agreed to. I decide there is surely no harm to giving my hair to this creature so I pluck them out and hand them over. He snatches them out of my hand and gobbles them up, to my surprise, then scurries past me into the woods.

"Hey! We had a deal!" I shout as he runs off.

"You never said *when* I had to lead you out of the woods!" I hear his distant voice shout back.

"Bastard!" I yell back, standing there in shock. Granny Mog's warning about the fae realm being a tricky place pops into my mind as I start to walk in the direction I had been going before this strange encounter. *How was I to know what* kind *of tricky it would be?*

I walk on, scanning the woods for more cheeky little wood sprites, not wanting to repeat what had just happened, when I am suddenly whacked on the back of the head. I stumble forward, just catching my balance, and I turn around to see that there is nothing there.

"What on Earth –"

Whack! I'm hit across the back again and I look down to see the tree roots are moving and slithering their way towards my feet. I whirl around and start to run, realizing in a panic that the *trees* are attacking me. I only get a few more metres before I'm tripped up by a root wrapping around my ankle. I fall to the forest floor with a big thud and am swept up into the air, dangling by my foot as more branches twine around my body.

"Let me go!" I scream, swinging my sword around, managing to chop down some of the roots but not quickly enough. Soon my entire torso is being covered and a branch whips my hand causing me to drop the sword. I let out one more scream before my head is enveloped in roots and I cannot move.

I am sheathed in darkness. I whimper at the thought that this may be how I die, smothered by tree roots.

No, no, no, this is not fair! I only just got here, please! I lose my ability to speak as a root is pushing at my mouth, trying to pry it open. I try as hard as I can to keep it closed knowing that if it succeeds, that would surely be the death of me.

It suddenly pauses its jabbing. A distant chopping sound reverberates through the wood. A low creaking groan comes out of the tree then the roots are quickly recoiling and I am dropped, head first, onto the ground. I let out a yelp and quickly scramble to my feet, scanning the floor for my sword. *Where is it? Where is it?*

"Looking for this, perchance?" a young woman with a

mess of red curls, a pert, freckled nose and a mocking smile says in a lilting accent. She stands in front of me, twirling my sword around by its handle. She has knee high leather boots over her brown trousers and a dark green hooded cape draped over her white blouse. I notice a gold clasp in the shape of a flame holding it together across her chest. Her outfit reminds me of something a prince would be wearing in one of those classic fairy tales where the distressed damsel is locked up in a tower and can do nothing but sit there looking pretty.

She stops twirling the sword and cocks an eyebrow, giving it a once over, looking impressed by the blade. She tosses it to me and I clumsily catch it before pointing the tip back at her.

"Who are you?" I ask, more wary with this encounter than I was with the last. She lets out a sharp laugh.

"I am the female who just rescued you," she scoffs and crosses her arms. She looks like a regular human to me. No strange coloured skin or pointy ears. I wonder whether she is fae or human when she answers my unvoiced query by blasting a flame jet out of her pointer finger at a root that was trying to snake its way back towards my ankles. It snaps back with a little whimper.

"Eeek!" I shriek and scamper away from the roots, towards the woman who wields fire. Not entirely sure which I should fear more. Colour stains my cheeks, I recalculate and take a small step away.

"Um thank you... That was crazy! That tree tried to eat me!" I exclaim, looking into her hazel eyes. In that moment,

I have a brief flash of recognition but I know there is no way I would have met her before.

"Well yes, you are in the Tanglewoods after all... what are you doing out here anyway?" She raises an eyebrow and gives me a sweeping look, pausing at my torn shirt, then at my wrecked shoes. I ponder if I should tell her the truth and decide that I desperately need to get out of here to find Marissa, so I take my chances.

"I need to get out of the Tanglewood Forest and find the boulder gnomes. Do you know the way out?" I carefully rephrase my question so as to not directly ask for help.

"I do know the way out, and I believe I know the gnomes you speak of. It is over a day's journey out of here though and I hadn't planned on leaving until I fulfilled my mission," she says as a small smile tugs at the corners of her mouth. "I *can* guide you in exchange for that fine sword you carry though," she says, giving me a wink, looking a little too pleased with herself.

"Can you guide me *right now*?" I clarify, learning from my past mistakes.

"Yes, right now," she answers brusquely, sounding annoyed.

"What of your mission? What was it anyway? Perhaps I can help," I offer, trying to get on her good side.

"The mission can wait. It may well be completed on our journey. I am searching for someone but that is none of your concern," she says as she turns around and starts walking away. "Come on, let's go! I told you it's over a day's journey," she says over her shoulder, I sheathe my sword and hurry after her.

"Hey, my name is…" I try to speak but am suddenly shushed by the woman.

"It is not wise to share your name so freely. You do not even know if my intentions with you are pure!" she scoffs.

"If you had malicious intentions I feel like you wouldn't have told me that. You can call me Nuri," I say, hoping my light attitude and tone will ease her clearly tightly wound nerves.

"Ugh… I'm Oleander," she sighs, surely resigning to my charm, before she picks up speed and starts jogging through the Tanglewoods. Perhaps some caution should be taken with this one. Her namesake speaks of delicate petals and a sweet aroma but the poison beneath the facade is not to be trifled with.

IT TAKES MOST of my concentration to keep up with her and not trip on the slippery, moss covered roots sticking up everywhere, so our conversation ends up dying off. Every now and again I catch a glimpse of something fearsome and am glad to have found a guide who can shoot fire from her hands, even if she does scare the crap out of me.

Spiders the size of golden retrievers skitter overhead, the occasional wood sprite peers around the trunks of trees, clicking their twiggy fingers on the bark and licking their lips. I swear I even saw a bush full of glowing eyes tracking our movement. *This place gives me the creeps.*

I can feel my newly healed feet starting to blister again and can't help the slowing of my pace. We have been jogging for half the day and I have drained my bark water vessel already, so I stop at a nearby creek to refill. The water looks harmless enough, but as I bend down I notice some white, glowing oyster mushrooms nearby that are giving off their sparkling spores which seem to be landing directly in the water. I think twice about drinking it. They could be ghost oysters, a poisonous look alike to the edible ones that wouldn't kill me. Considering where I am and the hum of magic in these woods, I don't doubt that they are more dubious than the ones in the human realm.

"Wait, do not drink that," Oleander says, sneaking up behind me. "The water within the Tanglewoods has a particularly nasty effect on those who do not hail from here."

"What does it do? I need water…" I complain, looking down at the fresh, bubbling water and feeling my mouth go dry.

She lets out an exasperated sigh. "All right, well then we will have to find a water sprite, now won't we?" she says, as if I should already know that. She trudges upstream scanning the bank as she goes. I worry at what this water sprite will do as I remember the all too fresh interaction with the maddening wood sprite. *Are they all the same? Will this one ask to eat my toe as well?*

We trek up stream until we reach a miniature waterfall. There, just under the falls, is a blue, shimmering creature with big fish eyes, leaning back, with the watery tendrils of its hair melding with the cascading water. Its scales gleam, mimicking the way water reflects its surroundings. The sprite sees us and quickly disappears, becoming one with the water.

I look at Oleander with wide eyes, she smirks. "Little sprite, little sprite, we have a secret to tell," Oleander calls in a melodic voice. "You must tell her a secret and she will fill your vessel... Go on, we don't have all day," she whispers in my ear then pushes me forward. I lean down to the water's edge and the sprite pokes her little head above water, turning her pointed frilled ear towards me.

A secret? I think to myself, *what secret might I tell?* I ponder about it for a moment but can tell the sprite is growing impatient as she slowly starts descending back into the water, so I say the first thing that pops into my mind.

"I am wanted by a wolf," I whisper, the sprite's eyes grow even wider as she looks from me to Oleander then back to me before snatching my water vessel and disappearing under the water. I look back to Oleander to see if she heard but she has donned a mask of indifference, arms crossed, foot tapping. I look into her eyes, trying to hear what she is thinking, but I am met with silence. I wonder at the shock of the sprite and hope the secret was not too big to tell when she pops back up with a giggle and a splash, handing me my water vessel.

"This will never run empty as long as you are within the Tanglewood Forest," she says in a sweet, high pitched voice, before she disappears under the water once again. I stand up, taking a big gulp of the cleanest water I have ever tasted and peer inside the bottle to see it filling back up.

"That must've been some secret." Oleander smirks, raising an eyebrow. "Come on, we've wasted enough time, let's go." She turns on her heel and starts out at a jog again. I groan and race to keep up.

WE KEEP GOING for a little while longer before my ripped up feet become unbearable and I slow to a hobble. Oleander looks back and lets out a big sigh before reluctantly trudging back to me.

"Let's make camp for the night. You need to find some better footwear when we are out of the woods. In fact your whole attire is rather strange," she says, flitting her hand at me. I look down at my paint stained, black linen overalls with my white t-shirt underneath, which is more brownish-beige now, and realize she is right. I may need to find some more inconspicuous clothing when I finally get out of the forest. Judging by Oleander's attire I would say my fashion choices are a few centuries ahead.

We find a bit of a clearing to settle down in, trying to keep well away from the roots of the trees and the little hiding places of the lurking creatures. Oleander instantly sparks up a big flame in the middle of the clearing with the snap of her fingers and instructs me to stay close to the fire throughout the night. She leaves me alone in the clearing for a few minutes and comes back with two limp, fluffy rabbits slung over her shoulder.

"I didn't think there would be something so cute in these woods," I say as I watch her gut and skin the first one. The sight doesn't bother me as I've seen many rabbits and geese gutted from my hunting excursions with the Jones boys. She looks at me and smirks to herself then lifts the rabbit's lip to show long, needle-sharp teeth jutting out.

"They feast on blood," she chuckles at the shock written on my face. I inch a little bit closer to the fire. She efficiently finishes gutting and skinning the second one then grabs two big sticks for us to roast them on like marshmallows and the smell of roasting meat soon makes my mouth water.

I have never experienced hunger like this before, not knowing when my next meal will come, and a wave of sadness at the thought of my mom and dad washes over me. All of my worries and issues of the past seem so trivial now and I pray for my mom's home-cooked meals. The longing for ignorance threatens to pull me into despair. I try to distract myself from the black hole of anxiety and dread threatening to pull me under by turning my attention to Oleander.

"So... Do you come here often?" I cringe, *stop being so awkward, Nuria!*

Oleander looks at me as she rips into her roasted rabbit. "No. Most try to avoid these woods," she says back between bites.

"Right, makes sense. So where *do* you come from?" I

ask, thinking I sound friendly enough but am met with a glare.

"Why are you asking so many questions? I do not know you and as I said before about the names, information is valuable. I do not trust you yet," she quips back.

"*Yet*," I mostly say to myself, earning another glare from Oleander. We slip back into an uncomfortable silence. I refrain from asking more questions about why all interactions with the creatures of this world seem to have a price tag. I don't want her to suspect I am from the human realm, but perhaps my clothing is already a dead giveaway. After she is done with her rabbit, Oleander lies down with her back to the fire and goes to sleep.

I stare off into the dark as I finish my last few bites and shudder at the glowing eyes I can see blinking back at me. *Stay close to the fire and you'll be all right,* I reassure myself as I curl up into a ball with my back to the fire as well and try to get some sleep.

I have a fitful night filled with dreams of a sharp toothy smile coming from the face of a wolf and the distant screams of Marissa. I wander aimlessly in the Tanglewoods, the dangling moss sways like a woman walking and for a moment it looks like Marissa walking away from me in my white linen dress. I call out to her but am met with flames and gnarled trees with red glowing eyes trying to grab me. I wake up with a gasp.

I look over and Oleander is still sleeping. She has a steady rise and fall to her chest that indicates a deep slumber but I'm too disturbed by my dreams to close my eyes again, so I lay awake, staring at the small sliver of night sky above us. *At least the stars are the same here*, there is a slight comfort knowing I am still on the same planet.

I wonder to myself whether the whole earth was like the fae realm before *The Divine Mother*, as the fae call her, split it in two or if it had been more mundane and subtle like the human realm. The forest here has a certain sentience to it, and though I do love the Wildwood back home, it has never felt like it acknowledged my presence. Here, I feel seen by *everything*, and I swear the ground even has the faintest thump of a heartbeat. I even feel... *more* here. It is hard to describe but every cell of my body feels... *awake*.

I wonder whether the world is actually divided in two and our maps just don't show it or if this realm is somehow overlapped over the other, hidden in the in-between spaces.

There are so many questions I fear will go unanswered. I long for the ignorance I had just a few days prior. I had always believed in a higher power and felt the wild places to be the closest I would come to divinity but finding out there is an actual entity with power to divide a planet is a chilling and humbling thought. I envision this ethereal being looking down at us all and moving us around like little puppets but have a deeper understanding that *She* is among us rather than removed.

My eyelids are getting heavier and heavier, the questions start to slow in my mind but I flutter them open, fighting the encroaching sleep. When I open them again I am met with a full view of the night sky, no gnarled branches block the shimmering expanse. I look to the side and see that the menacing trees of the Tanglewoods are gone.

I am lying in a grassy knoll, beside a big, black horse. The rise and fall of its body is slow and calm as it breathes, letting out little snores. I scrunch my eyes shut, not believing what I am seeing and when I open them again the same small sliver of sky and the familiar gnarled trees are once again enclosing me. *Was that a vision? I haven't had one of those since the night Marissa was taken.*

I shake my head and glance over to Oleander to double check if this is real and stifle a scream. A tall figure is standing in front of her, just outside of the glow of the fire. The smell of wet dog is thick in the air.

I try to pretend I am still asleep as I slowly feel for the hilt of my sword. The creature leans in to sniff at Oleander, its furry face with a long snout and long jagged teeth comes into view. *Is this a varg?* My heart thunders in my chest. I suddenly doubt whether I can take this thing on but I know that if I scream now it will just slash out and probably kill Oleander before she has a chance to fight back. So I grab firmly onto my sword as I see the varg lift a long arm with a clawed hand into the air, as if to strike Oleander, and I jump to my feet and run at the monster, sword first.

I manage to catch it by surprise and it stumbles back, letting out a deep growl, crouching down low and lunging for me. I block its striking hand with my blade and hear it yelp out, it swings its other arm at me just slowly enough for me to spin out of its reach, slashing its forearm as I turn.

I hear Oleander get up behind me and yell, "get down!"

She gives me a split second to drop to the floor as a blast of fire roars above my head, stinging my back with its intensity. The varg screeches and runs off into the forest, the smell of burning hair fills the air.

I turn around, still crouched on the ground with Oleander between me and the fire we were sleeping next to, and from this angle she looks as if she is a hot glowing ember, her features dark like coal. Her fingers are still on fire but soon sputter out, one by one, as she takes a few deep breaths and looks down at me.

"You saved me. I owe you a life debt," she drops on one knee in front of me, head bowed.

"Hey now, no need for all that. I need my guide alive after all," I laugh nervously, trying to shrug off the insane events that just transpired. I look down to see my blade coated in dark red blood and shudder. I have never harmed anything before, all my swordsmanship has been for tournaments and shows. I am grateful that muscle memory took over for me but I do not think I would have forgiven myself if I killed the thing.

"Why is everything a transaction here anyway?" I mutter to myself, realizing too late that I spoke that question out loud. Oleander narrows her eyes.

"You aren't from here... You're human? You mask your scent well." She sniffs the air, "what are you doing here? No wonder you've been so hopeless," she says as she stands up and offers me her hand. I tentatively grab it as I look into her eyes to gauge whether she holds malice or sincerity.

She smells like the other one, yet different somehow, I hear her voice in my head, my eyes go wide. I pull my hand away and quickly look down so she cannot read my thoughts.

The other one? Does she mean Marissa? I wonder as I try to figure out a way to find out what she knows without her knowing of my powers. That information seems too important to share; besides, keeping this a secret could come in handy, so I decide to let her think I am human. It also dawns on me that I haven't been able to read her thoughts until now because I hadn't touched her yet; more pieces of the puzzle of my powers slotting into place as I stare at the hand she had just touched.

"How do you know what a human smells like?" I question, looking her in the eye, knowing what she says out loud probably won't be the truth.

"I have Metamorph blood and have encountered one or two before." *She cannot know of my mission but perhaps she will lead me to the other one.* Both responses are almost simultaneous so I have to scrunch my face to concentrate. From what I could hear, she has Metamorph blood, like Durga, and the person she is searching for is most likely my sister . I wonder what this woman could want with her and become decidedly more wary of her. I try to keep my face as neutral as I can.

"Do humans often come through to the fae realm? Has another one recently come through these woods?" I ask as nonchalantly as I can, trying to make my question sound like a general curiosity.

"It doesn't happen often but yes, there is rumor that one recently passed through. There are certain scents I can detect," she says as she sniffs the air again. *What are the odds that two would come through within days of each other?* I can hear Oleander's thoughts layer over her spoken words as she gives me a questioning look. Before I can respond with another question, we hear the howl of several wolves, or I'm guessing vargs, and look at each other, eyes going wide.

"We should probably go!" I say, putting a pin in this sly interrogation to get as far away from here as possible. Oleander gives me a nod and snaps her fingers which instantly douses the fire. We both start out at a little faster than our jogging pace of yesterday, all too aware of the multiple horrors that are now searching for us.

I'm surprised to feel that in the short hours of sleep my feet have healed again, much quicker than in the human realm. I am also able to keep up with Oleander as we try to put as much distance between us and those vargs as we can without making too much noise. *Am I getting stronger? Or is it this realm...*

She is much lighter footed than I am and I can tell she knows her way around the forest as I stumble and curse my way through. After a long stretch of silent running we realize we cannot hear any more signs that we are being pursued so we slow down to a jog to conserve our energy. Although I am unsure if Oleander's energy stores will ever wane. She still looks fresh and bright eyed whereas I can feel my unruly hair plastered to my forehead and neck with my copious amounts of sweat and I know my stench is quite horrific.

"How are you not tired?" I ask as we stop for a breather, entirely for my sake.

"My mother was a deer Metamorph. I cannot transform like she could but I suppose some of her traits passed on. Not every child of an Elemental and Metamorph couple inherits both gifts, some barely receive anything at all. I have my father's gift mostly," she explains and I'm caught on the word "could" as I look into her eyes and see a glimmer of sadness.

"She is no longer alive?" I ask, cautiously. Oleander gives me a glare back. "My mother is dead too. She died giving birth to me," I blurt out. I expect a retort about giving too much information away, instead Oleander gives me a sympathetic look and squeezes my shoulder.

"We should keep going. We aren't far from the forest's edge." She looks off into the distance as if she can see the actual edge and we keep going, at a much more manageable pace.

Chapter Seven

The sun is just starting to peak over the soft rolling hills that stretch out in front of us as we finally emerge from the darkness of the forest. The stark contrast between the dense Tanglewoods, and the treeless expanse of hill and stone ahead of us is a welcome change. Oleander and I give each other a look and collectively let out a big sigh. For someone who seemed so comfortable in the gnarled woods I can tell she is relieved to be out. I look forward to my sunny destination with a big smile on my face and go to take a step forward when Oleander stops me with an outstretched arm.

"Wait, be wary of these gnomes you speak of. They have lived in the fae realm their whole lives and, judging by your willingness to trust, the gnomes who inhabit the human realm are a lot gentler than these. Careful with your words Nuri, look to me if you are unsure," she says as she removes her blockading arm and gives me a half smile.

Is she offering me help? Is she being nice to me? I can't seem to fight the cheesiest grin, she huffs through her nose and mutters under her breath.

"You're staying with me? What happened to your mission?" I ask, she shrugs in response.

"It may yet be fulfilled on this path," she says cryptically. A warning bell chimes about the same hunch I had from before about our missions being one and the same. I try to concoct a way in which she will come clean about her mission but I can tell it will be hard to extract that information. I bide my time until I can think of the perfectly worded questions. In the meantime, I look out to the horizon and start my search for the boulder gnomes. *I'm coming for you Marissa.*

AFTER TRAVERSING a few of the wind swept hills, I start to notice more and more rocks littering our path, so every now and again I stride up to one and give it a little knock to see if anything will stir awake.

"Um, excuse me... are you a boulder gnome?" I say, feeling as ridiculous as I look, tapping on rocks. Oleander just keeps her distance, every now and again stifling a laugh. This carries on for a long while, with the sun now nearly overhead, I am sweating and very aware of my stench.

Oleander sidles up to where I am hunched over a cluster of boulders. "Why don't you take a break? I think I saw a river off past that next hill. Besides, the gnomes do not usually enjoy answering to being summoned. They will find us," she says, probably reading my hot and annoyed expression.

I nod and take one last glance at the scattered boulders around us and yell, "if any of you are gnomes, I have been sent by Granny Mog. Please come see me by the river... Thank you!" Before abandoning my search and following Oleander.

As we crest the little hill I halt, completely awestruck by the serene sight. A lazy, flowing river winds its way through the surrounding grassy hills with scattered weeping willows at its bank, providing the most welcoming shade. The occasional yellow spattering of hypericum and little white daisies, that would be perfect for the creation of the flower crowns of my youth, are poking their cheerful little heads up through the grass. I can hear the distinct call of a chickadee and spot a mated pair of goldfinches flitting in and out of the tall, purple heads of flax. Atleast, I believe that is what they are. I take a pause to wonder if the wildlife of the human and fae realms are the same. I breathe in the fresh cool breeze as it lifts my hair and a little laugh of joy escapes my lips. Oleander smiles at me before giving me a little nudge with her elbow, beckoning me to give in to the elation that is bubbling up. We both run down the hill laughing, like school girls running for the empty swing set.

Once we reach the soft, babbling river she immediately starts to undress and I can feel the heat rise to my cheeks as she faces me, bare-chested, with a questioning look. I try to not look as though I am staring at her breasts with rosebud nipples that have risen with the sudden cold exposure, so I make, what I am sure feels like, very awkward and intense eye contact instead.

"Will you not join me? You surely smell as if you need a wash," Olander laughs as she removes her trousers, now standing stark naked in front of me. I have never been around any naked women and it takes me a moment to stop staring. She looks completely unbothered by my gaze and I can even see the slight twitch of her mouth as the edges of her lips curve up. The elegance of the lines of a woman's body makes me yearn for my paints as I take in her soft curves and strong arms. She has light skin with freckles dappled all over and I notice a little tuft of orange hair poking out from under her arms that matches the rest of her body hair.

No one would dare go swimming naked in the creek back home, not that they would ever swim anywhere other than their chlorinated pools in the first place. The only person I have been naked in front of as an adult was Benji and even then, it would often be in a darkened room.

Oleander gives me a wave to come join her as she turns around to wade into the glistening river. A little gasp escapes her lips as she enters the cooling waters and I can't help but admire the gentle swish of her long curls against the dimples in her lower back and the ripple of muscle in her strong thighs as she walks. I take a deep breath for courage as I start to tentatively peel my clothes off to join her.

When I look up, Oleander is hovering under the water with just her nose and eyes above, watching me like a crocodile. Her red hair is flowing in the current, reminding me of a bright piece of kelp that I once saw as a child when we visited the ocean. She stays perfectly still as she watches me.

I quickly undress, feeling the weight of her gaze but when my clothes are left in a heap beside my feet I find I already feel lighter, freer. I see her eyes snap to the necklace my birth mother left for me before she dunks herself under the water. I run into the river diving in and dunking my head under the sweet cool waters and emerge feeling bright and new. Oleander laughs and gives me a splash before she scoops up a handful of white, sparkling sand to scrub herself clean with. I follow her lead and can feel the multiple days' worth of grime and dried blood being washed away.

When we are done scrubbing ourselves until we are pink all over, Oleander motions for me to turn around with the twirl of her pointer finger, and I obey. Her hands reach over my shoulders to grasp my long hair and she sweeps it onto my back. The light touch of her fingers on my skin makes me shiver, I tell myself it must just be the cold water and nothing more. *Surely nothing more...*

She works her fingers through my extremely tangled hair, then efficiently gives me a braid to better keep it under control. I can't help but let out a little moan at the soft scrape of her nails against my scalp as she pulls back sections of my hair for the braid. A blush stains my cheeks at the intimacy of having someone tend to me in this way. Our closeness leaves me feeling even more naked but I am unsure if it is in a good or bad way.

After she is done I dunk my head underwater to cool the

heat from my cheeks so she does not see my blush. When I emerge she is already exiting the water but turns back to suggest I give my clothes a rinse too. She says they will dry quickly in this heat so I acquiesce and we both end up lying naked under the willow tree as we wait for my clothes to dry in the sun.

I am lying like a starfish, looking up at the waving branches of the willow tree, completely entranced by the simplicity of the moment. I swear the wind is consciously moving the branches for my own viewing pleasure. The honeyed sun moves like a mesmerizing kaleidoscope, dancing through the leaves. Oleander is sitting up, running her fingers through her hair to detangle it. I can feel her looking at me so I turn my head, the sun is reflecting a golden halo through her coppery hair and the sight steals my breath away.

"I've never met someone like you," I say, looking in her eyes. *Shit, that was supposed to be in my head.*

"What's that supposed to mean?" she laughs, *she shouldn't trust me so freely. I do not deserve it,* I can hear her say, picking up on a twinge of what sounds like sadness. I furrow my brows and shake my head.

"I mean... you're just so free and sure of yourself," I say back, trying to avoid eye contact. I don't want to accidentally transfer my questions about the meaning behind her thoughts.

"Huh, well to be truthful, it is abnormal in this realm for the women to be carefree. Most of us are in servitude in one way or another. I just decided to shirk my familial responsibilities to serve The Divine Mother instead. She wants all of her children to be happy and comfortable within her embrace and serving her feels more noble," she says as she smiles up at the tree. I feel the conflict within me about her true nature pulling at my seams. What she says rings true within me but what she thinks is making me worry.

I turn my gaze back up to the branches as well. "Back home I am one of few in my town who seems to respect nature. I always felt so out of place. It's comforting to know that there are people on this earth who actually care and that someone... or something is listening. There is no higher being that watches over us in our realm. Or that is what most believe anyway." I glance back at Oleander whose expression has turned very serious.

"You humans do not honour the creator of this earth? You do not know of The Mother?" She raises her eyebrows and blows out a sigh, "how sad and lonely your lives must be."

I hum my agreement. "If only you knew," I force a laugh. I feel a bit too seen and annoyed at the spiritual lacking in my upbringing so I change the subject. "What family responsibilities did you have?" I ask, keeping the conversation flowing as I return to thinking of a roundabout way to ask if she is hunting down my sister.

"My father serves the new king and, as his only daughter, I had a duty to become the wife to one of The King's lords to secure my father's position. Let's just say, I quickly disappeared to avoid such a fate. I am no one's *wife*," she jokes, as if it is a normal occurrence.

"As if people still do that kind of shit!" I exclaim and am met first with shock, then with a little smile. I see my opening and quickly add, "so is this person you are tracking down a service you are doing for The Divine Mother?" Oleander quickly glances at my necklace, then back to me.

She wears the crest of the old king's line, her thoughts flood in and I can't help my expression of confusion at her mention of the crest of a king as I grasp my necklace and wonder who exactly my mother was and why she would have such a thing. She clocks my movement and her eyebrows raise. *Can you hear my thoughts?* I hear her think as her eyes widen in astonishment. Just as she opens her mouth to say something we hear a loud, splashing noise behind us and turn to see several large boulders springing to life.

"You called and we have answered!" a large boulder gnome with a long swishing beard made of the same ghostly moss that was in the Tanglewoods exclaims as he tumbles towards us.

"Uncle Chomsky at your service," he says, sketching a bow. I give Oleander a quick glance and am suddenly aware that we are still naked so I bunch my knees up to my chest. Oleander doesn't seem bothered by her nakedness.

"Um... Hello." I try to reach my toes over to where my clothes are but they are *just* out of my grasp.

"How may we be of assistance?" I realize that I need the guidance of these gnomes to find my sister and can no longer hide my mission from Oleander. I doubt she would leave to give us privacy to talk so I try to be as vague as I can.

"Have you, by chance, seen a... hairy creature and a...

blonde woman pass through these parts?" I cringe, meeting Oleander's widening and understanding eyes, seeing that my vagueness did not work in the slightest.

"Ah, you mean the varg and the human girl?" *Well, if she didn't know before, now she certainly does. Great.* "Yes, they passed through here a few days ago. She seemed to be putting up a good fight but we could do nothing to intervene," he says and the other gnomes around him shudder at the mention of the varg. Oleander and I exchange glances and all pretenses about both of our missions melt away.

"Ok, let's not deny it any longer. We are both looking for Marissa," I say, crossing my arms and raising my eyebrows at Oleander.

"Marissa," is all she says, as if she is testing out the name on her tongue. "What is she to you?" she says, snapping out of her reverie. All of the warmth from our interactions before has gone cold.

"She is *my* sister! She was taken on my watch, I have to rescue her!" I say, glaring back. I turn to the gnomes and ask, "where are they headed?"

"They seemed to be heading towards Inverdell, but of course, it is hard to tell out here. We don't often leave the safety of our hills so we do not know much of what lies beyond the small village," Uncle Chomsky says, shrugging his big shoulders. "How does my cousin Mog fare?" He perks up at the memory of his cousin.

"She is well. I mean, they seem happy enough..." I say as I briefly let myself remember the warm hospitality of the boulder gnomes, then turn to give Oleander a glare. She was too quick to judge these gnomes, they are lovely. I catch her with a puzzled look on her face as she stares at my necklace.

"Pray tell, where did you get that necklace from?" Oleander asks and I can see where her mind is going. Perhaps this necklace is somehow traceable to my mother, so I lie.

"I found it in my sister's room." At which Oleander slowly nods, furrowing her brows and looking sceptical but having no way of calling my bluff.

"Hmm, all right we must be going, thank you for your assistance gnomes," Oleander says abruptly, as she gets up and tosses me my now dried clothing. I quickly pull on my shirt and overalls, still very aware that I am naked in front of a bunch of male gnomes.

"Wait, my dear. The girl dropped this as they passed through our knoll. Perhaps you can find a Metamorph to help sniff her out," a chunkier gnome pipes up, handing me a heart shaped, golden earring as I am finishing strapping on my sword. My eyes catch Oleander's and I quickly grab the earring and shove it in my pocket as she lunges for it. I jump out of her grasp and draw my sword.

"Why do you want my sister?" I shout at her, shuffling into my fighting stance. She has seen me use this sword before on the varg that tried to attack her so knows I am no novice. She takes a step back with her hands up but I wonder why she does not retaliate using her fire.

"I do not mean you or your sister any harm. Your care for your family is admirable but I can track them and you will only slow me down. I caught wind of a plot to kidnap the child of a long disappeared noble lineage with *particular* powers from the human realm and I could not let her fall into the wrong hands." She sounds sincere but still, I do not trust her. *What do my powers have to do with this?* I wonder but don't have time to prod as I see Oleander readying herself to attack.

"Either we do this together or I will throw the earring into the creek and the scent will be lost to us both." It is an empty threat, but she does not need to know that.

Oleander sizes up the distance between me and the water, most likely thinking she can tackle me to the ground before I can toss it. "Please! The life debt you owe me will be paid, just help me save my sister!" I say, not lowering my sword even an inch. She blows out a breath.

"All right, all right, we do this together," she tries to placate, her hands still up. "Just try to keep up. I believe I may know where they are headed but cannot be sure without the scent," she says, eyeing my pocket.

"You have to *promise* to rescue Marissa with me," I say, knowing now that the fae must keep their promises.

"*Fine*, I promise not to rescue her without you. Now you must uphold your promise!" she says, looking at my sword, raising both eyebrows. I take a breath and hesitate but there is a strong pull within my hand and a sudden pounding in my head that forces me to throw her the sword.

I truly do have to keep my promises here... noted. She did fulfill her end of the bargain by getting me out of the Tangle-woods after all. She catches it easily and we both take a unified breath to dispel the tension.

"Let's go get your sister."

Chapter Eight

I am left waiting behind a haystack just outside of the small village, as Oleander goes to find me some proper clothing. She said I would raise too much suspicion and there may be more vargs lurking around looking for anything unusual. I peak around the hay and from what I can see, Inverdell is a quaint little town of farms and tradespeople. The town itself is surrounded by a stone wall that looks to be around ten feet tall, perhaps it had once been a garrison. The wall is crumbling in places now though, so I doubt it would keep an army out. Many people, or what I think are people as it is hard to tell from this distance, are exiting and entering carrying various goods which makes me think this might be a hub, even though it is small. There are quite a few farm houses outside of the wall and my question from before, about whether or not this realm had similar animals, seems to be answered when I notice a few herds of sheep and cows lazily grazing on the lush green grasses. I am tapped on the shoulder from behind and whirl around, hand going to where my father's sword once sat. Oleander casts me a questioning glance and holds up a dark red dress with a lace up corset, a frilly white blouse, as well as some well-worn boots. Her eyes dart to where my hands went, a frown of hurt flicks across her face for the briefest of moments.

"What on earth am I meant to do with that?" I ask, noting the impracticality of such big skirts.

"This is what all the ladies are wearing these days. Come on, pop it on we don't have all day!" She shoves the clothes at me and takes a step back, watching with anticipation. I grumble something about the hypocrisy of how *she* gets to wear trousers as I undress, then slide first the blouse then the dress on over my head. I notice the dress has pockets and am pleased that at least the ladies' fashion has *one* practical element to it.

Oleander steps up close to me and grabs the strings of my corset and starts lacing me up. I can feel her breath as she leans in closer to better see and our closeness makes my cheeks heat as I remember our interactions in the creek. *Why am I blushing?*

"These look well worn... did you steal these?" I question as I lift up the torn hem of my skirts and the soft boots.

"Do not worry, they won't be missed." She gives me a wink as she pulls hard on the corset's strings causing me to stumble into her. I receive a gentle push back as she looks up at me through her long eyelashes, the corners of her mouth curling up slightly. She gives the strings one more quick yank then ties them in a little bow.

"Besides, I left a hair pinned on the washing line. That is ample payment, so I believe a thank you is in order," she says as she steps back, giving me a sweeping look, admiring her handiwork. The cinched waist of the corset makes my hips and breasts appear much larger than they usually do and I instantly feel uncomfortable about my femininity.

"How is a hair ample payment?" I ask, wondering how currencies work in this strange land.

"A hair is a promise of a small favour," she explains matter-of-factly.

"How will she know it was you who left a hair?" I ask, wondering if her hairs are particularly magical.

"If she keeps the hair on her somewhere she will just know when she sees me. But I'm not planning on staying here long enough to have to pay up right now," she snickers. My stomach drops as I am brought back to the deal I made with the wood sprite when I first entered the Tanglewood Forest.

"Shit, and what if someone were to give five hairs *and* an eyelash!?" I question, panic clearly written all over my face.

Oleander bites her bottom lip. "Oh no, to whom did you give such a gift?" she responds, crossing her arms and raising an eyebrow. "The eyelash is a promise of a kiss," she chuckles.

"A wood sprite in the Tanglewood Forest!" I wail, washing my face in my hands. She looks at me and bursts out laughing as she places one hand on each shoulder and gives me a little shake.

"I guess you should avoid the Tanglewoods then," she grabs my wrists to pull them away from my face. The heat from her hands tingles up my arms and soothes me, we both look up from my hands and into each other's eyes. For a split second I swear I can see flames in her irises and a sudden flash of our lips meeting pops into my mind before I pull my hands back and look away.

Was that from my mind or hers?

"Let's go ask around at the farmhouses to see if anyone has seen Marissa," I say, trying to act as if nothing happened as I look off into the distance. Oleander clears her throat and takes a step back.

"We do not need to ask around. All I need is the earring," she holds her hand out and I nod, fishing around in the pocket of my old clothes to give it to her. Oleander brings it up to her nose and closes her eyes as she inhales deeply.

Her eyes flip open, pupils expanding, she looks towards the village. "They were here... or are here. Her scent is very strong in the wind!" she exclaims with wide eyes.

We both start running towards the entrance of Inverdell.

I have to gather my skirts in my hands to prevent myself from tripping and falling flat on my face so my speed and ability to keep up with Oleander's long legs is greatly diminished. *Ladies need to be able to run!* I think back to my mother telling me otherwise and scoff at the inconvenience of running in skirts.

We stop a little ways back from the entrance to the village and slow to a walk so we don't look too suspicious in our haste. The steady flow of civilians entering the village is easy to meld into and I notice that not all appear to be in their humanoid forms. There are many who show slight changes into their Metamorph forms. The small group of females we are walking behind have holes cut into their skirts to make way for various different variations of tails. Perhaps house cats or some sort of big cat, I can't quite tell. We pass a male with a humanoid body but two legs of what might be a goat or a deer and another male with big, white, feathered wings on his back.

"Why do some Metamorphs retain parts of their animal forms?" I say to Oleander and she gives me a quick glance as if to tell me to shut up but instead, leans in and whispers in a barely audible tone, her warm breath on my ear sending shivers down my spine.

"Only those with higher power can fully transform out of their animus. Most get stuck with one or more features. My mother looked human except, instead of skin, she had the soft brown coat of a woodland deer. It would be best to not ask any more questions while we are here. Someone might suspect you come from the human realm." I nod but wonder why it would be so bad for them to know where I come from. I decide to hold onto that particular question for when we have more privacy.

As we walk under the big stone arch of the outer wall and into the village proper, I am met with a colourful and boisterous market. The shock of sounds, sights and smells takes me by surprise because the village appeared fairly calm, even slightly run down, from the outside. The space is packed with socializing fae going from stall to stall of what appears to range from mundane goods like flour, grains and milk to the much less mundane, such as fluorescent powders, strange caged creatures and organs floating in jars. Oleander sees my shock and hesitation and grabs my hand, most likely worried I will get lost in the bustling crowd.

"We have to get past the market, I can't pinpoint her scent in here, there are too many smells," Oleander says as she holds tight and pulls me through the chaos. I try to keep my eyes down because scenarios like this are usually what causes my brain to be overloaded with other's thoughts, and I have never been somewhere so crowded before. As long as I make sure not to brush up against anyone I should be alright, but in such a crowded space that seems to be a difficult task. My curiosity soon gets the better of me, though.

"Chump Chops, get your chump chops here!" a pig-nosed fae calls as he turns what looks like really massive worms over a spit fire.

"Miss! Miss, over here. This fabric would do wonders for your green eyes!" a female with the head of a tiger and an exotic accent calls to me as she holds out a shimmering roll of dark green fabric that changes to sea green as it catches the light. I give her a meek smile and shake my head, quickly looking down to avoid being bombarded with offers for something I have no need of at this moment.

"Charms, for your lovey!" I hear next but cannot see who is speaking.

"Down here, deary! A charm for you two?" I look down to see a toad sporting a red silk vest and finely tailored trousers addressing me whilst holding out a heart shaped vial with some swirling red smoke inside.

"Oh... ah, no thank you, we aren't together..." I stammer and blush as I look at Oleander, who is also blushing. We hurry on, passing several stalls selling produce and meats but a stall selling baked goods makes me slow my pace and tug a bit at Oleander as I smell the delicious scent of homemade bread. She stops and chuckles at my longing look.

"All right, just wait here," she reads my hungry expression and pushes past the crowd to get us some still warm pastries.

"Yum! What are these called?" I laugh as I take a big bite of the flakey, buttery pastry.

"These are fairy crescents," she says, taking a big bite. I notice that the inside is slightly glittery.

"Just one will keep you full for most of the day, and they are pretty delicious," she garbles around a full mouth and I laugh at all the crumbs on her face. I brush them off her cheek and pause with my hand resting on the side of her face, our eyes meet.

Oh Mother, what is she doing to me? I can hear Oleander's plea within my mind and quickly lower my hand. The excitement that flutters within my gut from the longing in her tone catches me off guard. I have never felt this kind of attraction towards a woman before and wonder what it is about Oleander that is drawing me in. She is an insanely beautiful woman that could incinerate my ass with the snap of a finger but there is something soft about her as well that makes me want to get to know her more. I try not to stare as we finish up our fairy crescents then keep on pushing through the market, trying not to get distracted by the multitude of wonders. I find I am more aware of our touching skin than anything else as she guides me through.

When we are finally out, Oleander pulls me into a quiet alley so she can pause to smell the earring again.

"She was definitely in Inverdell. I suggest we go check the inn to see if the scent is any stronger over there."

We continue on, weaving our way through tight cobble-stone streets. We pass doors with colourfully painted wooden signs overhead, depicting different trades such as a seamstress, a cobbler and a herbal potion maker that I make a mental note of. *I'd love to have a look in there.*

There are a few haggard looking fae loitering in the darker corners that we try to avoid as we navigate through the narrow lanes, Oleander keeps a hand on my father's sword and one at my low back as we scurry past. All the twists and turns have me feeling slightly dizzy and claustro-phobic until we round a corner and step out into the bright, airy main square.

Across from us there is a big building with a bell tower and various little shop fronts lining the square. There are a few fae milling around a white marble carving of what I am guessing is The Divine Mother, although she appears to be birthing the Earth, rather than being the Earth itself as I had assumed. She is seated, leaning back on her hands with her head tilted up to the sky. Her hair is carved to look like cascading vines of flowers and ivy and she is looking up with an ecstatic look on her face.

"I thought the fae considered the Earth itself to be The Divine Mother," I say, turning to see Oleander's frustrated, jaw clenched expression as she looks at the statue.

"Some do, but more recently, in the last century, there has been a rising popularity of a new faith. The new popular belief is that the Earth was birthed by a fae goddess that they still call The Divine Mother. The more powerful fae have been indoctrinated by the new king and in turn, have been working at indoctrinating all those beneath them into believing they, the Elemental fae, are all powerful like The Mother. But The Mother made us all a part of her. We come forth from the land itself, not from a bloody fae goddess," she seethes as she directs us past the statue. We get a few stares from the fae that have come to worship this version of The Divine Mother but Oleander doesn't stop to react.

"I'm guessing your father is a supporter of the new belief?" I ask, checking on her from the corner of my eye. She just nods her head and keeps walking.

This guy sounds like a real piece of work.

We turn off onto a wider road and at the far end we notice a pack of vargs pacing in front of a large, multi-storied building. Oleander quickly grabs my arm and pulls me back around the corner and into the square before they can see us.

"Shit! Do you think they saw us?" I start to panic, "wait, would they even know who we are? Maybe we should just casually walk up there..." I start to suggest, but Oleander covers my mouth with her hand and shakes her head. She brings one finger to her lips to signal me to be quiet as she removes her other hand from my mouth and motions for us to duck down the adjacent alleyway.

When we round the corner she lets out a breath, as if she had been holding it in, and says, "they know who I am. Those are The King's minions."

"Are they searching for you? Is Marissa in there?" I question, grabbing both of her arms with my hands and giving her a little shake. A fae couple walks past the entrance to the alley and I quickly drop my hands. We both try to look like we are just loitering but I can't help the panic that washes over me as I wonder what they might be doing to my sister in there and why they even took her there in the first place.

"No, my father gave up caring about me years ago. The King would not waste resources on tracking down a long gone runaway but I am *known* by the vargs for my disruption of The King's plotting and have been known to associate with the group of rebels who call themselves the Order of The Sylvans. Your sister's scent is very strong here and judging by the amount of guards I would say she is in there, although why they would stop in Inverdell rather than going straight to the Palace, I am unsure. The Palace is on the opposite side of this mountain range," she explains, furrowing her brow and biting her thumb nail as she thinks. I am grateful for her honesty for once.

"Tell me about this new king, what are his plans? Why are you plotting against him?" I ask, dropping my voice low so no curious civilians can hear us.

"He usurped The Owl King; a kind, benevolent king

who had been ruling the main landmass of Earth for centuries, the longest reign in recorded history. The Wolf challenged his beliefs and ways of ruling and amassed a following of zealots who believed in his claims of being a prophet of the new religion, sent by The Mother herself. They were preaching this new religion throughout the Continent until enough of the public were swayed and demanded a duel. The right of the duel hadn't been invoked in thousands of years and it had widely been forgotten. However, it was written into the code. Fae cannot deny the code." Oleander swipes a hand down her face, the memory of this clearly agitating her. "Sadly, there was no competition between a wolf and an owl. The Wolf had enough sense to abolish the tradition of the duel soon after his ascension to the throne." Another fae couple passes the alleyway and Oleander grabs onto my hips and shifts me so my back is to the square and she is hidden behind me. The spot where her hands grabbed me tingles, a minor distraction from the terror rising in me, threatening to burst out of the cage of my chest.

Once the couple passes she continues in a hushed tone. "I had been a devoted student of The Owl when I was a small child and I cannot stand by while The Wolf continues his reign. He believes that we have become complicit to the suffering of our land and thought The Owl too docile. He preaches that the lack of control the fae have over the lesser creatures is one of the causes. He is amassing some of the most powerful Elemental fae to aid him but I am unsure what they are planning or what his exact plans are for your sister, but I will do whatever I can to get her back!" I look down to see that my hands are shaking. The mention of The Wolf evokes the image of a wolf headed man sitting on the throne, snarling. The rising fear has me shaking and gasping for air.

"Nuria, look at me." Oleander tries calming me as she cradles my face in her warm hands. My whole body is quaking as I lift my eyes to meet hers. I am just now noticing their soft golden flecks, hidden amongst the swirling browns and greens and I momentarily forget myself. Before I can read her thoughts she is pressing her lips to mine. I close my eyes and kiss her back.

Her lips are soft but almost painfully hot. She parts her mouth enough to give my bottom lip a little bite. I hear myself moan from afar, as if I am removed from my own body and watching from above. Our bodies meld together as she gently backs me into the alley's wall and I shudder, feeling the cool stone on the palms of my hands contrast the heat of where our bodies touch. My shock is soon replaced by a trembling wave of warmth, radiating from where our lips meet, down to the space between my legs. I start to relax into the sensation but then she pulls away, ending our kiss just as abruptly as she had begun it.

"Well that worked," she says, with a little laugh and a cheeky half smile. Her smile drops when she notices my shocked face turn into a scowl. "You were having a panic attack. Nuri, your sister is close and I think I may have a plan to get her back. We cannot falter now, we are too close," she says, and continues telling me her plot as I just stand there, embarrassed and confused.

FOR PHASE one of Oleander's surprisingly simple, yet genius sounding plan, we cut back to the market to purchase a charm that changes my scent enough to confuse the varg guards and a few other items that might assist me. The vargs have never seen my face so shouldn't be on watch for me. The plan should work, hopefully.

I am wearing the musky scent of a male buffalo Metamorph, which to me smells vaguely of blue cheese. None of the guards give me a second glance as I walk straight past them and into the Inn. The ground floor is a busy tavern full of rowdy civilians and the occasional varg lurking at the corner tables. I avoid the front desk and bee-line it for a table with a bunch of empty tankards scattered on top. Turning away from the nearest varg to pull out a little white, frilly apron from my pocket. I tie it around my waist before snatching up the cups and making my way towards the kitchen.

The kitchen is way more chaotic than the tavern scene and I feel I am immediately in the way.

"Put those down over there girl!" a plump, greasy looking female with a duck's bill for a mouth squawks at me. "Wait, I don't recognize you. Do you work here?" She crosses her arms as she gives me a once-over. *Crap that was fast, ok think Nuri think...*

"I've been specially hired to care for the... asset," I say, giving a little wink to the duck lady whilst lifting my chin a little higher, hoping that I look more sure of myself than I feel. "She must not be kept waiting, she has been asking for her lunch for over an hour!" I snap at the woman, impressed with myself for my acting skills.

"She got her lunch ages ago! I bet those stinking vargs ate it! Here bring her this stew; it's all we have left until the dinner service. The poor thing looked like she was only skin and bone," she says, shoving a bowl of greyish brown slop into my hands. I grimace at what looks like a tentacle floating in the liquid before giving her a nod and promptly exiting the kitchen.

I can see a staircase at the far side of the tavern on the other side of the door that I assume leads to the rooms. I swerve and weave my way through the raucous revellers trying not to spill the slop on myself as I go. I have to dodge the grasping hands of drunken fae male more than a few times and scoff at how behind the times this realm feels. *Pigs...*

Once I am at the stairs a varg steps into my path and growls at me.

"Where do you think you're going, sweet thing," he says, sniffing at me. He quickly pulls away with a crinkled snout, no doubt due to my delectable buffalo musk.

"I have been sent with refreshments for... the asset," I say, giving him a look as if I am in on their secret.

"Asset you say?" he says, looking sceptical and showing me his teeth.

"You were ordered not to harm her and malnutrition counts as harm," I take a chance snapping back and suppressing my wince, hoping he doesn't rip my head off for the tone.

"Erg... Very well, but you better be back down here in a few minutes or I will personally come see to your demise," he snarls back, stepping out of the way, allowing me to slip past and run up the stairs.

There are three levels so I take my chances with the upper level, guessing from my knowledge of fairy tales, that they would lock her in the highest tower. I reach the top of the stairs and am dismayed to see six doors on this level and no indicator of which one she is in, so I begin with the closest one, knocking on the door.

"Room service!" I call out, hoping that inns in this realm have a similar concept. I am met with a tall, extremely buff man with horns sticking out of his head looking down at me angrily.

"Sorry, wrong room!" I squeak and run down to the far end of the hall trying to get as far away from him as I can. Thankfully, he slams the door behind me. I halt in front of the farthest door on the left side of the hall and take a centring breath.

"Room service..." I call out, a little less sure of myself, I hear the faintest response in return.

"Come in, it's open," I recognize the voice immediately and rip open the door.

"Marissa!" I wail, stepping into her room.

She is tied to a chair at the back of the sparsely furnished space and looks as if she has been dragged through the mud. My linen dress is in tatters and covered in brown stains. Her perfect blonde curls look like they have turned into one big matted mess and she has huge dark circles under her eyes. I quietly shut the door behind me before tossing the bowl of stew onto the little round table in the centre of the room and running over to her.

"Nuria?" I hear her cracked voice squeak, sounding as if she doesn't believe I am real. A sob breaks loose from her scrunched up face and I am already at her feet untying the rope that is holding her down. The knots are impossibly tight so I pull a little ivory handled knife that we got at the market out of my pocket and cut her free. As I move on to her hands I can see a stream of tears streaking down her dirty cheeks and pause to cup her face in my hands.

"I'm here to save you little sis!" I say, making quick work of cutting her hands free. She nods, ever so slowly and stares at me through wide, watery eyes. Her bottom lip quivers, like it used to when she was on the verge of one of her sob sessions when we were kids. I hack away at her bindings as quickly as I can, hoping to free her before she cries out. When Delia wasn't around, I was hopeless at soothing her and I doubt now would be any different.

As soon as the rope snaps she flings herself onto me and gives me the biggest hug I have ever received from her. She pulls back to look into my eyes but keeps her arms wrapped around me.

"You came for me!"

"Don't sound so surprised, Mar. You're my sister." I

place my hands on her shoulders and look her over. Thankfully she appears unharmed.

"I just... after the party and what happened with Benji, I thought you hated me." Her bottom lip starts to quiver again.

"Never, Mar. I will always come after you when you get stolen in the night by terrifying monsters. It's what sisters are for. Right?" I try to ease the tension but the words sound as ludicrous coming out as they did in my head. Her lip stops quivering. An awareness snaps into her eyes that was not there a moment ago.

"Nuria, where the heck are we? I thought I had been dreaming or drugged! There are talking animals and strange people with animal parts! And that thing killed Benji! And how did you find me? And how do we get out of here!?" she shrieks, letting her panic escalate and not letting me get a word in. Her breath is coming in heaves and I fear one of her old panic attacks may be coming on so I panic as well and I do what I have seen done in many movies to rectify this sort of situation...

I slap her.

"Ow! What the fuck, Nuria!" she yells and slaps me back, but it seems to have worked because she is just staring at me completely alert with her usual sassy Marissa look.

"Sorry! I panicked..." I bite my lip.

Marissa lets out a sharp laugh. "Maybe I deserved it." She pulls back and looks me up and down. "What on Earth are you wearing?" Her eyebrows raise nearly to her hair line as she looks at my frilly blouse and ridiculous amount of cleavage. I scoff and give her a little shove.

"We don't have time for questions! The varg guard will be up here checking on you any moment," I say, looking around for a solution for our escape when I see the only window on the left side of the bed looks big enough for us to squeeze through.

"Quick, to the window," I point and Marissa nods and runs over. She tries to push it up but it seems stuck so I get my hands on it to help her push.

"Hey, maid! What's taking so long?" I can hear the varg guard call from what sounds like the top of the stairs as we finally get the window pushed up. My heart starts pounding as I look out the window and down to the cobblestone alleyway, three stories down.

That would for sure break some bones. I look around for other solutions. To the left, the adjacent room has a balcony and the room below it also has a balcony. There is a small ledge just outside the window that I hope we can grab ahold of to help us inch our way over.

"You first Mar," I say, giving her an encouraging nod. She has always been brave and doesn't think twice before shimmying through the window and grabbing onto the ledge. When she is nearly halfway to the balcony I can see Oleander creeping her way up the alleyway from behind the Inn, I give her a big wave. She looks up and smiles waving back. I start to pull myself through the window when the door behind me whips open. Two vargs growl and run in after me.

I am only half way out of the window before one of them grabs my feet. I only have a moment to look into Marissa's panicked eyes before I am yanked back into the room.

I tumble to the ground and mentally curse Oleander for taking my sword but I still have the speed I use in fencing on my side. I quickly roll out of the way of the slashing hand of one of the vargs and kick out my legs to trip up the other. He falls with a loud crash, hitting his head on the wooden frame of the bed and doesn't get up.

Please don't be dead, please don't be dead!

I am still down on the ground when the first varg lunges at me, both hands grasping forward. He is met with my foot in his stomach, sending him sprawling backwards. I jump up onto my feet and dive towards the window, getting my head outside in time to see Marissa jump down from the second balcony into the alley way. She pauses and looks up at me with worry written on her face and I can see Oleander run up behind her and whack her on the back of the head with the pommel of my sword. She catches Marissa and tosses her over her shoulder, giving me one backward glance while mouthing, "I'm sorry," before she slinks away, into the dark alley.

My moment of stunned shock from the betrayal is enough for the still conscious varg to grab me from behind and smash my head into the wall, making me see spots as I slump to my knees before him.

"I told you I would destroy you!" he roars as he lifts a

sharp clawed hand into the air, gearing towards slicing me in two.

"Wait... I'm her sister!" I yell as I lift my arms to shield my face, not knowing whether that information would be valuable enough to save my life. *Please be valuable enough!*

"Her sister eh? Hmmm... interesting. All right then, you're coming with me!" the varg grumbles as he lowers his hand and pulls out a thick handled knife from the belt around his waist and knocks me on the head, like Oleander had just done to my sister. My vision goes dark.

Chapter Nine

I come back into consciousness, gasping. My eyes flutter open but my vision is blurry and shaded. I can taste the metallic tang of blood in my mouth and it takes me a few moments to realize that there is a dark sack over my head. I wiggle and feel that my arms and legs are bound tightly and judging by the sharp thing jabbing me in the gut and the jostling up and down I am guessing that I am slung over the shoulder of a varg.

"She's awake. We will be there soon enough, sweet thing, quit wriggling." The varg laughs at my grunt and gives me an extra hard jostle for good measure. I can hear the snicker of a few more vargs around us.

How long have I been out? Oleander betrayed me... Did they make it out of the village? Why did she do it? Where am I being taken? Why am I not dead? They only had orders to not harm Marissa... thinking she was me. Do they know I'm the one they were supposed to kidnap... Oleander betrayed me!

Thoughts are endlessly racing through my head as I helplessly hang over the varg's shoulder, unable to move or fight back. The anger and shame I feel for trusting Oleander makes me want to lash out but I know fighting back would be fruitless. I must bide my time until they inevitably let me down at our next destination. That is, if they aren't taking me directly to The Wolf.

Don't panic, don't panic...

After a while, I wish I was still unconscious because all the blood is now pooled in my head and my feet are tingling from being suspended for so long. The sharp pain in my stomach from the varg's boney shoulder has long since eased into a dull throb but I know I will have a particularly nasty bruise there tomorrow.

I hear a few of the vargs call out what seems to be a signal before I am flopped down onto the ground. My teeth clang in my head at the impact and I groan as I roll into a seat. I try to get my bearings by using my remaining senses. It smells damp, a bit like the rotting leaves of a forest floor and I hear water running nearby.

The hood is ripped off my face and it takes me a moment to register my surroundings. We are indeed in a forest that looks similar to the Wildwood Forest behind my house back in Easthelm and, for a moment, I am confused as to whether all my encounters in the fae realm have been a dream and I am back in the human realm. Then I see all the vargs milling about, and the happy illusion is crushed.

The sky is that purplish grey that could mean it is either dawn or dusk and I have no idea what day it is or how long I was unconscious. The sound of the water consumes my attention as I feel how dry and acrid tasting my mouth is, it also feels like there is crusted blood on my face and the spot where the varg hit me is horribly itchy.

"Please... water," I croak, feeling my throat burn at the lack of use. *I must have been out for a while.*

A shaggy, grey coated varg comes up to me with his canteen and grabs my chin to open my mouth, pouring some water in. He pours it too fast and I choke and sputter, rolling over to the side to spit it out. He just laughs and places the open canteen down beside me, leaving me to figure out how to drink it with my hands tied behind my back. I manage to lean down and wrap my mouth around the opening to lift the bottle up with my teeth and take a few deep gulps before I let it drop back down to the ground.

"Look fellas, she's good with her mouth," one of them snickers, and the others look at me and snicker. All their eyes are giving me a predatory once over that thoroughly disgusts me. I spit at their feet in defiance.

"You'll regret that!" I hear one of the vargs say from behind me as I feel its claw slice deeply into my shoulder. The feel of my skin ripping apart elicits a blood-curdling scream from my lips.

"Now you've done it Garr! We weren't supposed to hurt her!" one of the vargs exclaims, and I sense a note of actual fear in his trembling voice.

"We were ordered to not hurt her *sister* fellas, we can do what we want with this one," the one named Garr snarls.

The terror I feel at the thought of what they might do is bigger than anything I have ever felt before.

Fuck, I can't defend myself. Why am I here! Someone help me!

"I would advise against that, *dogs,*" the drawl of a posh male voice cautions the vargs but cannot see who is speaking.

"Oh! Uh... we were just joking around, Adviser Nerius. It won't happen again. Please don't report us to the Master!" Garr pleads to the man that I cannot see.

"See to it that she is cleaned up before you arrive. *He* has been impatiently waiting for days now. What took you so long?" the Adviser demands. It sounds as if his voice is coming from the direction of the water. I try to sit back up to look but the searing pain in my shoulder keeps me hunched over.

"There was a slight hiccup... Uh this is the target's sister," Garr speaks up, bowing his head at their blunder.

"He will not be pleased! Report directly to his study when you arrive. I will let you explain yourself then," Nerius barks at the vargs. I hear a splash and the vargs start muttering to themselves.

"Well you heard him, get her cleaned up and let's get a move on fellas!" Garr orders the others and I am scooped up in one of their arms and tossed into the water.

The shock of cold takes over my body's movements for a moment and I can feel myself sinking to the bottom, when a big hand shoots down and grasps me by the arms and pulls me back up.

"There, that ought to do it," the varg who is now

standing in the water with me calls back to shore. Garr gives him a quick nod before I am tossed over this one's shoulder and hauled out of the water. The pain in my stomach is intensified from the slight break it had from being repeatedly bumped on a bony shoulder and I can feel my fresh wound burn as it starts to slowly stitch itself back together.

I had never been aware of the healing of my body before but perhaps the feeling only comes when the wound is this large. It feels as though thousands of tiny hands are stabbing miniature sewing needles into the rough edges of my flesh and pulling them back together. The dark sack is pulled over my head once again and all goes hazy. I am left with only the various pains along my body and the grunts and stench of the vargs to tell me I am still alive.

We carry on for a few hours and I now know that the purple-grey sky from before was indeed dawn because I can feel the searing midday sun on my back, drying my soggy clothes, turning me into a ball of steam. I am suffocating in this sack as each inhale is full of condensation.

"Please, I can't breathe. I have no idea where we are and won't run away, please remove the hood!" I beg, the varg carrying me grunts as he pulls the sack off my head. We left the shade of the forest behind a while ago and the blaring sun makes my eyes water. From this distance I can see that the vargs must have hiked down a mountain similar to the Easthelm Mountain when I was unconscious.

This is all so familiar... are the two realms mirror images of each other? I couldn't tell we were at such an altitude when we were in Inverdell, it was so warm. Similar to Granny Mog's glen I suppose...

I am trying to decipher the layout of this realm as we all come to a halt and I am set down on my feet. The feeling of standing upright after being airborne for so long has my feet feeling like there are a thousand needles sticking in them and I sway forward, losing my balance.

The varg that was carrying me grabs my arms and his big claws dig in almost to the point of breaking skin and I wince at the pain in my left shoulder.

"Release her hands and feet. We are close enough now and we don't want the Master to think we *mistreated* the girl," Garr chuckles, signalling the varg who is holding me to untie my bonds.

"You even *think* about running and I'll whack you across the head again," he bares his teeth.

I rub my chafed wrists and give my feet a little shake when they are finally free and turn around to see an expansive estate sprawling before us. The soft rolling hills level out to a small lake with swans and geese floating on top and fluffy bulrushes swaying in the breeze. A herd of majestic horses similar to Durga, except black, roam freely, grazing on the waving grasses. Past the lake there is a gravel road lined with big oak trees that lean over the path like lovers reaching for an embrace, leading up to a massive red-brick house.

The house itself is stunning, with dark wood trimmings around the windows and two pointed towers on either side. I can see some smaller buildings to the left of the house, slightly removed, which I guess are stables or housing for servants. I have only ever seen such places in period piece movies with frustratingly slow-burn love stories. Delia loves watching them. I know that this is definitely not that as I am shoved in the back by a hairy snarl-toothed varg.

"Keep walking!"

I snarl back at him. "Who is this *Master* anyway? What does he want with me?" I say with a little dash of snark in my tone, feeling not so afraid of the vargs after the commands they received in the woods. Whoever that Nerius guy was, I owe him big time.

"He does not want *you*, little creature, so I would watch the tone. Master Pyralis is a force to fear. He is one of The King's trusted advisers," Garr replies in his usual snarling voice, but I also sense a note of pride in his Master.

These are not The King's minions as Oleander had thought. They belong to this Pyralis guy. I wonder why I am being brought here instead of directly to The King.

The house looks much grander when I am standing directly in front of it on the gravel path. There are three floors with small wooden framed windows all along its length and big floor to ceiling glass on the bottom level of both of the towers. The apex of each tower holds a beautiful stained glass window, as does the large window spanning from the second to the third floor in the centre of the house. I would bet that is where the staircase leads within its walls and can imagine the beautiful colours washing the whole interior in rainbow as the sun sets. The large front door is made up of a sturdy dark wood with large iron bolts and curved, elaborate iron handles.

A smartly dressed man with dark skin and tightly curled hair is standing in front of the bottom of the steps, waiting for us. His face is bleak and stern and I guess that this must be Nerius, awaiting our arrival. How he got here so much quicker than us and looking clean and well rested is beyond me.

"He is waiting for you in the study. Garr you will do, the rest of your ilk may skulk off somewhere," Nerius says with his chin lifted high and his nose crinkled at the gathered vargs.

"You heard him, to the kitchen lads," Garr chuckles as he dismisses the others. He grabs onto the back of my neck and gives me a shove, causing me to stumble in front of Nerius.

"A pity," Nerius says, looking down at me with one eyebrow raised, then stepping ahead to lead the way into the house. Garr takes up the rear as we walk in single file. Nerius swings open the huge double doors sending a gust of deliciously spiced aroma coming from within the house into our faces. It smells of crackling fires and winter baking, even though it is the middle of an extremely hot summer.

As we step inside, we are met with an open foyer with high ceilings that open up to a red velvet-lined staircase directly across from the front door. I tilt my head, taking in the grandeur of the space, noticing the many doors lining the halls on each of the floors.

Nerius directs us through a set of doors to the left which opens up into what I believe is called a drawing room, a term also gleaned from my mother's period piece romance movies.

The walls are painted a dark red, with matching red, straight-backed, uncomfortable looking sofas and elaborate red rugs that partly cover a hardwood floor. There is a low table set in between the sofas in front of a large, white stone fireplace. An enormous painting of the wolf headed king standing next to Pyralis sits proudly on top of the mantel. I can now confirm that the menacing figure in my vision was indeed this same king and try not to shudder at the memory. In the far right corner there is another door which we are being guided to. Nerius pauses before giving it one swift knock.

"Enter," a deep voice replies. I can't avoid my audible gulp.

Nerius opens the door and walks in ahead of us to announce our arrival. We step into the room and I can see a fierce looking man in his forties, with close cut, red hair sitting in a high back leather chair behind a large mahogany desk. He has a well-groomed beard and a face that is all sharp angles. He looks as if he wouldn't know the meaning of a smile.

The room itself must be the bottom level of the tower because I notice the floor to ceiling bay windows, and I wonder if there is a hidden staircase somewhere in this room. I look around but all I can see are walls lined with books and Pyralis' large desk with two smaller leather chairs sitting in front of it. I wonder what the nature of his work is and catch the smallest glimpse of maps spread over his desk.

"I present you Garr and...?" He turns to me, raising an eyebrow.

"Oh, uh, Nuria," I say, bowing at the waist. I realize a

moment too late that the bow is silly. I straighten up clumsily, already blushing.

Pyralis momentarily has a look of shock on his face as I step up to Nerius' side, which turns into a smile I can't quite read but it makes me decidedly uncomfortable. He stretches his hand over his desk as if he wishes to shake my hand and I look at Nerius in confusion. Nerius widens his eyes and gives me a swift nod so I step up to the desk and grasp Pyralis' hand, giving him a swift shake. His hand is so hot it nearly burns me but I swallow the yelp I feel bubbling up my throat and dip my chin before stepping back to my place beside Nerius. *That was strange, perhaps a show of dominance?*

"And Miss Nuria is the *sister* of our... target, Master," Nerius says, scowling at Garr.

"I see, and what, pray tell, happened there Garr? My sources said you had taken one from the human realm that fits a different description to this one, meaning you did not make the mistake from the beginning. So how on Earth did you lose her?" Pyralis questions Garr. I catch flames crackling in his eyes. *Strange...*

"Well, you see, Master Pyralis... this one here pulled one over on us. She broke her sister out but... but I caught her and brought her here!" the varg stammers and I suddenly wonder how I was so afraid of this fool. Pyralis only glares at him then holds out his hand, flames dancing within his palm. *Fire wielder!*

"Unacceptable," is all he says in a very cool tone as he snaps his fiery fingers and Garr bursts into flames.

His scream nearly pops my ear drums but he does

nothing to run away or put them out. I just stare, dumbfounded at the horror, and can't help my cough at the stench of burning hair. I stop myself from covering my ears but the overwhelm to my senses is bringing tears to my eyes. Not that I particularly care about this beast that kidnapped me and my sister, I still can't stand watching this level of suffering.

I turn away from the horror to glare at Pyralis, whose gaze snaps to mine. I try to tap into his thoughts but I am met with a wall of flame within my mind that makes my eyes burn. I try not to wince but I have to break our eye contact which feels like a defeat.

This carries on for another painful few seconds before, out of thin air, a deluge of water encompasses Garr and the fire is put out. Garr is left with barely any hair left on his body and lots of angry red sores that I am sure will turn into huge blisters later. I can only imagine the pain he is in right now and pity fills my heart for this creature that I harboured hatred for only moments ago.

He felt so much pride in his Master, how could someone treat their employee like this? I know my face is crumpled in pure hatred for the man seated in front of me and I don't feign to hide it.

I look around to see where that water came from when I notice Nerius suspending a little water droplet in the centre of his palm before he quickly closes his fist and turns to face Pyralis.

A water Elemental and a fire Elemental...Wait, is this Oleander's Father? I can suddenly see the resemblance.

What did he want with Marissa... or me rather? Did Oleander know?

"Thank you Nerius. Garr you are dismissed," Pyralis says nonchalantly as he flicks his fingers, motioning for Garr to leave.

"Yes Master, thank you Master," Garr says before walking away, whimpering slightly as he goes.

"Now, what shall I do with you, Miss Nuria. You appear to have stolen something from me so we must think of a fitting punishment," he says, steepling his finger-tips. I can't hold back my rage at what he has claimed.

"*I* stole from *you?!* She is *my* sister! And your minion literally kidnapped her! If anything I should punish *you!*" I fume, starting to take a step towards him as if I could, in any way, fight this man. All memory of the pain he just inflicted on Garr is wiped from my memory as my anger rises to a point. Nerius catches me by the shoulders and pulls me back. Shockingly, Pyralis starts to laugh, a laugh that doesn't meet his serious eyes and I am taken aback by the outburst.

"Feisty little human, I like your fire! After all, like speaks to like, but you are terribly mistaken. She *let* herself be taken in the first place. It is perhaps an unwritten rule of the fae that you would not be familiar with but unless she managed to escape by herself, she has technically been stolen from me and since *you,* her saviour, have now been caught, a debt is owed!" he says, his laugh turning to thunder.

"I believe fifty years of servitude would do the trick," he says, snapping back into his steely cool demeanour from before. His ability to instantly switch from pure fire to pure ice within his emotions frightens me.

"Fifty years!?" I exclaim, trying to shake Nerius' grasp.

"Or until your sister is returned to me. A human lifetime for a life seems only fair. Humans do make the best servants I find, so docile, so eager to please. Fear not, you will be looked after well enough. I'm not a monster." He snaps his fingers and a small flame sparks to life, hovering over his pointer finger. *Did he say there are other humans here?*

"Now this may sting a little," he says indifferently, and my attention is snapped back into focus. Nerius grabs my wrist and twists my arm to show it to Pyralis. The next thing I feel is a searing hot burn on the inside of my arm and I can't help the whimper that escapes my mouth as I try yanking my arm away. It is over in a moment and I look down to see the letter P enclosed in flames, imprinted into my skin.

"You can try and run away but every fae on the Continent will recognize that mark and bring you back here immediately. I suggest you settle into your new life, Miss Nuria. You are dismissed," he says, waving his hand at us like we are hovering flies.

Nerius lightly grasps my elbow to steer me out of the room. I allow him to guide me as I just stare, mouth agape, down at my branded wrist in disbelief.

How did I get myself into this mess? Fifty years for trying to save my family?! Screw all these stupid fae rules! He branded me like a piece of livestock! I start to shake in my rage, feeling completely helpless.

Once we are out of the study Nerius softly closes the door behind us and gives me a little tilt of his head to say, *follow me.* I comply with gritted teeth and tears threatening to spill over as he leads me out of the drawing room and across the foyer to the other side of the house. As we pass the stairs I look up and catch the eye of a little girl in a grey dress poking her head through the bars of the railing. As soon as our eyes meet she darts out of sight. *Human or fae?*

Nerius opens the mirroring door to the one of the red study and inside there is another drawing room, except this one is all soft greens and blues with woodland motifs on the walls. The sofas look much more welcoming, plush even. The low table in front of the fireplace has a beautiful tea set with whimsical tea cups with mushroom designs on. In the right corner, near the window, there is a wooden grand piano with ivy vines carved into the legs and a tableau of frolicking winged creatures on the front panel. I notice there are tiny boxes made of wood, shell and stone on nearly every side table making me want to run around and peek inside. I feel as though they would all be hiding treats of some sort.

"Does Pyralis have a wife?" I ask, noting that a fiery man would probably not select such décor.

"That is *Master* Pyralis to you, and no. His most recent wife... died a few years ago. It would be in your own interest to never mention her in his presence," Nerius responds curtly.

I look around as I am led to another door in the back corner of the room and notice a little framed painting on a small side table. A beautiful woman with soft auburn curls and what appears to be fur for skin inhabits the frame. She has a very familiar pert nose and slanted smile.

This was Oleander's mother's space. I give the room one more sweeping glance, feeling strange about the intimacy of knowing a bit more about her mother. I can picture her as a little girl sitting alongside her mom at the piano and wonder how old Oleander was when she died.

Nerius opens the door and ushers me into a fairly empty room. The walls are painted white, there is no art or decorations and the lace curtains that frame the window are pulled shut, giving the room a grey pallor. There are a few pieces of furniture covered by white sheets that make it feel like it is inhabited only by ghosts. There is still a clean and light feeling to the space as if it is cared for and dusted frequently.

"What was in here?" I ask. Nerius looks irritated at my presence and sighs.

"Someone we do not speak of..." he trails off, pausing mid-sentence then clears his throat. "Not for you to know, now hurry along." He leads me to the back corner where I can see a little golden doorknob shaped like a flower jutting out of the wall. Nerius twists and pulls on the knob and the door swings open to reveal a spiraling stone staircase leading up to the top of the tower. I wonder to myself whether the hidden door is in the same location in Pyralis' study, but doubt I will ever get the chance to find out. Once we are in the hall of the staircase I notice there is another door, directly across from the stairs.

"That leads down to the kitchens, where you will report

for duty in one hour. Up here is your room." He motions as we start to ascend the stairs.

"We had prepared for the arrival of your sister so you should count yourself lucky that you will be graced by this grand room. The servants quarters are full at the moment but believe me, as soon as a space opens up you will be out of this house," he says, making it sound like I am dirt beneath his boot.

"For now, you will travel only from this room to the kitchens. I do not want to find you snooping around," he says as we near the door. "I am the only one who addresses the Master, the rest of you report to me. I am *your* Master and *he* is mine. Keep your head down and fulfill your duties and you may find that life in the fae realm is not so bad."

Not that you have any reference, I roll my eyes, feeling that life in this realm will unquestionably *not* be pleasant *at all.* Nerius pushes open the door, which makes a loud creak, and makes way for me to pass him before shutting the door behind me again. I can hear his footsteps fade as he descends. I am finally alone.

Chapter Ten

The room is quite spacious, but plainly decorated. Faded spots occupy the walls where paintings would have hung and the scuff marks of furniture that once filled the space litter the floor. What is left is a large four poster bed, which I am sure, gets bathed in the light of the stained glass window when the sun is setting. To the left there is a tall wooden bureau and a lattice room divider with a clawfoot copper tub perched behind it. Directly in front of the round window is a little desk with a chair that I am currently fantasizing about sitting and painting at, but am met with the reality that I will probably not have time or access to paints in my new prison.

Ugh, how have I gotten myself into this mess?

I run and flop onto the bed, the softness of the mattress hugging me like a cloud. A little moan escapes my lips from the bliss of having a bed after many nights on the cold, hard ground. Maybe I will just stay up here, hiding in the blankets for the rest of my miserable life.

I wish I could just dissolve into mist, tossing away all responsibilities and just becoming one with the water cycle. Alas, I am solid and living and have others relying on me.

Visions of Marissa and where on Earth Oleander may have taken her are clouding my mind when a little *tap tap tap* on the door brings me back to the present. It is so faint that I wonder if I am just hearing things and settle back into my cloud of misery.

Tap tap tap, I definitely heard it that time.

"Hello? Um...you may enter?" I say, sitting up and hoping it isn't anything too menacing waiting on the other side.

"Ooo hello, I heard another human had arrived and I wanted to see for myself!" The head of the little girl I had briefly seen earlier in the day pokes around the squeaky door.

She looks to be around ten years old and has two messy braids hanging down her servant's uniform, a plain, grey pinafore with a white blouse underneath. I am surprised to see a human so young in this realm and cannot fathom how she got here, surely not through the same Gate as I.

"I'm Lillian," she says, hopping fully into the room and spinning around, wide eyed-mouth open, looking in awe.

"I have never been up here before, this must be our little secret or Mistress Smudge will surely tell on me," she whispers, skipping over to where I am seated on the bed.

She seems so trusting and happy for someone who has experienced what, I imagine, has been a difficult life if she grew up here. I can't see a brand on either of her wrists so I wonder whether she is here of her own free will.

"Hello Lillian, I'm Nuria, it's very nice to meet a fellow human," I say, holding out my hand for a shake, telling a lie that comes easily to me as it was only a few days ago that I discovered my true heritage. She beams up at me and grabs my outstretched hand with both of hers and shakes our joined hands wildly. My hand is now her prisoner.

"Oookay, well I believe I am meant to be heading down to the kitchens soon. Would you accompany me?" I ask, laughing at her enthusiasm as I try to pull my hand away from her, but she holds on tight with a big toothy smile. I notice one of her front teeth is either half grown or chipped which gives her a sort of harmless and comical demeanor.

"First you need to change into your uniform and actually, I probably shouldn't accompany you because then Smudge would know where I have been, silly! I have to go find my brother Jacob, anyway. He is probably lurking around the stables. Smudge needs him to run an errand for her in the village," she says, finally releasing my hand and skipping over to the bureau. She pulls out a grey uniform with a long sleeve white shift and tosses it on the bed. "You should hurry so she doesn't get mad. You do *not* want to see an angry kitchen Gromlin. Not a pretty sight. anyway good luck on your first day!" she says as she bounces back towards the door.

"Wait! Lillian... how did you end up here if you are human?" I ask, concern written in my scrunched up eyebrows.

"I can't remember, you'd have to ask Jacob," she says, turning back to the door. She lets it slam on her way out.

I flinch at the sound and hope she doesn't get herself caught for it, but I have a feeling she has her ways of sneaking around this mansion fairly undetected.

Kitchen Gromlin?

I am left in silence, wondering what they might look like. I can already feel that a Lillian sized hole is left in the room. The slight comfort of a normal, albeit tornado like, human interaction with a child gives me a momentary sense of ease and I am reminded of Marissa at that age. So similarly lively and friendly, making everyone love her. But the feeling of nostalgia is quickly traded for dread when I look down at my uniform laying on the bed and I start worrying about the thought of what sort of work might lay ahead of me.

I have to figure out a way to escape. I have to find where Oleander took Marissa. Perhaps I should get to know this Jacob person; Lillian said he has access to the stables. I think that he may be my only ticket out of here, as I change into my uniform.

Find Jacob, find Jacob, find Jacob...

I hurry down the steps, not wanting to be late for my first shift, but stop at the door to the white room, my curiosity at what lies beneath the white sheets momentarily taking hold of me. *Was this Oleander's room?*

I crack open the door, hoping to have a little sneak peak, but my plan is foiled by a varg with his back turned, standing guard at the door to the drawing room. Ever so softly, I shut the door, hoping he did not see me.

Great, they are having me watched. I huff a breath through my nose. Any plans of escape will be near impossible if I can't get past the vargs.

I turn to the door of the kitchens, pausing to take a breath and steel my nerves.

Ok Nuria, play along. You will *get out of here but for now, just try and fit in.*

I creak open the door to peer around it but am met with a long dark hallway made of stone that slopes down to another door. I rush down there and swing the next door open, thinking there will be more hallways and more doors but am met with a kitchen full of pointy-eared green creatures staring at me.

Kitchen gromlins...

"What is the meaning of this?! Trying to scare us half to death! Come down here!" A stout Gromlin with a bumpy nose, hair tufting out of its ears and a frilly apron yells at me, waving their rolling pin in the air.

With a quick glance around, I notice the kitchen itself is quite large with a long wooden work table in the middle of the room, two stove tops with six burners each and a big wood fired oven.

The room appears to be half underground but there are thankfully two windows high up on the walls in the back of the room as well as steps leading up to a door to the outside.

To the left there is another set of steps leading up to a door that perhaps goes to another part of the house. Off to the right there looks to be a store room and beside it a door half slanted into the floor which must be the cold cellar. *I guess there are no refrigerators in this realm.*

"So sorry, it's my first day and I didn't want to be late." I wince, looking down at the snarling creature.

"Harrumph, well you would do better to not frighten gromlins. You're lucky it didn't flip us all over the edge," she bristles and I wonder what she could mean by that.

"I am Mistress Smudge, also known as Chef, to you. I was only informed this morning that I would be having an addition to my crew so we have a special job for you," she says and I can hear the other gromlins chuckle, there's an inside joke I am missing.

"If you would kindly go down into the cellar to peel and thinly slice all of the onions that would be greatly appreciated. Master has a lunch scheduled tomorrow with a lord and his family from a neighbouring estate and all of these onions were gifted to him from their farms. He wishes for three different dishes using them so chop chop, off you go," she says, smiling and tapping the rolling pin in her palm as she walks away.

"Back to work, the lot of you!" she snaps and the rest of the gromlins scatter to their various duties.

I can cut some onions, no problem, I think as I pry open the cellar door. I am met with an icy blast of air and am shocked at how chilly it is as I walk down into the dark room. There is one candle lit in the far corner but it is enough light to illuminate the mountain of onions piled on the floor.

"You're joking!" I say out loud and someone slams the cellar door closed behind me.

I hear a muffled call say, "Don't let the cold air out!" I am left in the dimly lit food dungeon, by myself.

The monotonous task allows my mind to wander and I can't help but dwell on the betrayal of Oleander. The flow of tears brought on by the onions paves the way for actual tears as I sit in my rage and embarrassment.

How could she? Was the connection we had all in my head? What did she want with Marissa...or I guess, me, anyway? She mentioned The King wanted me for my powers but how could anyone know what I can do? Was my mother an Etherealist? I could drive myself crazy with all the unanswered questions. All I know for now is that I am stuck in this place and doubt I can get any answers while sitting in a cellar.

When I finally emerge, cheeks tear stained and eyes all red from the onion fumes, I notice it is dark outside and there is a delicious smell emanating from the oven. My stomach gurgles as I inhale deeply.

"I never want to see another onion again in my life," I say, mostly to myself, but the nearest gromlin chuckles from its work station.

"Ah, finally. I want to get started on the onion soup. You may now peel and dice the potatoes. Shoo shoo." Smudge waves me back down into the cellar and I moan as I turn and trudge down the steps to tackle the pile of potatoes I had noticed earlier.

I am left alone with my intrusive thoughts once again. *I'm stuck here... There is no way out... Marissa needs me... Oleander betrayed me... I'm a fool for feeling anything for her.*

When I emerge from the cellar, much later, shivering from the prolonged cold, I walk in to see all the gromlins sitting at the big wooden table about to dig into a delicious smelling dinner of what appears to be multiple chicken pot pies. It must be nearly midnight and I am shocked to see how lively the bunch still seems.

"Come take a seat, you're just in time for dinner. We are done for the day." A smiling Gromlin with a pointy nose and big black eyes waves me over to an empty seat.

The kitchen is spotless and there is only one big pot left steaming on the stove. They must have served dinner to the household ages ago. I can't resist my yawn as I slump down in my seat. A big helping of pot pie is plopped onto my plate and I dig in immediately, savoring the beautiful flakey crust, creamy gravy and soft, comforting root veggies.

The gromlins dig in too but continue to chat away about local gossip from the neighboring estates and the village. I have no ability to focus on anything other than the steaming food in front of me, so all that they are saying is not registered in my very tired brain. When I am starting on my second helping I realize Lillian is not present.

"Does Lillian usually join you for dinner?" I ask the Gromlin next to me.

"No no, all the other servants eat in the servant's hall. They think they are above us because we cook their food," the creature scoffs as it heaps a spoonful of pie in its mouth.

Damn, how am I going to meet her brother if they never even come in here? I'm starting to feel dejected as my plan from earlier seems more complicated than I thought. I decide I will just have to bide my time for the moment and wait for when he and I can speak privately. *Surely I will meet him soon...*

"Are the other servants gromlins as well? Are you all indebted to Master Pyralis?" I ask, genuinely unsure who the fae tend to employ and what those contracts might look like.

"Gromlins only work in the kitchens silly. We have to stay hidden because of the danger if we flip. Happens a lot less when we are amongst our own kind and no, none of us are indebted, we are paid a fair wage. The Master is only one of few major household lords that stayed true to The Owl King's ways. The Wolf King has allowed the other lords to use fae and creatures-of-fae as slaves," the Gromlin on the other side of me answers and I catch it glance down at my wrist where Pyralis branded me.

Am I the only one who owes him a debt? I look down at my wrist before pulling down my sleeve and hiding it under the table. When I look back up the gromlin looks as if he is starting to shake and his eyes are changing from black to red.

"Simmer down Olaf, go dunk your head!" Smudge calls from the end of the table and Olaf nods, rushing over to the sink to pour some water over his head.

"What happens when gromlins... flip?" I ask as I look at Olaf's head steam under the running water.

"Ha! Just wish you never find out girl," is all the response I get in return from another gromlin. I eye the large group of them warily and truly hope I never find out.

After dinner I find myself helping with the dishes, trying not to sway too much from the exhaustion from minimal sleep I have had over the past few days. Smudge gives me a sweeping look before she graciously scoots me out of the kitchen so I can go to bed.

My feet feel like bruises as I climb the stone steps to my room, the door creaks loudly as I push it open. The space is illuminated with candles in sconces that I hadn't noticed before and my bed looks newly made. There is a clean white nightgown on top of it, and I can see the bathtub is full of sweet smelling, steaming water.

Where did all of this come from? I wonder but am too tired to reflect on it as I peel my uniform off and step into the deliciously warm waters. I groan, rejoicing in the heat as it seeps into my aching back from being hunched over all day.

I untangle the braid that Oleander had given to me days ago, giving my scalp a little massage to release the tension. I nearly fall asleep in the bath and it takes all of my will power to pull myself out, put on my nightgown and flop on the bed. I don't even get under the blankets before I fall into a deep sleep.

Hazel eyes ensconced in soft flickering flames fill my mind, my tense muscles relax in their glow.

You are safe there. Wait for me, his deep voice comforts me.

~

RATHER THAN FIND a way out of this place, I just wait. What I am waiting for I am not sure. Perhaps I am waiting for the joke to end or to wake up from this dream. More disturbingly, I think I am waiting for the man of my visions to come rescue me, for Embrys to come rescue me...

The worst part isn't the cutting of onions or scrubbing of dishes. It's waiting for some external force to come and get me out of here. The worst part is expecting something different, and yet all I do is sit and wait. *He said to wait. Why am I listening?*

The next two weeks are much of the same, although I eventually graduate from peeling and chopping vegetables to assisting with making doughs and sauces when Smudge notices I am somewhat competent at cooking. I have Delia to thank for that skill; she was always an amazing cook.

Am I already resigning to never seeing her again? I try not to think of my parents and Easthelm. The panic is not helping my headspace.

So I keep my head down, hoping for a day that Jacob might walk into the kitchen but I haven't even seen Lillian again since that first day and I am starting to lose hope. Only a few servants dressed in much nicer frocks than ours come in and out during meal times to fetch the platters of food. They barely even acknowledge my presence.

I am often too tired and busy from my work to even think about plans to escape anyway. My thoughts always seem to return to where Marissa might be and if she is all right though.

All visions of Embrys have ceased, although I find myself searching for his fiery eyes in my dreams almost every night. He said I am safe here but what danger was he alluding to? I just feel stuck in here while Marissa is out there.

I FIND out from one of the gromlins named Lorn that the water of the house is heated by Master Pyralis' magic and the constant source of water is from Nerius' skills at bending the flow from the water shelf beneath the land. I am grateful for the hot bath every night but sometimes wonder at this never ending supply of water when I haven't experienced a single rainy day since I have been in this realm.

I am slowly getting used to the workload which allows me to split my focus more and join in on the conversations with my fellow gromlins, which helps pass the time. They are turning out to be quite the bunch of gossips. I find the social workings of gromlins to be similar to that of high schoolers which makes me miss the days of walking in on Marissa and her cronies giggling on the living room couch.

There has also been some more serious talk amongst the gromlins lately of local farms struggling to grow their crops because of the relentless drought and a strange eerie haze in the air, curling in from where the bigger cities are.

"It's a curse upon the land!" one of the gromlins speculates. I can't help but wonder at the similarities between the issues that have been plaguing the human realm in the past few years and am not sure if it is a curse that is to blame.

The days start to blur and I can't help but submit to my fate and feel like I am turning into a kitchen Gromlin myself. Every now and again I try to think of an escape plan but my every move is watched by either the gromlins or the vargs. My hope is waning.

What my poor parents must be experiencing worries me, the guilt at what I have gotten myself into pulls me further into my slump. I have no calendar here but I think it must be nearing the beginning of September which means university will be starting up soon, but this information has no relevance to my current situation and only adds to my depression.

I think of Mr. Bugg waiting for my emails that will never reach him again and my unfinished guide to mushroom identification. Little things that felt so big, so important, only a few weeks ago, have no use to me now. I'm still unsure if I can ever cross The Gate again.

A FEW WEEKS or perhaps months in, when I have stopped trying to peek through doors I shouldn't be or trying to wander off, Smudge notices my low mood and trusts me enough now to graciously let me fetch eggs from the chicken coop in the mornings. A small mercy.

This is the only time I get to be outside and I start to notice my skin has turned a milky white colour from the lack of sun. The brief respite from the kitchen walls always gives me a moment of joy as I stand towards the warm rays, feeling it tingle on my face. When I dally too long Lorn is sent out to fetch me, snapping me out of my reverie.

One such morning I am squatting in the coop collecting eggs when I hear a horse gallop nearby and a man calling out, "fetch me Nerius!" As the horse comes to a halt.

I hear the crunch of boots on gravel as he dismounts. Through a little wire window in the coop I can see the back of a man that has shoulder-length, wavy red hair. He is broad shouldered and has a beautiful sword strapped diagonally along his back over his brown vest. His white sleeves are rolled up to show his muscled forearms that I notice tense as he grips the reins as he looks to where another set of boots are now crunching in the gravel.

I lean into the window in an attempt to get a closer look but I accidentally trip on a chicken and stomp on its foot, causing it to let out a big squawk.

I quickly duck down so the man can't see me. Thankfully, when I peek back through the window he is facing away from me again, stroking his horse. Nerius is striding over to where they are standing, his face scrunched in agitation. I duck back down so he doesn't catch me spying. Although he saved me from the vargs' abuses when they were hauling me to the estate, I still fear him and do not wish to get on his bad side.

Nerius stops a healthy distance away from the massive

horse and crinkles his nose at the fresh droppings it just let loose. "Where have you been, young Master? We had expected you back weeks ago when we sent word out that *she* had been captured," Nerius says.

"I thought I caught wind of my sister's whereabouts. There were reports of a rebel group being seen in the forest not an hour's ride south-west of here. I trusted you had everything under control here and I had only received word of the girl being taken from our men when I stopped at Inverdell last night. I rode home as soon as I could when I heard we apprehended her sister instead," the man explains, sounding annoyed. I recognize his voice but do not know where I would have heard it before.

His sister... Does Oleander have a brother? I tuck that question away, the piece of information that sparks my interest is of Oleander's rebel group possibly being nearby. It must be the Sylvans, how many rebel groups could there be? I hold onto this information with dear life as my mission is sparked within me once again. *How could I have sat here not doing anything for so long? This is a sign, this is my chance.*

"Ah yes, the sister... There is a development on that but I will let your father fill you in. Regardless, it is good you are home now, Master, as Lord Galeheart and Lord Clayborn are arriving this afternoon and will be staying for the next few days to discuss the recent climate events and how trade has been affected. You are needed by your father's side to tell us of your discoveries on your travels and what reports you have from the Palace. There will be a formal dinner tomorrow evening in which they will be making plans regarding these issues," Nerius informs as he grabs the reins of the man's horse and directs them around the corner and out of my earshot.

He's been to the Palace, is that where The King is? Has he come to take me there?

I run out of the coop with a quick glance to the kitchen doors to check if Lorn is around but I find I am alone. I hurry to the side of the building so I can better hear, being careful to not crack the eggs I have held in my bunched up apron.

"Where is the girl? Did the vargs harm her?" the man questions with what sounds like concern in his tone as they walk in the direction of the stables.

At that moment the recognition strikes me like lightning. I know where I recognize his voice from and confirm it as he turns to Nerius, sweeping his hair behind his ear and exposing his profile to me.

The man from my visions.

Embrys... Is Oleander's brother? I feel a physical tug to chase after him but before my body can betray me the kitchen door creaks open.

"Nuria! What are you doing? Get back here or we are both going to get in trouble!" I whip around to see Lorn's big, green head sticking out of the kitchen door and frantically waving me back inside, in my surprise I nearly drop all of the eggs, hissing as I right myself.

I glance at the spot where Embrys had just been before shaking off the shock of being so close to the man who has been with me since childhood. Sudden doubt sours my gut when the thought enters my mind that perhaps he does not actually know me and everything has been a figment of my imagination. It should not matter to me, as escape is at the forefront of my mind, but it does.

All I just heard has sparked the beginnings of a plot for my escape and hope blooms within me once again. An hour's ride to the south west should be doable if I time it right.

I'm coming for you Marissa!

Chapter Eleven

L ater that evening, while I am in the bath, mulling over my plan, I hear a little *tap tap tap* at the door.

"Come in, it's open!" I call out, recognizing the knock even after weeks of not seeing her.

"Nuria! I am so sorry I haven't been around. Mistress Colette caught wind of me traipsing around the house and put me on strict servant quarters duties for weeks! It was so boring! I am in her good books again so I came straight here," Lillian giggles as she races over to the tub and starts flicking water at me.

"Pretty necklace, where did you get it?" She pulls the pendant out of the water and examines it like a crow playing with something shiny.

"It was my mother's," I say and she makes an *oh* shape with her mouth before carefully placing it back against my chest. "Do you think it is wise to be once again *traipsing* through the house Lil?" I laugh, splashing her back.

"Lil... I like it. No one has given me a nickname before," she giggles and sticks out her tongue. "Perhaps it's not so wise to be up here, but most of the servants are in bed by now anyway, they won't notice I am gone," she says, a mischievous grin spreading on her face but then the corners of her lips turn down into a scowl.

"Nuria, why did you lie to me? There has been gossip in the servant quarters that there is a fae girl working in the kitchens. I thought you were human?" she questions with a little frown and a pout tugging down her bottom lip as she rests her chin on the edge of the tub.

"How did they know I am fae? I mean... I grew up in the human realm and I just assumed everyone thought me to be human," I ask, wondering what gave it away and if that means Pyralis has known who I am this whole time. *What's his game?*

"Juniper is a deer Metamorph and she says you smell funny. Like a fae wearing human perfume. I'm human though so I can't smell you. " Lillian replies, taking a big sniff in my direction.

So he must know what I am. Why has he led me to believe otherwise? Panic starts to rise when I think this may affect my plans of escape.

"It's ok, I forgive you." Lillian gives my hand a little pat. "What kind of fae are you anyway?" She blatantly scans my naked body in the water, probably searching for some sort of animal part.

"Can you keep a secret?" I ask, Lillian nods her head,

leaning in close. I wonder whether she would know what an Etherealist is and try my luck. I hold onto her hand and look her in the eye.

I am an Elemental fae.

Her eyes go wide and she squeaks in response. "Wowie you're pretty special! I've never met someone like you before," she says.

She does not prod further about the topic though which I am unsure how I feel about. I wonder what she knows about Etherealists and if there are others like me. She said I am special but how special could it be? Perhaps she just hasn't encountered one from within the confines of this estate.

"I also heard you almost caused Olaf to flip? You've got to be more careful Nuria!" she scorns, waving her finger at me like she is the adult here.

"What did I do? I was just asking whether the gromlins owed Pyralis a debt like me," I say, showing her my brand.

She makes a humming sound in her throat. "Well, that would've done it. That's not just a sign for a debt. It's a slave brand. The gromlins are very touchy about injustice. What did you do to Pyralis to get such a mark? He doesn't usually do that to his servants," she asks, sounding worried. She reaches out to touch the scar but thinks twice and pulls away. "This ties you to him for life, or until he removes it," she adds with a big pout on her face.

"I did nothing! He is the monster who tried to kidnap my sister! I freed her from his vargs and for that I have been enslaved!" I say, trying to keep my temper under control so I don't scare her but internally I am envisioning setting Pyralis on fire and watching him burn like Garr did.

There is no time for revenge, escape is the only goal. I reassure myself, but still allow a brief moment of imagining Pyralis getting a taste of his own cruelty.

"Wow, so you're like a princess locked in a tower who needs her shining knight to come rescue her! Jacob used to tell me bed time stories of princesses just like you," Lillian giggles, clearly unable to fully comprehend the situation and using fairy tales to make sense of it.

"Except I am no princess and my shining knight will have to be myself. Besides, not every woman needs to be rescued, Lillian. Sometimes we have to watch out for ourselves and I'm doing just that," I say, reaching out to grab her little hand to give it a squeeze.

"You're leaving aren't you?" Lillian says, pulling her hand away and frowning at me.

"Lil, I can't stay. My sister is still out there and I need to find her. I don't belong here; I belong in the human realm," I say, looking into her eyes. She is hurt by my not wanting to stay. I wonder if she has ever had a friend.

"Will you take me with you?" she asks as she chews the end of her braid, looking at me with hopeful eyes. My heart sinks.

"It is too dangerous, and would you really want to abandon your brother? If you aren't indebted to Pyralis you two can just leave. If you come with me you will be seen as aiding an escaped slave," I explain, clearly disappointing her but also seeing her resign to my logic. She lets out a big sigh.

"I don't know anything other than this life... but perhaps if I had someone from the human world to guide me...?" she asks, but I just shake my head. I'm not even sure if I can return to the human realm, but I do know that my escape plan does not include towing along a child.

"Well, if I can't join you, I can still help you!" she says, her bright demeanor returning as she does a little hop dance. "Tell me what to do! I can be your shining knight too," she giggles at the thought. Her hopeful face reminds me of Marissa and melts my heart enough to accept her offer.

"All right Lil I trust you, here's my plan." She leans in close, eyes wide. "I have tracked when the vargs settle into their evening meals and there should be a brief window of overlap during the important dinner with the visiting lords tomorrow night. I will only have a window of a few minutes but if you can get Jacob to have a horse saddled and the stables unlocked I should have enough time to escape. The vargs are fast but not faster than a horse," I explain my plan to Lillian. She tells me the little information she knows of the rebels that I hope to find in the forest.

I pray the plan works, it has minimal room for error but if I time it right it should work. If not... then I don't even want to think of what Pyralis might do to me.

AFTER LILLIAN HAS DEPARTED with her part of the plan to sort out for me tomorrow, I am left lying in my bed, staring at the pointed, wooden ceiling, wondering whether it was a wise choice to trust a ten year old. My still damp hair is creating a stain on my pillow that I can feel creeping towards the back of my neck, giving me a chill but the plans for my upcoming escape are plaguing my mind and I can't be bothered to get up to grab a towel.

Thoughts of what I may find in the forest haunt me. *What if they are hurting Marissa, what if I have to fight the rebels? I have no weapon...*

Holes are already forming in my plan but I cannot dwell on them. Tomorrow is my opportunity and the wheels are already in motion. I close my eyes and try to slow my breathing, willing sleep to come, when I start to hear a woeful song being played on the piano downstairs.

At first, I think that it is the ghost of Oleander's mother singing her lament. The song starts out slow and sweet but is now moving towards a heartbreaking crescendo and I can feel myself being physically pulled by the notes as I sit up and walk towards the door.

What am I doing?

I open the door and poke my head out into the stairwell. No one is there, so I tiptoe my way down the steps and reach the door on the left. I have never left my room at night before and the feeling of wrongness causes my heart to pound.

I should go back.

I look up the stairs but my hand has a mind of its own

and grasps the door knob, pushing the door open. No one is in here but the melancholic music fills the dark room filled with ghostly furniture and pulls me in.

When I get to the door of the drawing room I have to physically stop myself from swinging it open and turn my back to the door instead, leaning my head against the wood and closing my eyes.

The music winds its way around my limbs and swirls into my heart. It speaks to me of a warm motherly embrace. The feelings I had when I first put on my mother's necklace are perfectly captured within the notes. I lift my hand to my cheek and feel it is wet from tears I did not know I needed to release. At the acknowledgment of my own sorrow, I let out a little sob.

The music abruptly stops. I hold my breath, hoping whoever is on the other side did not hear me. I go to tiptoe away, when a deep voice sounds from the other room.

"You do not have to hide. I won't turn you in," a familiar voice says softly. *Embrys.*

"This was a song I played when Elora, Oleander's mother, died. My father cannot bear to hear it, so I only play it when he is asleep. I never knew my mother. She died in childbirth... Elora treated me as if she was mine but father always reminded me that she, in truth, was not. It is nice to have an audience for once," he says, as he starts to play, very faintly, for a few bars. I can picture his fingers delicately caressing the keys for a brief moment before he cuts himself off again, the light thud of the lid sounds as he closes it.

The scrape of the piano bench warns me of his

approach as he stands up. His footsteps are soft and swift as he strides over to the door I am hiding behind. I have no time to turn around and run, or maybe I just secretly don't want to, before he wrenches the door open and looks down at me.

I gasp at the sudden reveal and go to take a step back but feel I am glued to the floor. *Why are you betraying me now, legs?* He looks down at me with a soft knowing smile, breaking up the hard features he inherited from his father. I can feel the magnetic pull that I felt at the chicken coop drawing me towards him.

What is this connection? Does he know of my visions? The light cast behind him sets his red hair aglow. From this lighting I am unable to tell the minute colouring of his eyes, however, I do notice their movement.

He looks down at my body briefly, lingering at my breasts and I follow his gaze to see that my still wet hair that is draped over my shoulders has now seeped down, making my white nightgown nearly translucent and my nipples taut. Our eyes snap back to each other and, where I once would have been embarrassed, I feel the warmth of arousal blooming at his noticing.

"Nuria..." His breath hitches as he takes a small step towards me, "you're everything I thought you would be." He reaches out his hand as if he was going to brush my hair out of the way but my legs finally obey and let me move. I slowly back away, shaking my head at him and turn on my heel to run back through the dark room to the safety of my stairwell. I do not hear him come after me as I run up the steps and into my room, closing the door behind me and slumping against it.

What on Earth just happened? I am everything he thought I would be? What does that even mean... I try to settle myself but my pounding heart is threatening to burst out of my chest. My body *needed* to touch him to feel fulfilled. He knows my name, which means he *has* been sharing visions with me.

How can someone feel that way the first time they meet? Why did I run? I have been waiting for this. For him. Right?

I try to remember how Benji and I's attraction started but come up short realizing that compared to what I'd just experienced I'm not sure if Benji and I shared anything remotely similar. This all seems too ridiculous to be true. This isn't how this is supposed to work. Things like this should take more time...

Just go to bed Nuria, after tomorrow you will never see him again. I feel I am being tested on where my loyalty lies. He is the son of my captor. He is the catalyst for my escape, and I know I need to get out of here to find Marissa. Why couldn't he have been someone else's son? Why could we not have met elsewhere?

I can't get distracted from my path now, so I hurry back into bed, pulling the covers over my head, but as I try to sleep, my dreams keep going back to his smile, the fullness of his lips, the beauty and sorrow in his song and the way he said *my name.*

His strong hands play the keys of the piano so delicately and I dream of those same hands touching me, just as softly.

Caressing and stroking me into submission. I drift off into sleep, with his song winding its way around my heart.

Nuria, I hear his deep voice say my name.

I wake with a start and can feel the evidence of my arousal between my legs. *What is happening to me?* I groan at my longing and rollover to bury my head in my pillow, letting out a frustrated scream before trying to go back to sleep. Eventually exhaustion gives me sweet release from this foolish pining and I drift off, into dreamlessness.

Chapter Twelve

The next morning, after breakfast service, the gromlins and I are working away at preparing the evening's dinner: roast goose in a red wine sauce with honey glazed carrots, rosemary roasted potatoes and a creamy parsnip puree. There's a peaceful silence while we labour. I am elbow deep in the goose's cavity, smearing the garlic and herb butter all over, when one of the fae servants that usually ignores my presence steps down the stairs and calls over to me.

"Nuria, you are wanted as a servant for tonight's dinner. Clean yourself up and report to Mistress Colette in the servant's quarters," she says, holding her head high and looking down her nose at the kitchen crew before giving me a curt nod and climbing back up the steps.

I quickly remove my hands from the goose and wipe the greasy mess on my apron as I look to Smudge for approval. *Shit, what do they want me for? This isn't part of my plan!*

Smudge doesn't even look up from her work and just waves me off. I have been here for ages and have never been asked to attend any other part of the house before but I make the assumption that the servant's quarters are located in the separate building I saw when I first arrived. I make my way out the back door and around the back of the house.

As I round the corner I notice a beautiful flower garden that I had not seen before. It is nearer to the far left side of the house and out of view of the chicken coop which I had only strayed from yesterday, when Embrys arrived.

There are roses and dahlias in shades of yellows, pinks, and reds swirling in a large spiral garden bed. Rudbeckias of a deep orange, the shade of a sunset when a storm is rolling in and bright white daisies poke their sunny heads up here and there. Lining the outer edges of the garden beds is some sort of well-manicured hedge that gives the garden a well-kept contrast to the bright colours of the flowers.

I can see some elderflower and perhaps apple or pear trees further back, creating a border between the gardens and the expanse of forest that encompasses the back acreages of the estate. In the centre of the flower spiral there is a pergola covered in variegated ivy and the sight of Embrys sitting on the iron bench stops me in my tracks. His silky red hair is tucked behind one ear, showing off his strong jawline. The dappled light casts shadow and dancing sunlight across his face and I can see a hint of a frown knitting his eyebrows together as he concentrates. I catch myself twirling my hair with one finger and chewing on my lip before I realize how ridiculous I look.

Stop swooning you idiot.

He pops his head up as if he senses my stare and gives me a little wave, his other hand closing his book with a *snap*. I smile awkwardly and when I go to wave back I am interrupted by someone clearing their throat. Looking up towards where the servant's quarters are, I see a sour-faced woman with a painfully tight bun and furry tufted ears glaring at me from the doorway.

Mistress Colette I am guessing? Great. I hurry on without looking back at Embrys, my cheeks heating from the embarrassment of being caught staring like some sort of giddy schoolgirl.

"There will be none of that, Miss Nuria. You have been promoted, yes, but you are *not* one of them." She motions me to hurry inside. "Now, I am not sure why exactly you have been requested for tonight's dinner but we have some very important guests that we must impress. You will follow all of my rules and will not put one finger out of line to make me look bad, understood?" she says as she leads me through a tight hallway. I grunt in response.

Some of the doors we pass are open and I peer in to see sparsely furnished rooms with sets of bunk beds and plain wooden bureaus. We turn down another hall and end up in the laundry where a few older women, some noticeably fae from their various animal parts sticking out and some I am unsure about, working away at washing, folding and ironing.

A crisp, three-quarter sleeved black dress with a white

knee length frilly apron is already laid out for me on the work table. Miss Colette motions for me to put it on.

"Hurry up now girl, we do not have all blooming day to wait for you," she says, arms crossed and foot tapping. I nod and undress right there and then.

As I finish buttoning up the dress and tying the apron, one of the laundresses helps me undo my sloppy, half fallen out braids and pulls my hair into a tight, high bun like Mistress Colette's.

"Much better," she says, sizing me up and giving the laundresses a nod of approval. "Now, come with me. You will be stationed with the girls, preparing the dining table and polishing the silver until it is time for service," she says, turning back down the hallway we came from then taking a left turn to a larger room where a few fae servants are seated having tea and scones.

They stop their chatting to stare up at me and I have a memory flash through my mind of a morning not too long ago where I was still at home, in the human realm, walking down the stairs to see Marissa and her friends gossiping conspiratorially on the couch in the living room. A twang of homesickness punches me in the gut but I quickly shake it off, feeling that this bunch might jump at any sort of weakness. Their scowls say it all, I am not wanted here.

"Juniper, please see to it that this one is useful. I will check in on you periodically and when you least expect it," is all Miss Colette says before departing, leaving me with the sneering fae.

"You heard her ladies, I am in charge," the one named

Juniper says, puffing herself up. She is the deer fae that came to fetch me earlier. She has dark, tan skin, the colour of Oleander's mother's fur and dark hair pulled up in the servant's fashion. She has little horns coming out of the top of her head and hooves for feet. I ponder whether her whole legs are that of a deer and catch myself staring. When I meet her gaze she looks utterly unimpressed at my blunder and rolls her eyes.

"Right, well come on then, let's get to work." She motions me to follow her as the other girls stay behind to clean up their meal.

WE ARE LINED up along the back wall of the dining hall holding our designated platters when the lords and ladies walk in. They are dressed in their finery; the women in elegant floor length dresses made of jewel toned velvet with black lace up corsets over top and the men in three piece velvet suits with long coat tails and shining metallic buttons on the front.

The opulence of this party leaves me feeling paltry and drab in my servant's clothing. All I want is to get Embrys to look over just once.

Come on Nuria, stop swooning over a man, this isn't like you.

I know I have to focus and figure out how to adapt to the change of plans but so far I am coming up blank. As they enter and find their seats they don't even glance our way and

I can feel my annoyance rise as even Embrys won't look at me. Their conversation from the drawing room carries on as they slowly file in.

"The lack of water seems unprecedented. Even our staff water diviners are coming up short. The King's theories about the link between both realms must have some merit, but he shows no signs of action to remedy it. Perhaps we should take matters into our own hands. We must send some of your vargs over to see what they can find out about what the humans are up to." A tall, gangly man with a sharp nose and long, white hair gestures to Pyralis.

"The humans would never accept a varg into their ranks, or any creature-of-fae, for that matter. Besides, they are all idiots, Gaelheart. Has The King mentioned his plans to address this problem?" Pyralis responds, looking over his shoulder to the tall, sharp featured lord. From the swirling, silver crest embroidered on his suit jacket I recognise him as the Lord of the House of Wind, a prominent family of Elemental fae that run the sprawling, wind swept lands that are east of The House of Flame. We had a briefing before the dinner on who everyone is so we could address them appropriately if we were beckoned to speak.

"No, he has been shut in the Palace, supposedly pouring over old lore texts. He has called in the Seers of Mount Aethel but will not share his plotting as to *why* with any of us. I would have thought he had included *you* in his inner workings Pyralis," Gaelheart says, peering down his nose at the Lord of the House of Flame. "If we cannot send your vargs then perhaps we could send one of Clayborn's many daughters to do the job. They aren't useful for much else and there are far too many of them to marry them all off successfully. Why not Eunice?" Gaelheart says, raising a questioning eyebrow at Clayborn, the portly, red-faced head of the House of Soil. Clayborn chuckles and nods along, not even denying that his daughters are good for anything other than marriage and breeding. I am trying to keep my expression trained into a neutral mask but have to bite my lip to stop from shouting at these lunatics. I see why Oleander left.

"Come now, Gaelheart, she would be stuck with the humans and have to live out a mortal life. Even you are not that cruel," Embrys replies nonchalantly. I try to catch his eye but he ignores me as he walks towards his designated chair. His association with these men irks me. *How can I be attracted to someone who believes in this treatment of women? Is he just playing along? I bloody hope he is...*

A male fae pulls out the chairs for each guest and as they are seated the servants with the selected wines move forward to fill the goblets. It is all a very well-orchestrated dance and my part is up next. I have to take a steadying breath to be able to convince my feet to move and my hands to serve.

I start with the wife of Lord Clayborn, a sickly pale woman with black hair and red stained lips. My task is to scoop potatoes on their plates until a hand shoots up as my signal for when to stop. I nearly drop the whole platter in Lady Clayborn's lap because she was inches away from slapping me in the face but I managed to do a little twirl to keep my balance, making it all look like part of the show. I hear a low chuckle and look up to catch Embrys' eye for a brief

moment before he continues his conversation with Gael-
hert's wife.

I make my way around the table, counterclockwise,
without any word from either Embrys or Pyralis but as I
reach Lord Gaelheart he suddenly grasps my wrist and pulls
me closer, nearly knocking the platter out of my hands.

"Now where did you get this fine specimen, Pyralis? I
thought you did not partake in the keeping of slaves but alas,
you have outdone us all. She is a beauty, not a single animal
part to be seen. Unless it is hiding underneath," he says,
eyeing up my body with a prowling sweep of his eyes.

I can feel my cheeks go red but the rage I feel trumps the
embarrassment. His wife's face remains cool and distant.

"She's not human though is she? Those are even rarer to
come by. I *will* win that young one off you one day."

*Does he mean Lillian? How dare he? What is this back-
wards realm?* I clench my jaw to keep from growling in his
face but am met with his disgusting thoughts instead. *I will
steal this one away later; I will find out for myself what hides
beneath that frock,* I hear before I can peel my eyes away to
keep from hearing the rest.

I catch Embrys' eye and he subtly shakes his head. *Leave
it be Nuria, go back to the kitchens.* His low, soothing voice
rumbles through my mind and I look down to see that my
hands are trembling.

I can't be here anymore without throwing these potatoes at the heads of these revolting fae so I turn to leave
through the back door but Juniper steps in my way, blocking
the door.

"Turn around and act normal or you will make us all look bad. You can go fetch the dessert in a moment," she whispers, nudging me to get back to my spot along the wall.

Pyralis scoffs at Gaelheart's last remark. "She owed me a debt. It is true, I do not go out of my way for slaves, Gaelheart, but this one seems to have fallen into my service," he says as the lords and ladies laugh at my predicament. "And unfortunately for you, Miss Lillian is not for sale. She is not my slave but rather my employee and I have taken a liking to her," he adds.

I stand still, staring at the wall, envisioning the whole table on fire until Juniper finally dismisses me to go fetch the dessert platter.

I burst into the kitchen seething, tears streaking down my cheeks. The gromlins all stop their work to look up at me and I can see the concern written on all of their faces.

These creatures care for me... Ok, new plan. I storm down the steps and bee-line straight to Olaf, my best bet, as I let my tears and rage fully take over my expressions.

"Nuria! What has happened?" Olaf says, dropping the dough he was just kneading, dusting his hands on his apron.

"I am a slave Olaf! Look!" I show him my brand, and can see the signs of his impending flip already taking shape as his hands start to shake and his eyes go wide.

"Wh-what? What did they do?" he says with a shaky voice, and I have a split second of guilt about what I am about to do before I keep pushing.

"They laughed! One of them said he is going to take me to his rooms later tonight and hurt me, Olaf!" I say, my voice reaching a high pitch of feigned hysteria. Olaf's eyes turn red, steam is shooting out of his ears and I can see the gromlins closer to him start to shake, as well.

"Olaf! Dunk your head, quick!" Smudge yells from across the room, but I cannot let this trainwreck stop now so I spin around with my wrist in the air so the whole room can see.

"They keep gromlins as slaves too! Imagine the horrors they do to your brethren!" I yell, feeling like the brave leader of a rebellion riling everyone up for a revolt, but in truth I am just an agent of chaos. "Will you just stand-by and do nothing?"

I am unsure what a room full of flipped gromlins will involve and realize I should probably get out of there so I don't find out. Before I can even step towards the back door I hear a roar come from behind me and turn to see Olaf, in his fully flipped form.

He is twice his regular size, now taller than me, with bulked arms, sharp protruding teeth and red, piercing eyes. His erratic breathing and darting eyes show me that this is no longer the Olaf I know and have come to care for. I duck down, crawling under the work table and can see the feet of the surrounding gromlins transform one by one as the whole room flips.

The chaos is more than I could have wished for. Anything they can get their hands on is thrown, smashed or ripped apart. Sauces are being painted on the walls, ceramic plates and bowls are crushed into dust and they have all ripped their aprons off and set them on fire, waving them around like the flags of rebellion that they are. When the kitchen is left in tatters they start running up the steps of the servant's entrance and spilling out into the house, hooting and roaring in their frenzy as they go.

"Well, that bloody worked," I laugh, unbelieving at the sight of demolition, as I poke my head up from under the table to make sure they are all gone. I allow myself only the briefest moment to take in the destruction before running out the back door.

I cannot see any of the vargs patrolling outside so I creep my way along the back of the house, stopping before each illuminated window to peer inside to make sure no one is looking but all I see is ruination. The vargs are running around the house, throwing buckets of water at the flailing gromlins and the lords and ladies are cowering in various corners, begging the gromlins not to hurt them.

I hope the gromlins will be all right... I worry about what their punishment might be but hope that since this is in their nature that Pyralis will see it as his own risk for employing them. I take one last look through the window then I stay true to my course and make my way to the stables, where I hope Lillian managed to enact her part of the original plan.

Arriving at the stables, I see there is a horse already saddled and ready to go with a sword strapped to its side. *You good man, Jacob!* I look around but neither Jacob nor Lillian is in sight. *I hope they aren't in the house!* I pause, looking back at the house full of pandemonium but know that this is my only chance, I cannot go back.

I turn to the horse and pat its nose while looking in its eye. *I am Nuria, I need your help. Please will you help me?* The horse snorts, blasting warm air on my face, and nods its head but does not verbally reply to my request. It seems to have understood but perhaps this is not a Metamorph as Durga was and is just a regular horse. I'm entirely not sure how my powers work. Perhaps I cannot communicate with regular animals.

I step up into the saddle, feeling brave and ready for what lies ahead as I give the horse a little kick and we shoot out of the stable at a full gallop. I don't look back but for a moment I swear I can hear Embrys' voice in my head. *Nuria, where are you? What have you done?!*

Chapter Thirteen

We make our escape at a full gallop. I don't dare let go of the reins to wipe away the tears streaking my cheeks from the rushing wind in my face. Whipping tendrils of my uncoiled hair flow behind me like a cape in the wind and my howl of freedom rings through the night like a wolf's lonesome ode to the moon.

The strong muscles of my steed tighten and ripple with each leaping step as he gallantly carries me onwards on my rescue-turned-escape mission. We are a shadow in the waning moon light and I trust his senses to carry us safely on.

Only weeks ago I would have been terrified of being on the back of a horse this size, but now, after all I have experienced, I feel my courage taking shape and overpowering all fear in the name of rescuing my little sister.

I'm a badass!

I imagine myself swooping into the forest to save Marissa, and her stunned look at me riding in as her shining knight, like how we used to play make-believe with our father as children.

The outline of a forest starts taking shape in the distance and I urge my steed to slow his pace so we can scope out the place before busting in. My fantasy of charging in to play hero is probably not the best idea when wanting to confront a most likely lethally-trained rebel group.

Upon entering the tree line, I slide off the horse and unbuckle the sword from the saddle to strap it around my waist but notice the belt is massive. Lillian must not have told Jacob who this horse was for but it makes no difference to me what tale she told, so I sling it across my chest instead and unsheathe the large sword.

It's got some heft to it but I have practiced with heavy swords in the past to strengthen my arm enough so that the fencing epees would feel like air. I feel ready to use it if necessary but take note that precision will be of the utmost importance so I don't tire too quickly. I give it a few practice swipes and upon doing so, I notice the pommel has an intricate flame design and the letter P inlaid in gold.

Well if Pyralis' brand doesn't give away where I have come from then this sure will.

I grip the sword and crouch down, creeping my way into the forest, scanning for any signs of the rebels. So far I am met with complete silence, not even a whisper of wind or creak of a cricket. These woods don't feel malicious like the

Tanglewoods but they do have an ancientness about them, almost a sadness even.

I have the same feeling of being watched by the trees but don't feel that they want to harm me. I imagine they have observed hundreds of years of passing fae and creatures and would have some grand stories to tell as I marvel at their massive trunks and high reaching branches. The ferns here are so huge that the unfurling fiddle heads are bigger than my fist and the moss is so squishy that in some patches my feet are swallowed whole. I stop for a moment at the trunk of a colossal cedar to listen for any movement and look back through the trees towards where I had left my steed and can see another horse, identical to him, riding in from the direction of Pyralis' estate.

Shit, that was too fast! How could they have known where I went? I wait to see if more have followed this figure but it appears to be alone, thankfully no vargs in sight. While they might be dumb, I still wouldn't want to be caught having to fight off a pack of them.

I duck behind the tree, crouching down lower as I watch the cloaked figure dismount his horse. My steed whinnies in response and walks over to him and starts nuzzling his neck. *Pfft traitor...* The low rumble of a laugh echoes through the silent woods, *wait a second...*

I grab my sword and turn the pommel over to see a big letter E inlaid in gold on the other side, *Embrys*. I look back up at the cloaked figure and now recognize his build and gait. This is Embrys' sword, and that must be Embrys' horse.

Did Jacob not set that horse up for me? What happened to him and Lillian? Did he refuse to help her? I wonder at the luck of Embrys' horse still being saddled and ready to go, thinking perhaps he had had plans to leave that night anyway. He is scanning the woods, so I duck back behind the tree to hide, peeking just my head out to see.

"Nuria!" Embrys calls out, cupping his hands around his mouth. "I have to bring you back, please just come with me and he will never know you have left. The house is in chaos and they won't realize you are gone for a while but we have to go now!" He takes a few steps towards the trees. "My father means well, believe me, we are protecting you. Do not make this harder than it needs to be. I swear your conditions at the estate will improve, please!" he calls out into the dark, scanning side to side, showing me that he hasn't pinpointed my location yet.

He pushes his hood back and turns his head to the side, as if he is intently listening, I hold my breath and try not to move. I can feel a familiar fogginess in my head and scrunch my eyes closed trying to clear it but when I open my eyes I am seeing from Embrys' perspective, looking into the dark forest, scanning the trees for my whereabouts.

"Gah, get out of my head!" I yell out as I try to shake the vision off and am transported back into my body. When I look back up to where Embrys had been he is gone, only the two horses remain, shifting from leg to leg in restlessness, their hot breath sending plumes of fog out into the crisp night air.

Where did he go? I scan the forest but it is too hard to

tell if the shapes I am seeing are trees or man. If he is able to see through my eyes when these visions happen then he knows where I am. I have to move, and quickly!

I jump up from my hiding place and run towards the horses, hoping to make my escape once again but I only make it a few paces before the shadow of something whooshes by the corner of my eye. I whip around to find Embrys, standing only three strides behind me with his hands up, in a sign of non-hostility.

"Please Nuria, I mean you no harm," he says, taking a tentative step towards me. I take an equal sized step back and point the stolen sword at him, squatting down, into my fighting stance as I narrow my eyes, trying to give him my meanest death stare. A stare I know Marissa would have made fun of.

"You mean *me* no harm? Then why send the vargs to kidnap me in the first place? Or were you just following *Daddy's* orders?" He scoffs at that, I flare my nostrils, "I will be no one's *slave*! I must rescue my sister. I mean *you* no harm but I will do what I have to do without remorse, *Embrys*," I say and hear his sigh followed by a chuckle at my outstretched arm.

His cockiness and miscalculation at my seriousness gives me a surge of rage that I will gratefully use to fuel my attack and douse my fear. "Go on, try me," I say, prodding him to make the first move so I can figure out his weaknesses. I was always particularly good at goading on my opponents and causing them to attack foolhardily, giving me time to learn their moves.

"I am not going to fight you Nuria. You would surely lose. Come now, this is ridiculous. Give me back my sword and we can be on our way." He goes to take another step forward but I have had enough of his coaxing and lunge, waving my sword in an arc towards his body. He leaps back and curses, then draws his own sword. *Finally.* I step back and tauntingly draw a line in the dirt of the forest floor just in front of my feet with the tip of my boot.

I show him my teeth like a wild animal. "You will not cross this line."

Fencing has always been the only time I truly let myself go. The decorum of the sport often left my opponents bewildered at my feral behavior but there are no explicit rules against it and it usually worked in my favour.

Occasionally I would go a bit too far and end up with a penalty. Like the time in ninth grade when I told Carson Nugent that his inevitable tears of defeat would fill my chalice of victory, earning myself a yellow card. Hunt's look of disappointment is still one of those memories that makes my gut sink whenever my brain decides to reminisce.

This was a real fight though, no penalties and no Hunt here to disapprove.

I hear Embrys' chuckle again, the most irritating chuckle that doesn't require words to elicit its meaning, as I have heard it from many male opponents before. I am often misjudged initially. He thinks I am a foolish girl and this will be easy for him.

I fume at his arrogance but hold back my urge to swipe at him. He feigns boredom as he looks at his sword, flipping it around in his hand a few times before suddenly, he lunges at me slashing towards my chest.

I quickly block using both hands on the hilt to take the weight of his hard blow before I spin out of his reach and swipe towards his open back. He is quick on his feet, ducking under my high swing and sweeping his leg back to knock my two legs out from under me.

I land hard with a grunt and can see him stand, sword in hand, plunging it down to my chest but he is met with my foot in his balls which causes him to stagger back, crying out in pain. *What the fuck! Is he actually trying to harm me?* I scramble to my feet, not letting my shock steal any of my focus, and sit back into my fighting stance once again. He growls and straightens up, ready for our next blows. *Real fight! Real fight!*

We are met strike for strike, parry for parry in an elaborate sequence of feet and singing steel as we dance around each other, unable to land anything effective. I can feel myself tiring at the prolonged fight and the heavy sword. Sweat trickles down my face and the beginnings of blisters are forming on my palms.

I will not give up, this is for Marissa! I push on, but it feels as though he is not tiring at all and my confidence starts to wane.

"I must admit, you are a worthy adversary, but I see you are tiring," he says, grunting between breaths and narrowly missing the tip of my blade at his cheek as he leans back, out of my reach.

"Give this up Nuria."

I falter for a split second and am met with a slice in my arm. I cry out but do not allow myself to stop as the warm gush of blood starts to soak into my sleeve. He winces at the slice as well and backs up a step, shaking his head.

"Gah! You bastard!" I jump back, out of his reach. I have experienced some small pokes and slices from my tournaments before but nothing as deep as that and the searing pain is too distracting. I have to end this soon.

In my fury I see an opening as he backs away and lifts his hands up. I tackle him to the ground, not giving into his feigned submission, crouching low, hitting him below his waist to topple his centre of gravity. We crash down as a united tangle of bodies, the impact knocking the sword out of his hand.

I try to sit up as I straddle him and get the longsword across his neck but its size has me awkwardly having to lean back to pull it across his chest, my arms too shaky now to fully lift it up. Embrys uses this moment to wrap his surprisingly nimble legs around my waist and flip me onto my back, pinning me to the ground and knocking the sword from my slackened grip as he takes both of my hands in one of his massive ones and restrains them above my head. He pushes his other forearm into my neck and leans in close.

"Had enough fun?" he jokes, but I can tell that it was also a struggle for him as his breath is coming in heaves and sweat is running in rivulets down the side of his cheek.

His strong body pushes against mine and I know that from this spot I will not be able to throw him off. Our eyes meet. My heart stutters for a moment. He sucks in a breath, his cocky grin drops.

Damn, he has beautiful eyes. They are exactly as I have glimpsed in my visions, yet so much more. I can see the browns and greens of the entire forest in fall and the raging fires of the dry season in his serious gaze.

A part of me submits to our closeness and does not want him to get off, inwardly purring at what else could be done in this position and sparking the memory of my dreams last night. His strong hand holding me down sends flashes of his touch shivering down my body, but I scrunch my eyes closed and give my head a little shake to dispel this ridiculous longing.

Not the time for this Nuria! The other, stronger willed part of me is pissed at losing this fight and won't give in so easily so I strain my arms and writhe underneath him, trying to wriggle at least one limb free so I can escape.

"Marissa! Maaaarriiisssaa–" I shout, hoping she is somewhere in these woods and my shouts will bring out the rebels, one enemy traded for another, but I am cut short by Embrys covering my mouth with his calloused hand. I hear his breath hitch and he closes his eyes, turning his head away from me.

"Don't writhe around like that," he growls as he releases my mouth, letting his thumb brush against my lower lip. When he looks back at me I can see flames dancing in his eyes.

His lowered tone hits me in the sensitive spot between my legs and I freeze my movements as I feel the heat rise in all the places our bodies are touching. It lingers between my legs and I can't help but bite my lower lip to restrain the moan that wants to escape at the exhilarating sensation I feel igniting all my nerves.

His gaze flits down to my mouth for a split second before meeting my eyes again. I cannot seem to pull away from his locking stare and for a moment, in our shared consciousness, I see a flash of our naked bodies entwined and can hear his voice sighing my name. We both gasp simultaneously.

"How do we do that? Why do we do that?" I ask, looking into his bewildered eyes. "Why have I been sharing visions with *you* my whole life?"

He sighs, looking at me with furrowed brows, a muscle in his jaw twitching as he clenches it. I can sense the inner cogs working out what to tell me and am surprised when he lets go of my wrists and sits up.

"I knew your mother, Inanna." That was the last thing I expected him to say.

He sweeps a hand through his luscious red hair, and I feel a moment of envy, wishing I could do the same.

"Nuria, you and I... share a bond of sorts," he says as I prop myself up onto my elbows, still painfully aware of his strong legs hugging my hips, keeping me in place.

Inanna... I mouth the word. This is the first time I have heard her name and it feels like a puzzle piece has found its place in the gaping hole in my heart.

"You look like her," he adds, rubbing the back of his

neck and giving me a half smile as he studies my face. *No... he doesn't get to look at me like that. Like he pities me.*

"Well I never knew her. She died giving birth to me," I snap. His face crumples for a moment before I look away. This man in front of me knew my mother more than I did and it doesn't feel fair.

"Wait, how could you have known her? You look like you're my age." I look him up and down, searching for some sign of age.

"I was a boy when she... disappeared. The fae don't age as humans do. We slow down the aging process in our early twenties and sort of just linger there for an extra hundred years or so."

I chew my lip, contemplating both of these shocking pieces of information and pondering what that means about my own life span and what would have happened if I just continued living in the human realm. Would I have just stopped aging?

"We should head back to the estate. Before anyone realizes you are gone," Embrys says, looking off towards the horses nervously, as if he can see all the way back to the house and the pandemonium that is unfolding there.

I take this moment, and my newly freed hands, to try and stealthily reach over my head for the discarded sword but before I can grasp the hilt, Embrys' head snaps back towards me and he is on top of me again in a split second, pinning my hands against my hips, tucking them in with his knees then bracing his hands on either side of my head.

He hovers over my face, his red hair curtaining us off

from the world, brushing the sides of my cheeks. I can't control my pounding heart and the gasping of my breath as he leans in even closer; leaving our mouths just inches apart.

"Would you like me to tie you up?" he asks, mischief glinting in his eye, his mouth curling into that infuriating half smile.

Something about this man irritates the crap out of me whilst also making me want to rip all of his clothes off. That smile makes me want to bite his bottom lip hard enough to make him bleed. The electric pull between our lips brings us closer until I can feel his bottom lip brush mine, the tether between us feeling more and more tangible, more and more irresistible. I fight it, because I *cannot* fall for my bloody captor, no matter what my body wants, no matter what he meant to me before I met him. *Family comes first,* I reassure myself. Perhaps this feeling just scares the crap out of me...

"No," I say in my driest tone, not giving into the pull I know we are both experiencing. He stops smiling and snaps a cool mask on as he pushes himself up onto his feet, grabbing my hands and pulling me up with him.

"Good. Let's go," he says, without looking at me as he leans down to grab his sword. He tugs on my wrists, pulling me along with him to the horses. I glance behind me hoping to see someone, anyone, coming to my aid but all I see are trees.

My stomach sours as I accept the failure of my mission. My heart breaks all over again from losing Marissa but I'm not even sure if she was here to begin with. Just a fool's hope.

As I look forward, resigning to my fate of being carted back to my captor's estate I hear a high pitched whizzing sound and something zooms within inches of my ear and lodges into Embrys' shoulder. The sound of Embrys' yelp scares the horses, causing them to whinny and gallop off back in the direction of the estate. *Perfect.*

I see what hit him and my jaw hits the floor.

An arrow is sticking out of his arm and he curses colourfully as he spins around, pushing me behind him and drawing his sword. "Stay behind me Nuria!" he says, scanning the forest. I just stare, in complete shock, at the arrow sticking out of him, and the blood that is pouring down his arm, before realizing we are under attack.

I snap back into focus. "No way! We need to get that extra sword!" I say, lunging forward, but am met with another arrow sticking out of the earth at my feet, stopping me from taking another step.

"Wait! Hold fire! That's my sister!" I hear a wonderfully familiar voice call out of the dark. Marissa runs towards me, accompanied by three hooded figures lingering just outside of the shadows of the forest.

She is dressed in brown trousers and a white blouse with a green hooded cloak around her shoulders and a sword strapped to her hip. Her blonde, curly hair bounces behind her as she sprints towards me, grinning ear to ear. The hooded figures make no move to restrain her. She looks well... happy even.

"Marissa!" I call back and meet her half way, our bodies

colliding together in a bear hug, now the second time in our life that we have ever hugged like this.

"You're alive!" I say, pulling away and cradling her perfect face. " I'm so sorry!" I turn her head side to side looking for any damage but she looks as if she has fully recovered from her kidnapping. She rests her hands on my forearms and I see the twinkle of her eyes as she blinks back tears.

"I thought they killed you! Nuria, we were coming to avenge your death," she says, in a whisper as she grabs my hands and lowers them from her face. *Avenge my death?* I choke on a laugh. She looks over my shoulder to see Embrys yanking the arrow out of his shoulder and winces at his grunt of pain, ignoring my outburst. Her waggling, raised eyebrow is question enough for me to roll my eyes and shake my head.

"Do not move another inch," another familiar voice calls out from one of the hooded figures as they approach with another arrow pointed at Embrys.

"Ollie?" Embrys says, squinting in the dark and tilting his head to one side to try and see under the hood. The figure motions for the other two to go to Embrys with a nod of the head, which causes the hood to fall back, revealing the unruly red curls of Oleander.

"How did you locate us?" Oleander does not even deign to look at me and just keeps her very lethal looking stare set on her brother.

"Um... hello, hi," I say, waving a hand in her face while still holding Marissa's hand with my other one. "What the heck Oleander? You traitor! You left me for dead and *stole* my sister. You made a promise! How were you even capable of breaking it?" I say, stepping into her space. She slowly peels her eyes away from Embrys and meets mine. I feel my face burning with rage and accidentally squeeze Marissa's hand really hard in my anger.

"Ouch!" Marissa pulls away and steps up beside Oleander.

Wait a second, I look between her and Oleander. "You're working together? She literally knocked you out and kidnapped you Mar!" I seethe.

Oleander cocks an eyebrow. "First of all, I said, and I quote, *I promise not to rescue her without you.* Honestly, one would think you would have learned by now that semantics matter in this realm. I did not rescue her without you. You just unfortunately got left behind once the rescuing was done," Oleander says and I go to smack her but she catches my hand mid-air and holds on tight, pulling me closer.

Her eyes soften slightly but she does not relent in her grip. "Look, I am really sorry but the place was swarming with vargs and you were about to give away my location. I got her out of there, and to safety. The knock on the head was just a security measure so she wouldn't alert them to our whereabouts. I did not exactly have time to explain who I was now did I? And it is your fault for not telling me who *you* really were. If you were honest from the start I would have still helped you to free your sister," Oleander says, still holding my wrist. I can feel her heat running up my arm from where our skin meets. I yank it away and cross my arms, denying the thrill her touch just gave me.

Seriously Nuria, you're into siblings? Get it together.

"Well... shit," is all I can say as a reply because her logic is annoyingly sound and her touch has me all flustered.

I can hear Embrys struggling behind me and look back to see him trying to fight the other two rebels but clearly losing since he can barely move his right arm. I try to ignore that issue for now and turn back to Oleander and my sister.

"I wasn't even sure *who* or *what* I was in the first place all right? I only knew that my birth mother was fae and I had just found that out not even twenty-four hours before meeting you. You never told me *why* you wanted Marissa so how could I have trusted you with the truth? And why is she still bloody here? Did you have no decency to just return her home?" I say, finding my words again.

"I didn't want to go. Nuria you were either dead or imprisoned and you came all the way to a different flipping realm to rescue me! I had to stay and fight for you. No way I could let you upstage me, right?" Marissa chimes in, giving me a wink. Her cockiness that usually infuriates me is a comfort, making me smile instead.

I'm so happy you're ok, I think as I look her in the eye and her jaw drops.

"I heard that. You were right, she *is* an Etherealist!" she says, turning to Oleander with wide eyes.

"How do you know what that is? And how do you know *what* I am?" I ask Marissa, then Oleander.

"I've been with the rebels for over a month Nuri, I know

everything," Marissa says, flipping her hair over her shoulder and rolling her eyes. *Same old Mar.*

Oleander cuts in, "look we can stand here and chat all night but I would rather not wait and see if *his* furry minions show up to back him up." She tilts her head to a now subdued Embrys. "So if you would kindly follow us, I will tell you what you want to know in a more secure location," she says, waving the other two over who now have a shackled, blindfolded Embrys held between them. *Now that's a nice sight.* I raise an eyebrow and bite my lip. Oleander catches my eye and I clear my throat and look away, as if I was not just checking out her brother.

"Fine, let's go." I nod, giving one more glance back to where Embrys and I had fought. I notice a patch of white flowers that I swear were not there before, but Marissa links her arm through mine, giving me a little tug to follow Oleander before I can inspect them more closely.

Chapter Fourteen

We are being led through the forest, keeping quiet by Oleander's strict instructions, until we are far away from where Embrys found me. All I can hear is Embrys tripping and cursing as the rest of us walk along in silence. I keep my hand locked in Marissa's the whole time, feeling that if I let her go she is going to be taken from me again, and still not quite believing that I found her... or she found me, I guess. I continue to stare at her and squeeze her hand a little harder. She looks back and gives me her cheeky little smile, squeezing my hand in return.

She looks so sure of herself and comfortable playing this new role of rebel. I think I never really knew her before. *Was that popular girl act fake? Do we have more in common than I thought?* The Marissa I thought I knew would have been grossed out by the dirt under her nails and the bulky clothes that don't show off her assets. *Who is this girl?*

I really like her.

Oleander halts by a moss covered stone wall and lifts her hand, motioning us to all stop. She knocks three times on the stone, one slow and two fast, and then waits. The stone makes a grinding noise as a door that was perfectly concealed within the designs of the moss and lichen rolls open, revealing a hole, barely big enough to fit me standing upright.

We squeeze in, some having to crouch, as we make our way down the pitch black tunnel, single file. The floor is fairly even and the walls nearly hug my sides so it is easy to feel our way through. I can hear the grinding of the stone door as it closes behind us, leaving us in true darkness as it shuts with a suctioning sound. The tunnel turns a few times, first right, then left, then right again before straightening out. The rasping of breaths and shuffling of boots are the only sounds.

"Stop," Oleander says, and I halt, unable to see anyone or anything and just trusting that we are all still together. I can hear her repeat the knocking pattern of before and another door swings open, letting the bright orange light of dozens of candles flood into the tunnel, momentarily blinding me. The sound of many voices overlapping signals a room full of people.

"We are here," Oleander says as she moves into the large cave that houses the rebels.

The cave itself is three times my height and is deep enough to fit two long wooden tables flanking the left side wall, with cut up stumps for chairs and a woodless fire, no doubt Oleander's handy work, with logs for seating situated in a circle in the middle of the space.

To the right there is an alcove that appears to be some sort of communal kitchen space with a big stone slab jutting out of the wall for a work table and little shelves dug out for storage. On one end of the alcove there is a little waterfall pouring through the rock and into a carved out trough that then drains back down into the stone floor. I wonder if this is natural or being manipulated by a water Elemental like Nerius did at the estate. I can see the openings to two more tunnels at the back of the cave that I assume lead to sleeping quarters or perhaps an alternative exit.

The place is full of fae, and creatures-of-fae, some sitting at the tables and some around the fire all conversing and filling the space with sound. When we enter the chatter quickly dies down and Oleander motions for another large fae male with foxy looking ears and grey curly hair to come assist with Embrys.

"Well, now you know where they live so is that enough of a show of trust, Nuria?" Marissa says, pulling me down the stone steps, towards the fire. "Oleander means well... she's just a little brutish sometimes," she says as we sit down on a log. She fusses with my hair, flipping it over my shoulder and smoothing down my fly-aways while making little *tut tut tut* sounds with her tongue. "You've let yourself go a bit feral big sister." I meet her eye and she gives me a little wink, *just kidding!* she chimes down the connection of our mind.

"I'm still getting used to that. I guess it could come in handy, eh?" I say, taking a moment to study her face, seeing the same little sister but feeling that she has changed so much from the sister I knew in Easthelm.

"Mar, I feel like you are a completely different person. What happened?" She just rolls her eyes and levels her sassy stare at me whilst blowing out a sigh.

"Easthelm is a bitch-eat-bitch world Nuri. I did what I had to, to survive. Not all of us *mere mortals* can just not give a shit like you." *She thinks I don't give a shit?* "I felt as if I had been living in Mom's shadow my whole life. I'm sorry, I know this is harsh but you are the adopted daughter... no one had any expectations on you from the get go. Everyone saw me as a mini Mom and expected so much from me. Dad expected so much of me..." The sass has been wiped off of her face and is replaced with something softer, more vulnerable.

A whole new understanding dawns on me about our childhood. She had never felt she fit in either... but just mastered her mask better than I. I knowingly nod at her then look over her shoulder, watching Oleander stride up to us after having conversed with a group of gnomes near the kitchen. She seems to be something of a respected figure amongst the rebels and I wonder how old she was when she joined their ranks, when Pyralis tried to marry her off.

"We may continue our discussion if you wish." Oleander sits down, keeping some space between us. She gazes into the fire, leaning her elbows on her knees. The flames dance and leap in her presence, as if they had missed her while she was gone and are dancing for her return, like a puppy who was left at home all day.

"Where did you take Embrys?" I enquire, trying not to sound too interested. "How much of our conversation did you hear?" I turn to look at her. She keeps watching the fire and I can't help but stare at her wild beauty. Her cascading hair is fire incarnate and it is changing colour in the flickering light of the flames.

"He has been taken for questioning by Fenrick, our senior Metamorph. I heard enough to know it was not The King's minions that took you, as I had once thought, which is why our rescue missions were fruitless. We were searching in the wrong place. Why my father wanted to apprehend you in the first place is what I am unsure about," she says, peeling her eyes away from the fire and looking at me. "I also *saw* enough, Nuria..." Fire dances in her irises.

At the utterance of my name the flames dim and skitter as if the coldness in her tone might threaten to douse them. As she meets my eye I am met with the flash of an image of Embrys on top of me and our mouths nearly touching. I clear my throat, dropping our eye contact, feeling my cheeks flush.

"I'm not sure what you *think* you saw but whatever it was, it meant nothing." I raise my eyebrows, "I needed information from him, I still do, but he bested me," I say, but I don't know why I feel the need to explain the moment Embrys and I shared. It's not like Oleander and I mean anything to each other. She did use me after all, but I see what I think is a flash of envy cross her face as she furrows her brows and glances down at my mouth for a split second. *Interesting...*

"And let me get this straight, we don't know exactly why The King wants me and we don't know why Pyralis wants me but...why did you guys want me?" I ask, tilting my head to the side in question.

Marissa butts in, pulling my shoulder a bit so I will look her way. "They wanted to save you and recruit you into the Order of the Sylvans, Nuri. The Wolf King is a tyrant that is dividing the fae into classes. This new religion makes the Elemental fae out to be superior but they... *we*, were all made by The Divine Mother as her children. Equal in rights but all with our own unique talents," Marissa says, lifting her chin, sounding as if she is reciting the facts from a textbook. I look at her, one eyebrow raised, in shock at her sudden interest in the rights of living beings and the wellbeing of the Earth. *Definitely a different Marissa.*

"Well, I see they have brainwashed you..." I narrow my eyes at Oleander. "Seriously Oleander, she is a sixteen year old *human* and our parents probably think we are dead!" I turn to my sister, "Marissa, what about Mom and Dad?" I ask, knitting my brows together as the thought of their broken hearts and panic resurfaces yet again. Marissa winces and looks down at her hands.

Oleander chimes in. "She is grown enough to make her own choices. I was younger than she when I left home," her eyes brazenly flare. "She has also shared that she witnessed her mate being murdered in front of her eyes. No one should have to experience that. She needed to fight back, seek retribution, and this is her way of doing so. A noble cause I might add." Oleander nods at Marissa and Marissa beams at the compliment. "Your realm would not make sense to her right now," Oleander says, looking back at me with slightly more sympathetic eyes. I can understand her point, returning to Easthelm after finding out this fairy tale realm exists would feel strange and I know Marissa is just as fierce with a sword as I am. But the thought of her getting injured or worse is just more than I can handle at the moment.

I blow out a breath through pursed lips. "First of all, ew, I sincerely hope Benji was not your *mate*," I grimace at having to say the word. "Benji was alive when last I saw him, bleeding a crazy amount from his chest, yes, but still alive! Second, she will have to return sometime and the longer you are here the higher chance you will get caught and hurt. What if you get taken as leverage to get to me? I couldn't live with myself if something were to happen to you, Mar!" I plead, only noticing now that more fae and creatures have joined us at the fire and are intently listening to our conversation.

"We will protect her!" a gnome calls out and is met with calls of agreement from various fae around the fire.

An older looking fae woman with cat eyes and a swishing, grey tabby tail interjects, "she is never on the front lines anyway. Our more skilled and senior members stage the coups." She leans in to see me around Oleander's shoulder.

"What coup? How can a ragtag band of fae do anything against a king that supposedly has accumulated a massive following?"

A fae male that has white stripes in his hair pipes up from across the fire, "we have been freeing our enslaved family members if you *must* know!" I cringe at my blunder.

Of course they are, just as the gromlins said, the Elemental fae are taking slaves.

"Ok, well now we are reunited so we can just return to the human realm, correct? There is no reason for us to be here anymore, we can just forget all about this place and go back to... normal," I say, but as I say it, it feels wrong. Easthelm never felt right to me and the thrill of my escape from Pyralis' estate is the most alive I have ever felt, but looking around at all of these fae fighting for their families leaves me thinking of mine with more than a twinge of guilt.

What would I even be going back to? Mom and Dad should be enough, family should always be enough, right? I already know my answer. I left a perfectly fine relationship with Benji *because* of my answer.

Oleander studies her hands for a moment before looking at me, "Nuria, I am afraid it is not that simple. Our spies inside the Palace have told us The King has been calling in the Seers to aid him in opening The Gates. There is some word of a prophecy he has discovered in the ancient tomes within the Palace that is the key to reversing the curse. He means to infiltrate the human realm. We don't know why he wanted you but for some reason you are integral to this. From what we have been told, he does not have any Etherealists in his army so we assume that is why he seeks you. The ability to bend the minds of one's foes is formidable and feared. They were once greatly respected amongst the Houses. The Seers can feel the tethers of the Ether, although vaguely and loosely, as they are of the same Elemental house. They would have been able to tell whether an Etherealist heir lives. We cannot let you try to return, you would surely be caught. There may already be traps in place for you," Oleander explains, looking apologetically at Marissa and I. *Does that mean we are stuck here?*

My fists clench, nails digging into my skin. "I don't even know what an Etherealist can do! What, my random visions and the little blips I get into other people's minds is really something that is valued? I can't *meld minds*. It just seems useless and confusing to me!" I throw my hands up in frustration, "I thought The King was not aware of my arrival into this realm? It was all Pyralis' doing was it not? How could he know I am here? And what is this prophecy?" I ask and receive Oleander's same sympathetic look from before. *Annoying.*

"Someone tipped him off, likely someone that my father employs. It makes sense that The King would have planted a spy at the residence of the only head of an Elemental house that didn't deny him when he overthrew The Owl."

I wonder who that spy might be, doing an inventory of all the faces I saw in my time at the estate. *How would they have known who I am?*

Oleander continues, "as for the prophecy, this remains hidden even from our most adept spies. The King has supposedly been shutting himself in his study and requesting only the presence of the Seers."

I remember the lords mentioning something about that at the dinner, I recall whilst chewing the inside of my cheek.

I wonder if my mother was the only one before my birth who mastered the ether, other than the Seers. "Why are there so few Etherealists if they were so respected, as you said?"

"The Owl had lineage in the House of Ether. After he died, no one from the House of Ether would swear fealty to The Wolf. So he hunted them all down in his rage. I suppose he is regretting that now if he indeed needs your gifts for some purpose." Oleander shrugs, looking at me with weary eyes. Marissa gives my shoulder a squeeze as I am sure she sees the hurt flit across my face. I can't help the sinking feeling in my gut at knowing that I don't have any living relatives in this realm because of this bastard of a king.

Was this fate the thing that my mother was running from? Durga warned her not to let me enter this realm... is that why? I mindlessly grab for my mother's necklace. A habit I've recently formed whenever I think of her.

Wait a second...

"You said this crest belonged to the royal house? It was my mother's." I pull the necklace out from under my dress to show them.

"I never said that to you..." Oleander's eyes widen, "you must have read my thoughts." She shakes her head, observing me carefully. "This proves she was of the House of

Ether but it does not narrow down her direct lineage. Just as this clasp shows I am of the House of Fire. Although, that gem in the centre is rather peculiar..." She leans in a bit closer. *Great, another dead end.*

"So what are Marissa and I supposed to do about it? It doesn't sound like you have enough information about what my purpose in all of this is... unless you're hiding something, *again.* We can't just hide out here forever," I say, my annoyance at all of this is starting to get to me. *Why us?*

The conversation I overheard the lords having at Pyralis' estate chimes in my mind, "wait didn't you mention that The Wolf King kicked the owl guy off the throne because he was ignoring the warning signs that the land was sick?"

"He *murdered* our beloved King!" one of the fae calls out.

"Right, sorry..." I cringe, "well, I overheard these lords talking at Pyralis' estate about droughts and strange fogs possibly causing crops to fail on the Continent. Similar climate events are happening back home. What if The Wolf is right? What if he just wants to open The Gates so the fae can help the humans fix what they have done? Ask Embrys, he was there!" I cross my arms, a smug little smile spreading across my face, feeling like I just solved everyone's problems.

Oleander shakes her head and rolls her eyes. "Nuria, I am not hiding anything," she says while looking me straight in the eye, *go on look for yourself,* she challenges me to scan her memories which I'm not even sure is something I can do on demand, or at all, so I scoff and break eye contact.

Oleander grunts then continues, "do you really think he

would want to *play nice* with a race he sees as *beneath* him?" Her eyes dart to Marissa then back to me. "His first order as King was to create hierarchy and classes based on our magic!" Oleander stands, raising her voice so all the rebels can hear as she scans the room, looking like a mighty leader about to give a call to arms.

"He sanctioned the creatures-of-fae to be slaves, he has forsaken The Divine Mother! Even the creatures have magic to some degree. What do you think he will do to the magic-less humans? Come on girl, use your brain." She taps the side of her head, looking back down at me, "this is not an action of peace. It is an action of war and we must rise in the defense of the oppressed!" She finishes her speech by looking out to all those that have gathered and the group hoots and hollers in agreement, Marissa joining in the action by pumping her fist in the air, causing me to do a double take.

I look around the room and can see so many different types of creatures all fighting for their families' freedom and my heart sinks at my selfish desires to just bury my head in the sand. Oleander's reasoning means that my parents are at risk of succumbing to the wrath of this king as well if he figures out how to get those gates down, but I feel lost about how on Earth I could be of use.

What is it about my powers as an Etherealist that is so special? Surely there are other people out there like me. I crumple from my dread.

As the cave succumbs to the revving up of the rebels in their excitement about Oleander's speech, I notice Fenrick is returning from wherever they are keeping Embrys and leans in to whisper something in Oleander's ear.

She nods and looks down at me. "He has requested to see you, Nuria. Refuses to speak to anyone else... Well, he requested I join but I might just let him flounder a bit longer," she says, winking at Fenrick, at which a sly, foxy grin spreads across his face.

Fenrick waves for me to follow him and I look back at Marissa who is now dancing around the fire with some gnomes, a drink in hand. *Are they giving my little sister alcohol too?* I will have a word with Oleander later about some conditions that need to be met if we are to stay here. Not getting Marissa drunk will be high on that list.

Fenrick leads me down the tunnel on the left, it is much more illuminated than the entrance tunnel with free floating flames flickering in stone cut outs, carved into the walls themselves. I wonder if it is Oleander who is syphoning power into these little fires all the time and how tiring that must be for her just to give her fellow rebels light and warmth.

We walk on for a little while and I notice doorways leading to rooms with bunk beds, a room filled with books and comfier looking chairs and other rooms that are too dark to see what is inside. We turn down a tighter, less lit tunnel to the left and stop in front of a door made of iron bars.

"You guys have an actual jail in here?" I scoff, but am actually quite impressed at all the material they have managed to sneak through these caves.

"I'll be just at the other end of the tunnel. Try to get him to tell you why Pyralis wanted to apprehend you. Call out if you need me," Fenrick says, turning to leave.

"Wait, aren't you going to open the door?" I call out and he tosses me the keys over his shoulder.

"Open at your own risk, like I said, I'll be just at the other end of the hall," he chuckles then disappears around the corner. I turn to the dark cell. *Why would this be risky? Surely Embrys wouldn't hurt me. Or perhaps I am thinking there is more to our bond then there actually is... I swear I saw shock on his face when he sliced my arm during our fight...*

"Nuria, thank The Mother! Get me out of here, they won't listen to me," Embrys says from the dark at the back of the cell. "I need to see Oleander, did she come with you?"

"No, I don't think she wants to speak with you just yet. What did you do to her that made her hate you so much?" I ask and he stumbles forward, coming into the light.

His hands are still restrained behind his back and I can see through the hole in his shirt where the arrow struck, it doesn't look like his wound has healed yet. I also see he has some bruising starting to form under his eye making me think that Fenrick wasn't over here just asking him questions.

"Shit Embrys, what did he do to you?" I ask, quickly unlocking the door. He wobbles on his feet as if he got up too fast. Our bodies collide as I lunge out to catch him, slowing him down as we both sink to the ground. I immediately regret my choice as his massive weight lands on my lap.

Why am I helping this prick? I bristle at the memory of him stabbing me in the arm.

"What, this? It's nothing," he laughs, giving me his infuriating half grin as I try to push his weight off of me, which proves to be quite difficult with his hands tied back. He winces a bit when I grab his injured shoulder and give him a shove.

"I deserved it." He looks over to me and I catch him studying my face for a reaction, but I give him none. He sighs and nods his head. "I didn't protect Oleander when we were younger. She was only fifteen when The Wolf requested her to be married off to one of Gaelheart's slimy sons... Something about the correct breeding of fire and air making something even stronger for his army. She was terrified and I just looked the other way, thinking it was the natural course of things which, I know now, it was anything but. The rebels took her in and cared for her like I could not, I suppose." He slumps forward in his shame.

"I've been searching for her for years. Not for my father's sake, but for us... her and I. When Elora died we leaned on each other in our grief while my father pulled away from us completely. She is my baby sister and I would do anything to have her in my life again. I know I don't deserve her but I will find a way to make up for it." He looks up to meet my eye, the ghost of a tear streaks down his cheek.

A strong surge of yearning bores into my heart causing me to wonder if the emotion is his or mine to claim. I have to mentally restrain myself from brushing that tear away. He looks away, perhaps noting my internal struggle.

"Why do you support your father Embrys? He's not a good man. I sense some goodness in you... or at least remorse. Why not leave when Oleander did?" I ask, lifting his chin up so he meets my eyes, *and don't lie to me, I will know.*

His eyes widen and he nods his head. The scratch of stubble on his chin makes me want to run my hand along his jaw but I resist the urge. My gaze slips down to his lips for the briefest of seconds before I release him.

"Unfair little trick," he says as he blinks his eyes, trying to break the contact, giving me his half smile. "He's not all bad I swear. He spiraled after Oleander's mother died and swore to do whatever it took to save our family. Unfortunately, in saving us from The Wolf executing us, as he did to many other heads of the Elemental houses, our father pledged allegiance – at the cost of Oleander's trust. He beat himself up about it for years but his heart break has just solidified into resentment over time. He believes she should have married Gaelheart's son for the good of the family," he explains, holding my eye contact. "But he isn't like the other lords. He doesn't keep slaves and he actively supports his subjects who have been suffering from the droughts. I stick around to help the villages and farms in our lands. I make sure the other lords don't step out of their lands and enslave any of the creatures-of-fae that are within our care." I look at him, eyes narrowed and sucking on my teeth as I ponder his sincerity.

"He *was* parading me around in front of those lords

though, wasn't he? It was a show of status to have a fae slave," I say, my disgust for Pyralis returning.

"Yes it was to show you off, but he had to make them believe that he is following suit. He would *never* take a slave, but he had his reasoning for keeping you with us. Giving you that brand also ensured the other houses wouldn't be suspicious of the sudden new addition to our household." He looks down to my wrist where the brand is poking out of my blouse. I follow his gaze and tug my sleeve down to hide it.

"Well, what were his reasons then?" I splay my hands out, lifting my brows in exasperation. He just shakes his head and averts his eyes.

Is he blushing? What his father could possibly want me for evades me and Embrys doesn't seem like he will readily give up the information either

"I was not privy to his plotting. I only knew that in keeping you, we were protecting you from *something*. He knew your mother too Nuria, I would even say they were friends from what I remember, I was quite young when she disappeared. Perhaps in his own perverse way he thought to save you from whatever it was she ran from," he says, keeping his eyes averted, *definitely hiding something*. I grab his chin again and force his eyes to meet mine but he suddenly reaches both his hands around and grabs my wrists, fire erupts in his eyes.

"How did you get unshackled?" I try to yank my hands away.

"Little sleight of hand when you helped me down to the

ground." He winks, I grunt in exasperation at being bested by him once again as he clasps the shackles down on both my wrists and yanks me up to stand with him. "Now stay quiet, or I will have to do something I really don't want to." I feel the shackles heat and burn my wrists in his warning as he peers around the doorway but I scream out anyway and yank on the chains as I slide to the ground to sweep out his feet. The metal burns even hotter and I scream again but this time in actual pain. *Help! Help, fuck, help me!*

Within moments Fenrick is there and deals a hard blow to Embrys' temple that has him crumpling to the ground.

"Thanks," I say as Fenrick grabs the keys from the floor and undoes the cuffs. There are angry red blisters where the metal singed my skin. *If that was a warning then what was he prepared to do to me?* I give Embrys a kick with my boot with the intention to see if he is unconscious but I may have let my leg swing a little harder just for good measure and am met with a groan.

"Quick, shackle him again. He can sit in here and stew for all I care. Asshole." I stick my tongue out at him as we close the metal door behind us. I catch Embrys with his eyes open giving me his half smile.

"Sorry, you caught me by surprise when you knocked me over. It was just a scare tactic, I didn't mean to actually harm you Nuria. Can you blame me for trying to escape?" He winces as he sits himself back up, looking genuinely sorry. I have no empathy for this brute. I scoff and turn around to walk back towards the main hall with Fenrick, leaving Embrys in the dark cell.

Our conversation runs through my mind and I am confused at his escape attempt. It felt as though he was starting to open up to me. If he wants to gain his sister's trust then surely he would have just complied. What is he hiding? I need to know more about Pyralis and my mother. Why did he want to protect me? Did he know who my father was? Is he still alive, or was he among those that were slayed by The King?

I'm lost in thought as I return to the communal fire, and don't register my surroundings as I sit down in a huff. I stare blankly into the flames whilst chewing my nails, trying to find some sort of connection between all I have learned of Pyralis and The King when I hear Marissa's laugh sound from one of the tables at the far end of the cave.

She is sitting with Oleander and another fae boy that looks to be closer to my age, although who knows how old he actually is with this whole prolonged lifespan thing. He has darker skin and tightly curled black hair and a big dimpled smile but I can't see any visible signs of what kind of fae he might be.

They all appear to be having a good laugh and he claps Oleander on the shoulder before standing up and heading towards the kitchen. Oleander and Marissa continue on in the conversation and I notice they look like old friends, sisters even, and I feel a little joy at seeing the normalcy of their interactions. Marissa leans over to give Oleander a hug before racing off after the fae boy, *typical Mar.*

As if sensing my stare, Oleander turns to look directly at

me, giving me a little nod before standing and making her way over.

"What did he do?" she says with a knowing look as she sits next to me, sliding a little closer than the last time. I roll my eyes and look at the fire.

"He opened up to me then tried to bloody capture me again! As if he could escape this place with me in tow," I laugh, shaking my head and knitting my brows together in my still very present confusion about our interaction.

"I see, he has a certain charm does he not?" she chuckles, rolling her eyes. "I recall that he would make me laugh and feel seen as a child and then snap to cold whenever our father would enter the room. As if he could not be seen acting like a child." She sighs, looking into the fire.

"He said he wants to make amends and that he regrets not protecting you. He really did sound sincere but why he wouldn't just join you here I don't understand. What is it about your father that makes him so loyal?" I question as I study her expression. I can see a flash of pain cross her face as she looks down at her hands. She blows out a sigh through her pursed lips and turns to face me head on.

"He knew our father before my mother came along, and he saw what our father... did to my mother." She looks down and shakes her head, redness rising in her cheeks.

"What do you mean, 'did to your mother'?" I raise an eyebrow, she takes a steadying breath. I haven't seen this vulnerable side to her before and I am unsure what to think of it.

"Our father was madly in love with her." She pauses, her

eyes flitting to my face then looking away again. "Embrys told me that our father's love softened his heart, he was such a different man to what he had been before my mother entered his life. He started caring for all creatures and was a dedicated servant to The Divine Mother because of my mother's caring nature and her love of the Earth. He would do anything to please her. If you have been in that house you may have seen the room devoted to her. He even helped paint it." She bites her thumb nail as she recalls what I can imagine is a painful memory.

"Their love was also... passionate," she cringes, "I was too young to understand what had happened but Embrys explained it to me before I ran away. It was an accident but one he could not undo." She pauses again to look at me and I give her my best, *go on,* nod, trying not to look too eager but also trying not to look bored. I have always felt unsure about what my face and hands should be doing when people have serious conversations with me but she seems to not be bothered by my weird half-smile and says what I was absolutely not expecting,

"Pyralis burned her alive one night during... uh..." Oleander suddenly looks away and shudders whilst looking down at her clenched hands.

He burned her alive? During....

"Oh!" Understanding dawns on me, my eyebrows shoot sky high, "and Embrys... saw?" I question, imagining a young Embrys walking in on a gruesome sight and blanch at the horror of it. I grab her hand, not knowing the right words to say to comfort her.

"Embrys had been so proud of the man our father was and understood what had happened was a horrible mistake. He wanted to protect him. Our father was a ghost of a man for years after my mother died and Embrys stepped up. . . He is the one who hired Nerius so that nothing like that would ever happen again. He cared for me and for the people of the villages and took on all of our father's work. The Wolf saw Embrys as a young threat but our father snapped out of his grief long enough to step back into his role, committing himself to the servitude of The King to spare Embrys, who would have fought to keep the old ways and surely gotten himself killed for it. I suppose he feels some sort of debt is owed to our father for this." She finishes and gives my hand a little squeeze.

My view of who I thought Embrys to be is completely wrong. I originally saw him as just the lackey of his evil father but I see now how wrong I was. Memories of our shared visions come to my mind. We often connected when things were tough for me at home. He would show me beautiful images of life in his realm, giving me an escape. A particular favourite was of little winged creatures playing in the rustling heads of the bulrushes on the shore of a small lake. The lake, I realize now, is the one at Pyralis' estate; the creatures were probably wind sprites. I wonder if I unknowingly did the same for him when he had it rough. Could we feel each other's distress?

"Thank you for telling me that. I'm so sorry about your mother," I say, squeezing her hand back. I have never had a friendship with a woman that was anything other than surface level and it feels very raw to have someone trust me with something so tender.

"So now that he has found you... what will you do?" I ask, becoming very aware of our hands still touching. The heat from the last time we touched doesn't feel as strong but I feel a different level of ease wash over me. The ease that might be what friendship feels like... I hope.

"Well, leaving him in there overnight won't harm him, now will it?" She winks at me and removes her hand from mine to push her hair out of her face. She turns to the fire, leaning her elbows on her knees.

"Can you forgive him?" I study her profile for a second before also turning to watch the flames dance and leap towards her outstretched hand.

"I've come to learn that forgiveness is the only noble way forward. Resentment is a festering sore that, if left unchecked, will devour the attention of those who pick at it. I know he has been searching for me for years and I have seen from afar the work he does to keep his people safe. I forgave him a long time ago. But my purpose is not to be a brood mare so I *will not* return to the estate with him. Our work here is too important. If he chooses to join us I will welcome him. The arrow in his shoulder was just some sibling tension that needed to be released," she says with a little smirk on her face, closing her fist on a little flickering flame that was dancing in her palm.

She tilts her head to the side to look at me from the corner of her eye. "Will *you* join us, Nuria?" I meet her eyes for a brief moment before looking away. My usual insecurities bubble up.

"You don't think I'm a freak... weird, strange... creepy?" I can't bring myself to look at her.

She grabs my chin, forcing me to. "Who on Earth would think such a thing of one of The Divine Mother's creations? Nuria, you are magnificent. We want you here. I want you here..." She lets go only when I give a little nod of understanding.

I look around the big cave at all the different creatures gathered in their various conversations. All these creatures that have worked past their differences and banded together to keep everyone of this land free, and now I have been asked to join, to be a part of something greater than myself. Somewhere I am accepted and wanted.

I look at Marissa who is mock-fighting a little boy with wooden swords and can't help but smile at the woman that is unveiling herself before my eyes. A woman that once seemed to only care about material things now also has a higher purpose. She is brave, funny and caring. I look back to Oleander who is by far the coolest person I have ever met. *This badass wants me here? Wants me as an ally? How could I say no?*

If this is the only force that is standing between The Wolf and the destruction of my home and my parents... then how could I say no? I give Oleander a big smile, beaming from within at the feeling of purpose and belonging flooding my system but before I can give her a reply a tall, pointy-eared, green fae bursts through the entrance tunnel's door screaming.

"Fire! The forest is on fire!" The green fae halts at the top of the steps and I can see the bottom of his cloak is smoking. He does a quick scan of the room, Fenrick and another man, who looks like he could be his brother but with black hair and ears instead, race up the steps to meet him. Oleander shoots up from her seat and runs up the steps as well, I follow close behind.

"It's Pyralis, he is torching the woods!" the messenger says and Oleander looks back at me for a moment with furrowed brows.

"Quick, go find Celeste! She's our only water wielder," Oleander directs Fenrick, but before he can depart the green fae man shakes his head in a panic.

"No, it's too far gone! We have to evacuate. He is searching for her!" He looks at me with a scowl as if Pyralis' temper is my fault. *I mean, he's not wrong...* The fox brothers look to each other with concern then nod before splitting up to gather everyone for an evacuation. Oleander looks at me and puts both of her hands on my shoulders.

"It's not your fault. His temper is no one's fault but his own. My mother would be mortified at the destruction. This forest is thousands of years old," she says with a crack in her voice, hanging her head. I pull her in for a hug and hear her sniffle.

"You are not him. This is not your shame to carry. You heard the guy, we have to get out of here." I pull back,

Oleander steels her expression and gives me a nod. The leader is back.

"You and Marissa gather the children and mothers and head out the northern exit. The tunnels span a ways and hopefully the fires haven't reached that far. I will get Embrys," she says, looking to the tunnel where Embrys is being held. I run down the steps to relay the orders to Marissa.

The entire cave is in a frenzy as the fae run around and gather the minimal supplies they can carry. Children cry at left behind toys and mothers with babies are only able to carry their child and nothing more. The kitchen supplies are scooped into sacks and slung over shoulders, and the last of Oleander's flames sputter out, leaving the once homely cave dark and cold. One last quick glance is all I have time for. My heart sinks at the loss of the Sylvans' home... Almost my home. *Is this all my fault?*

We all make our way out of the north tunnel in a slow, bumbling mass. Fenrick and his brother direct us into groups as the tunnels branch off so we don't all exit the same spot and alert Pyralis and his vargs to our whereabouts. There is minimal conversing as everyone's fear appears to be trumping all else. The sniffling noses of children and the cries of babies is all the sound that fills the dark tunnels as we make our escape. I've already lost sight of Marissa. I pray she will meet me when we exit into the forest, I refuse to have lost her so quickly after reuniting.

When the group I am with finally emerges through a stone door, similar to the one we had entered through, I am met with the chaos of hot flames turning the forest into a bright orange inferno. Fae and forest animals are running in all different directions. Clearly the fire has spread, my heartbreak at the pure destruction of such a beautiful haven momentarily stuns me.

How could anyone intentionally destroy this place? This is all my fault!

I snap back into focus, watching Marissa run ahead holding the hand of two small boys. I take a step to run after her, when out of nowhere, a buck jumps in front of me and I am knocked on the head with its large antlers. I hit the ground hard and everything goes hazy before my vision starts to darken. I feel something warm and wet slide down my temple before losing consciousness completely.

Chapter Fifteen

The flames scorch my back as I run through the forest, increasing in heat with every step I take. I leap over logs and fly around trees with an ease I have never felt before and when I look down I see that I have the legs of a deer.

Have I transformed? My confusion is causing me to slow my pace but, as I slow, I can hear the deep laughter of a man coming up behind me. I whirl around to see Pyralis standing there, his head crowned in fire and each hand encompassed in flame. Beside him is a man with dark brown hair, green eyes and an eerily familiar, toothy smile holding his hand out towards me.

"Nuria, come to me..." They call out simultaneously, their voices melding together into one deep, sinister growl as they slowly walk towards me.

My feet won't let me run and I look down to see flames licking up my legs. I can hear myself scream, as if I am removed from my body and I can feel the heat increasing with every second that passes. My name is being called out again but this time from somewhere far away.

"Nuria!" I wake with a gasp and sit up straight, smashing my head into Embrys'.

"Divine Mother! Ouch! Nuria, what are you doing down here? We have to go!" Embrys rubs his forehead and I rub mine before looking around to see I am still in the burning forest. Pyralis and the strange man are nowhere to be seen. Embrys grabs my hand and pulls me up then puts his hands on my shoulders and looks me over as if he is a worried mother looking for injury, turning my head and wincing as he spies the spot on my temple where I was hit.

"Are you all right?" I nod, not entirely sure if I am or not. "Can you run?" I nod again but then feel a wave of dizziness wash over me, I lean into his hands to steady myself. "Shit, no you can't," he says then places my arms around his neck and sweeps my legs off the ground and starts running, faster than is humanly possible.

I can't see any of the other fae around as we barrel through the forest but I notice the flames have grown exponentially in the time I was unconscious. They are closing in on us too quickly. Embrys banks left and I can see that he is aiming for a large waterfall in the distance that tumbles down into a small lake. I bunch my fists into his shirt and my breath quickens, the smoke nearly chokes me.

As the flames grow even higher around us Embrys runs into the lake and only slows his pace when the water rises to his thighs. He wades in further, to what should be the deepest spot but it only reaches his waist.

"I don't think this will stop the fire, Embrys! We'll boil!" I start to panic, my breaths coming in even quicker as I look around, seeing flames on all sides of the small lake and big trees falling over, blocking any hope of escape.

"Shit I know, I know, all right! There was nowhere else to go!" He holds onto me tightly, not daring to let me down, but I lower my foot enough to feel the water is already very warm which doesn't bode well for us.

"I'm sorry, Nuria," I pull back so I can scan his face. His panic is palpable and I wonder where the strong, cocky man of earlier this night has gone, when the image of his burning stepmother scars my mind. Her screams echo in my ears.

"It's not your fault," I cup his cheek and feel the muscles of his jaw tighten, his nostrils flare.

"I can't let you burn. Not like her!" A tear streaks down his cheek, and I realize who he is talking about, that I tapped into his memories just then. I lean my forehead against his in solace.

"You are not your father," I say, for the second time tonight, and can hear him let loose a sob. I lean in and kiss his cheek where the tear had fallen and my fear at the encroaching fire is momentarily put on the backburner as my heart breaks at witnessing this man unravel in front of me. He pulls back, looking a bit stunned. His gaze lowers to my mouth and my breath hitches as I think he is about to kiss me when, instead, he whips his head towards the waterfall.

"Did you hear that?" he says, turning his head and squinting his eyes at the falls. There is a thick cloud of steam rising from the lake now so it is hard to see but I look over to where he is searching and swear I can see a hand poke out from behind the waterfall and wave at us.

"Yoohooo! Over here! Quickly!" The hand pulls back into the water.

"Yup I heard ... and saw that. Come on, let's go!" I say. *Is this our salvation?*

I push out of his arms but when my feet hit the water the temperature feels nearly boiling, causing me to yelp and scramble back onto Embrys, leaving me in an awkward bear hug with my legs wrapped up over his forearms, my hands grasping his shirt and my backside hanging in the air. I am very aware of the ridiculousness of the position and Embrys raises his eyebrows and looks down to where our bodies meet. *Is he blushing?*

"Ok... just... stay there, I guess," he grunts as he carries me, wading through the scalding lake to the waterfall. As we near the roaring water the hand pops out from the edge of the falls this time and frantically waves at us so we skirt around to the side and peer in to see that there is a cave behind the falls and a little old man with a wispy beard and curly grey hair sticking out of his head standing there.

"Come now, make haste. The falls will keep the fire at bay." He scurries farther into the cave.

Embrys steps up onto a rock ledge and out of the water. I unhook my legs from his arms and slide down his torso, painfully aware of our bodies touching and my skirt riding up from the strange angle of my legs as I do so.

Blushing, I step away from him and flatten my skirts. I turn to face the old man but all I see is his back as he disappears around the corner of a tunnel. Embrys and I look at each other with matching expressions of shock then hurry after him, leaving the fire behind us.

The rock in this cave feels much cooler than the rebel's cave, I'm guessing from the water insulation above us which makes for the perfect place to hide out. The old man is surprisingly quick for someone who looks so ancient and the tunnels are dark and winding. As if reading my mind, Embrys lights a flame in his palm so we can see where we are going. It still shocks me every time a fae wields one of the elements and I forget that I too have this power within me; although, occasionally being able to read someone's thoughts doesn't feel as cool or useful as being a living flame thrower.

The old man suddenly stops dead in his tracks and laughs out loud before racing ahead once again and Embrys and I nearly topple into him and exchange looks of, *what the actual fuck,* before racing off after him again.

We make another sharp turn and then step into a large open cave that is illuminated by what appears to be glow worms. Their twinkling lights of yellow, blue and green make the space feel oddly festive, like the lights we string up around the house for Winter Solstice. The area is around half the size of the rebel camp and has an alcove with a bed, a library built into the rock wall and a kitchen space carved out as well. The floor is compacted mud with a few rugs scattered here and there. It looks just like a regular home, everything quite commonplace, except for a small cave right at the back wall that is entirely encrusted with purple shimmering crystals that draws my attention. I can't help but stare and feel like my vision is tunneling towards only that space.

My necklace is making that same humming sound from when I first put it on and I swear I can hear whispers coming from the small cave. I squint as I lean forward but am met with a hand in front of my face that snaps its fingers right in front of my nose. The glow worms all douse their lights at the snap, casting us in complete darkness, then slowly reigniting one by one.

"Do not stare at it. You are not ready." I shake my head and look down to the old man whose hand is still outstretched in front of my face. *What is this place?*

"Who are you?" Embrys chimes in, looking from the crystal cave - to me - to the old man.

"I am Gaius," he says matter-of-factly as he smooths down his long moustache with his thumb and forefinger.

"Well, thank you for saving us. I was not looking forward to being turned into a charred human... *fae* soup back there," I joke but am actually still pretty shaken up by our almost very gruesome death... Although, Embrys did not seem phased by the near boiling water. I wonder if fire wielders burn.

"Burn burn burn, not by his father's hand," Gaius sings to himself as he walks down the slope, into his cave. *Did I say my last thought out loud? This guy is a nutter.*

As he enters the space a rabbit hops out to greet him followed by a waddling beaver and some small birds that come flitting down from the ceiling to land on his shoulders and head. From the back of the cave a doe and her fawn come striding out of a tunnel I did not notice before, straight to Gaius, cautiously observing Embrys and I.

"Ah, my furred companions, we have company!" Gaius bends down to scoop up the rabbit and gives the beaver a little pat on the head. "They sought refuge from the inferno, just as you have," he says, giving the bunny a little scratch behind the ears before placing it back down on the floor. Many more creatures start popping their heads out from behind the furniture. There is even a large, grey, lone wolf who lifts its head up over the back of the sofa and glares at us. I don't dare take my eyes off of it as I am unsure if this is a Metamorph or an animal. Either way, my relationship with wolves is not very trusting.

"She will not harm you. She has vowed to keep her fangs to herself while she seeks sanctuary." Gaius must have seen my wary glance.

"Wait a second, how would you know what her intentions are?" I know the fae have certain lesser magics but I wasn't aware talking to animals was one of them. "Can you speak to animals?" I turn to Embrys who just raises his eyebrows and shakes his head, which is now the chosen seat of a fluffy chickadee that looks very content pecking at his thick hair, and wrapping it around itself to create the beginnings of a nest.

"The fire's heat should abate within a few days' time.

You may remain here while you await its passing." Gaius ignores my question and waves us toward the tunnel that the deer had entered from.

"A few days?!" I look at Embrys with raised eyebrows, "we can't stay a few days! We have to find where everyone else went... if they are ok." Gaius just shakes his head before disappearing around the corner, into the tunnel. We follow him, watching our footing so as to not step on one of the multitude of small forest creatures skittering around.

"Embrys, I can't just stay here. We have to go find Marissa and Oleander," I plead, he just pushes a breath out of his lips and shrugs.

"I'm sorry, Nuria. Gaius is right. It won't be safe for a few days. We are lucky to have found him. Oleander can hold her own in a fire and I believe the rebels have a water wielder or two. They will be safe," he says and we stop behind Gaius at the doorway to a small room.

"I have this chamber which I trust shall prove sufficient for your stay. I am not accustomed to entertaining guests, save for those that are of fur and feather." He waves out two foxes that were curled on the bed in the small space.

I am keenly aware that there is only one bed in this room and pretty much zero floor space. I blush as I catch Embrys' questioning eye.

"There is a bathing chamber at the end of this tunnel. Perhaps the waters will even be warmed by the fires outside." Gaius taps his fingertips together, grinning under his bushy moustache.

"Well, I am not sure about you, but I am exhausted.

Thank you Gaius for your hospitality." Embrys nods to him and Gaius looks between us, waggling his eyebrows, before scurrying back down the tunnel.

"Um... maybe you can go sleep on the sofa or something?" I suggest, watching as Embrys enters the room and takes his cloak off whilst kicking off his boots. He jumps onto the bed.

"Not a chance. Besides, there would be no room out there with Gaius' horde. I do not sleep in barns. Nor do I sleep with animals." He sits up, raising an eyebrow while giving me his vexing half smile.

He starts to unbutton his tunic, popping one button open at a time without breaking eye contact, as if he knows it will catch my attention. I just roll my eyes and head towards the bathing chamber. I am truly exhausted from this never ending night as well but a cold bath feels like a smarter option than jumping straight into bed with the guy I have been sharing visions with practically my whole life. After what Oleander shared about his past and our near kiss moments ago, I'm not sure how I truly feel but what I *do* feel, is my restraint faltering.

The bathing chamber is steaming from the heat of the fire, as Gaius predicted, and it takes me a moment to be able to see my surroundings. There is a dark central pool that looks big enough to fit ten people with a little creek running into one end and exiting the other, constantly circulating the water. There are a few rock ledges around the room that house little colonies of only the yellow glow worms, giving the space a nice warm radiance.

I take a quick glance behind me to see if anyone has followed and when I feel I am truly alone I peel off my smoky clothes. I know I will have to put these back on but at least I can wash the grime and soot off my skin.

I dip my toe in to make sure it isn't boiling and I am met with the perfect bath temperature that contrasts the cool air and rock of the cave. It sends a delightful shiver up my spine as I slide all the way into the waters. The moan that escapes my lips is entirely involuntary as the warmth covers my shoulders and immediately relaxes the tension I had been holding on to.

I give my face a little scrub and notice the crusted blood from where I got hit, washing off in a deep red slurry that is whisked away in the gentle current. *Surely I have some sort of brain damage from all the times I've been hit on the head since being here.* I give my sore temple a gentle rub prodding to see how large the cut is but I find none. *Huh, super speedy healing, this whole fae thing is cool.*

I close my eyes and lean back against the cool rock, sinking down so just my head is out of the water and I start to drift off, the exhaustion fully taking hold of me now.

I feel like I am falling and open my eyes to see shimmering purple crystals surrounding me. I am floating, mid-air, in a cave covered in them, with sharp little points glistening on all surfaces. I can hear voices whispering but they are so faint and overlapping that I cannot make out what is being said. A few sound as if they have an urgency to them though, I lean in to better hear.

"What are you saying?" I call out, thrashing my arms and

legs around, trying to find something to grab onto to get me out of this suspension, but the walls of the cave seem to be expanding out of my reach whenever I get near them.

"Help!" a voice comes in clearly and I swear it sounds like Oleander.

"Where are you?" I call back, looking around at the crystals but only seeing hundreds of my own reflections looking back.

"They think it was me! We are surrounded... Quick, hide!" I hear her call out again but this time sounding much further away.

"Wait! Who is surrounding you? How do I find you?" I thrash around but the connection goes silent.

"Nuria.... Nuria!" I can hear a different voice calling to me now and the walls start to shake as if an earthquake is ripping through the cave.

"Nuria!" Embrys' deep voice rumbles. I flick open my eyes to see him in front of me in the pool, shaking my shoulders."Thank The Mother! Nuria, you must have been dreaming. When I came in you were under the water." He leaves his hands on my shoulders as if he thinks I will sink under again, I can feel the calluses in his strong grip rub against my bare skin. I notice he is fully clothed and look down, remembering that I am not, and wrap my arms around my breasts.

"I'm ok," I wriggle out of his grasp and sink a bit lower until my chin is resting just on top of the water. "I was in the purple crystal cave. Except it was massive and I was floating and there were voices..." I stare blankly at Embrys' torso as I recall the strange dream. He sinks down so our heads are on the same level and our eyes meet. "Wait... why were you in here in the first place?" I raise an eyebrow at his intrusion.

"Would you believe me if I said I was just worried about you being gone so long?" he chuckles and takes a small step closer to me, giving me a teasing smile that doesn't meet his serious eyes. "There is something about this place that feels strange; a certain power hums in the walls. My fire feels wilder here... I did not wish to leave you alone..." He steps up even closer and I can feel the added heat of his body through the minimal water that separates us.

"Playing the protector instead of captor now, are we? Kind of cliché don't you think?" I joke but I think back to the way he stepped up for Oleander when they were children and realize it is probably just in his nature, and I kind of like it. *Is that so wrong?*

He blows out a breath as he sweeps a wet hand through his tousled hair, the motion does wonders for showing off his muscled arm.

Is he putting the moves on me? I am acutely aware of our proximity and have that awkward feeling of not knowing what to do with my face and hands again so I try and play it cool by leaning my elbows on the rock ledge behind me but, in doing so, I nearly expose myself, so I quickly drop my arms again, splashing us both. He chuckles and wipes his face with his hand but his expression goes from playful to serious in a second.

"I never wanted you to be our prisoner. I had been waiting my whole life for the woman I have been sharing visions with to appear, and when you finally did... I failed you. Just like I did with Oleander. I do not agree with how my father handled the situation and I am trying to remedy that. We wanted to keep you safe but all we have done is push you away. I am here now, for you and for my sister. I will protect you both, Nuria." I feel he is being earnest but it is hard to concentrate when the way he says my name makes my toes curl. I want this, whatever it is. I want to be close to him, it may just be a welcome distraction from everything but I don't care.

I take a chance between us, feeling courage bolstering my actions as I stand, allowing my breasts to breach the surface. His eyes can't help but dart down, lingering for a moment on my necklace, before meeting my gaze once again with irises full of flame. A cloud of steam rises from the water, momentarily shrouding him from my view but in the next moment he is standing right in front of me, looking down and dripping cool water on my chest from the tips of his hair.

He lifts his hand to touch my face but hesitates, his brows knit together and he goes to pull back, as if second guessing himself, so I reach out my hand and place it on his chest. We do not break eye contact as I peel off his soaked shirt, he lowers his hand to help with the other arm.

Damn, he is chiseled in all the right places. My gaze trails down to the lines near his hips that angle down into the water, hiding what I can feel my body pull towards. He has a large scar on his left peck that I trace with my fingers before looking back up to him with questioning eyes.

"My father," is all he says in explanation before taking my hand in his and kissing my palm before placing it around his neck. My breath hitches at the delicate brush of his lips on my hand, an unexpected tenderness from this man of fire. He trails his hands down the side of my body with a feather light touch that makes me shiver before landing at my hips, all the while holding eye contact.

Shit, that's hot. Benji was always so bothered by eye contact which made what we did feel wrong, but I won't lie when I say that *this* amount of eye gazing is a little bit intimidating. I break, looking down to his chest and swallow, hoping he doesn't see my insecurity. *Are we really doing this?*

He leaves one hand on my hip, firmly holding me in place, as his other hand trails back up my spine, before gently grabbing the hair at the nape of my neck to tilt my head up to him, making me meet his eyes once again. The cool, wet strands of his hair brush my cheek as he leans in, his lips just barely brushing against mine. I close my eyes, waiting.

"We've been here before and you denied me. What do you want, Nuria?" He pulls away just a fraction.

I open my eyes to see the flames in his irises burning bright and hot, pleading for my permission, but my words and breath are lost to me at such close contact so I grab onto the back of his neck and pull him down into a burning kiss, answering his plea.

It is a hard, greedy kiss that leaves me feeling engulfed in his flame. He tightens his grip on my hip and pulls me even closer and I lose all control, twining my hands through his thick locks, pulling him down for more. Our tongues meet in a searching flicker and I gasp at the ecstasy such a small movement can send through my body, careening down my spine and settling low in my belly. I can feel him through his trousers but his height has his need pushing into my stomach instead of the spot where I want him most.

As if reading my desires, he hitches my legs around his waist and backs me up against the pool's edge, giving me the most tantalizing pressure.

"Embrys," his name escapes my lips, sounding like a prayer.

I slide my hand down his chest, then abs, making my way to his trousers and fumbling for his belt but he grabs my wrist and pulls away from our kiss.

"Not so fast," he growls, restraining us both. His skin feels almost painfully hot to touch. I am so used to how Benji used to make love to me, hard and fast, taking it slow does not come naturally.

He unhooks my feet from his back and places my legs back down, hiding my sex below the water. He leans in to kiss me again, but this time much more tenderly, taking his time, as if committing the shape of my mouth to memory. I nip at his bottom lip trying to coax him back into the all-encompassing fire we had from before, he growls again and rests his forehead on mine, gripping my hips, steadying himself. I've never been thankful for my curves before but the way he grabs hold of me makes me see the soft, sensuality of my body in a new light.

"Patience, Nuria." I pull away to look in his eyes and give

a little nod, panting a bit from my longing but trying to be good and show restraint like he is.

"You won't burn me. I trust you."

His gaze ignites. I can feel a tight knot of energy form between my legs that craves release and whimper as he reads my desire again, giving me his knowing half smile.

He slowly trails his hand down the outside of my thigh then torturously brings his fingers back up the inside, making slow, tantalizing circles, until he faintly brushes me where I need him the most. I gasp at the contact and he growls in response, sinking his teeth into my neck as he sweeps his fingers back and forth over my sensitive spot, causing me to cry out at the immense pleasure and contrasting pain.

I bunch my hands in his hair and can't help my hips from moving in rhythm with his skillful fingers, *just as I had dreamed they would be.*

He nips his way up my neck, giving my earlobe a little bite before bringing our lips together again in a fiery kiss that burns deliciously. Our tongues intertwine and he swallows my moans as he brings me to my climax, holding me tightly against his chest as I cascade over in shivering glory. I break our kiss to cry out at the culminating wave, and take a few deep breaths before opening my eyes. I feel as though the breath has been stolen out of my lungs as I gasp in the thick, steamy air.

When my vision clears I look over his shoulder and am immediately pulled out of my bubble of ecstasy when I notice three brown ducks floating in the water, looking right at us. I burst out laughing at the absurdity and the duck in the middle quacks in response, which in my mind, sounded as if it was saying, *awkward...*

Embrys releases me and whirls around which scares the ducks, causing them to flap away into the tunnel, spraying us as they go.

"Divine Mother!" Embrys shouts, blocking the spray with his arms.

We look at each other and both burst out laughing. Embrys grabs my hand and pulls me back into his arms, looking down at me with an ear to ear grin. I feel all glowy and warm, basking in the light of his smile.

"Will you join me in our bed?" he asks and my heart stutters at the implication of *our* anything. I can feel my pupils dilate and my pulse quicken again at the suggestion. "We should probably just sleep, Nuria," he chuckles as he leans in to give me a kiss on the cheek.

Who could sleep after that? I blow a breath through my lips at the suggestion as he steps out of the pool in his soaking clothes and grabs my dress for me, holding it out so I can step out as well.

"How are you going to dry yourself?" I question as I step up and grab my dress to hide my nakedness, even though we just shared such intimacy, I still feel shy.

"Fire wielder, remember." He opens both palms and steam raises off of him in a sudden cloudburst and he is left with completely dry looking clothes.

"Huh, cool trick," I say as I lift my chin and walk past him, still holding the dress just against my front and very aware of his perfect view of what I know is a great asset as I walk down the tunnel. *Yes, I'm definitely starting to love my curves.*

I look over my shoulder to see his eyes widen as he stands in shock with his palms both still open before shaking his head and quickly following me back to our room, his heat dries my hair as we go.

When I turn to enter our room I stop dead in my tracks, locking eyes with the grey wolf who is now lounging on our bed. Embrys bumps into me from behind and places his hand on both of my shoulders to steady us from toppling onto the ground.

"Oh, hello," Embrys says casually to the wolf as if it is his pal. I can feel myself start to tremble at the memories of the wolf headed man in my visions. "Nuria you're shaking, let me grab you a blanket," he says and goes to step around me but I grab his hand to urge him to stay put.

"What's wrong?" I can feel him looking at me but I don't dare remove my eyes from the wolf. She yawns; baring her teeth to us then lets out a big sigh before jumping off the bed and sauntering out of the room, brushing my leg with her fur as she goes.

When she is gone I let out the breath I was holding and let my shoulders slump forward.

"Wolves. I don't trust wolves," I say and the memory of the vision I had back in the human realm of The Wolf King sitting on his throne flashes in my mind. Then I remember whose eyes I was seeing through in the first place and whirl around to face Embrys, "you know The King. You've spoken to him recently in the Palace!" I accuse as I back away from him. He puts his hands up and takes a tentative step towards me.

"I am his subject, yes. He called upon me to give reports on the climate events within our lands." He takes another step closer and I shake my head in warning but I am now against the wall so he has control over coming closer or not. He stays put.

"Nuria, I am not a part of his plotting. Please believe me, I can keep you safe." He drops his hands and gives me a pleading look. "Come, let's go to bed. It has been a long night." He reaches out his hand and I choose to trust him and let him lead me onto the bed.

He is so gentle as he tucks me under the covers, the tender action shocks me and leaves me feeling a strange vulnerability at the tenderness he is showing. He gives me a little smile as he stands and goes to leave the room.

"Wait, where are you going?" I call to him, all tucked in with just my head sticking out of the blankets.

"I'll stand guard. There does not appear to be a door to this room and I want you to be able to sleep." He shrugs, walking out into the tunnel. He slides down to sit on the floor and leans on the rock wall beside the door.

"If you really need to fulfil this 'protector' role, you know you can do it beside me... in bed. I won't bite, I swear," I say, trying to keep the mood light. Judging by the heavy sigh I hear, followed by silence, I gather that he isn't buying it.

After a few minutes of waiting awkwardly, thinking he is

ignoring my last comment, he says "I... I can't share a bed with you..."

"Oh. That's fine." *I didn't want you to anyway.* The sting of rejection hurts more than I'd like to admit. I thought he wanted me... in that way.

"I mean... I just can't. I'm sorry," his voice is quiet, withdrawn.

"Why? You can talk to me..." He goes silent for a long while. "Is it me, or..."

"No Nuria, I want to be with you. I just... I fear anyone I share a bed with will end up like *her*. I fear I will do... what my father did." *Oh shit, he thinks he will burn me? Is that why he kept us from going further?* I have to tread carefully here.

"Have you ever slept with anyone before?" I never would have expected this cocky man with a protector complex and insanely skillful fingers to be a virgin.

I hear his sigh. "No. I've been intimate but never... to the full extent. I couldn't put anyone at risk..." *Ok... ok, ok that's all right, I can work with this...*

"Embrys, I've said it once before and I will say it again, you are not your father. His power *is* something to be afraid of because his emotions run rampant and he uses his fire to harm others and gain control, but you aren't him! Do you wish to harm and control others?"

"No, never... but Nuria, my powers..." he cuts himself off.

"Your powers, what? I've only seen you create a flame for light and to dry your clothes. You're harmless, Embrys!" I so badly want to get up and hold him. This man that I saw as so strong, is scared – of himself.

"I'm not harmless, Nuria! My powers are greater than my father's. They started surpassing his when I was a teen. I tried to hide it but The King himself was even growing suspicious of my abilities. He would have seen me as a threat had my father not taken control of the House." He blows out a breath. "I'm dangerous. We shouldn't do... what we did, again. It isn't safe. *I'm* not safe." His last words are barely more than a whisper. *All right, that's it.* I wrap the blanket around my shoulders and roll out of bed.

"I'm not afraid of you." I slide down the wall, beside him, "look at me." He lifts his hanged head to peer at me through his hair. It's all ruffled, as if he had been running his hands through it.

"You should be, Nuria. I'm not even sure if the feelings we have for each other are real or if we were somehow tethered together. You shouldn't waste your time on me. You know what I did to my sister. For Mother's sake, I nearly burned your hands off with the handcuffs in the caves, remember? Why do you care about me?" His eyes darken, not even the slightest flicker of an ember within them. *I did forget about the handcuff thing...*

"I don't know if we were somehow connected by *my* mother or *The* Mother, but what I do know is that you *do* care about your sister. You also care about and fight for your people and *that* is what I respect. Let's just take whatever this is one step at a time. You don't have to hop into bed with me but don't let your fear of harming me be what stops you. Having power of any kind is a new concept to me but from what little I have seen, even *I* know that who you are, deep down, governs how your powers show up. You protect. Your father controls. It's as simple as that." I grab onto his hand and give it a squeeze. The faintest flicker reignites in his eyes. *A good start.*

To my surprise, he leans in and brushes a soft kiss on my forehead. "Thank you," he says, still from that quiet place within himself. I blow out a breath and give him my best interpretation of his cocky half smile.

"Now mister brave protector, would you please guard my door. There is a big bad wolf out there and I am in need of your services." I manage to get a chuckle out of him as he nods. I shuffle back to the bed and nestle in.

Part of me craves his closeness but I don't want to push him. This is enough. I probably wouldn't sleep if he was next to me anyway if I am honest with myself. The intimacy of sleeping next to a lover seems too daunting right now and with that wolf lurking out there it is nice to have him guarding me instead.

Wow Nuria, such a damsel in distress, I cringe at my acceptance of protection but I know this is what he is able to give, so I accept it. I suppose I don't *always* have to be my own knight in shining armour.

I throw one of the pillows out the door and get a grunt of thanks in response before I nestle down in the surprisingly comfortable bed.

Chapter Sixteen

I am back in the crystal cave but this time I am standing firmly on the ground, feeling the sharp points of the crystals prickling my bare feet. The cave spans double my arm's reach and twice my height. The colour of the crystals are fading and darkening in a constant wave going from nearly white to the deepest purple. The swirling colours hypnotize me, pulling me in. I shake my head to break the trance I am being lulled into and frantically look around for an exit, but find none.

What am I doing here? I try to take a step but my feet are stuck in place.

"It was not me! What is your proof? Unhand me!" I hear the same voice from my dream earlier calling out. She sounds as if she is struggling.

"Oleander? Is that you?" I call out but receive no response. I whip my head around, searching the crystals but all that I can see are hundreds of my own reflections looking back, so I close my eyes and listen.

I don't know how to explain it, but I can *feel* her presence in the crystals in front of my feet so I crouch down to touch them. When my fingers brush the point of the largest crystal within reach my fingers start to get sucked down, down, down into the ground. I try to pull back but next my arm is yanked under, then all of me.

My head pounds as I feel I am being squeezed into a too tight space, a loud pop sounds in my ear as I come out the other end of the floor, straight into a freefall. My stomach sinks as I plummet through a tunnel that is also coated in the sharp crystals, their colours flashing rapidly. I keep my arms hugged close to my body for fear of scraping up against them. The ground is approaching too quickly and I know if I reach out my arms to slow my fall I will rip them to shreds on the crystal's knife-like edges. My heart is pounding in my ears, all I can do is flinch and scrunch my eyes shut in anticipation of impact.

Instead, I am somehow righted and land flat on my feet in a bone-rattling thud and open my eyes to see that I am standing in a field, surrounded by people on large white horses and vargs. The sun appears to have just risen as the sky is all pink and deep purple and the air feels crisp.

There are two vargs grabbing both of my arms in painfully tight grips, snarling at me with dripping fangs. I look behind me and see the charred forest behind us and the damage is catastrophic. The thick smell of burnt wood shoves up my nose, nearly choking me.

Where am I? I feel a lump rise in my throat and tears sting my eyes at the sight of the destruction. *Did the animals manage to escape? Did the rebels get Marissa out?* I can feel rage ripple through my body. *The fae are just as bad as the humans. They don't care about nature, all they care about is power!* The tears are now pouring from my eyes in an uncontrollable river.

I turn back around and look down at my body and see red curly hair dangling down from my head and realize I must be seeing through Oleander's eyes. *I'm dreaming, I'm dreaming, I'm dreaming...*

Fenrick, the grey haired fox Metamorph, is lying face down in the dirt at the feet of the horses. Blood is pooling underneath him and I feel a sob bubble up my throat at the realization of what that amount of blood means. I try to yank away from the vargs but my struggle is fruitless. They have me, or Oleander, well and truly captured. Pure panic seizes my body, coiling around my guts like a boa constrictor and a need to escape from being so near to the lifeless body of a man I had just met, not even twenty four hours ago, causes my breath to come in heaves and my hands to start shaking. *Is this real? Please don't be real!*

"By the order of The King, you are under arrest for the destruction of the Heartwood Forest. There are eyewitnesses from the Pyralis estate that validate the claims. We are taking you back to the Palace to await your trial." An uppity looking fae reads from a scroll atop his white steed, looking down at me with distaste.

"Who? Who is this eye witness? It was my father, not I,

let me go!" Oleander's voice comes tumbling out of my mouth as I struggle in the varg's grip again. A fresh stream of tears slide down my cheeks and Oleander's rage sears me deep within my chest, like the white-hot fire that it is.

"Save it for the trial." The fae waves his hand, shooing us away like flies, signalling the vargs to place shackles on my – her – wrists. I look behind me one more time in a desperate attempt at escape before getting roped to one of the horses and yanked along behind them. Marissa pokes her head out from behind a boulder and I – Oleander – shakes her head, signalling for Marissa to stay put. *Safe... she's safe.*

One moment I am looking down as we pass lifeless Fenrick and start to shake as sobs take over my body, the next moment, I open my eyes and am sobbing and gasping in my bed, back in Gaius' cave.

"What? What happened?" Embrys startles from his sleep at the door and comes rushing over to me, wiping the sleep from his eyes as he stumbles to my bedside. I touch my face and feel the tears that had been freely flowing during my vision and shudder at the memory of seeing Fenrick's body in the dirt.

"They... they killed Fenrick. And they took Oleander!" I rip the blankets away and go to get up off the bed, as if I can somehow run and save her right now.

"Wait, wait, Nuria! Who has Oleander? What do you mean? How could you know?" Embrys grabs my arms and sits me back down, kneeling in front of me with confusion knitting his brows together. I take a breath and notice I am completely naked and wrap the blanket back around my shoulders.

"It was like the visions we shared, except I don't think she knew I was there. I dreamt I was in the crystal cave again and it transported me into her body!" I know I sound crazy, but Embrys was right about this place. There is strange magic here and I think I have been unwittingly tapping into it.

"The King's men *arrested* Oleander. They are blaming her for the fires. We have to do something!" I grab on to his forearms and give him a little shake. He drops his hands to slide the blanket back up over my shoulders then sits back on his heels, blowing a breath through pursed lips.

"My bloody father put the blame on her. I know it! " he curses through clenched teeth, bunching his fists in his lap. The flames in his eyes are wilder than the ones I saw last night and I can feel the same rage that I felt within Oleander emanating off of him. "How could he?" His shoulders slump forward as he hangs his head, his hair shields his face from me. I slide down onto the floor until our knees are touching and lift his chin so our eyes can meet.

"What are we going to do about it, Embrys?" I say, gripping his chin a bit harder. I need the man that gets shit done right now, not the unraveling one. His eyes widen and I can see a little mischief glimmer in his pupils that I am guessing is the result of the tone that I am sure no one has dared to take with him before. His expression crumples a second later.

"Nuria, we are stuck here for a few days. It is too

dangerous out there for you." He opens his palms in his lap in exasperated defeat. Then I remember what Gaius had said about his father's flames not being able to burn him, he truly did seem undisturbed by the near boiling lake.

"No... *I* am stuck here. *You* are not. You won't be harmed by these flames. Embrys, you must go after her!" I plead and he pauses to chew on his thumb nail and stare at the floor. "Embrys!" I shout and give him a shove.

"I'm thinking, I'm thinking!" He puts his hands up. "I cannot just barge into the Palace demanding my sister be returned, Nuria. I have to play this smart. The Wolf is an extremely cunning man and at this point he believes me to be loyal to him," Embrys explains.

His eyes dart down for a moment, noticing my nakedness, so I reach back to grab the blanket that I left on the bed. *No distractions!* I look him in the eye to send my thoughts barreling down our connection. His eyes blink twice before he nods and clears his throat.

"I will have to return to the estate. I will say I had been searching for you but did not locate your whereabouts. My father most likely found out where you were from the direction the horses came from so I will have to lie about losing my horse as well." He resumes biting his nail as he thinks the plan through.

"But how will you save her?" I question, he takes another moment in thought before replying.

"I will find out what I can from my father then I will return to you in a few days. We will find the rest of the rebels together to formulate a plan. One does not just simply storm into the Palace. We will need the numbers and the combined magics of the rebels. We must also find some excuse for entry. Leave it to me," he says.

I nod and grab his hand to give it a little reassuring squeeze. "Will you be all right here Nuria? I don't want to leave you if you feel unsafe." He squeezes my hand back.

"You must, for Oleander. I will be fine with the old man. Don't worry about me," I say, giving him a playful little shove but I feel more than a little apprehensive about being left in this strange place, with this strange magic.

"If you run into Mar on your way to the estate can you let her know I am all right?" I ask and he nods, his eyes seem to have a new set determination to them which makes my heart flutter. *Damn, he is beautiful. This... this is what draws me in.*

"I should depart as soon as I can. My father will be suspicious if I am away much longer." He grabs my other hand and looks down at my mouth for a split second. *Is he going to kiss me goodbye? Are we people who kiss goodbye now?* I think I accidentally still have the channel of our thoughts open from before because he chuckles before leaning in to kiss me.

I let myself soften into it and bring my hands up to his neck as he places his hands down on my legs and leans in. *Oh wow, this feels good.* Before we can really get into it he pulls away and gives me a swift peck on the forehead before standing and heading for the door, wrapping his cloak back around his shoulders and sliding on his boots as he goes. "Stay safe," is all he says and gives me a wink before disappearing around the corner.

I am left, kneeling on the floor, staring out the doorway, feeling the tingle of where our lips met and immediately feel his absence. *How can I miss someone so much already?* I shake my head and get up to dress myself, wondering what my days of waiting will look like, already impatient for his return. Impatient to get out of here and find Oleander. I need a distraction or I will go crazy.

Perhaps Gaius needs help with the animals. I know enough about animal care from my summer at the Easthelm Wildlife Rescue that I could be of some use. I also think of the mess so many creatures would leave in a confined space for multiple days and shudder at the memories of cleaning the enclosures at the rescue centre. *It's for the good of the animals...*

When I am done tying up my dress and pulling on my boots I turn around and am met with the grey wolf, standing in my doorway, staring at me. I freeze and suck in a breath. *Shit...shit shit shit.*

Calm yourself. I stick by my vows to Gaius, I hear a feminine voice roll through my mind. My eyes widen and I blow out a breath I had been holding.

"How can I hear you? Am I still dreaming?" I pinch myself hard but am just left with an angry red mark while I am indeed still standing in front of the wolf.

Do not be senseless. Where has the large one gone? She shakes her head causing the dense fur around her neck to swish side to side. Understanding dawns on me as I register that I am able to hear her thoughts because she brushed up against me last night. My eyes widen at the implication of being able to read the thoughts of an animal.

"Gaius can hear your thoughts too!" I say, she just huffs a sigh and trots away. "Wait!" I call after her, running out of the room and down the tunnel that leads back to Gaius' space. I *will* get some answers!

I come careening around the corner, nearly tumbling into a doe, and have to grab the wall of the tunnel to stop myself. She lets out a little yelp in response and jumps out of my way, prancing across to the other side of the cave, her bambi following close behind, eyeing me warily.

"Sorry!" I whisper-yell as they retreat, so as to not scare anymore of the creatures. I scan the room for the wolf and see she is back on the sofa, her spot, and is glaring at me.

Be quiet, clumsy fae. Gaius is in trance. I hear her say as she tips her head in the direction of the crystal cave.

Gaius is floating, cross-legged in the centre of the small cave and appears to be humming to himself. *What in the actual* – His eyes snap open and he plops down onto his butt, his hair stays floating above his head for a split second before getting the memo about gravity and springing back into place.

"Oh, you have awoken," he says as he nimbly uncrosses his legs and hops out of the cave. He walks right up to me, leaning his face close to mine while squinting and scrunching his eyebrows together. "You have been in the crystals. I warned you, you were not ready!" he accuses, pointing his boney finger at me.

"I had no control over that! I was dreaming. Also, why

did you not tell me that you are an Etherealist?" I counter, pointing my finger back in his face.

He makes a *harrumph* sound and waves his hands by his head. "You never asked!" he chuckles. "The crystals came to you in a dream, you say? Hmm we will have to remedy this." He chews on his top lip, surely getting a mouth full of moustache as he regards me. I try to ask him how we would remedy that when he interrupts, "I see the fire wielder's son has departed. Good good." He seems to be speaking to himself but raises an eyebrow at me.

"How did you know Embrys is the son of the man who started the fires?" I ask, raising my eyebrow back at him and placing both my hands on my hips.

"I know a great many things, child." He turns and motions to the crystal cave. "I have not heard the term Etherealist in a long while, but I suppose you may claim me to be of the House of Ether. Others know me as a Mind Walker." He spins around and walks over to the sofa, plopping himself down next to the wolf.

I give her a wary glance, still not entirely trusting and she huffs, rolling her eyes, as she jumps down, making space for me to sit next to Gaius. I tentatively walk over and sit at the edge of the sofa, taking as much space as possible between me and the old man.

"I was told the House of Ether had been wiped out since the reign of The Wolf King, something about their allegiance to the late King?" I ask, looking at this man in a new light as I realize that I may be related to him. A bit of hope glimmers in my cracked heart.

"I absconded from my duties to the rulers of this continent long before The Owl even ascended to the throne. You
see, my talents were not particularly well suited to aiding the
royal line." He shrugs and I look around at his cave.

"You mean you've been *here* for hundreds of years? How
old are you?" The thought of how long a fae life could be is a
daunting thing.

"Most do not live to this age. I have been sustained by
my work with the crystals. I wandered for a great many years
after leaving my duties, before stumbling upon this cave.
This forest called to me and told me of its lore and its need
for help. In exchange for my protection of the animals, she
gifted me access to her magic." His eyes sparkle at the
memory. A bunny hops up into his lap and nestles in.

"What do you mean by '*leaving your duties*'?" I ask and
another bunny jumps up onto the couch and sniffs in my
direction, twitching its little nose, before deciding I am safe
and jumping into my lap; I flinch and keep my hands far
away from its mouth, remembering the blood thirsty bunny
from the Tanglewood Forest.

"This is not the kind you fear. The Tanglewoods have
their own special breed," Gaius chuckles and I visibly relax. I
give the bunny a tentative stroke then decide it is just a cute,
harmless thing that isn't vying for my blood. Gaius shakes
his head and continues on answering my questions.

"We are the advisers, my child. We see and understand
the weaving of all things." He waves a hand in front of his
face as if he is seeing and feeling the very same threads he
speaks of.

"The Divine Mother bestowed upon us the charge to guide the other fae and creatures in their actions of creation and destruction. She cultivated within us a deep longing to serve others and to act with unwavering justice!" He clenches his fist in the air, "otherwise our abilities would have been far too powerful. Although, there have been a few dark wielders in our land's history but they burn themselves out rather quickly." He seems to be lost in thought as he looks to the crystals and chews on his moustache again.

Is this why I am the way I am? Why I felt so at odds with those I grew up around?

"What are your *talents*? Why could you not be of use?" He seems to remember I am beside him with a little start.

"Oh, I get a bit lost deary. The animals draw me back to myself but if I tarry too long in the labyrinth of human and fae thought... well I am utterly lost. I served as an adviser in the Palace when Edmund, The Owl, was but a lad and... well suffice to say that I was not the most comforting fae to have in company. I could not direct my mind-walking and would find myself in the head of some far away creature and would forget who I was entirely. I was told I would be found walking the halls of the Palace talking to myself quite often. Not all of those from the House of Ether have the same abilities or control. We are quite a diverse bunch. Or... *were* I suppose." He frowns as he looks down to his lap, which now houses three bunnies and one chipmunk.

I am relieved that not all Etherealists turn out like Gaius but I wonder what that means about my own abilities. I know I can occasionally read and transfer thoughts and the visions or *mind walking,* seem to have been limited to just Embrys until last night. It doesn't feel like what I am able to do is of much use at this point. *What was my mother able to do?*

"I know you left far before her time but… would you know of my mother, Inanna?" A sliver of hope shines through my eyes but his small shrug and shake of the head quickly douses it. His face does a strange scrunched up thing, his expression slowly changes as he widens his eyes.

"Wait, I do recall in my wanderings The Owl lamenting for one he called Ina. *His* Ina. She had been stolen from him."

Did he say his Ina? *Could it be the same person?* He reaches out to touch me and I have an initial instinct to pull away but something deeper within yells at me to let him. As his old calloused hand brushes my cheek he gasps and his eyes roll back in his head.

"What? What do you see?" I grab his hand in mine and give it a squeeze. *Oh shit, is he getting lost?* I look around the room to the animals that are quickly gathering and make eye contact with the wolf as she pushes her way through.

He is traveling, we must wait, she reassures me and I look back to Gaius, seeing his eyes slowly roll back down and blink at me in confusion.

"Gaius, are you all right? What did you see?"

"Oh Ina, hello." He smiles and pats my hand.

"I'm not Ina, I'm Nuria. Gaius, did you see my mother? Are you able to see into the past?"

"The past… Was I in the past?" He looks around at the

animals surrounding us and nods his head as if he is listening to them speak. "Yes, I must go back into the crystals. Forgive me deary, I lost myself for a moment. Now I must go find what I lost." He gives me a blank stare and a little, dopey smile as he slowly gets up and shuffles back into the crystal cave.

Great, he really is a nutter. Was he talking to my mother? I wash my face in my hands. These past few days have been too much. This massive question mark that has been looming over my head for my whole childhood is being dissolved too rapidly and yet, not rapidly enough. My brain needs a moment to catch up, to understand. It feels as though there is a missing piece to my past that is so close to being slotted into place but I still feel lost and confused.

The connection I have with Embrys feels old and right, which confuses the crap out of me. He said he had been waiting for me, as if he knew I would come. I should have asked him more about his time with my mother and what could have possibly created this mental bond between us. We very well may have been tethered together against our wills.

Is that an ability of the House of Ether? Did she have unique gifts? Gaius mentioned not all Etherealists... or Mind Walkers, have the same abilities. Perhaps my mother was stronger at creating ties between people. I both want more answers, and for all the answers to stop to allow my head to stop spinning.

I guess my expression has my inner turmoil written all over it because when I look back around, the animals have inched closer to me. A fox has settled over my feet and the doe from earlier is resting her chin on the back of the sofa, near my shoulder. Several birds line the sofa's back and I can see the three ducks from last night waddling towards me from the kitchen, followed by a raccoon that appears to be holding a steaming cup of tea.

"For me? Why, thank you," I laugh, reaching out to grab the mug. The sweet and caring nature of these creatures brings tears to my eyes, tears that have been readily falling more and more these past few days.

"I'm all right, I swear. I haven't lost the plot, like a certain someone." I point my thumb towards where Gaius is now napping in the crystal cave and give the animals a wink. His snores rumble through the space and seem to accentuate my claim. The creatures chitter in response; *At least someone appreciates my jokes.* It may be possible that I am lying to myself. *Am I actually all right?*

With not much else to do but ponder the meaning of my life, I decide instead to enjoy my cup of tea and thoughtlessly stroke the bunny that is still nestled in my lap. *I am stuck here until Embrys returns. I need to do something... something...* I shake my head feeling lost once again but the rumbling of my stomach takes over my thoughts and I remember I haven't eaten in probably twenty-four hours. I gently plop the bunny off my lap and head to the kitchen, noticing some fresh duck eggs calling my name. *Breakfast is something I can do.*

Chapter Seventeen

I am lounging on the sofa, scarfing down my eggs and flipping through a book I found on some lore about The Divine Mother as I wait for Gaius, who is still snoring loudly in the crystal cave. It's a beautiful ancient looking tome bound in dark leather with golden embossed lettering. It feels like perhaps I should not be holding it with my grubby hands but I cannot resist, the curiosity pulls me in.

The book is written in English from a long forgotten time but I had a course in linguistics that I took last semester to help with my grasp of the ancient naming system for flora and fauna in the human realm. From what I can recall from the course I am able to grasp the general gist of this text, albeit very slowly. It is a fun puzzle to untangle and I feel the need to satiate my hunger for any sort of knowledge about this realm, the home of my parents. Possibly my home now if I can't pass back through The Gates.

From what I *can* understand, the text depicts a world in which the humans had just come into being at the hands of The Mother, shaped from the red clay of an abundant valley. The world was one big paradise, with a large land mass surrounded by many smaller chains of islands, much the same to what it is now. The humans seem to be the last creatures The Mother created and her reasoning was to have a creature with the power of the mind, rather than magic, to create beauty and wonders upon her.

The Mother loved all of the simpler animals that had not been gifted with the greater magics but felt she needed a companion that had the power of invention, a companion who could create like she could.

The fae seemed to be quite content using magic as their tools, which makes sense considering they seem to be stuck in some by-gone era rather than in the modern world of humans. They have all the comforts one could need at their fingertips, quite often at the snap of their fingers. They clearly had no reason to innovate and keep building new technology, no need for dreaming of what could be invented.

The tale goes on to describe the jealousy that the fae had of the humans' ability to create without magic and the love and guidance they had from The Mother. They felt, as The Mother's first born race, they should have been favoured by her. So the fae retaliated and began syphoning magic off of the Earth to strengthen themselves until they reached a breaking point, unable to contain what they had taken. Originally their magic was more subtle, as if they were attuned to the fabric of the Earth but they greedily desired more.

They attempted to embody the magic of all the elements and the gifts of the animal kingdom as well, but instead they shattered themselves into Elementals and Metamorphs, only maintaining a fraction of what they were seeking. Rather than being able to access the Earth's magic, they retained power in much more specified ways, creating The Houses. In The Mother's fury, she split the world and ripped the magic from one side, creating the realms and The Gates. The Mist was born from her tears of rage and regret, for allowing her children to grow so greedy.

Damn, that's one angry mom.

Did the Etherealists stem from the original fae?

I scoop another mouthful of eggs in my mouth, looking up from my focus on the book and am met with a grinning Gaius, standing a foot away from me.

"Jeez Gaius, give a girl some warning!" I catch my plate of half-finished scrambled eggs as I nearly topple them on the floor.

"The crystals have informed me that I must instruct you in the art of mind walking. It is your destiny!" He squints his eyes and points his finger in the air, rather dramatically. I swallow another bite of eggs and slam the book shut. Gaius' eyes snap to where I placed the book at my side on the sofa and I can see a muscle tic under his eye.

"Be careful with that! It is five hundred years old!" He scurries to my side to carefully grab it and places it back on the bookshelf, patting it and whispering something inaudible as he goes. *Five hundred years old!* I stare at my lap where the ancient text was lying a moment earlier.

"Wait, you want to instruct me? Is that something you can do?" I am not entirely sure that I want someone who was an outcast amongst the Mind Walkers for *getting lost* to teach me but I suppose some training would be better than what I am currently doing, which is absolutely nothing.

It is hard to sit still after the weeks I wasted at Pyralis' estate. These last two days have felt like a whirlwind... but in a sort of exhilarating and addictive way, even though my brain is still swimming with information overload. This world I live in is so much more vast and complicated than I ever could have known. Magic was once steeped in every crevice of the Earth and we managed to muck it up with our greed. It sounds all too familiar to what is going on back home in Easthelm, The Mother's precious humans making the same mistakes, albeit centuries later. If there isn't anything I can do there to change people's minds, perhaps there is work to be done here... with my *gift*. I nod my acceptance to Gaius' offer.

"The crystals shall provide the greater part of the instruction when you are ready for them. I shall be at hand to guide you on your path. Pray tell, what have you already achieved?" He waggles his eyebrows.

"Well, I can sometimes read the thoughts of others and transfer my thoughts to them but I have to touch them first and maintain eye contact. Also, up until last night I would randomly share visions with only Embrys but I think the crystals put me into my friend Oleander's mind this morning. Perhaps you can help me get back to her? Or to Embrys?" I shrug, knowing it isn't much and what I *can* do is pretty much out of my control.

"I see... A Mind Walker, like I." He strokes his beard and cocks an eyebrow.

Great, I'm like this nutter...

Ha! We shall see! I hear his voice spark in my mind. *For our first lesson, let us converse, but only within the mind. Tis' akin to a muscle you need to strengthen. With practice, mastery shall be attained. You cannot just jump straight into the waking lives of others, untrained. First, we practice with beings right in front of you.*

I really feel the need to check in on Oleander and Embrys but perhaps I should listen to advice on what *not* to do from the man that often gets lost. I give it a try, intensely looking him in the eye.

Are you able to read everyone's thoughts? I ask, he gives me a little excited clap.

Not all. Many have learned to shield, knowing that Etherealists walk amongst them, although now that they are perceived to be gone that may not be the case any longer. You do need to practice with an Etheralist, which would be quite the challenge with none around. Was there anyone who you attempted to read but there was a wall blocking you?

I chew my lip, trying to recall all the minds I have tapped into when I suddenly remember a scorching wall of flame.

"Pyralis!" I say, out loud. Gaius places both his hands on his hips, frowning at me.

Oh right! Um yes, I remember when I first met Pyralis

he had a wall of flame that I could physically feel the heat of. The memory of our meeting blazes behind my eyes and I can hear the screams of the varg as Pyralis just stared at me.

Hmm yes, he must be of an age that still encountered our kind, or had direct contact with one who guided him in the art of shielding.

"My mother!" I say out loud then pinch the bridge of my nose. *Sorry, this is hard. Embrys mentioned my mother and his father were possibly... friends.* The thought of my mother befriending someone such as Pyralis irks me. Although, if what Oleander said was true then there was a time when he was actually somewhat decent, but it is hard to believe after he just threw his own daughter under the bus for the mess he created.

"Wait! Before you went back into the crystals you thought I was someone named Ina. Was that my mother?" I switch back to talking out loud, cringing at my mistake. It's actually very hard to stay within the mind, I don't even notice the switch until it is too late.

Gaius makes a *tut tut tut* sound, crossing his arms. *I am sorry dear, what I may have seen was wiped from my memory. You must practice. I will leave you with the animals to converse while I attend to some things. I shall return soon to see how you fare.* He says before scurrying off towards the tunnel that we entered through.

I sigh out my disappointment at him losing the information about my mother. *If they are the same person then my mother was someone important to The Owl.* The frustration of feeling so close to her but still not having answers feels like it is consuming me.

I decide there is nothing I can do about it right now but, if my training goes well, Gaius will let me into the crystals and I can search for her myself. So I turn to look around for my first practice target and a bunch of the animals have surrounded me, no doubt taking orders from Gaius as well, to help me train. I can already feel a faint headache nagging behind my eyes but try to push past it and get to work, beginning with the creatures I have already touched, starting with the grey wolf.

HER NAME IS SELENE. I learned that she had been left as the runt of her litter and has been pretty much raised by Gaius. She wanders the forest but never strays too far from him. Her love for him is fierce and it seems she will do whatever is needed to protect him. *Nice ally to have*, I did not realize wolves felt such loyalty and I apologize to her for my original judgement. She reassures me that my fear in her is healthy for she would do *anything* to protect her love.

I move on to the bunny that was in my lap which is mostly just asking for me to scratch this one spot behind his ear that he cannot reach which results in a line up of animals who have particular spots of their own that need scratching.

By the time I reach the end of the line my *little* headache from before has turned into a full blown migraine and I have to lie down on the sofa with a blanket draped over my eyes to ease the pounding throb. The twinkling lights of the glow worms feel like knives sticking into my brain. The pain overrides the frustration but I cannot help the feeling of hopelessness slowly creeping up on me again. How could I possibly find my mother within the crystals when I am so *weak.*

I need to see if Oleander is all right and I crave for the connection Embrys and I have. The more I find out about my abilities the more I remember our little shared moments growing up. There was a certain comfort to them when I was younger, like an imaginary friend of sorts. He would show me snippets of this magical world and allow me into brief moments of his life and it made me feel like I had something that was just mine. I had a secret that my family had no way of knowing. I wonder if he knew what our connection was even from a young age. Did my mother guide him before she died?

My head starts pounding fiercely and I have to press my hands into the sides of my head to relieve some of it.

"This is why you are not ready," Gaius' voice sounds from somewhere near the side of the sofa. I sigh at how right he is.

"Not now, come back later." I swat at the air, unwilling to get up, the pounding in my skull is unrelenting. "Do other Elemental fae have to deal with this? Or do they just wake up one day and have their powers?" I groan as each word sends another throb through my brain. I picture a tiny Embrys burning the house down and hope that their powers don't manifest right when they are born. It would not be fun to birth a fire wielder.

"There is a moment, usually after the age of five, that the powers manifest. Sometimes, with the very powerful, it manifests right at birth which can be difficult on the mother. Most Elemental fae have their families to guide them from a young age so it grows gradually," Gaius says, sounding farther away from me now.

Great, I've got fifteen years of catching up to do.

Suddenly, I feel Gaius' hands on my head and before I can swat him away and ask what the heck he is doing I feel my migraine suddenly disappear.

I rip the blankets back and sit up, and am met with a smirking Gaius surrounded by four more deer. *Did they multiply?* "You healed me! Can you heal people?"

I do not heal, but I can trick your mind into forgetting the pain, one of my abilities.

"Cool. Can you teach me?"

"One thing at a time! Your mind needs to rest but your body does not! Come, help me clean the soot off of our new friends." He motions behind him and I notice the room is a lot more crowded. "Then you may scoop out the droppings from the backroom. They have all been courteous enough to use just one room as the toilet." Gaius claps his hands together as if the work ahead is something exciting.

Greeeat.

Chapter Eighteen

T he day is a hard slog but I am grateful for the work to distract me from my worries. Every so often my mind slips back to who Ina was, where Embrys might be and if he is safe at his father's estate, if Marissa is all right with the Sylvans, then to Oleander and what could possibly be happening to her in the Palace. The lone wolf seems to be keeping tabs on me though and comes to give me a little nudge whenever she notices my mind is wandering, possibly a task she has had to do for Gaius her whole life.

As a matter of fact, all the animals seem to be keeping tabs on me. Even at the end of the day when I went for my bath, those same three ducks from the night before accompanied me, making me squirm at the memory of what they saw, then blush at the thought of Embrys' hands on me.

I am now lying in bed, alone at last and can feel the exhaustion of the day taking hold of me. Gaius' healing touch wore off a while ago and the inside of my head feels like a construction site but when I close my eyes the pain eases a bit. The space feels empty without Embrys but as I start to drift I can feel his presence waiting for me in my dreams, as if he is still hovering and protecting me from afar.

I wake to the sound of metal scraping against stone. When I open my eyes it is dark and it takes me a moment to adjust to the sudden lack of glow worm light that I had grown accustomed to.

"Get up!" a deep voice rumbles and I feel rough hands clasp onto my arms and yank me out of my bed.

"Unhand me!" *That wasn't my voice.*

I am pulled into a hallway with iron sconces lining the walls, giving me more light to see by and I startle at the sight of vargs holding onto me. I look down and see I am in a crisp, white night gown and red hair swishes in front of me.

Oleander! Am I in the Palace?

Oleander is led up a few flights of stone stairs and through a high ceilinged room with doors lining the left side wall and floor to ceiling windows lining the right side, showing a twinkling night view of what I am guessing is the capital city. The floor is glistening, white marble and there are white statues depicting different motifs of The Divine Mother in the middle of the hall.

There is one similar to the one in the square of Inverdell, with The Mother birthing the earth and there is another one showing her holding a large drop of water in one hand and a clump of soil with a small tree growing from it in the other. The last, and largest, is a carving of a scene with many different creatures-of-fae bowing down to The Mother in her fae form, *the new religion.*

The door at the end of the hall is cracked open. I can hear voices arguing, male voices. Oleander allows the vargs to lead her to the door and is pushed through ahead of them, stumbling on her bare feet.

"Ah, Oleander. Pleased you could join us." She looks up to see a boardroom with a large wooden table housing around two dozen chairs, tucked in. Only four chairs at the very end are inhabited with Pyralis, Galeheart, a young man with slicked back, jet black hair and a sharp pointed nose and the dark haired man I recognize from my dream in the forest the other night.

"Not like I had a choice... your majesty." Oleander bends at the knees, curtsying.

Your majesty... The Wolf King!

"How dare you speak to his majesty..." Galeheart half rises in his chair but The Wolf snaps his fingers and points for him to sit back down. He levels a stare at Oleander and gives her the wolfy grin I have seen in my nightmares.

"We have come to an agreement about your future, child. Come, sit and join us." The Wolf motions for Oleander to come and sit in the empty chair beside him but she chooses the farthest seat instead.

"You have not given me my trial yet, so you cannot possibly have *come to an agreement.* He is the one to blame, not I." Oleander points to her father and I half expect to see him burst into flames but all I see in his eyes is sadness. *How could he frame his own daughter?*

"You have a right to your trial but we would like to give you an alternative offer instead. After all, I am not an unfair ruler. There are witnesses to your crime, Miss Pyralis. It would be wise to heed my warnings and choose the easier path. You have stated you do not know where the girl is so this is your only other option to bargain with." The Wolf says and I notice Galeheart sneer, looking Oleander up and down as if she is dessert.

I look to the young man beside him and start to see the resemblance between him and the head of the House of Wind. Although, where Gaelheart is all sleaze and fake smiles, this man is stone cold. His stare feels like it is boring into my soul through eyes as black as his hair. Oleander clenches her jaw and bunches up her fists at her side before slamming one onto the table, setting the crystal-ware that lies in front of the men trembling.

"I refuse! I would rather die than marry him!" Oleander seethes through her teeth. A wicked light gleams in the eyes of Gaelheart's son.

Marry him? This is the son that The King and her father wanted her to marry when she was fifteen! The thought of bargaining off his daughter when she was so young boils my blood. My only solace is in envisioning Pyralis set on fire.

"You should burn, you bastard!" Oleander yells then covers her mouth with her hand. I feel her shock at the outburst shudder through her. *I was the one who thought that! Oh no, no, no! Did I make her say that?*

Pyralis looks as equally shocked as I feel. He whips his

head to see the reaction of The Wolf with what looks like fear taking hold of his expression.

"Please, your majesty, excuse her outburst. She knows not what she says. I am to blame for her fiery heart," Pyralis pleads, bowing his head in subservience. *I never expected him to fear anyone...*

"Very well. Your trial will be the day after tomorrow, at dusk." The Wolf gives her a grin, showing his now elongated fangs before pushing up from the table, leaving through a backdoor that is camouflaged in the wood paneling without another word or glance at Oleander.

The day after tomorrow? That's too soon! Is this just a bloody business deal to him?

Oleander washes her face in her hands and looks up to see Galeheart and his son have also departed. She is left with Pyralis.

"Why? Why blame me father? Why not just let me be?" Oleander pleads.

"Please... Darling you must know it is for your own good. For the good of the family." He gets up and comes to sit right next to her, leaning in close as if he is hugging her. She glances at the vargs who had been guarding her but they are in conversation with themselves. Pyralis whispers in her ear, "if you know where she is you must tell me. Please, I only wish to protect her. Embrys can go retrieve her and bring her to safety." He clasps her hand as he pulls away but she sends a burst of flame through her hands, encasing both of their arms in fire. Pyralis just shakes his head and looks at her with pity. Oleander snarls in response.

"I wish you had turned out more like your mother, but you are all *me*," he seethes as he pulls his hand away and strides towards the door, signalling the vargs to bring her back to her room.

Oleander crumples from his words for the briefest of moments but when the vargs grab her again she ignites. Her whole body is covered in flames, causing them to yelp and pull back. Before she can make her escape she is doused by a deluge of water. Nerius appears from the hallway that Pyralis had just exited to and gives Oleander an equally pitying look before turning to follow his employer, leaving her soaked from head to toe and shivering from the icy water.

I gasp and open my eyes to find that I am back in my glow worm illuminated room. *The trial is in two days! I need to talk to Embrys, I need to warn him...*

The presence of the crystals hums through the walls. They are calling me. They know what I must do and now, so do I.

Chapter Nineteen

I quietly make my way to the main cave, not wanting to wake anyone but also unsure of what time it is. The constant glow worm light doesn't really help with that, it probably contributes to Gaius' insanity.

When I round the corner I see that the animals are indeed sleeping. They are curled up in various groups so I tiptoe around them, trying not to alert anyone of my movements. Gaius is snoring in his bed at the far side of the room, I'm grateful for the sound to cover up my sneaking. I am almost at the cave when Selene, the wolf, steps in front of me, blocking my path.

Where do you think you are going? her low, growling voice questions me.

I must enter the crystal cave. My friend's life depends on it. You will not get in my way! I try to step around her but she steps closer to the cave, blocking my entrance.

You heard Gaius. You are not ready. You will get lost.

I must try, please. A dear friend of mine is in danger and this is the only way I know I can help. You would do this for Gaius. The wolf bows her head then looks back to where Gaius is sleeping before stepping out of my way.

Thank you! Give me a few minutes before you wake him. I can read her intention to inform him but she nods at my request and sits down.

I look at the crystals and can feel their pull. The humming is growing louder and I swear I can feel my necklace humming in response, the metal grows hotter against my skin. I don't have time to consider what this might mean. I must find Embrys and warn him. I step up into the cave, crouching low and sitting down, cross legged like I saw Gaius doing. The points of the crystal are sharp but don't break any skin as I sit there.

Now what... I close my eyes but nothing happens. The necklace is growing almost painfully hot against my body and is becoming a big distraction so I lift it out from under my night dress so it is not resting on my skin but as I let go, it floats up in front of me.

A flash of light illuminates the cave, starting at my necklace and sparking to a large crystal to my right. I feel the burst of energy twang in my head like a hammer hitting a nail. My vision starts to blur and the last thing I see is the wolf jumping on to her feet and running towards the sleeping Gaius.

~

I'M IN A DARK PURPLE, swirling vortex with shimmering lights, like the glow worms, but I cannot see the cave any longer. A dense smoke clouds my vision. I sense that I am dissolving into the void within the crystals but strangely, I am not afraid of it. It feels natural and good. My task is completely forgotten.

Time is strange here. I both feel like I have been in this state for an eternity but also for only a few seconds. I find peace and slowness within the spaces between the in breath and out breath. Everything is simple here and yet so beautifully complicated. Everything is spun out of the same web and I am both of that web and spinning it at the same time.

It would be so easy to just let go of myself, so easy to let go of the notion of self. It feels like the warm embrace of a welcome home. *What was so urgent? What was I worried about?* I can feel the cells of my body merging with the soft tendrils of purple smoke and I want to just relax and melt away.

Nuria, a voice calls my name and I feel it like a jolt to the system. The necklace around my neck is tugging me up, up, up.

Nuria. I do not recognize the voice. It is neither male nor female but its urgency brings my awareness back into focus.

The purple smoke feels so thick now that it is making breathing a task I have to actively focus on.

Breathe in... breathe out. Where am I?
Breathe in... breathe out. Embrys?
Breathe in... breathe out. What have I done?

Breathe in... breathe out. Help!

The smoke is getting thicker, a panic attack starts building up in my body, closing my throat and threatening to rip my heart out of its cage. My fingers tingle, my hands start to shake and my breaths are now coming in heaves, which I know is not allowing me to get enough oxygen.

What have I done? Embrys... Embrys!

The smoke suddenly clears, I cough and gasp for the sweet fresh air to fill my lungs. *Thank The Mother!* I keep my eyes scrunched closed and double over to brace myself on my knees as I level out my breathing and feel my heart rate start to slow. I open my eyes to see I am standing on a gravel path.

Nuria? I can hear Embrys' voice call my name and I can't explain how relieved I am to hear it. I snap open my eyes and whirl around, looking for him but instead I see Pyralis' estate looming over me and no one is in sight.

I turn back around to see that I am in front of the stables. It seems to be mid- morning here judging by the height of the sun, but I had entered the crystal cave in the middle of the night. *How long have I been in there?*

"Embrys?" I call out, searching for him.

"Master Embrys? What is wrong?" A boy of about fifteen comes out from the stables with the reins of a large black horse in hand.

Was he talking to me?

Yes, Nuria... you're in my body. I hear Embrys' voice again.

Oh! How are you able to talk to me? Can you see through my eyes?

No, everything is dark. I can hear your voice, that is all. What is wrong? What is happening? Are you dreaming again?

No, I... entered the crystal cave. I had to reach you!

You what! Nuria, it isn't safe! What were you thinking? His voice booms so loudly in my head that I clasp my hands over my ears.

"Um... Master Embrys? Can I assist you?" The young man is staring at me with raised eyebrows.

Right... I'm Embrys.

"Oh, no I am all right... Carry-on with whatever it was that you were doing... uh..." I stammer, not knowing this servant's name.

His name is Jacob.

"Jacob." I give him a smile, he nods and goes back into the stables, giving me one more quick look of concern before closing the big door behind him.

That was Lillian's brother? Have you seen her? Was she all right after the gromlin flip?

Actually, she apparently fled and no one knows where she has gone. Jacob has been worried sick but strangely did not join on the search for her... Nuria, what are you doing here?

Right. I've come to warn you that Oleander's trial has been moved up to tomorrow at dusk! She refused The King's offer of marriage to Gaelheart's son. He said they have witnesses that say she set the forest on fire. Embrys, I'm worried she is going to be found guilty. What is the punishment for burning a forest?

The punishment is death, Nuria. To balance the lives lost

she will be condemned to death! I can hear the panic rise in his voice.

No! There must be something we can do. Embrys... I have to come. The Wolf said he wants me, he tried to bargain with her for her freedom, asking her to give up my location but she refused. I can save her. Use me to bargain for her release!

In the distance I can hear the clopping sounds of a horse approaching. I turn towards the gravel path leading out of the estate to see Pyralis galloping in. He stops and dismounts right in front of me and Jacob comes running out of the stables to grab the reins to lead the horse inside. Pyralis has dag circles under his eyes and his hair is wind swept and messy.

"Embrys, good. We must make haste; your sister's trial is tomorrow evening. I rode all night to retrieve you once I received word that you returned home. We must show a united front. You need to convince her to marry Elias. She still seems to look up to you, she must listen!" Pyralis grasps Embrys' shoulder and I have to restrain myself from shoving him off and snapping in his face.

"We both know it was *you* who set the fire. Why not just own up to it?" I seethe.

Careful Nuria...

Pyralis washes a hand over his face. "Come now, son. You know it was all Nuria's fault. If she hadn't run off I would have never lost my temper!" He clenches and unclenches his hands and flames erupt in his eyes. I see my opening to finally get some answers knowing Embrys cannot interject.

Nuria, don't!

"Why is she so important to you? Why not just let them both go?"

"You know why, son. You know who her mother was. We need her to fall for you. You have been playing along so nicely up until now. Her scent is all over you, which goes to show that our plan is working," Pyralis sneers, clapping Embrys on the shoulder. "You must return to her but only after the trial. She cannot go anywhere near the Palace until our family has been tied to the House of Wind. I already have the House of Water at my disposal through Nerius and you will secure the House of Ether through the girl."

You what?! You needed *me to fall for you? For what, a political alliance? Was everything a lie?* I squeeze my eyes shut and try to block Embrys out but I feel his energy push through my barriers.

"Embrys? What is wrong?" I try to tune Pyralis' voice out,

It is not what it sounds like! Nuria please! His voice sounds like it is fading and I can feel the tug of the necklace around my neck pulling me back to the cave as my vision starts to darken. I sink to my knees and the last thing I hear is Pyralis shouting for Nerius' assistance before everything goes dark.

Chapter Twenty

When I open my eyes, I am back in the crystal cave. This time I can see Gaius, anxiously pacing outside of the opening, stopping every now and again to give me a worried look. I try to call out to him but produce no sound. He doesn't seem to notice I am waving at him either but then I look down and can see I am being pulled away from my body. I am lying on the bottom of the cave with my eyes closed.

Woah, talk about out of body experience. Um... hey, me... wake up. Please, wake up!

I try to concentrate on moving a limb or even a finger but nothing happens. I wonder whether this is what Gaius meant when he said he loses himself, pure dread sours my stomach.

Oh no, oh no, Gaius! Help! Get me out of here! I call to him over and over, nothing happens. I try to focus on wiggling my pinky finger, nothing happens.

Where am I? I am caught somewhere in between sleep and wakefulness but I am paralyzed. Embrys was my anchor in the past when I had entered the crystals through my dreams but I don't dare call on him now, not after what I just discovered. *How could he...Come on, I have to get out of here. Oleander's life depends on it! Help!* I keep shouting to Gaius but he just keeps anxiously pacing.

Far off, in the distance, the faintest reply echoes. It sounds like the voice that had been calling me before...

Am I hearing things? Hello?

Nuria... Come to me. I definitely heard it that time. I look down to see my necklace floating mid-air and the crystal in the centre starts to glow.

Nuria... come to me. The voice is much louder now and I feel the warmth of the necklace around my neck pulling me back down into my body. *Is this my mother? Is she calling me?*

Mom! Mom is that you? Where are you? I need to speak to you... To see you. Please!

I am nearly back into my body and can hear the voice call out my name one more time before I am snapped back into consciousness, bolting upright and gasping for air.

Gaius startles and tries to crawl into the cave with me, "praise The Mother! Nuria!" I wave him off and clamber out on my own. When I try to stand I wobble and collapse into the side of a deer that has run up to my side to brace me.

"Thanks." I give her a little stroke on the head and look at Gaius. "How long was I in there?"

"A full day and a night." He is anxiously chewing on his

moustache and wiggling his fingers at me. "What did you see? Where did you go?" His eyes are wide and sparkling.

"That long! There is no time Gaius, I have to go! I have to get to the Palace. Embrys... He betrayed me... Oleander needs me..." I look down and realize I am still in my night-gown and turn to go to my room but my legs are all jelly and do not want to cooperate and my head starts to spin.

"Give yourself a moment, child. You have been sitting in one position for a long, long time." Gaius grabs onto my arm and leads me to the sofa, taking my weight by ducking his shoulder under my arm while the deer braces my other side. "Now, tell me... where did you get that necklace?" He warily eyes up the necklace that is sitting outside of my night dress. It is still faintly glowing.

"It was my mother's. It was found on her burial mound by the boulder gnomes. They took care of me when I was a child. My mother died giving birth to me." I thoughtlessly grab onto the necklace. "They thought I should have it..." I sit and accept a glass of water from a raccoon. My thirst suddenly hits me, my throat feeling like a sand swept desert. I gulp it all down in seconds.

I was in there for nearly two days?

"I have only ever seen two of the necklaces from the House of Ether that contained the crystal of consciousness in my days. Both belonged to the royal line and no one knew of their origin. More specifically, one belonged to Edmund and the other to his mother..." Gaius stares, mesmerized by the necklace and reaches out a tentative hand to touch it but pulls away at the last second. His eyes dart back to mine for a moment before he drops onto one knee and bows his head.

"Wh...what are you doing? Gaius, get up."

No way... there is no way my family was royal. Me? Nerdy, clumsy, grumpy... me? A royal? I shake my head and look down to the necklace and for a moment, it seems to glow a little brighter as if responding to my thoughts.

"I do not acknowledge The Wolf as king. The line of The Owl has ruled for millennia in a fair and just way. You are the true heir, Nuria. I am at your service... Although I may not be of the *best* service." He bows his head even lower. I grab his shoulders and help him stand back up.

"First of all, Gaius, you are amazing. The most talented Etherealist I know," *Not that I have met any other,* "second... I am no heir or ruler or anything, really! I'm just Nuria... I spend my days studying plants and painting and lying in beds of moss and being extremely socially awkward. I can't even convince people to join me in my pathetic protests in Easthelm. I can't be who you think I am Gaius!" I try to push up from the couch but I am suddenly feeling even fainter than before.

Perhaps I am dreaming. This must all be a dream. The raccoon that brought me my water has popped up by my side with another glass that I gratefully take and chug down.

"You already are, my child! There was a prophecy foretold by the Seers of Mount Aethel, my kooky distant cousins who have the gift of foresight as their tie to the Ether, that told of an heir raised in the way of humans being sent back to us to take their place upon the throne!" Gaius looks down to my necklace which is now glowing much brighter, as if it is excited by these revelations. "It had been foretold before my time and had been cast aside as hearsay when Alastair, The Owl's grandfather, was on the throne. He banished those very Seers to their now coveted mountain for suggesting such a thing, but the Seers must not have known it would be a child of the royal lineage, come for retribution!" Gaius' eyes are wild now, I just shake my head in disbelief.

Is this the prophecy that The Wolf has been told of? I wonder if he thinks it is about me. Perhaps he doesn't want me alive after all... I shut the thought down as I am already resolved in bargaining myself for Oleander's freedom. This realm needs *her*, not *me*.

"Look, I can't promise that I am everything that you had hoped for from this prophecy but I do know that I must go to the Palace and stop this trial. Oleander deserves her freedom and Pyralis and Embrys need to be put in their place!" I feel a surge of energy course through me and shoot to my feet. "Gaius, I don't have much time. The trial is this evening. Is it even safe for me to go out there?" I didn't really think this through. There was just a bloody forest fire that spanned on for miles and is probably still smouldering and extremely hot.

"It may not be safe for you alone but I know of one who may assist you. I will need to enter the crystals to try and reach him. I will do what I can!" I nod to him and we part ways. Gaius heads into the crystal cave and I go to my room to change.

When I get to my room I expect to find my old sooty servant's dress but instead there are a pair of trousers, a clean white blouse and a red cloak, waiting for me on my bed. The grey wolf is sitting beside them. *What the heck?*

I thought you might need something a little easier to move in for combat. I nod my head in thanks. *Protecting the ones you love is the noblest cause of all. Do not forget that.* She nods back before brushing past me and trotting off.

Combat... Shit, Embrys took the sword. What is it with the Pyralis siblings and taking my swords when I need them the most!

When I come back to the main cave, Gaius is already waiting for me and waving me over.

"He has answered and is on his way. Come, he will meet us at the entrance of the waterfall." I walk swiftly behind him, heading to the tunnel that Embrys and I entered through, what feels like, ages ago. I glance behind me one more time and give all the creatures a smile and a nod of thanks before disappearing into the darkness of the tunnel, my eyes catching those of Selene, grey wolf, one more time. *Thank you.*

Gaius and I hop down into the waters of the small lake, which feels more like a bath than a refreshing forest pool, and I look around for this mysterious person Gaius said was coming to aid me. The forest is charred and smoking and I can see embers still glowing on the ground. The destruction steals my breath away and I can't help the tears that start rolling down my cheeks.

"Gaius, the forest! It's all dead..." I sob. How anyone

could so callously destroy so much life for their own political gain is beyond me. The fae are no different than the humans.

Gaius must read my anger. He blows out a breath, causing his moustache to flap around before he grabs my hand and leads me to the shore of the lake. He bends down and brushes away some of the ash to show me a little sprout, already pushing up through the charred earth.

"The Heartwood is a mighty being. She will bounce back grander than she was before. She has seen fire in her past and will not perish from this one. There is enough good left in the creatures of this world that we will always fight and regrow. Do not forget it. Do not lose hope, young one." He gives my hand a little pat.

The resilience of this land amazes me. The regrowth in the human realm takes years and years but as I look around I can see green popping up from the ground and out of the side of burnt trees already, even though the wood is still smoking and the ground is hot to the touch. Gaius is right, and Oleander's words from a few nights ago chime in my mind. *Forgiveness is the only way forward...*

"Ah, Braun has arrived." Gaius straightens up, I look to where his gaze has gone and the largest buck I have ever seen is standing there, staring at us. He is nearly the size of Durga and his antlers are a mighty sight to behold. As he steps into the lake he transforms into his humanoid form which is just as colossal as his animal form. He has a head of thick brown waves and kind, golden, brown eyes that match the hue of his skin. I shyly avert my eyes but both Gaius and Braun seem completely unfazed by his nakedness.

"I have heard your call, Gaius." Braun claps his fist to his chest. "So this is the one the Sylvans have been searching for. I am Braun, a guardian of these woods and I will assist you however I can, small one." He bows his head and I awkwardly curtsey back.

"Um, hello Braun. I'm Nuria. You said the rebels have been searching for me? Is Marissa with them? She is a human, around this tall... blonde curls?" I reach my hand to her petite height and try to keep eye contact with him whilst doing so but his height is making it *very* difficult to avoid staring at a certain something. A very large certain something...

"Ah yes, she is with them and well. I am fond of that one, she has a sweetness to her. But also so fiery for such a tiny thing," he chuckles and I swear I see him blush. I cock an eyebrow at his response and what that might mean. *No, I don't want to know...*

"I need to get to the Palace before sunset, Braun. As much as I would love to go to Marissa and the rebels... There just isn't enough time. Can you get me there?"

"Yes, this I can do. Magath, the City of Her Divine Children, is a far distance but if we make haste we shall make it." He starts to shake and I watch as he slowly morphs back into his deer form.

It is an impressive sight to see and I know I am just rudely standing there, staring at him with my mouth hanging open, but this is not something one witnesses every day. Fur replaces skin and antlers grow like branches, the only thing that remains the same is the colour of his eyes.

When he is fully morphed he walks to my side for me to hop onto his back, which I do awkwardly, not sure if I am supposed to grab ahold of his antlers or just wrap my arms around his neck so I decide the neck is probably nicer for him and lean forward. As soon as I am settled, Gaius gives me a wave and bows his head before Braun leaps out of the lake and we take off. *I'm riding a talking deer... Never in a million years would have thought this was possible.*

"Thank you for everything, Gaius!" I turn to call back but whip back around to grab ahold of Braun's neck before he accidently bucks me off.

As we race through the forest I can see more and more evidence of it coming back to life. The wind is whipping my hair around in a frenzy, so it is hard for me to tell, but I swear I see some boulders rolling around, squashing out the embers. A vision... or memory, I am unsure, of gnomes gathering during a storm to help cut a new path for a creek flashes into my mind and a feeling of comfort that all will be put right washes over me.

We pass a winding creek and I see water sprites splashing around their surroundings, putting out little flames and wood sprites coaxing little saplings out of the ashes. The forest is still very much alive and all the creatures within it are doing their part to heal it.

Leaving my worry for the land and my sister behind, I look ahead to what I might face at the trial. Embrys and

Pyralis will no doubt be there trying to keep me from entering and I have to keep away from the vargs so I am not immediately captured and unable to attend the trial. I have no idea what a trial looks like in the fae realm so I must keep hidden and interject at precisely the right time. I have also never been to this 'divine city' so I have no clue where I will be going or how to gain entrance to the Palace.

Shit, why do I never think these things through? Trepidation creeps into my mind but I've made it this far with minimal planning. I just have to trust I will be able to get to where I need to go... I have to trust myself.

Chapter Twenty-One

When we leave the charred remains of the Heartwood Forest, we are met with a sprawling prairie that is dotted with shimmering lakes and marshes. Not the friendliest terrain for a hooved creature to be running through at full speed.

Braun slows his pace just enough to keep us from accidentally stepping into deceiving puddles that might swallow us whole but also attempts to keep us going fast enough so that he doesn't sink in the mud, it is a complicated dance. I have to hold on tight during the stop-start lurching motions but eventually he gets his stride and the jostling levels out.

These lands look like a water sprite's dream. I wonder whether this area is controlled by The House of Water. I never received a history or geography lesson on the makeup or divide of lands but this has water wielder written all over it.

The botanist in me takes a moment to appreciate the

fluffy bulrushes, with a few red-winged black birds flying in and out of the reeds and the soft purple petals of the lotus lining the lakes. As we race by, flocks of geese take to the air, lifting in unison like a fluffy cloud and the big white swans swim further into the middle of the waters to avoid us. A great blue heron pops his head up from his fishing ground and gives us a curious look, unafraid.

In a not so distant past, I would have thrown on my waders and collected some samples but unfortunately that side of me needs to take a back seat. The passing appreciation is all I can give to this space. Perhaps I will return and take my time with this place, that is, if The Wolf doesn't want me dead...

The natural places in this realm are truly remarkable. I can imagine the human realm once looked this way but a wetland of this size would have been drained and turned into farmland a long time ago. The closest thing I have experienced in the human realm was the boggy marshes near the university, where my class would go on excursions for sampling. They were nowhere near this magnitude and beauty though and there was indeed farmland surrounding it.

I sigh and look forward. A grand house is coming up on our right which I am assuming is the estate of the lord of these lands and the marsh land is starting to become dotted with many smaller houses. Some of the homes even appear to be floating in the middle of the lakes.

A man with what looks like a beaver tail is sitting on the porch of one such house with his fishing rod cast out. He waves out and I go to wave back but Braun has found a solid gravel path that winds through the marsh now and is picking up speed so I have to hold on tight and give the man a nod instead. This seems like a peaceful land. I wonder if the lords here take slaves. There has to be some good fae left, right?

The marsh land seems to span on forever and I start to worry as I notice the rise and decline of the sun. We are past midday and I am aching all over from riding bareback and holding on for dear life but there is no way we can stop, so I try and focus on what is ahead instead.

The wetland is slowly turning back into prairie and I can see a forest line far in the distance which, I bet, is the estate line. I hope this is the territory in which the Palace is because judging by the sun, we don't have much time.

The forest is sparse, mostly birch and aspen. It only spans for about a kilometre until we are back out in a pastoral landscape with farm houses popping up here and there and livestock grazing. I can see the spires and towers of a large city poking up into the horizon. A plume of fog seems to linger just overtop the city. It is still a ways off but I let out a sigh of relief that we are going to make it, hopefully with time to spare.

THE ENORMITY of the city of Magath shows its full glory as we near. There is a big wall of living vines surrounding the entirety of it. They are flowering in places, showing off bursts of whites and purples that add to the whimsy of the place. I can see taller buildings that are all full of points and curves popping up from behind the walls, giving the place a dark fairytale feel to it, but there are the same flowering vines growing off of many terraces which softens the sharp lines. The contrast of life sprouting on all surfaces and the dense looming fog confuses the senses. Something feels truly amiss here.

Braun stops a little ways from the front gate and lets me hop off before changing into his humanoid form. Again, he is unfazed by his nakedness and the various fae travelling towards the gate don't seem at all perturbed either.

"This is where I leave you, small one." Braun looks warily to the gates and I notice some vargs standing just inside the massive doors. "I must return to the forest and tend to the places I am needed. Stay out of trouble..." He looks back to me and gives me a nod before transforming back into his stag form and springing away.

I guess I am on my own... I bite my lip and look nervously at the vargs. *I need a plan...*

There are many fae walking in and out of the city but I need something to distract the vargs from looking right at me just in case they have been put on the lookout under Pyralis' guidance.

Just then I notice a woman of around thirty, with dark hair pinned back in a messy bun, stumble and drop a roll of fabric on the ground. Her arms are already full of rolls of fabric and a baby so she is noticeably struggling to pick up what she dropped, cursing quietly as she tries.

Perfect.

"Excuse me, ma'am, allow me to assist you." She gives me a big smile and blows out an exasperated breath, shaking her head at her own predicament.

"Thank you dear! This trip has been quite the struggle. Our cart got bogged down in the marshes and my husband stayed behind to try and get it out. I have to deliver these today so I ended up traveling the last hour with her in my arms." She bounces the baby on her hip who giggles at the movement.

I go to pick up the fabric but instead she shoves the baby into my hands and scoops the fabric up herself. "If you could just help me to my shops I would be most grateful!" She beams at me and starts walking towards the gate. I look at the wriggling babe in my arms and decide that this will have to do. Surely the vargs won't recognize me with a baby in my arms... right? I pull up my hood and cradle the squirming child, rushing to follow the woman.

The vargs sniff at me a bit as we enter but whatever smell is coming from the bottom half of the baby has done a great job of covering my scent up and they do not stop us.

When we are clear of the gate my eyes go wide with wonder at the beauty of this city. Only a few places on the Continent have been relatively untouched in the human realm, holding on to the old charm of a time long since passed, but the magic of this place far surpasses them.

There is a big, open, cobblestone square just inside the gate that is lined with two and three story brick buildings with shops on the ground levels that show signs of food vendors, bakeries, bookstores, herbalists, haberdasheries and more. Hung across the square are stringed-globe lights with suspended fires burning inside, which I can imagine makes this whole place light up with a beautiful warm light at night.

There are streets winding off from the square that have cute multi-story brick homes lining either side. The balconies and wooden window sills all have box planters of vibrant flowers and vines and there are laundry lines spanning far overhead across the streets with beautiful garments fluttering in the wind.

Children of both Metamorph and Elemental fae play in the streets and old hunched grannies sit, gossiping in the doorways. The feel of community is strong and wholesome, even so close to the Palace of such a pernicious ruler. Easthelm feels so lifeless in comparison to this place. I've never been one to enjoy crowded spaces but I can see myself living here... If I ever get the chance.

I make sure to keep up to the woman with the fabrics but can't help my curiosity as I sneak peeks into shops and down side streets as we go, my eyes drinking in everything I see. Even the alleyways have a sweet charm to them with little hidden cafes with tables outside and more string lights illuminating the spaces.

We turn down a large open street and I have to dodge carts that appear to be pulled by nothing as I keep up with the woman. We finally turn into a big shop with elaborate ball gowns in the window and she drops the fabrics down at the front counter.

"Thank you... Uh..." She smiles, arching a brow.

"Nuria, my name is Nuria. You're very welcome." I hand the now squealing baby back to her.

"I'm Fern." She smiles and kisses her wriggly baby on the cheek, "and this is Oakleigh." The baby gives out a loud squeak in response to hearing her name. "Is there anything I can do for you to thank you for your help?"

"Actually, if you could just point me in the direction of the Palace that would be super helpful."

"The Palace? Today is the trial of the daughter of the Lord of the House of Fire. Are you sure you want to go there?" she lowers her voice to a whisper as she covers her daughter's ears. "There may be an execution..."

"Is the trial open to the public?" She nods in response. "Then I must go. A friend's life depends upon it."

She knits her brows together, giving me a sympathetic look.

"Very well. I warn you... The Wolf King is no pacifist. The outcome may be gruesome. But I see you are determined. If you follow this road to its end and take a right turn, follow that road down past the Wishing Tree Gardens and over the bridge. You will know it when you see it." I give her a smile of thanks and leave the shop.

Right... Wishing Tree Garden, bridge, Palace.

The main street is crowded with carts and fae of all kinds busily going about their days or perhaps going home after a day's work. I'm not entirely sure what a day in the life of a regular fae folk would look like. *Do they have jobs? Do they go to school?* I am busy pondering to myself, keeping my pace quick when I accidentally trip over a boulder gnome.

"Oh! Please mistress, I beg your pardon!" The gnome bows its head low, nearly touching the ground.

Wait a second, wasn't that my fault?

"You stupid little creature, get inside!" A fae man with a finely tailored green velvet suit and matching top hat waves a cane at the gnome before turning to me and removing his hat to give me a little bow of his head. "Do accept my sincerest apologies. The good slaves are hard to come by these days. I've had to settle for gnomes!" His tone is joking. I can't help the look of disgust on my face that pulls my top lip up into a sneer. The fae man just gives me a little bow, probably thinking I was scowling in agreement to his belief that having gnomes as servants is lowly, and follows his slave into one of the brick townhouses.

Of course the main city would be rife with fae who keep slaves, but actually witnessing it and the poor treatment of the creature makes my stomach roil. I feel so helpless and small in the cause of freeing these beings, especially when I know those who are keeping the slaves have mighty powers that my silly mind reading abilities have no chance against. This makes freeing Oleander all the more important. I look to the sky and can see the beginning shades of a sunset creeping in and quicken my pace down the cobbled road.

When I pass the outskirts of, what I assume, is Wishing Tree Garden, I have to resist stopping and entering to marvel at the largest fig tree I have ever seen. The park looks to be the size of two city blocks and the entirety of it is this one tree. Its roots sprawl over the ground like large tentacles, creating arches and benches and even little tables all throughout the park.

Fae seem to be milling about having picnics or leisurely strolls around the outskirts of the park but in the centre, at the main trunk, there are dozens of fae leaning in to lay hands upon it. They look to be muttering to themselves and I wonder if they are sharing their wishes with the tree itself.

There are figs all over the ground and the many fae around the tree's trunk seem to be scooping them up and eating them. The blissful look on their faces makes it impossible to resist the urge to stop. Figs are so rare to come by in the human realm, mostly originating in the south islands, but the pollinators needed to create fruit have been steadily declining. So the marvel of such a large, abundant tree is enough to convince me to try for myself. I lean down to grab a plump fig and take a bite as I keep walking towards the Palace.

The first bite is pure, unimaginable delight. A tingling euphoria spreads from my lips down to my heart. It feels like a happiness drug and I immediately want more. *I don't remember them being this good!* I bend down to fill my hands with them and take delicious bite after delicious bite, letting the juices roll down my cheeks and stain my cloak. Before I know what I am doing, I find that I am sitting in a little alcove of the roots with a horde of figs piled in my lap.

How did I get here? What was I doing again? My brain feels like it is floating in a cloud but I don't seem to care because the joy I feel is mesmerizing. I close my eyes for a moment, mid-bite, savouring the sweetness. When I open my eyes again I have been transported into a dimly lit stone hallway with a solid metal door in front of me. The sudden change in scenery is very sobering, a chill creeps up my spine. *Where am I?*

There is a little window, smaller than my head that is open in the door that I step up to, to peer inside. Oleander suddenly pops up on the other side of the window looking extremely pissed off.

"Embrys, I don't care what you say, I won't do it. That marriage would be the death of me. He would use me as a brood mare then dispose of me. That was what our father did to your mother, was it not?" She bares her teeth.

I don't feel like I have control over Embrys' body as he responds with a growl. "You know nothing of my mother, Ollie. The King will surely kill you for this, and I know it was not you who started the fire, but there is a witness! What can we do?" He presses his hands up against the door.

"Embrys' mother was no *brood mare*. She could not contain his fire, my daughter. " I turn and see Pyralis storming down the hallway, fuming at the ears. "I did not use her as you claim. She was, regrettably, not strong enough to bear a child of fire and perished after birth. We mourned her loss but I was a new father and had to pull myself together for the sake of my child!" He clenches his jaw so hard I'm surprised it doesn't break. There is a silence as Oleander looks to Embrys with sadness in her eyes. She did not know. How many poor women has Pyralis' fire burned through? Embrys has lost more than I could fathom to his father's power, no wonder he fears his own, or perhaps he blames himself for her death.

"If you cared for both of our mothers then how could you possibly try and give me away to a man that will be nothing short of cruel?" Glowing handprints form on the metal door from where Oleander's hands are placed on the other side. Pyralis steps in close to the window and lowers his voice.

"You will not have to suffer for long, my child. We just need the alliance with House of Wind and then you will be free to do as you wish. I have secured the House of Water and Embrys has secured the House of Ether... nearly. House of Earth are all bumbling fools that will follow whoever holds the power. I could not share this with you when you were younger because you would not have understood but perhaps you can see now. This is for you, this is for us! With three of the four houses in our allegiance we can take the throne. You can call in your rebel friends to our aid and we will have the power!" His usual steely expression has been traded for one of pure fanatical desire. He truly thinks that this plan will work.

"You are mad to believe you can take the throne! You think you are a fit ruler? You abandoned us after my mother died. For years you were useless and now you're an unpredictable despot. You set The Heartwood aflame for Mother's sake!" Oleander's voice rises to a shriek as she pounds on the door in exclamation. "And you!" Her flaming gaze turns to Embrys, "how could you deign to use Nuria in that way?

You best beg for her forgiveness when she finds out. You do not deserve her!" She pounds the door again.

"Lower your voice!" Pyralis pounds back. "I will not rule. I know I am not fit. I know I have failed you but your brother... *He* could rule! And with the hand of the Etherealist girl he will have legitimacy to the throne!"

Like heck he will! I barrel down our connection and Embrys gasps in response. I can feel his mind look inward and see what I am seeing through my eyes on the other end.

"Nuria!" Embrys calls out and it is the last thing I hear before darkness consumes me.

Chapter Twenty-Two

When I open my eyes, I can see the sun is well and truly setting now. The sky is awash in pinks and deep oranges, I startle to my feet. My head feels clouded in a thick fog and I look down to see a pile of half eaten figs littering the floor around me.

What was I doing? There is a strong urge to eat more. My hand is moving to my mouth before I can think twice about it and I take a big bite. *Ah, that's better...*

I sink back down against the tree but before my butt hits the ground Embrys is in front of me knocking the fig out of my hand and grabbing my shoulders.

"Hey, I was eating that..." The words are sluggish as they come out of my mouth. I try to shake him off and lean down to grab another fig but Embrys pulls me up and wraps my arms around his neck and before I can protest, his mouth is on mine. *Oh, this is even better...*

I close my eyes and feel as though I am floating through the air. The kiss starts out warm but soon the heat between our lips starts burning. I gasp as I pull away and notice that he must have been carrying me because we are now on the outskirts of the park.

What was I doing? Suddenly my awareness of what just happened dawns on me. I pull out of his embrace and slap him across his extremely hard jaw, *Ouch*. I pace back and forth shaking my hand.

"What do you think you are doing? Get away from me!" I bare my teeth to him.

"Nuria, you were gorging yourself on the figs, I had to intervene. The fae know to dose themselves slowly with them. They contain pure euphoria gifted from The Divine Mother herself. This tree is sacred and has been here for thousands of years. Only the zealots who have been eating the fruit for years are able to handle the amount you just consumed, and even then, they stay in trance, muttering to the tree for hours, like those you see behind you." He gestures to the fae I had noticed earlier and upon closer look they appear to have lost the plot entirely.

"So you thought kissing me was the answer? Embrys, I want nothing to do with you! I need to go do what *you* could not, save your sister." I try to shake off my inner voice that is betraying me and longing for another kiss. I push past him, hurrying towards the big bridge that Fern described, praying that the Palace is not far off. The trial must have already started.

Embrys sighs and jogs up to my side. "I kissed you because I had a feeling it would irritate you enough to break you out of your stupor. I was clearly correct." I look his way only long enough for him to see my exaggerated eye roll.

"Huh, another irritating habit you and Oleander share," I scoff as I continue walking. Embrys falters in his steps for a second then catches up to me again.

"She did what?!" His fingertips burst into flames.

"Oh spare me. You do not get to be jealous." I keep storming forward. He just shakes his head and lets out a frustrated sigh. The fires wink out one at a time.

"Please, Nuria, it is not safe for you at the Palace. The King wants you; you cannot fall into his net. My father's plan could work. You are the rightful heir after all. I promise you do not have to marry me or even look at me again but stand with us and we will stand behind *you!* This realm needs change and you have come on the eve of revolution. You must be the answer." Embrys keeps pace with me but doesn't try to get in my way. I can hear genuine worry in his voice, however misguided it might be. I spare him a glance and see his wrinkled brow. I also notice his hair is half out of its binding and he is sweating, as if he ran at top speed to find me. Again trying to play the hero no doubt.

Wait, did he say I am the rightful heir? I stop walking and step into his space, he nearly collides with me and has to put his arms up for balance.

"You knew all along who my mother was and you kept it from me?" I point a finger into his chest. *It is just lie after lie with these bloody fae.* "I am not who you think I am, Embrys! I do not wish to be an *heir!*" I give him another hard poke. "I do not trust your father any more than I trust The King. All I know is that Oleander has done more for the creatures of this realm than any of you and what I can do right here and right now is free her so she can continue on with her mission. The King won't harm me, he needs me," *I hope,* "who knows, maybe I can reason with him. Perhaps I can make him promise to free the slaves and leave the human realm alone in exchange for me and my powers." I meet Embrys' eye for only a moment and catch his apologetic look. He just nods, lost for words.

Finally voicing my plan out loud makes me realize how ridiculous I sound, but it is all I can do to save my friend and to hopefully save my family. If The King needs me then surely he will be amenable to a bargain, right? *Oh Mother, I hope so.*

I shove my self-doubt down into the darkest parts of myself and continue walking to the big bridge that stretches over a wide emerald river. Embrys is silent beside me but keeps up stride for stride and I feel a pull towards him and a yearning to reach out and grab his hand, *are these my desires or his?* I notice his fingers flex from the corner of my eye.

The Palace comes into view as we reach the crest of the bridge. Fern was right; I would definitely *not* miss this. The Palace looks as though it has been raised from the Earth, Herself. It has towering spires of sparkling white, uncut rock with little oval shaped windows scattered unevenly throughout. The white flowers of my mother's burial mound carpet the surrounding ground that I notice none of the fae walk on. Moss hugs the walls and living vines spread their tendrils across the rough white stone, reaching for the sun and even crawling into some of the open windows. I can see the main entrance which consists of a huge vine arch with wisteria cascading down, creating a suspended veil of white. The scent of the succulent flowers hits me, even this far back. Embrys stops me by taking my hand in his. I almost pull away but the tender look in his eyes and the half smile I have grown to enjoy stops me, even though I am thoroughly pissed at him.

"I will not try to stop you if this is what you wish. I know you do not feel you can trust in me after what has happened. Believe me when I say nothing I have ever said or done with you was in pretense. I care for you more than you know and I will stand with you against The King if that is what you wish." He cautiously reaches to cup my cheek in his hand, checking my face for any sign of anger but I relent and soften, allowing his touch. He lied to me multiple times and I am unsure if I can trust him ever again but I really, really want to. Only his future actions will determine that. Only his support for Oleander and the Sylvans will change my mind.

"Embrys, you must promise to leave with Oleander when The King takes me. The two of you together will be unstoppable, and he does not suspect you to be a rebel. She will need you as guardian for The King's guard to fully release her." He studies my face for what feels like a long time. His brows knit together and he clenches his jaw, fighting his own stubbornness. I stare into his hazel eyes. *I do not need your protection. You owe me nothing but the truth moving forward. Please, can you do that?* A muscle in his jaw tics but he finally nods in agreement. I let go of his hand, turning towards the castle.

Chapter Twenty-Three

There is a crowd pushing through the main arch which obstructs the view of what is beyond. If this is a public trial then I am guessing that is what they are all trying to see, making my swift entrance just a bit more challenging, *great*.

As if reading my thoughts, Embrys walks ahead of me with a ball of flame floating in his hand and the crowd immediately parts for us to pass through.

"Thanks." I keep up behind him.

Startled fae glare at us but none try to get in our way. When we are through the arch we climb the white stone stairs to the main doors and push our way through the crowd. The main foyer is grand, with high dome ceilings and white marble floors housing designs of green vines mosaiced into the large tiles. The walls are covered in sprawling ivy and there is a magnificent chandelier that looks to be a golden and shimmering upside down tree floating mid-air. Lights twinkle from the tips of the branches and I can imagine the beautiful disco ball effect it must have at night. *I wonder if they have balls here. That's a fairytale thing, right?*

The grand room has been transformed into a court-room. On tiptoes I can see at the far end of the space is the dark haired man from Pyralis' painting, and my nightmares, up on a dais, sitting on a throne made of a living tree resembling a miniature version of the Wishing Tree.

He wears a golden crown of ivy with what looks to be fangs pointing down all along his brow, *nice touch*. The balance of delicacy and fearsomeness I am guessing is a special addition, courtesy of The Wolf.

We push through the crowd far enough so we can see the backs of Oleander and Pyralis' heads. They are seated at the base of the small platform that holds the throne with vargs on either side of them. Oleander doesn't appear to be restrained but it is hard to tell from behind. There are three rows of seated fae directly behind them, two seats I recognize are inhabited by the thin, white haired head of Gaelheart and his black haired son, Elias. As if sensing that Embrys is here Pyralis turns to meet his eye. As he turns, Embrys shoves my head down so I am hidden behind a portly fae man that has a pig's tail sticking out of his pants.

Stay hidden until The King calls for objections, my father will try and intercede otherwise, Embrys says. My eyes widen as I realize that we were not sharing eye contact. I wonder whether my powers have somehow grown since my stint in the crystal cave, or if it is just our connection that has grown.

Embrys releases the back of my head and walks forward

through the crowd. I peer around the shoulder of the pig fae and watch him take his spot on the other side of Oleander. She shows no signs of acknowledging his presence. *Shit, she must be freaking out.*

"Loyal subjects, we gather you here this eve to bear witness to the trial of one, Oleander Pyralis, who has been accused of the destruction of the sacred Heartwood Forest, by means of her Goddess given gift of fire. We will hear her plea." The voice of The Wolf carries far but he does not shout. He is somehow amplified whilst keeping his tone cool and calm. There is some murmuring in the crowd at his mention of the destruction of the forest, his simple gesture of lifting a hand silences the crowd instantly.

"She has her right to a fair trial and a right to representation on her behalf. Miss Pyralis, please do stand and introduce who your representative will be." The Wolf nods, a show of respect to the order of things. Oleander rises and Embrys watches her closely, sparing a quick glance back to where I am crouched.

Stay there. Stay hidden.

"Your majesty, I thank you for the opportunity to prove my innocence. I will be representing myself." *There is no way she would have had time to find someone to help her. This isn't fair!*

Whispering breaks out amongst the gathered fae again, this must not be an orthodox method. I can see Embrys tug on Oleander's hand and say something I cannot hear but she just pulls her hand away and stays standing, facing The King.

"Very well. You may be seated. On behalf of the Heartwood Forest, *I* will be standing as a representative," The King says and the shocked whispering has turned to outright exclamations. This is clearly not a normal occurrence either, for The King himself to stand against an accused. This doesn't seem fair and I want to barge right up there and yell in his face but it appears Embrys has beaten me to it, *foolish man.*

"On what grounds do you have the right to stand for the forest? You are supposed to be our ruler, our keeper of peace and justice. If you are standing against my sister you cannot be a fair judge!" Embrys walks up only one of the steps before two vargs grab him, holding him back by the arms. The King waves them off and slowly rises. His cool and calculated smile makes me shiver.

"Mister Pyralis poses a good question. I do not suppose to play both judge and accuser. I am a fair and just King after all, am I not? Thus, my most faithful citizens, I pose onto you the duty of being my voice of reason. Hear us both and choose if this young woman shall bear the burden of guilt or if she shall be granted exculpation. It is not an easy weight to bear but someone must pay the price for the devastation of such sacred life. I trust you will be pragmatic in your decision." I look around at all the nodding heads and exuberant faces. Having The King ask such a thing from his people is clearly making them feel important. Not a good start for Oleander.

"As for the grounds on which I may speak on behalf of the forest herself, I invoke the ancient right of my direct ancestor, Silasi, protectress of the forests of both realms, as appointed by The Divine Mother herself." Whispering breaks out amongst the gathered crowd, Silasi's name being traded around in shocked tones. *Who is this person? What is she to the fae?*

The Wolf sits back down on his throne and leans forward, placing his elbows on his knees, as if he is about to tell a tale to a group of eagerly listening children.

I scoff but as I look around everyone is dead silent and are indeed, eagerly listening. I can see how this man won over a nation by preaching his fanatical new religion. His way with words and with a crowd is scarier than the monster he morphs into. Embrys shakes off the vargs and bows his head, silently resigning back to his seat.

The Wolf motions to Oleander to join him on the dais. Oleander rises from her seat and steps onto the first step. The vargs do not try to apprehend her as she takes one more step up and turns around to face the crowd. The sight of her determined face pulls at my heart. I can tell she is being brave but her fire is ever lingering behind her eyes, waiting to be set free. I wish I could run up there and stand with her against her accusers.

"Gentle fae, please hear me when I say I am innocent. I have been a protector of the natural world all my life. All the creations of The Divine Mother are worthy of life and I would never purposefully destroy her blessed design." Oleander scans the room, keeping her chin up.

"I was deep underground, within a system of caves in the Heartwood Forest with some companions, when word got out of a rapidly spreading fire. At this time I aided in bringing my friends to safety. The fire was too far along, so we had to evacuate rather than try and fight it. I have been wrongfully accused based on my gifts from The Mother and resent the prejudice that is based on my birthright. Unfortunately my companions could not be here with me today but my brother was present; I call upon him to attest to my character." Oleander gestures for Embrys to join her on the dais. *Why doesn't she accuse her father right away? He is to blame!*

Embrys' shoulders rise and fall slightly as he takes a steadying breath then gets up from his seat to join Oleander. His long legs take both steps in one stride. With them standing side by side I notice their height difference. Embrys truly is a large presence but Oleander makes up for her height with a smouldering fire that seems to always be waiting, just under the surface of her skin.

"My sister left my father and I seven years ago to pursue her devotion to The Mother," *more like ran away,* "she had always been a student of the natural world and wished for nothing else but to protect it. I do not believe she has it in her to harm any of the creatures upon this Earth unless provoked in order to protect one that is more vulnerable. I, Embrys Pyralis, vouch for her character and do not believe that she has done what she is accused of doing." Embrys nods his head to the crowd in finality and goes to step back down to his seat but is halted, by the upraised hand of The Wolf.

"A moment, Mr. Pyralis. I have a query of my own to pose upon you before you take your seat." The Wolf stands and approaches Embrys and Oleander, buttoning his suit vest as he walks.

"Now what a shining description of your dear sister's temperament, I truly do admire sibling adoration." The Wolf smiles to the crowd, heads nod in agreement. "Is it not true though, that she had you imprisoned within this network of caves?" The Wolf has a feigned look of concern. Embrys slowly nods in response, eyes shifting to where I am still crouched down in the crowd.

"Well, and what may I ask was your crime to have been placed in such a place? If she is as caring towards nature as you have described, how could she treat her own flesh and blood with such disrespect? Unless you truly do deserve to be imprisoned, in which case we would be most happy to take the law into our own hands here at the Palace." His slow spreading grin and slight tilt of the head reminds me of a jackal about to pounce on a newly found rotting carcass.

"There was no crime, your majesty. It was simply... Uh... sibling rivalry. See I had done wrong to her when we were much younger and I suppose she just needed to make a point. I played along." Embrys looks to Oleander, who is still looking straight ahead trying to keep her cool. I can see flames flickering behind her eyes and pray that she can keep it together. She would surely write her own death sentence if she exploded on any member of the court like she did with her father a few nights ago.

"I see... Sibling rivalry." The Wolf stretches out the words, earning a few laughs from the crowd. "Extreme, but I suppose if you went willingly then that was your own prerogative. Nevertheless this has just proven that you were incapacitated at the time of the origin of the fire and would not have had any means of ascertaining who started it. Therefore, my esteemed citizens, you must take his account as one of judgement of character only." The Wolf's grin has turned into another feigned look of pity as he opens his palms to the sky and shrugs his shoulders as if to show he is sorry that this is the case. *Shit.*

"And *if* I find there is any untruthfulness to your words, Mister Pyralis, believe me there will be just punishment." Embrys' face goes pale but he keeps his chin up and nods in acknowledgment of the threat.

Embrys looks to Oleander and takes her hand in his, whispering something inaudible before he leaves to sit back in his seat. Oleander lifts her chin a little higher and squares her shoulders to the crowd. *Bless her strength and stubbornness.*

"I call my father, Lord Pyralis, to the dias," she calls out and judging by the way that Pyralis' head swivels from side to side, he is shocked. He slowly rises and walks up the steps to stand between her and The King. Fear emanates off of him. *Good, be afraid!*

"Father, is it not true that you apprehended and enslaved an Elemental fae recently?" *Oh Mother, what is she doing?* Pyralis' eyes go wide with flames as he stares at his daughter. There is a long pause before Pyralis clears his throat and turns to the crowd.

"An Elemental owed me a debt so we agreed upon a time

period of servitude as her repayment," he says through gritted teeth.

Agreed upon, my ass! They both seem to be avoiding the usage of my name and which Elemental house I belong to, *thank The Mother.*

"Right, and did she not escape your household on the very same night that the Heartwood fire started?" Oleander's tone has turned cool and silky, the fire in her eyes still blazing. It is scary how similar she and her father can be when provoked.

"She did leave the same evening, yes," Pyralis' tone turns into a warning.

"And judging by which direction the horse she had stolen returned from, would you say she fled to the Heartwood Forest?"

"The horses came from the south-east, yes but she could have gone anywhere in that direction or she could have left the horse and changed course on foot. There is no way of knowing for sure."

"Yes, of course, but would it not be the first place to look if you were to search for her, as it is the biggest landmark south-east of your estate?" Oleander's smug grin says it all. She thinks she has him cornered.

"I suppose. I sent my men out to search for her. I had other pressing matters to attend to at my home; our gromlins had a united flip that needed to be resolved," Pyralis scoffs, waving his hand at her as if she is an irritating child asking useless questions. I don't think I told Oleander about the gromlins and I can see the cogs turning in her mind as she ponders this new piece of information. It gives him an alibi I bet she did not expect. A moment later I see her cool and calculated grin form on her lips once more. She has found the solution.

"I am through with my questions. Thank you." She nods to Pyralis who looks to The King for his confirmation before returning to his seat. The Wolf does not question Pyralis about whom the Elemental fae was, I am not even sure if they are allowed to enslave the Elementals. *Why is he letting that slide?*

"If I may, to bolster these statements, I will call Lord Clayborn to the dais for a few questions. I believe he was present that evening as well," Oleander says coolly. Pyralis pauses before taking his seat. He is facing the crowd and I can see the split second of worry cross his brow before he turns and sits. The portly Lord Clayborn, who had been sitting a few rows back, waddles up the steps and takes his place. He gives The King a nervous bow of the head at which The King shows his teeth, something halfway between a smile and a snarl. Clayborn starts shaking.

"Lord Clayborn, we have established that there was a gromlin flip the evening of the forest fire and I would just like you to help us with the timeline. How long did the situation take to resolve?" Oleander is speaking more gently to Clayborn, as if he is a scared child she is trying to coax the information she wants out of.

"Yes, it was a frightful event. I hid under the dining room table as the servants handled the gromlins. It took around an hour for all of them to be doused."

"An hour you say? Well now, that is fairly quick. You have very efficient servants, Lord Pyralis." Oleander smiles and narrows her eyes in her father's direction. "Did you happen to see Pyralis after the event?" Clayborn starts wringing his hands and looking to The King for direction. The King merely stands there with plastered on pleasantry.

"Y-yes, I saw him mounting his horse and taking off with a small pack of vargs." Clayborn is now visibly sweating.

"Which direction did he go, Lord Clayborn?" Oleander's excitement is now palpable.

"S-south... east." He bows his head, avoiding everyone's gaze. The crowd gasps and a whispering murmur spreads.

"Thank you, Lord Clayborn, I have no more questions for you. As you can see, my fellow fae, Lord Pyralis, the head of House of Flame, was seen riding towards the Heartwood, in an angry pursuit of his Elemental *slave*. You decide for yourselves whether a man who was seen riding towards the forest with reason to burn it in order to smoke her out is more likely the guilty person than I, someone who had no motive and who has always cared for The Divine Mother's creations." Oleander does not hide her smug excitement, she even goes as far as crossing her arms and tilting her head as she looks at The King as if to say, *bring it on.*

She would have made a good lawyer in the human realm. I am now vigorously chewing my nails and looking back and forth between The Wolf, whose smile has turned sinister, and Oleander who is still exuding smugness.

"A fair argument, Miss Pyralis. You may return to your seat Lord Clayborn, I have no further questions for you,"

The Wolf snarls, Clayborn quickly stumbles back to his seat. "Instead, I shall call upon my chief witness to attest to Miss Oleander's crime." He claps his hands together and narrows his eyes at the crowd. *He looks like he is up to no good. Who is this witness they have been going on about?* I am now destroying the nails on my other hand with my nervousness.

"I call upon Miss Lillian, a servant from Lord Pyralis' house, who claims to have seen Miss Pyralis in action." I am the only one who audibly gasps. I duck down behind the pig fae again to hide from The Wolf, who is now searching the crowd for who made the sound.

Shit... Lillian? Is she the spy that Oleander mentioned? She knew of my plan to escape... She knows what I am!

Lillian appears through a side door that leads onto the dais. She is no longer in her servant's uniform but instead is in a dusty pink gown that cinches at the waist before it puffs out into a long tulle skirt. Her hair is braided into a coil on top of her head and she does not prance in like I half expected, she walks, with poise. *Who the heck is this version of Lillian?*

"My dear Lillian, might you recount the events of the evening of the horrific fire for us all?" The Wolf motions for her to step beside him and gives her a gentle, fatherly smile while placing a hand on her shoulder. They look awfully comfortable around each other and my confusion about the difference between the Lillian I met and this Lillian is making my head swim. If she was planted in the Pyralis estate, I wonder if The Wolf knew of me all along.

"I will do my best, your majesty, as it was a very frightful evening indeed." She clasps her hands in front of her and lowers her head. *An act? Or is she scared of The Wolf? Is he forcing her to do this?*

"I was busy helping some of the servants polish the silverware and keeping out of the way of the fancy dinner Lord Pyralis was holding, when I heard a loud racket coming from the lower levels of the house. I peeked around to the servant's hallway and saw massive gromlins tumbling out of the kitchens! They were frothing at the mouth and flailing their arms in the air. You see, when a gromlin is flipped they are huge, maybe three times bigger than me! So I did what anyone would have done I suppose...Well any ten year old – I ran away." Her acting is very convincing.

"I went straight for the stables, because that's where my brother Jacob usually works and I thought I could find him. He was not out there though, and when I looked back through the windows of the main house I could see servants running and screaming and gromlins setting fires and flipping tables! Vargs were running around with buckets of water trying to douse both the fires and the gromlins but there were far too few of them. Everything was getting out of hand quickly." Lillian is quite the actress I must say, the whole crowd is enthralled by her recounting of the night so far. To be fair, I did not see her at all that evening so perhaps this part is still the truth.

"I – I was really scared! The door of the stables was already open so I went in and saddled up the pony that Pyralis has been allowing me to ride. You see, he wants me to become a lady and all ladies know how to ride." She smiles down at her hands.

"anyway, I rode her right out of there! I haven't gone far from the estate before and I was not thinking straight so I just let my pony lead the way. After a while I realized I had no idea where we were and got really scared. It was so dark out and no one was around. But then I saw it, a huge flame erupting ahead of us in a forest! The pony kept its distance but we were close enough for me to see *her*!" Lillian dramatically sweeps her arm to point at Oleander. "She started the fire!"

The crowd erupts, shouting accusations at Oleander and pushing forward to get closer to the dais in their outrage. She shakes her head and tries to speak but the crowd's voices drown her out. I am trying to keep my cool and stay within the angry mob but the smug grin that is slowly spreading across The Wolf's face sets me over the edge. The chaos he has sown is a contagious disease spreading too quickly. He knows what he is doing. That conniving, devious man staged this whole farce to entrap Oleander. I cannot let this go any further. I see red.

In the next moment, I am charging forward, pushing my way through the crowd and past the row of seated fae nobles.

"You liar!" I run towards the steps but am met with two vargs instantly pulling me back by the arms, lifting my kicking body into the air.

"She lies! I can prove it! Let me go and I will show you!" I kick and wriggle in their arms, their grips tighten and I know they will leave huge bruises.

The Wolf's predatory grin drops the moment he lays eyes on me. He does nothing to hide his shock. "Let her go. I will allow it!" The crowd stills, the vargs release me.

I snarl at the vargs then straighten out my now disheveled clothing before I step up to stand beside The King, eyeing him warily. The man that has been haunting my dreams, that has been lurking behind the fear of my new found friends, is here... beside me. He is only a few inches taller than me but his presence seems to take up all the air in the room. His green eyes can't hide their shock and what looks like... sadness? Or is it longing? *He recognizes me...*

Pyralis' shock and rage has him fuming from the ears and he looks like he is about to run up here after me, but Embrys grabs his forearm to keep him in place. I clear my throat and look at Embrys who is barely containing himself.

I will be all right. I know what I am doing. He drops his hand from his father's arm and nods his head. Steeling himself for my sake, following my lead like he promised.

I look to Oleander who does nothing to hide her outrage and fear for me. She is shaking and steaming. She keeps her eyes locked on mine. *What's happening? Nuria he will imprison you! Go now while he is still in shock. I will be fine...*

I reach out and give her hand a little squeeze. It singes a little to touch but I don't flinch. *No, you won't be. This is the right way, Oleander. You have to continue to fight for the freedom of the fae. Embrys will help you. He loves you. Let me do this.* I turn to face the crowd.

"My name is Nuria Piedmont. I was there with Oleander in the caves when we were informed about the start of the fire. She brought me down to the caves after finding me in the woods, which were very much *not* on fire at that point. She was in the caves with us the whole time and could not have started the fire. I *promise* that it was not her." They all know that invoking a promise ties me to my word. Everyone is silent and looking to The King for his next move. "I believe that Miss Lillian must have mistaken Lord Pyralis in her fear and confusion. Red hair does, after all, run in the family as you can see." Even though I bet Lillian is working for The King, I do not want to incriminate her. I don't know her reasoning for what she has done but perhaps she was coerced. I cannot be the reason for any pain or suffering inflicted on a ten year old, so I leave it at that; just a confused and scared child, not her fault. Lillian's hands are clenched at her side and her gaze is darting between The King and I.

The Wolf finally shakes off his shock and looks to the expectant crowd, plastering on a smile. He looks as if he is about to speak when he is interrupted by Lord Pyralis shooting out of his chair.

"She is the servant who ran away from my estate. You cannot trust a word she says, your majesty!" The vargs block him. The look that The Wolf lays upon Pyralis is one of impending pain. The foolish man just admitted to apprehending me, and if The Wolf truly knows who I am then Pyralis is in deep shit for hiding me from The King.

"Well, well, this is a tricky situation indeed. Lord Pyralis, what is your proof that she is untrustworthy? She invoked the promise of her word. Going against it would physically hurt her. Does she look pained to you?" Pyralis fumes but cannot deny that I have spoken true without bringing further attention to himself, so he sits back down.

"Miss Lillian, we have no further *purpose* for you. You may leave." The King grinds out behind clenched teeth. Lillian ducks her head and scurries off the dais. Her betrayal stings but I sincerely hope she is not punished for failing in her task.

"Now, Miss Piedmont, it was very noble of you to come to your friend's aid this afternoon but I am afraid, while we may not yet know for certain whether she ignited the catastrophic fire, we do know she was aiding in a known rebellion group. There have been reports of them hiding in those very caves." His toothy grin is back and I feel my jaw clench hard enough to crack a tooth. *Shit, did I just reveal that somehow?* "The confirmation of your presence was all we needed to validate a previous statement that was ascertained from a member of this rebel group that was captured, running from the scene of the fire. Unfortunately he did not survive the wounds he incurred from said fire, so could not join us here today."

"Who? Who was it?" I demand, not caring about the tone I've just taken with the literal king.

"Mr. Fenrick."

Images of his limp body, bleeding out in the dirt, flash into my mind. I want to scream that it isn't true but I have no way to explain that I have seen through Oleander's eyes without giving away my lineage. I look at Oleander who appears as if she is about to explode. We are still holding hands and the fire rising in our palms causes tears to stream down my cheeks. She pulls away and the fire is immediately doused behind her eyes as she realizes the pain she was causing me.

Oleander, I know it must not be true! They killed him. I saw him dead on the ground in front of his soldiers. I saw through your eyes!

I don't know, Nuria. He was already there when I ran from the forest. I trusted him with my life but I have no way of knowing! I cannot deny it; it will dig my grave further if I admit to knowing him...

Her face crumples at her inability to defend her friend's honour but she is right. If she claims to know of him then she will definitely confirm her part in the rebel group, so she shakes her head.

"No, I... I do not know of him," her voice cracks and she hangs her head to hide the tear I see glisten down her cheek. The Wolf snarls.

"It appears we have come to an impasse on both accounts brought forth today. Perhaps it is time to hear the verdict of our peers. With, of course, my say in the final judgement and punishments required." Both Oleander and I whip our heads towards The King, scowling.

"You said the civilians would decide!" I raise my voice.

"I said that they may share their thoughts. I, at no point, said they had the final decision, my dear."

Both Embrys and Oleander's hair burst into flames but The Wolf is quick, as if expecting such a reaction and snaps his fingers which signals a hidden water wielder to dump a small deluge on top of them, leaving their heads smoking and sizzling.

"Come now, if you cannot control yourselves you will be detained for your recalcitrance." Embrys and Oleander make no further move against him.

"Good. My esteemed civilians, will you please raise your hand if you believe Miss Oleander to have started the fire of the Heartwood Forest?" Most do not raise their hands, *thank The Mother!* I grab onto her shaking hand again.

"I drop the claims against Miss Oleander, in agreement." Embrys' cheer pierces through the silent crowd. Pyralis' face is red and I can see a vein pulsing in his forehead from all the way up here.

"Raise your hand if you believe Lord Pyralis to be the one who started the fire of the Heartwood Forest." Almost all raise their hands.

"I am also in agreement with this verdict." The Wolf's smile is wicked as he turns his attention to Pyralis.

"Lord Ignacious Pyralis, you are hereby charged with the destruction of sacred life. There is an order to the ecosystem. Without the apex predators, everything tips out of balance. I take it upon myself, the apex predator of this realm, and your king, to seek retribution. The punishment is death." In an instant Pyralis shoots to his feet in protest, but he is too slow. Beside me, where The King once stood, a massive, black wolf with gleaming green eyes is now crouched and ready to pounce. Pyralis makes it one step before The Wolf is upon him.

Chapter Twenty-Four

The moment between breaths is such a small measure of time. In this small space, big things can happen and in this particular moment, Pyralis' body finds itself suddenly without a head. My world has slowed as I watch the massive wolf clamp his jaws down, eliciting a squelching crunch. Blood sprays, hitting the first two rows of fae and coating Embrys entirely. A coppery stench shoves its way up my nose and I try not to vomit. The slow slump of Pyralis' body feels like it takes too long but it must only be one breath later. The spot on my wrist where his slave mark was branded tingles for a moment and I know, without having to look, that I have been released from our bond.

I can faintly hear Oleander's shriek and feel her pull on my hand as she lurches forward. Her searing hand snaps me out of my reverie and our grip on each other is so tight that she pulls me forward with her, nearly flinging me down the steps. Vargs step up to grab us both, holding us back.

Embrys is just sitting there. *Why is he just sitting there? Embrys!*

His eyes snap to mine. *Nuria? Wh – what happened?*

Don't look down, Embrys. The Wolf... he killed your father.

He looks anyway. His lament bubbles up from deep within him and splits the air, our only warning before his whole body ignites. Before he can do anything stupid, watery shackles are wrapped around his wrists that slowly spread up his arms and legs, encasing his entire body in liquid. He struggles but stays seated. Perhaps he cannot move enough to stand, I'm not sure, but he does not cease his struggle.

I lose my grip on Oleander's hand as she is held down by some vargs, the same water shackles are spreading across her body as well.

The Wolf turns back to the dais and takes one big leap that lands himself by my side once more. I don't dare show my fear, but instead look him straight in the eye.

You monster!

Something akin to sadness flickers behind his eyes and he lets out a barely audible whimper before shaking and shifting back into his humanoid form. Vargs quickly surround him with a green velvet cloak to cover up his naked body. I catch a glimpse of something shimmering around his neck but he wraps the cloak tightly around himself before I can make it out.

"Justice is swift and exact in this realm. He has paid in full for his crimes so that his children will not bear his debt to the natural world. Lamenting his demise will not prove fruitful. We are not finished here! Let us all regain our wits," he calls out to the crowd.

Pyralis' body and head are swiftly removed from the room and the crowd turns to The King as if nothing has happened. *Is this a normal occurrence? Is brutal death really something that just... happens? In a bloody court?!*

"Moving on to our last charge. Raise your hand if you believe Miss Oleander Pyralis to be a part of the rebel group that had been reported to be hiding in the caves within said forest." As if completely unfazed by what the punishment may be, around half raise their hands at this. *Shit. I can't watch that again. Not my friend!*

"No, no! I propose a bargain! Take me in her place! " I blurt out, before The King has time to dole out his exacting punishment onto my friend. I hear Oleander sob from where she is still pinned down on the ground.

"And who says you are payment enough for her crime?"

"I know you have been searching for me. I am one of the last remaining members of the House of Ether. Your lore speaks of a fae, raised by humans, returned to this realm to guide you. I am the one you seek! You may take me in exchange for Oleander. Let her and Embrys go free." I hear gasps and exclamations spread through the crowd. Is this prophecy widely known in this realm? I stand strong, but don't dare look at Embrys or Oleander. Embrys promised to not stand in my way and to help his sister, a promise he is bound to, but I know if I look at either of them, their broken hearts from seeing their father killed and now seeing me taken away might sway my courage.

"I... I cannot just release a known rebel..." The Wolf lowers his voice and takes a step towards me, the closest he has been to me yet. He smells of the forest in autumn and crisp dewy mornings, his scent is dizzying and my body betrays me by leaning in a little. I notice a small light near his collarbone shine through his cloak. He looks down at his chest then to mine. I can feel my necklace heating against my skin. Recognition dawns on me. *Does he possess the other necklace?*

He catches my questioning stare and before I can say anything he interjects –"I agree to your bargain. I will accept you in place of Miss Pyralis. She and her brother are free to go until the sun rises next morning, at which time they will *both* be known as being part of the rebellion against the crown and will be hunted down. I thank you and I take my leave." He looks to the crowd, which applauds at the swift conclusion of the trial.

Before I can do or say anything, The King has signaled for his vargs to grab me. He turns and exits the room through the side door that Lillian had entered through. I am swiftly ushered along and pushed through the same door without getting to talk to or even look at Oleander and Embrys again.

Chapter Twenty-Five

T he Wolf whirls on me as soon as we are all squeezed into the dimly lit hall. "You draw too much attention to yourself, child!" He reaches towards me as if he wants to caress my face but pulls his hand away, shaking his head, no doubt from my snarl of disgust. He has an expression of actual concern which confuses me. Did he not just agree to take me prisoner? Did I miss something?

"Take her to one of the green rooms in the right wing. One that locks." He nods to the vargs. They shove me past him and when I glance over my shoulder he is already disappearing through a side door, green velvet trailing after him.

I stop struggling as I am hauled through many different halls, some made of dark, damp stone and some bright and airy, containing floor to ceiling windows showing the twinkling lights of the city at night. So many fae are inside their homes right now, enjoying dinner with their families. So many fae that did not just see a man beheaded. I do not register much of my surroundings as my mind turns to what on Earth just happened.

I gave myself up. I am captured and have resigned to the whim of this monstrous king.

He won't harm me, right? Otherwise he would have done it right out there in front of all those fae... right?

I came all this way to save my sister and have somehow ended up joining in a rebellion against said monster. Am I a fool? Or just foolhardy... My sister is safe, I think, and Oleander and Embrys are safe, for now.

Between the two of them, I trust they will evade The King's guards and join back with the Sylvans. I know in my heart that Embrys will keep his word and do everything in his power to support Oleander. He will step up like he did when they were children, only this time he doesn't have his father here to sway his judgement. He is good hearted and brave and kind and I made the right choice ensuring that he and Oleander are together... I did this for them.

They will free the fae... *Will they free me? Will Embrys free me?* Part of me wishes they would, another part of me wants to scream off the rooftops to tell them to leave me behind and burn everything The King has built to the ground. I have work to do here. While they free the fae I need to keep this tyrant away from the humans.

I did the right thing... I did the right thing.

My breathing is reaching panic level so I close my eyes and allow the vargs to guide me as I search the strange corridors of my mind for Embrys. I search for his warm glowing ember in the dark purple swirl of my psyche; the warm glow that has been there, below the surface all my life. The presence that was somehow passed on from my mother, a woman I have never known, into him. I open my heart and search, just to know that he and Oleander are all right.

Instead I feel my necklace heat around my neck and the emerald green irises of The King pop into my mind. With a gasp, I open my eyes. The vargs push me through an open door and swing it shut with the snick of a lock behind me.

My internal workings pause for a moment as I take in the grandeur of the room I have been placed in.

It is lush, to say the least. In the centre of the room is a four-poster bed that is actually... a *tree*? There is a canopy of leaves overtop of the white, linen bed and the wooden posts are twisted and look to be rooted to the floor. The walls are lined with large potted monstera deliciousas, philodendrons, and an actual whole wall panel of moss. The big bay window to the right of the room is framed in hanging pots of vines and succulents. My legs have a mind of their own as I wander over to the moss wall and sink my fingers into the fluffy softness.

Oh wow, every house should have a moss wall...

"I don't mean to intrude," a small voice calls out. I startle as I am caught pressing my face into the moss. I turn to see Lillian has entered the room.

A varg reaches to close the door behind her. "The King has requested your presence at dinner this evening and I have been sent to be your lady in waiting." I see her blush and bow her head. She clasps her hands in front of her, the picture of subservience. I step away from the wall, brushing off my cheek and straightening myself up.

"So what? You're working for The Wolf? I trusted you."

"I am so very sorry Nuria! I did not wish to be so deceitful with you. You were so nice to me when all the other servants despised Jacob and I for how Lord Pyralis favoured us." She steps closer to me, wringing her hands.

"Then why? Why did you betray him and me?" *What is it with this realm? Is everyone just taught that betrayal and bargains are the only way to interact with another person?*

"The King took us in when our parents died. He cared for us and asked us to help him by spying on Pyralis. He did not trust him, so we were sent to keep a close eye on him." She shrugs.

"You were born in this realm?"

"Yes, we both were, but our parents were not. My brother said they were both professors, whatever that means, who studied ancient texts and went searching for this realm. My mother had Jacob in her belly when they found their way through."

"And how did The Wolf cross your path? Why did he take you in?"

"My parents were supporters of his teachings of the new religion and followed him wherever he went. Eventually he accepted them as servants when he took the throne. You see, they had come to this realm together, chasing the lore of the magic of The Divine Mother and he showed them the way."

I wonder if they knew of his plans to infiltrate the human realm.

"Well they were crazy to come searching for this place. It is not kind to humans... or fae raised in the human realm for that matter. How did they die?"

"I do not know. I was very young and The King just said it was an accident. I – I never thought to question it." Lillian's head hangs down again, but I can see she is peeking up through her eyelashes to see my decision on whether I will let her stay or not.

I sigh at the forgiveness I am about to give to yet another friend of this realm. I never had many friends back home anyway, but surely this is not normal. Plants and animals never betray me. Perhaps I should just stick to befriending them in the future...

"Fine, you can be my lady in... whatever." Lillian immediately perks up and bounces on her toes, grinning ear to ear. "But don't think that we are cool, Lils. Don't lie to me ever again. I think you need a friend that doesn't only care about themselves and it seems they come few and far between in this place." She nods emphatically and draws a line across her throat with her thumb.

"Wha – what does that mean?" *Did she just threaten me?*

"It means I swear or lose my head!" she giggles, as if I am ridiculous for not knowing that. *Fae version of cross my heart and hope to die?*

"Right. Well... I've witnessed enough beheading for a lifetime, so please keep your word."

"I promise... and not just a human promise, but a real fae one." She winks. "Now, first thing is first, you need a bath." She grimaces, looking me up and down. I suddenly feel the lingering stickiness from the figs I had gorged on and give myself a sniff, smelling Braun's stag musk mixed in with rotting fruit. *Yup, I need a bath...*

Lillian opens a side door I had not noticed before that leads into a bathing chamber. I nod my thanks and she leaves me to bathe in peace. When I am finally alone and scrubbing my sticky skin clean, the walls I had firmly placed around what had just occurred come tumbling down. I literally watched a man's head get ripped off. I heard the crunch of his spine... and the rip of skin.

I'm going to be sick...

I shut down the image as best I can but my body does not get the memo and the shake in my hands is making it difficult to scrub anymore. So I just sink down into the hot bath until only my nose and eyes are above water.

I wish I could just transform into a frog or better yet, a lily pad. Then I could just float and not think. I could just float and photosynthesize and make a flower. That's it.

Alas, instead I am here, a bloody prisoner once again. At least my friends are out there, with their heads intact... For now.

Shit... Marissa! I bolt upright in the bath as I realize the Sylvans will be in even more danger now that The King's guards will be out looking for them. I should have had the sense to tell Oleander and Embrys to get Marissa out, to get her to safety. Easthelm isn't a safe place anymore though... Nowhere is. She most likely would not acquiesce to being sheltered somewhere either. No, Marissa will fight. She was always stubborn but the person she has grown into in these past few months would never back down. I have no way to protect her from here, but perhaps she does not need my protection anymore. Perhaps she never did...

When I emerge from the bathing room Lillian is still there, sitting on the bed beside an elaborate, floor length ball gown. Her huge grin reminds me of Marissa whenever I let her play dress up with me... Terrifying.

The dress is a dark green tulle fluff ball with golden embroidered leaves covering the torso. The neckline plunges modestly but with a tight enough bodice that makes my cleavage uncomfortably noticeable and with nowhere for my necklace to hide.

Why is it always a bloody dress? I sigh as I look at my reflection in the mirror that is on the front of the wardrobe, Lillian is beaming behind me. *I want my smelly trousers back.*

I have always resisted and tried to hide my femininity but my curves always gave me away. I prefer to be covered in dirt rather than polish and jewels, but after meeting Oleander I've come to realize femininity can mean many different things. Her wildness is uniquely feminine and her curves do not speak of softness or weakness, they speak of freedom and strength.

Perhaps I can grow to love mine as well... but just preferably not in dresses. I hope I am reunited with her soon. Her closeness brings out a version of me that I feel has been hiding away behind the aloof mask I had mastered back in Easthelm.

"Any chance there are some dinner appropriate trousers or overalls?"

"What is an *over-all?*" Lillian asks as she tries to tame my wild hair into a braid. I blow a breath through my lips.

"Never mind. I think that is as good as it is going to get Lils. I should probably get going." I am sure it is nearing midnight and despite the dread I am feeling at seeing The Wolf and facing what may come, my stomach is still gurgling away and I swear I could smell chocolate wafting in from the hallway earlier.

Lillian nods and gives me a quick hug. She gives me such a pitying look when she pulls away that it is making me wonder if I should just try and escape through the window now and face a pack of vargs hunting me down rather than facing The Wolf.

Surely I am not walking into my certain death if something chocolatey is on the menu...

She opens the door and the vargs go to grab my arms again but I step back and raise my chin, holding my hand out to them in protest.

"Surely that is no way to treat a lady. Look how I am dressed! You will ruffle my tulle." I channel my best Marissa impression and the vargs look at each other and bow their heads, allowing me to pass. I know she would be proud.

THE PALACE IS a maze of tight domed hallways and grand open courtyards with marble columns lining the edges. I have no idea where I am within this place and am sure I would die of old age before I could figure out how to get out. Eventually, we end up in a grand dining hall, with a long wooden table that could fit fifty taking up the middle. The sides of the room have high arches with doors behind some and statues of fae and the Divine Mother behind others. Another enchanted chandelier of vines and branches hangs above the table, offering the space a warm glow.

The whole table is set with gold and silver and decorated with massive pine cones, beautiful logs with mosses and bright red and orange fungi growing out of it, and little globes with suspended flames dancing with them.

Upon closer inspection the little flame in the globe closest to me looks like it has legs and arms and is frantically waving at me.

Imprisoned fire sprites? Why would he imprison sprites when a fire wielder could just create flames in those globes instead?

This is a show of power. I suppress the urge to run down the length of the table smashing all the globes and freeing the sprites when I see the only occupant of the long table grinning at me.

Those green eyes pierce me.

The Wolf is sitting at the farthest end of the table dressed in an impeccably tailored, dark green velvet suit with black lapels and little golden leaves embroidered on the cuffs. It nauseates me that we are matching. *Am I now his little play thing? Like a doll to dress up and parade around?*

"Nuria, please join me." He gestures to a seat beside him. I go to pull out the chair that is the absolute farthest from him instead but a varg growls at me and shoves me in The King's direction.

"Such a stubborn little one, so like your mother. Come sit and eat. You must be absolutely ravenous." The Wolf laughs as he raises his goblet in the air.

Did he say I'm like my mother? His casual mention of her has me fuming. Of course he must have known her if she was a member of court. *Were they friends like she and Pyralis were? I sure bloody hope not.*

I pull out the chair that is two over from him, refusing to be that close, and he does not object.

The food in front of us is modest, which is not at all what I expected. I thought he would have curated some elaborate banquet in which there would be no earthly way two people could consume, just to prove his wealth and power. Instead there is a small roast chicken with some potatoes and a leafy green salad in which I recognize more than a few edible weeds.

I am guessing my facial expression has my confusion written all over it because The King laughs, a laugh that crinkles the corners of his eyes; not reserved or forced, but one of unabashed amusement. He gestures with his fork and knife for me to help myself. *The Wolf King has dimples when he smiles...*

"I know what you were expecting of a king, but contrary to belief I live in reserve. I could not possibly exploit my position when we are all facing drought and food shortages together."

So you condone slavery but share your food... Asshole.

"Noted." I dig in because I truly am quite hungry and I am too angry to engage in conversation.

We eat in silence for a long while, or at least it feels uncomfortably long to me because I am tensely awaiting my punishment, but none comes. He seems unconcerned with my being here and even hums a little when he eats.

The suspense is becoming too much, I have to break the silence.

"So, what am I here for? I've been told numerous times you have been searching for me. Well here I am. Can we get on with it?" I drop my silverware and cross my arms. He is leaning forward, mid-bite when I see it, the glint from the necklace I had noticed before. As if in recognition my necklace responds by heating and levitating up off of my chest like it had in the crystal cave. In reply his necklace lifts itself out from under his shirt and reaches towards mine.

"What on Earth? Why do you have the twin necklace of mine? You do not deserve to wear that! It belongs to *my* family!" I grab my necklace and press it back into my chest.

Mine! This is all I have of my mother. Panic that he is going to steal this one too begins to set in.

It is astounding the value one can place in an object when it represents a lost loved one. This piece of metal and crystal ties me to my heritage and to a life I could have had. I know the rage I feel about someone also having a piece of it is irrational but in this moment I find myself grasping my dinner knife in my hand and pointing it at The King, as if this tiny steak knife would be any match against a larger than life wolf.

No one will take her from me!

He calmly places his silverware down and softly presses his necklace into his chest.

It is of my family as well, his voice echoes in my head.

"What...what do you mean?" I can feel my whole body start to shake. *No, no, no!*

"Nuria, your mother gifted this to me on our wedding night. This is why I have been searching for you, my child. I am your father, and now that we are united we can finally begin our work."

Acknowledgments

Hello pals, Elena here.

Where does one even start in thanking all of the incredible, mystical creatures of this human realm for their support? This project kept me sane through a very painful recovery period from a spinal injury and has grown into so much more than I could have ever dreamed.

The genesis of my characters, Nuria and Embrys, came from a creative writing prompt from my dear friend Kelsey Lloyd. She created a wonderful somatic card game called Perfect Diction that is a game of unraveling our sensual curiosity via word play. She challenged a few of her nearest and dearest to birth a creative writing piece based on twelve words she randomly selected for us from the game. I of course was intrigued, and from these twelve words, a deliciously spicy scene with Embrys and Nuria emerged. This was the first time I had ever written something like this... and I loved it! I did not end up using this scene in the book but the spark to write was largely coaxed out of me from this exercise. Thank you, thank you, thank you Kelsey for igniting my creative flame!

This spark happened to coincide with a spinal injury that knocked me flat on my ass for around three months.

Through the boredom, the incessant need to be productive, and working through the pain, I birthed the first draft of Heir of Ether in eight weeks. Throughout this whole time I was so insanely lucky to have the most supportive partner, Geoffrey, who not only took care of me but also the farm we live on. He has been my biggest cheerleader throughout all of this. There have been many tears that he has held me through and so much joy that he has celebrated with me. Let me tell you, writing is not for the faint of heart. He was there for all of it and continues to help me and cheer me on as I write book two.

Heir of Ether would never have gotten to the stage it is at without the help of my alpha reader/beta reader/editor, Jarrah. This amazing creature was my hype girl from the beginning as well. I tentatively sent her a few of my chapters when I was just starting out and her response was filled with so much excitement that I found the drive to keep going. She has been editing and giving me feedback all throughout her postpartum time with her newest bubba and I am so inspired by her. She is an amazing mother of two children under five, living the homestead life, and also somehow still finds the time to respond to my crazy messages about my mythical realm. You are a legend!

My writing journey has also been witnessed and supported by my amazing online writers group, The Imposter's Club. This rag tag group of writers banded together, thanks to our founder Rob, and has been supporting each other through all the highs and lows that comes with navigating the wild west of being creative and publishing a book. There has been so much invaluable advice that I have received from these people and I honestly feel like I could share absolutely anything with them. Thank you for being my online rock!

I would like to thank my cover artists over at Etheric Designs. They were so lovely to work with and captured my vision of the Tanglewood Forest so perfectly.

Krystal my PA over at @aussieindiepa on Instagram helped me get my ARC copies out and saved me from the techy headache of it all. She also eased me into the Australian/New Zealand indie author scene which has been so special to be a part of.

Thank you Susan Mackie for answering all my self-publishing questions and for formatting my book! You have achieved so much as an author and you inspire me to keep writing and keep self-publishing!

Lastly, I would like to thank all of you. It amazes me that someone read something I wrote, and enjoyed it, I hope! Thank you to my beta readers, my ARC readers, and to everyone who has taken the time to get to know these characters and dive into their realities. I look back on my time writing this and I honestly do not remember most of it. To me, that shows that this art came through me rather than from me. Therefore I believe it belongs to whomever it touches. Thank you for reading, feeling, and being your unique selves.

Your pal, Elena Huebert.

About the Author

Elena was born and raised in the suburbs of Winnipeg, a flat, dusty city in the middle of Canada. She moved to Australia in 2017 where she met her love, Geoffrey during her very last month on her Working Holiday Visa. She made a leap for love decided to make the big move and dive head first into living in Australia to be with him. Fast forward 8 years and they are happily living on the land in rural Australia, raising chickens and ducks, hanging out with their donkeys, goat and horse and exploring the bushland with their fur baby Nelly. The natural world has always been a big part of Elena's life and passions which can be reflected in her pauses between the action in her writing to appreciate the beauty and curiousness of nature.

Stay connected for book two in the Her Divine Children Duology!
Elenahuebertauthor.substack.com
Facebook: Elena Huebert Author
Instagram: @elenahuebert_author

www.ingramcontent.com/pod-product-compliance
Lightning Source LLC
Chambersburg PA
CBHW020513260626
47156CB00006B/1990